BELINDA MISSEN is a reade
When she's not busy writing o
ling the Great Ocean Road and beyond looking for inspiration. She lives with her husband, cats, and collection of books in regional Victoria, Australia.

Lessons in Love

BELINDA MISSEN

ONE PLACE. MANY STORIES

This novel is entirely a work of fiction. The names, characters
and incidents portrayed in it are the work of the author's
imagination. Any resemblance to actual persons, living or
dead, events or localities is entirely coincidental.

HQ
An imprint of HarperCollins*Publishers* Ltd
1 London Bridge Street
London SE1 9GF

This edition 2019

1

First published in Great Britain by
HQ, an imprint of HarperCollins*Publishers* Ltd 2019

Copyright © Belinda Missen 2019

Belinda Missen asserts the moral right to be
identified as the author of this work.
A catalogue record for this book is
available from the British Library.

ISBN: PB: 978-0-00-833089-7

MIX
Paper from
responsible sources
FSC™ C007454

This book is produced from independently certified FSC™ paper
to ensure responsible forest management.

For more information visit: www.harpercollins.co.uk/green

Printed and bound in Great Britain by
CPI Group (UK) Ltd, Melksham, SN12 6TR

All rights reserved. No part of this publication may be reproduced,
stored in a retrieval system, or transmitted, in any form or by any means,
electronic, mechanical, photocopying, recording or otherwise,
without the prior permission of the publishers.

This book is sold subject to the condition that it shall not, by way of trade
or otherwise, be lent, re-sold, hired out or otherwise circulated without
the publisher's prior consent in any form of binding or cover other than
that in which it is published and without a similar condition including this
condition being imposed on the subsequent purchaser.

Erin & Michael
Thanks for the laughs

Chapter 1

If Queen Elizabeth were to narrate my last year, there's every chance she'd call it my *annus horribilis*.

While my castle hadn't exactly burned to the ground, I had lost my job. There was also the tiny detail of my marriage falling apart. And by that, I mean my husband tripped and fell into my best friend, which meant *she* was also out of the picture. So was the mutual friend who was acting as sentry for their rendezvous. If only all love affairs came with a lookout, I may not have ended up here in the first place.

My dad had taken off on a European backpacking sabbatical, which had evolved into a spiritual hike of the Camino de Santiago. All of this without his girlfriend, who was less spiritual and more surgical. When her first reaction to his holiday plans had been, 'Over my dead body', his response was, 'Tupperware forever'. She called time on their romance very shortly after that. As for Mum, well she hadn't changed. She was still living it up in Sydney with her yachting weekends and Pantone apricot orange-coloured husband, Barry.

There *was* light at the end of the tunnel though and, by some miracle, it wasn't an oncoming G-class diesel locomotive. It was a job. At home.

I was moving home.

Well, not technically *home*, per se, but within a few hundred feet of said residence. Despite his continual offers, I wasn't prepared to move in with Dad, his pumpernickel bread, health supplements, or yoga retreats. I hoped that, one day soon, the Great Penis Drought would end, and that I'd get to bring a man home for a little health retreat of my own. There was little to no chance that I wanted to try and sneak a boy down a darkened hallway like a teenager, lest I get stuck for a lecture on contraception. No, Dad, it's not just like putting a condom on a torch, no matter how illuminating the penis may be.

Instead, I was moving in with my cousin Penny and, for that, I was ecstatic. I honestly was. She was more a sister than a cousin and had been the first to call when she'd found out about the shit hitting the wildly spinning marriage fan. *Live with me*, she'd said. *Pack it all in and get back to the beach.*

While her offer had been tempting, I'd managed to resist for nine months. I was hellbent on the notion of proving to all and sundry, and then some, that I was perfectly capable of surviving without my husband, his bank account, or morbidly obese property portfolio.

During that time, I lived in a sixth-floor apartment in the centre of Melbourne with two other couples and a vertigo-riddled cat. Fast-forward to August, when I was made redundant from my job in the city library, and the decision to move home suddenly became a lot easier, and somewhat necessary, especially if I didn't want to end up paying the landlord in that special nudge-nudge, wink-wink kind of way he initially suggested when I was twenty dollars short for rent one week.

When I was first married, I was the library teacher in a school of more than one thousand students. I eventually swapped that for the glamour of a public library, author speaking events, and working in the repairs room. Now, I was trading it all in again, leaving the bustling high-rise library for Apollo Bay Primary School, tucked neatly into Victoria's Great Ocean Road. Not only was it my childhood school, it also had a much smaller library with one floor, and only a nth of the books I was otherwise used to. The fact Penny worked there as the receptionist was a welcome bonus.

The job application process began within minutes of receiving my redundancy slip and had been relatively painless. Several interviews and background checks later, I got the phone call I'd been waiting for – I wasn't a criminal! Also, I'd been offered the job. There'd be less books, less people, less drama; all the things I'd been hoping for. I was also looking forward to being closer to family again, catching up like old times over a pot of tea, a back fence, or a passive-aggressive social media post.

It didn't matter that I was leaving my so-called life behind. Most of my friendship circle had disappeared in the great marital purge, so I didn't feel bad leaving any of that. Those who had clung to my friends list had either told me that moving was a bad idea or supplied a constant stream of unhelpful gossip. They said I was running away with my tail between my legs and admitting defeat. It was throwing the toys out of the pram.

Ladies and gentlemen of the jury, I respectfully disagree.

Everything was going to be just fine. Mired in paperwork, I'd had addresses changed, mail rerouted, and I'd done the big social media call-out announcing my new address to the select few who might one day need it. Not that I was holding my breath – anything outside the City Circle tram route seemed a little too over the hills and far away for most of them. When everything was done, and all my bills were squared off, I began the drive home.

Now, as I sat in my car outside Penny's house, all that was left to do was get on inside, unpack, and make it through my first day at my new job. By six o'clock tomorrow night, I'd either be celebrating with a glass of fizz, or re-evaluating my life choices.

Currently, that life was crammed into a few boxes in the boot of my car. There wasn't a lot to show for ten years of marriage. All I had left were some clothes and shoes, and not even my best ones, a few precious books, and some bric-a-brac. The divorce hadn't yet been finalised. In fact, it hadn't even been filed, but leaving a marriage was no different to fleeing a burning building – I took the important stuff and made a run for it before the roof caved in.

I curled my fingers around the black leather steering wheel of my Audi convertible and looked up at the split-level unit. For a moment, everything was peaceful. With the top closed and window cracked, I could hear the crash of the ocean at the end of the street, the low thud of bass from a party a few houses over, and the static of my car's radio station – no longer in range after three hours winding around the Victorian coastline. It was perfectly calm. I wound the window down a smidge further and let the sea breeze wash over me.

When my car door closed with a pop, the front door of Penny's apartment flew open. She bounced down the stairs, past the lone palm tree decorated with twinkle lights, and a 'Santa Stop Here' sign that still hadn't been removed from Christmas and had faded almost beyond recognition.

Twelve months younger than my thirty-six years and stylishly soft around the edges, she had deep-set brown eyes that were Disney large, a button nose, and a Milky Way of freckles across a lightly made up face. Her dark brown hair was pulled up in a messy but subtly styled ponytail. Today, she accessorised with a smile brighter than the Las Vegas strip.

'Ellie!' she squeaked.

'Hello.' I lumbered towards her, shaking out the hours spent in the driver's seat.

'Finally! I'm so excited!' She threw her arms around my neck and I sank into her hug. There was no competition: she gave *the* best hugs in the world – and she never let go first. I could definitely get used to this kind of reception. 'Not about the whole divorce thing, that's very uncool and incredibly sad but, yay, housemates!'

'I'm sorry I'm so late.' I pouted. 'Brunch ran on a little long.'

Penny dismissed my concerns like someone clears the air of an offending fart, with a quick waft of her hand and a curled top lip. 'It's fine, seriously, gave me time to clean your room, make it look like I wasn't inviting Walter White for tea and powdered sugar. Oh, and I've grabbed some things for dinner.'

And here I was prepared to murder what was left of my credit card balance in favour of the local Thai takeaway. 'Fantastic!' I pipped, feeling the knot between my shoulders begin to unravel, glad to finally be here. 'Gosh, it's good to see you.'

'You, too.' She rubbed my upper arm. 'Come on, let's get you settled in.'

The boot of my car looked like the outtake from a Macklemore video, a jumble of clothes tossed on top of my belongings and wrapped around delicates. T-shirts threatened to twist themselves into knots befitting skeins of wool if not moved soon. I hooked an arm underneath what I could carry and trounced up the creaking stairs behind Penny.

As I crossed the threshold of my new life, it became apparent that my cousin lived inside a disused set of an Elvis film. In the corner of the living room, right behind a beanbag, was a fake palm tree doused in more drip lights. A ukulele rainbow lined the wall, and hula girls were dotted about the room, along with tikis and all things pineapple. One sniff, and you could almost smell the piña coladas and that coconut scented suntan oil everyone used in the early Nineties. Even the white dress she was wearing had multicoloured cocktail umbrella motifs dotted about the hemline. Then again, I was surprised it wasn't a grass skirt.

Penny gestured to the first door on the right. 'Okay, so you get the room at the front of the house. I don't know why, but I just picked the other one when I first moved in.' She tapped at her chin. 'That's right. If I squint, stand on my tiptoes, and stick my head out of the window and catch the breeze on my tongue, I can totally see the beach. The good news is, you get a bonus ceiling fan.'

Despite her assertions, my room didn't seem to be the pick of the bunch. It was different shades of cream, beige, white, off-white and ivory, and I was sure a sauna crammed with sumo wrestlers had more airflow. I tossed my pile of clothes in the direction of the bed, and the breeze it created was officially the only one in the room. The window, trimmed with gloss white plantation shutters, opened with a tired yawn.

A salty sea breeze rushed into the room. After a morning spent driving the winding roads from Melbourne, the crash of waves and brackish sea air mixed to create a soothing balsam. It was quickly turning me from Ursula the Sea Witch to Ariel the Little Mermaid, but without the fantastic hair, banging bod, dinglehopper, or seashell bra.

'Are you sure it's okay for me to stay here?' I turned to face Penny, whose brows were raised, and lips pursed. 'The landlord said it was fine?'

'The slumlord was no problem at all.' She bounced on her feet. 'In fact, he only raised the total rent by one hundred dollars a week. He's good like that.'

'Slumlord?' I narrowed my eyes. 'Really?'

'He *hates* it when I call him that.' A facetious smile took hold. 'It's fine, I promise. I sorted the lease with him last week over a pot of tea and fruitcake.'

If you spent ten minutes listening to Penny talk about Patrick, you'd think she was describing a recently beatified saint of the rental world. He wasn't greedy and kept rent to the lower end of the scale, he let her hang pictures, kept out of her hair, mowed the lawns, helped the local junior football team, and donated his business time and energy to charitable projects, all while running his own construction company. As if that wasn't enough, this place was modern and clean, and had a soft homely charm about it. I felt at ease already – I loved it!

'Now, what do you want to do first?' she said. 'Unpack? Drink? Do you need something to eat?'

'No, hell no.' I patted a full stomach. 'Brunch was epic: bacon, eggs, black pudding—'

Penny gestured with her fingers down her throat. 'You're so

gross.'

'It was lovely,' I pressed. 'Seriously, you don't know what you're missing out on. Crusty sourdough toast, farm fresh butter, tomatoes, spinach, you name it, we had it. Oh, and bottomless cups of coffee.'

'The coffee I *can* do.' She finger-gunned me. 'Want one?'

I pulled up a wicker stool by a Munchkin Land-sized breakfast bar in the kitchen. Railway tiles and modern appliances made the space look slightly less tropical than the rest of the house. That is, until I reached across the counter and flicked at a dancing hula girl toy. We watched her gyrate against a jar of Blend 43.

'That's Lula the Hula.' Penny jiggled the plastic toy. Her head flopped about wildly and her painted-on smile stayed resolute. 'I like her. She doesn't talk back.'

I looked away and laughed into the palm of my hand. 'It's a bonus, I guess.'

'It is.' Two mugs landed on the bench with a thud. I was about to drink coffee from the top of Elvis's head. Did that make it a coffee-flavoured lobotomy? A lobo-coffee? 'So, tell me about your last night in Melbourne.'

As part of the Farewell Ellie Tour, as if I were moving to the next country and never returning, my flatmates insisted on a Saturday night party. What began with crackers and beetroot hummus soon devolved into too much wine and Cards Against Humanity. We rounded things out with a late-night coffee and cake blitz through St Kilda, a stroll along the beach, and an early morning taxi fare home. After just enough sleep to take the edge off, we yawned our way into the closest café for breakfast at our regular table in the corner.

'Can we go up to Melbourne one night? It's been forever since I went. It might have been that day we did lunch and looked at the Myer Christmas windows.'

Also known as: The Week Before Everything Went to Shit. Ah, the ignorant bliss.

'Really?' I said. 'Of course, absolutely. We may as well do an overnight trip, make the most of the drive.'

'See a concert?' she suggested.

I nodded, enthused. 'Definitely.'

After a few moments of silence, she clicked the kettle on. 'So, Ellie returns home, huh?'

There it was – that wisp of disappointment people tried so hard to hide, with a smile, a cup of coffee, or a gentle enquiry gift wrapped in a statement that sounded more like a question. Friends had hinted as much when I decided to leave Melbourne. *Are you okay? Are you having trouble coping? Are you sure there's nothing you want to talk about?*

'It's not all bad news, you know.' I folded my arms over on the counter. 'It was months ago—'

'Long enough for ...' She cradled an invisible infant.

Don't think I hadn't thought of that a thousand times over. Tick-tock-biological-clock. 'Thank the gods we didn't make it that far. Honestly, I'm fine. I've dealt with what I needed to, and I'm happy. Sure, it still stings a little, and it might look like I'm running home with my tail between my legs, but at least I have a job—'

'Bonus!'

'—and, really, it just felt like the right time to make a fresh start.'

It also didn't hurt that I'd had several weeks without the responsibility of a job to simply enjoy life again. It had been a welcome break, a chance to re-evaluate life, and work through my plan of attack. Money was tight, but the rent was paid, and I had enough to see me through to at least the first payday or two. It really wasn't the worst thing ever. After all, I'd been through worse.

'Everyone at school is peachy keen to meet you. I caught up with some of the girls last weekend. We should all go out for dinner. Why don't we do that tonight? Should we?'

I waved a hand. 'Not tonight. I just want to rest.'

'Good, good.' Water sloshed up the sides of the coffee cups as she poured, one after the other. Milk, sugar, and sewing tin biscuits.

'Maybe next weekend?' I tried. 'Let me get settled in first.'

'Speaking of settling in.' Penny slinked away towards the front door. 'Let's get you unpacked, that way it's done, and we can relax.'

Squeezing past each other like rabbits in a warren, we ferried my belongings inside one box at a time. Initially, we stacked them neatly by the door, careful not to make too much of a mess. By the final drop, full of bric-a-brac, I didn't care. I tossed my armful on the bed and hoped for the best.

The last battered cardboard box, held together by rounds of red electrical tape and a bit of luck, bounced a little as it landed on the bed. A picture frame spilled out onto the duvet, anxious to escape. Not today, Satan. He of wandering penis was not welcome in this bed or near this house, lest he curse this new life, too. I snatched the rose gold artefact up and, before I could stuff it back into the box or set fire to it like it rightfully deserved, I looked at the carefully posted photo.

It was nothing too dissimilar to your average, spent-way-too-much wedding photos. The suit and tie were worthy of *Casino Royale*, crisp and cut in all the right places, and the white dress that had been painstakingly made over weeks, months even. It was sleek and modern, no garish beading or bones poised to turn my body into a cocktail frank on the receiving end of a toothpick at a moment's notice. It was all just perfect, blissful, happiness.

Until it wasn't.

Penny appeared by my side, snatching the frame from my hand.

'Why?' She waved it about like a bag of freshly laid dog turd. 'Just ... why?'

'I have zero idea.' My shoulders hugged the bottoms of my

ears. 'There was probably a nanosecond in which my not-so-romantic-anymore heart thought things could be fixed. A brief second of weakness where, maybe, if he'd told me he'd simply tripped and fallen into her, I might have believed him, and things would be okay again.'

'Tripped and fell into her?' she squawked. 'Ellie, you deserve better than a stupid excuse like that.'

Firm, but fair.

'I don't know,' I tried.

I snatched the frame back from her and tossed it into the waste paper basket beside the bed without a second thought. The brittle glass finally gave way and cracked, feathery webs spread almost faultlessly down the centre of the photo, across smiles and up-dos, vows and promises. Perfection be gone.

'Nice shot.' She gave me an upside-down smile and left the room. 'Well done, you.'

* * *

While I busied myself sorting belongings onto shelves, clothes on hangers and shoes into racks, Penny kept herself occupied with dinner. I thought of suggesting takeaway after all, but a quick check of my banking app suggested it may be best if I skipped the credit abuse and waited until payday.

As the afternoon sun dipped lower in the sky, we set ourselves up on our small deck. It was just off the side of the small dining area and sat smartly above the carport. In one corner, a single-serve barbecue, and a faded wooden table in the middle. All the rattling and cursing that came from the kitchen had given way to steak, garlic butter, and a pineapple infused coleslaw.

'I do at least have a bottle of champagne.' Penny gave the bottle a violent shake. I cowered as it popped with little more than the excitement of a dead toaster. Warm cola had more fizz.

'Oh well.' I took the glass from her. 'It'll do.'

'Sláinte.' Penny chinked the edge of her glass with mine.

'Huh?'

'It's Scottish for health,' she explained proudly. 'Learned it from my Mr December, Richard.'

'Your who now?' I laughed.

She gave a wistful Hallmark sigh and gazed up at the heavens as if they'd suddenly part and drop this magical Richard back into her lap. 'Richard, aptly named for what I was using him for, was visiting the area, surfing, travelling …'

'Shagging,' I laughed, glass pressed against my bottom lip. 'You're … I have no words for you.'

'A multicultural woman of the world,' she declared, finger poking at the air. 'Speaking of which, let me catch you up on the people of *our* world.'

Had I really been gone that long? It certainly hadn't felt like it. I still came back for Christmases, birthdays, Easters, long weekends when I could wrangle Dean away from his job. Then again, when you're busy inside your own bubble, it can make the outside world a little hazy. Because, as Penny began rattling off happening and incidents, it became apparent just how much I had missed.

Our cousin Sam was married to Mary. I was sure I'd been at that wedding. It involved a rustic barn in Dean's Marsh, hurricane lamps and an oversized Polaroid frame fit for the hashtag #SNMWedding on Instagram. Not surprisingly, it hadn't caught on. But now he had kids? I really *was* out of touch. The realisation was sobering, and I quickly downed the contents of my glass.

'One, with another on the way.' Penny pushed her steak around the pool of garlic butter on her plate. 'And Sophie, his sister, has had three boyfriends in the last twelve months. Each of them were "The One", mind. We were rolled out every time for dinner to meet Huey, Dewey, and Louie.'

'That old chestnut,' I grumbled. 'How about your parents?'

'My parents are as they are.' She shrugged. 'Nothing really

changes with them. Dad wants to retire, but I don't think he wants to spend all day with Mum. Not that I blame him, of course. Mum has a new hobby every second week.'

'What is it this week?'

'Sewing. I'm not so secretly loving it, because she's making me a heap of dresses.'

'I would be, too,' I agreed. 'Do you think she would make me some?'

'I think she would be thrilled.' Penny refilled her glass and waggled the empty bottle about. 'Want me to grab another one?'

'No more tonight.' I placed a protective hand over my glass. 'I'm not sure bloodshot eyes and reeking like the back end of a wine barrel is a great look in front of the principal.'

'Come on, he's a lush from way back. You remember all those Friday mornings, watching teachers smuggling bottles of wine and slabs of beer into the staffroom. It was like a reverse walk of shame. No, kids, we're totally *not* getting wasted after the 3.30 bell. No, siree.'

'I do remember that.' I nodded. 'Very well.'

'Are you prepared?' she asked. 'How are you feeling? Excited? Anxious?'

'Positively shitting myself,' I laughed nervously. 'Please tell me it won't be too painful?'

'You'll be fine,' Penny soothed. 'You've survived worse.'

She was right. If I had managed to get through the last nine months without having myself committed, this next week was going to be a walk in the park. I mean, I'd taught before. How hard could it be?

Chapter 2

'Perry?' Penny narrowed her eyes at the name scribbled on her takeaway coffee. 'I didn't say Perry,' she whispered, thrusting the offending cup with orange marker scribble under my nose.

'That looks like a Penny to me.' It really didn't. 'And this says Eleanor, so it's definitely the right order.'

'And, look, he even drew you a car.' She pointed at mine. 'A car!'

'Oldest trick in the book.' I took a sip and checked my watch.

If I'd heard it once, I'd heard it a thousand times. It was a lucky year when someone didn't question the origins of my name. No, I wasn't named after a car. My Dad, however, had a massive political crush on Eleanor Roosevelt, so that was something. At least it wasn't Eleanor Bradley, nude model. Imagine explaining that to people. At this point in life, I was happy to take the small wins where I could get them.

'Come on, this looks like a penny to me.' I pointed out the squiggles beside her name. 'See, you have a coin there. He drew a coin.'

'I thought it was a smiley face.' She leaned in and whispered, 'Do you think we should stay for breakfast?'

I shook my head. 'Nah, I'm okay.'

'All right then. Are you ready?'

I'd been ready for hours. Awake long before the rest of the world, I'd sneaked a few slices of toast and watched the sunrise while curled up in the egg chair on the deck. Breakfast television was out of the question; Penny's Elvis obsession stretched to her television, which looked like it would have been new when the

King ate his last sandwich. That meant subtitles were out, and I could not lip-read for shit.

Had my brain been in gear, I might have nicked the bathroom before she got out of bed. As it ended up, we squashed ourselves in front of the mirror, shoulders over elbows and hairdryers in each other's eyes as we did our best to not look like *Game of Thrones* extras. Oh, and we agreed that perhaps it would be best if one of us showered at night, and not in the morning. I volunteered for night shift. A clean body in clean sheets? Yes, please.

My mousy-brown hair had more pins in it than an angry woman's voodoo doll. One wrong move and I'd either scalp myself or pull my brain out through the back of my Nordic braid. But, combined with my very favourite navy wrap dress and heels, I was ready to take on the day.

School was a twenty-minute walk from home, thirty minutes if we went via the café. The first trickle of nervous sweat made its way down my back as we traipsed through the rippling bitumen of the car park. It had seen better days; shrubs had grown from weeds and created tectonic rifts in the surface, and the once vivid white lines were nothing more than faded rubble.

A time capsule to my youth presented itself in a carving on the trunk of a pinkish-grey eucalypt by the main quadrangle. What were the odds Josie Smith still loved Trevor Reeve, the kid who told everyone Superman was his uncle?

'That would be a negative,' Penny explained. 'Last Christmas was the season for cheating, or so it seems. Trevor took off with a barmaid and is currently living in Warrnambool.'

So much for "tru luv".

The winds of time had taken a barren school oval and replaced it with a football field, used by the local team on weekends and training nights. An ochre running track encircled the field, and newly upgraded demountables were dotted around the main building – the Pentagon, as Dad used to call it.

It was neither five-sided, nor did it hold huge secrets. It was a giant red-brick square. A library, staffroom, and admin block sat at the heart of it all, and nests of classrooms branched out at each corner, creating bricked-in walkways that were perfectly cool on hot summer days.

'You ready?' Penny stopped, hand on the front door.

'Nope,' I squeaked. 'Not in the slightest.'

She laughed. 'Yes, you are. You've got this.'

After a hall lined with current class photos, we walked into the teachers' lounge. The early Nineties décor remained, white tiles with crumbling grout and stucco walls, and a café bar that was miraculously still bolted to the wall. It was already feeling the effects of providing cheap coffee grinds for a horde of perpetually exhausted teachers, and brown grains littered the bench like ants across a picnic blanket. I made a mental note to bring my own coffee tomorrow.

A heavy grey door swung open to my left. Phillip Vine, the same jovial white-haired principal I'd had, and had come up against in several scrapes, stood before me with arms outstretched. 'Eleanor Manning.'

'Ellie, please.' I leaned into his hug. He was *still* an Old Spice man. 'It's so good to see you again.'

'And it's nice to see you didn't skip the country before the start of term,' he teased. 'Welcome to the team. Officially, anyway.'

'Thank you so much.' I wrung my hands and tried to take in as much of my surroundings as possible which, despite my history, was likely going to be very little today.

'Or, should that be: welcome back?' He fixed me with a curious gaze before laughing at his own joke. 'I wasn't entirely sure which one to run with.'

While Phillip launched into an explanation of what was going to happen over the course of the day, Penny disappeared towards reception, chirping excited greetings to anyone she ran into. Her bright infectious laughter could be heard through walls and doors and, when she returned, she was jangling a set of keys in my direction.

'Let's go check out your office.'

'Please do.' Phillip squeezed my shoulder. 'Just make sure you're back for the staff meeting in here in ten minutes?'

'Sure.' I wiped sweating hands against my sides. I angled myself towards Penny. 'Lead the way.'

Like that, I was whisked out of the staffroom via the swinging door, and into the adjoining library.

Growing up, I'd always wondered what it would be like working in this library. I'd sit in class and daydream about having students of my own, stacking shelves and stamping the return cards in the front pocket of each book. I didn't have to imagine any longer. Did this mean I was living the dream? I guess it did, except for the fact that return cards were now obsolete. Thanks a lot, technology.

After wading through an information technology degree at university, I shuffled into a teaching diploma and took up a position in the library of a central Melbourne primary school. Oversized classes, under available resources, and a handful of firebugs, who'd found joy in old books and magnifying glasses, gave new meaning to the term burned out. No matter how many times they tried, I couldn't buy the excuse they were simply trying to rid the room of ants.

After that, the public library became my refuge. I worked in the repairs room, spent my days fixing broken spines and wrapping books in protective wrap. Solitude stopped being satisfying when I began feeling like I was wasting my brain. After all, I had a qualification and I knew I was a good teacher. What good was my university tuition debt when I was spending my days gluing books back together instead of teaching? I soon yearned to get back into a classroom, and this role popped up at the perfect time. Getting that phone call from Phillip had been one of the rare fist-pumping moments in the last twelve months.

Tucked away in the belly of the not-quite-Pentagon, with a door that linked to the staffroom, my new library smelled of tannins, vanilla, and dry-cleaned carpet. A small courtyard at the rear of the space still looked like an upscaled terrarium. Wisps of rubbish and overgrown weeds spun about in the warm wind like a bite-sized tornado.

Stacks I used to hide between stood solid like tin soldiers, now with a comforting beanbag at the end of each aisle. I not so silently wished we'd had them during my time; they would have made lunchtimes in the library much more fun.

Penny nattered excitedly as she unlocked the door to my office, a glass-fronted room tucked in the front corner of the library. It looked like the aftermath of an evacuation. Books were strewn across benches, blue and yellow streamers hung from the roof, and random football-themed drawings were tacked to the windows. My attention kept floating back to a caricature of a dark-haired footballer holding a trophy aloft.

'I guess someone was in a hurry,' I mumbled.

'You've got no idea.' The right corner of Penny's mouth twitched into a smile.

I ran my finger along the spines of DVDs, in numbers heavy enough to cause sagging in the shelves against the wall. An empty table with a large roll of book covering held in place on a dispenser sat under the window. The old workbench brought back memories of lunchtime chats with Mrs Coates. Often, our debates descended into discourse over which Roald Dahl book was the best.

I never did understand her adoration of *Royal Jelly* until I was an adult. Sick, sick woman. I tossed my handbag under the bench, thrust my hands against my hips, and tried to take in this adult version of a childhood memory.

'What do you think?' Penny asked.

'It's a little surreal, isn't it?' I said. 'We couldn't wait to get out of here as kids.'

'Oh, yes,' she chuckled. 'And for someone who was so desperate to get out of here, you spent a lot of time in detention.'

I rolled my eyes. 'That's the best you can do?'

It wasn't my fault I kept scoring higher than Jarrod Sims on maths tests. For so long, he'd been ego-stroked into believing he was some sort of Pythagorean prodigy. When we ended up in the same class, it was a constant tussle every time he took offence. It made my last year of primary school interesting. It became even more tangled when he developed a crush on me in high school.

'Anyway, time for me to play fairy godmother.' Penny tapped my shoulder with a ruler. 'Come, sweet summer child, let's go make some new friends.'

Chapter 3

A tiny cheer rose from the sofa by the window as we entered the staffroom. Four women, all squeezed up against each other and inspecting phones, leapt to their feet like a choreographed greeting party.

'Please tell me this is Ellie!' A magazine-thin brunette pushed herself up out of the depths of the sofa and crossed the floor in loud heels.

'This is she.' Penny waved her arms about like a game show host. 'Ellie, these ladies form the bulk of our junior class teachers. This is Grace, and we've got Emma, Gemma, and Jemima.'

They almost sounded like an Austen novel. I did my best impression of someone who knew what they were doing, stepped forward, and made my way along the couch, shaking hands and uttering greetings.

'What's happening on the sofa this morning?' Penny asked.

'The usual.' Emma used a sole fingernail to tuck a lock of platinum blonde hair behind her ear, her mouth last seen on the back end of our neighbour's cat. I'd seen that face before on numerous GIFs. 'Just looking at You Know Whose Facebook, ogling football photos, the usual.'

'Who what now?' I looked between the two of them. Then again, did I *really* want to know?

'I'll explain later. We're on a whirlwind tour of the isles. Bye, ladies.' Penny grabbed me by the elbow and dragged me in the opposite direction. 'They're lovely girls, they really are, but their thirst is real, and their class is sometimes not. Come on, let's go meet some more people.'

'Who were they talking about?' I whispered.

'You'll see,' she muttered, tugging harder.

Where I thought I was going to hide in a corner – I even had a spot picked out at the corner table – Penny made like the amazingly sociable, bubbly person she is and introduced me to anyone she could get a word in with, pushing into twosomes and creating threesomes. With each new conversation, she remembered to include a helpful Brief History of Eleanor. *Eleanor is a past pupil, she studied teaching and computing in Melbourne, and has recently returned home. She enjoys knitting, long walks on the beach and world peace, and she once played in an orchestra. Oh, and she's my cousin. Ask her about the time I broke her arm.*

I was both delighted and put at ease by the conversations this started. And the broken arm story was accurate. I was fourteen, and she was trying to demonstrate her best karate chop. With a stick. In hindsight, it may have been the offcut of a railway sleeper. Snapped that bone right in two, she did.

First lesson of the day: I could learn a thing or two from Penny about simply getting out there and being the life of the party. Whatever that special something was, she had it in overflowing buckets and then some.

Phil was busy in conversation with someone else, his bald head gleaming under artificial light, shining eyes lined in laughter. Others milled around and took their spots, echoes of tired greetings and holiday stories repeated ad nauseum while they waited. Eventually, somewhere around the sounding of the first morning bell, we all came to rest in seats and on table edges in some late-thirties game of musical chairs.

'And a very good morning to my favourite team.' Phil clapped his hands together, the only person ecstatic about the end of holidays. 'Welcome back, commiserations if your chosen team lost the Grand Final, and all that buzz. We have one day before the onslaught of final term begins, so I guess it's heads down today as we prep lesson plans.'

The room was so quiet you could hear stomachs rumble and coffees slurp. The Zip instant boil clung to the wall and sighed as the tank refilled.

'Look at *all* that enthusiasm. It's not that bad, we've got a curriculum, we know what to do. We've walked this path before.' He glanced over as the door adjoining my library opened, and three men wandered in confidently late. Leading the pack was an irritatingly handsome man. He was far too attractive to be relegated to a classroom all day.

Around me, women sat up straighter. The mystery of who 'You Know Who' was had been solved.

Phil clapped his hands together. 'Marcus, good afternoon, thank you ever so much for joining us.'

Marcus, who was met by a round of applause, bowed and made a beeline for caffeine.

'It's lovely to see you're still raising our dress standards singlehandedly after such a stellar performance on the football field. Well done on the trophy.'

'I do my very best.' He pressed his hand to his chest and took a sip of his coffee. He winced and stuck his tongue out in disgust. Yes, the coffee really was that bad.

The high-pitched wheezing I could hear was either the women at my table, gearing up like pressure cookers at a potluck, or the sound of the local fire station calling for help. Marcus, with his navy suit jacket stretched tight across his shoulders, looked like he'd leapt from the pages of *GQ* in a scene reminiscent of an old A-ha video clip, cuffs ready for shooting and shoes so polished I was surprised we couldn't see up his inside leg. Not that that would be entirely offensive, it had been a while, and I was running out of options. Either that, or he was one Jimmy Olsen away from writing for the local paper.

He was beautiful in a way that was not possible. At least, not by any of the standards set by my life experiences. He was tall, so much so that most could use him as a maypole and still slip under his arm with room to spare, and I was sure I could stack bricks on those shoulders. Brown hair and bottle-green eyes were accentuated with laugh lines that he wore like some men wore suits – perfectly charming and wonderfully naturally. The glint in his eyes, and the squared-out shoulders told me he knew this, too.

'And good morning to you,' Penny mumbled beside me. I held my mug to my mouth in the hope it hid my laughter.

It didn't.

Scanning the room looking for a place to land, Marcus turned, and offered a tight smile to our table. There was a mouthed greeting mixed somewhere in there, but I couldn't quite make it out. I made the broad assumption it was aimed at everyone, and not solely at me, because we did not know each other from a bar of soap, and I bet he used expensive soap. It probably also smelled of fresh pine forest and sex. Really, really good sex. He and his two accomplices took the empty seats at the end of our table.

'And before I forget, I want you all to welcome Eleanor Manning to the team.' Phil recaptured my attention, imaginary spotlight burning up my face. What's behind door number two? The new girl! As much as I expected it, warmth still pooled in my cheeks and my skirt ruffled up my thighs as I slipped a little further down into my chair. 'Ellie is taking over from Cathy in the library who, as you'll remember, took off like a bat out of hell at the end of last term. Ellie is making me feel incredibly prehistoric today, as I was her principal when she was a student here.'

Was that the sound of surprised gasping? It may well have been.

'And, boy, do I have some stories,' Phil chuckled.

'Please don't,' I laughed, hiding my face behind my hands.

'No, I won't do that to you today. The Christmas party will be here soon enough.' He smiled softly. 'It's good to have you back, Ellie. But, speaking of Cathy, has anyone heard from her?'

'Currently sipping cocktails in the Bahamas,' came a chirpy voice somewhere to our left.

'Half her luck.' Phil made a point of rolling his eyes. 'The most I could manage was a glass of Passiona by the swimming pool after the Grand Final. Even had a little purple umbrella. Anyway, please give Ellie the support she needs as she settles in.'

I gave a quick wave and looked out at a crowd of expecting faces. On first inspection, they looked mostly bored. A few people were checking phones, and Penny was picking at muck under her cadmium-yellow fingernails. Marcus continued to peer into his coffee cup, as if its murky contents could read his fortune. Then again, it was a stroke of fortune to drink the coffee supplied and not die, so maybe he was on to something.

So far, so good.

When the meeting was over, I scuttled for my office, avoiding getting caught up in too much chatter. I was full of the type of nervous energy that either propelled you forward or paralysed you if you thought about it too much. I wanted to get moving before it turned into the latter.

Returning to primary school all these years later, it was an *Alice in Wonderland* moment to realise how small the furniture looked. Chairs that once felt like thrones now barely grazed my knees. My eyes caught spines of books I recognised and, besides the occasional hello from teachers who used the library as a thoroughfare, it was quiet and calm. It felt right; peaceful, even.

I switched on the office light, felt around the computer for the on switch, and wondered exactly where the hell I was supposed to begin. It was all well and good to have the lofty notion of returning to the classroom until I had to actually do some work. The not knowing was no better than bobbing about at sea, life jacket on, but nothing in sight but bright blue horizon.

'How are you feeling? Ready?' Phil appeared in the doorway, a bunch of well-worn clipboards clasped to his chest.

I took a deep breath, and felt a quiver climbing my spine again.

'I think so? I was just planning on cleaning a bit before I got stuck into things.'

'Yeah, sorry about that. Cath was feverishly excited about getting out of here. I hoped she might stay until the end of the year for handover, but nothing was convincing her.' His eyes scanned the room quickly. 'No idea why.' He winked. 'Now, we don't have your password yet. Matt in IT will get you sorted at some stage today, so let's get you introduced to everyone while we wait. Thankfully, Cath was a dab hand at record-keeping, so you should be able to check back through her stuff and work it all out easily. She's organised everything for the Book Fair. I think that's the only big thing on your calendar. All you'll need to do is take delivery of the books and sort the displays out ... oh, and deal with the mess on the day.'

To be fair, if I were Cathy, I'd take the tropical holiday over teaching the new girl, too. One of the positives of my redundancy was escaping that responsibility of handover altogether. I was out the front door so quickly I only had time to collect a few scant personal belongings and my coffee cup. It looked like Cathy had the same idea. Clever girl.

Phil and I had been in contact in the last few weeks, emails pinging back and forth, as he detailed the first few weeks of term, so I felt confident I wasn't completely in the deep end. I'd done the teaching gig before. Hopefully everyone's bike-riding metaphor was right, otherwise I'd be heading straight into a prickly bush of mistakes and mayhem.

Those exchanges pulled back the curtain of the theatre production. As a student, you don't think of nearly half the things that need to happen in the education system. You see work and deadlines, but you don't see the jigsaw puzzle of trying to get all your ducks in a row, teaching what needs to be taught, while still maintaining some semblance of fun. It was a challenge, but one that I'd always loved.

With blank paper, a pen, a heart full of hope, and a bladder full of coffee, I followed Phil down hallways, where we mused over murals, both the old and new, and reminisced over my years as a pupil. Things were simpler then, he explained, easier to handle with what felt like less rules and red tape.

We slipped into each of the classrooms, shook hands and mingled, until I had met almost everyone I could. Random jottings quickly filled my notepad, requests for films, documentaries, books, and stationery orders. Despite my brain feeling a little bogged down by the unrelenting pace, it was great to be useful again.

'Ruddy hell, Ellie Manning!'

Our final stop for the day was the Grade Six block, where I froze at the sight of a familiar face. 'Mick?'

Michael Buckley was arguably the best teacher I ever had. Big call considering the number of classes I'd taken in my time. In my final year of primary school, he was maths mad and perpetually grumpy, but made all of us feel important. Often, he would stay late to chat with someone who was slower to leave class or looking a little more anxious than usual. At one point, he called my dad to voice his concerns that I was 'less rambunctious than usual'.

As it turned out, having a cold would do that to me.

I peered around my old classroom in amazement as he urged me to follow him. Tables and chairs formed a ring in the centre of the room. Thoughts and plans had been scribbled on the whiteboard and crossed out again. Last term's artwork dangled from ceiling tiles and clung to windows.

Phil took his leave as we sat on the ledge of a table facing the centre of the room. I was more than capable, he reasoned, and I didn't disagree. Mick was a familiar face. I had this.

'What on earth possessed you to come back here?' he asked. 'Returning for family?'

'I heard you still made a great coffee,' I teased. I don't know that I'd ever seen him without a coffee cup in hand, either. 'Plus,

I thought you could do with checking in on.'

'See, the coffee has fallen to Marcus now.'

'Ah.' I turned towards where Mick's attention was held at the back of the room, three men scuttling at the realisation they'd been caught spying. It was a Monty Python sketch as they bumped, shuffled, and passed paperwork to each other like synchronised jugglers. Marcus crossed the glass-windowed office, mug to his mouth and watching from the corner of his eye. Busted.

'Clowns, the lot of them,' Mick said quietly. 'And, if I point at them just so, they'll think I'm talking about them. Egotistical little shits.'

I pulled the folder up over my face and laughed loud and free.

'I'm sorry I missed the meeting this morning.' Mick elbowed me gently. 'I saw your name on the roster but wasn't sure if it was you, or if someone by the same name just felt like orbiting the area for a while.'

'Surprise.' I grinned, throwing my arms out like P. T. Barnum on a slow morning, then scrambling to pick up a packet of crayons that tumbled from my hands and scattered to the winds. 'How have you been?'

Mick gave a small shrug. 'You know, just slogging around here, keeping kids out of trouble.' He slipped from the table and nodded towards the office. 'Speaking of trouble, come with me.'

I followed him into the small office, which looked like it had been used by the same four men for a few years. It had that old, comfortable look and smell that screamed 'Keep Out: Boys Only'. Desks were well settled into, a coffee machine had its own small altar in the corner, and family photos lined desks and noticeboards.

'Ellie, these gentlemen here – and I use the term 'gentlemen' loosely – are Tony, Roger, and Marcus.'

'Hello.' I gave a tiny wave at the three smiling faces, all seated around one desk in the middle of the room. One by one, they stood, introduced themselves again, and shook my hand. Roger was quick and jangly, much like his bony arms. Tony was limp and damp and looked like he needed to pat down his forehead with a handkerchief before heading back into battle. Marcus, despite being warm and solid, left me with the distinct impression I was being sized up. Did everything have to be a competition? I avoided his continued gaze and turned my attention at the others. 'I'm just here to meet and greet and take requests.'

'Kicking ass and taking names,' Tony tittered.

'Bingo.' I set my belongings on the table and watched as they shuffled through papers and pulled out ready-made lists. It wouldn't have surprised me if they'd stocked up on requests in anticipation of slipping things past the new girl.

'How has today been for you?' Mick glanced up from his seat.

'I'm ... yeah, just taking it all in again.' I pushed myself up on the balls of my feet. 'It's making me vastly aware of the years that have passed, and I'm suddenly feeling rather ... inferior.'

'Try being me,' he joked. 'Not only is my past coming back to haunt me in the form of you, but Jack is now teaching here.'

'No,' I laughed. 'He is? I don't think I've met him today. I'll have to go and find him.'

'He is.' He nodded. 'He was probably in the meeting this morning. You'll find him down in the music hut cultivating his beard and apparently fashionable man-bun. God knows it's a mess, and his mother hates it, but you can't tell him these things.'

I snorted. The last thing I'd have pictured him with was a beard. Jack would come in and help Mick on his days off school. As a teenager, helping involved not a lot more than supervising some quiet reading time, or re-enacting a Shakespearean scene to give Mick another ten minutes on lunch break. He was quite the rock star to the small handful of pre-pubescent girls in our class. I wondered if Mick ever understood that. Probably. It's not as if twelve-year-old girls were renowned for their subtlety, after all.

'I'll make sure to tell him you're here. He'd probably be keen for a catch-up.'

'If he remembers me,' I noted, looking around the table. 'Now, does anyone need anything else from me?'

Silence. One by one, they shook their heads in turn. Only the scrawled lists I'd been given? Nothing more than pencils and glue? Good.

'No ... oh, wait. Yes.' Marcus peered up at me, brow knitted. 'I'd like to change my library session. I want a morning, preferably Monday. Could you make sure that happens?'

I blinked twice and stared hard at he who would be Clark Kent. 'No.'

'No? Is there a reason for the no?' He rested his chin in the palm of his hand. I'll bet that look worked on all the ladies.

'I've been here not quite a day, and I have zero desire to turn this place into a snow globe just yet. I would like the opportunity and support of my colleagues as I settle in. I'm sure at the start of the new year, we'll look at changing time slots.'

Tony snorted, then hid his mouth behind his hand quickly. My heart gave a bass drum thud, and annoyance prickled at the back of my eyes.

'I'd really love a morning session though. Do you think you could get another class to shift?' Marcus pressed on. It didn't at all surprise me that he didn't understand the word 'no'.

'You can try if you want, see if someone wants to swap,' I said.

The office was so quiet you could hear my heart using my ribs as a xylophone if you concentrated hard enough. Please, do not put me in this situation, I thought. Not on day one. Yet, there was always one, wasn't there?

'Could *you*? Please?' he asked. 'I'll be so busy with curriculum all day. It's not like it's a difficult request.'

I recoiled a little. Did anyone just see my shoulders curling in on each other? The words were so bloody familiar that it made me think the universe was just laughing at me. It was every night I'd ever tried to get Dean out of his office. Often, I was greeted with a combination of, 'Can't you see how busy I am?', followed with a chaser of, 'And what are you doing all day while I'm working?' Anything further was met with, 'Whatever.' I wanted to turn around and walk out. Except I couldn't do that here without looking like a total strop and not the team player that I'd prattled on about in my job interview.

'Funny about that, so will I.' I gathered my pile from the table. Papers slipped from my fingers and out onto the table. It felt like I spent the next few moments grabbing at air before Marcus took pity and handed them back. 'If there's someone you'd like to swap with, you're welcome to ask them. If they say yes, you can have your morning. Otherwise, no.'

'Ha!' Roger clapped his hands in delight. 'Boy Wonder doesn't often hear that.'

'Is everyone else done?' I asked. 'I also have work to do.'

Marcus huffed, hands clasped in his lap. Far from the polite and confident look he carried this morning, he'd now shown me an entirely different person. I stepped into the corridor, took a steadying breath and thought about tearing back in there and giving him a piece of my mind. But what would that prove? I decided to get on with my day. It was day one, something like this was bound to happen. Attitude clashes were the stumbling block of any new job, and he appeared to be a Lego in the middle of the night.

I shuffled back to my office to find a password tacked to the top of the computer screen. That was nice. Exactly where was I supposed to begin? I imagined my inbox would be backing up quicker than a toilet stuffed with paper and cherry bombs. I pushed my planner to the side for a moment to try and tidy the room.

As I moved about, familiarising myself with everything, my brain threw out questions. Was I supposed to fire up the borrowing system and run a report for overdue books? Maybe I needed to do a complete stocktake before doing that, just in case.

But school wasn't back yet, so it was kind of pointless. I thought back to what I'd done previously and decided I would do that tomorrow, once students were back and the school was alive again. Curriculum first, got it.

It was amazing how quickly things began snapping back into shape. Still, with each email I deleted, ten more popped up in their place. I almost wanted to kiss Grace when it turned out her four o'clock email was nothing more than a ladies' lunch invite because, by that time, I'd started to reconsider every life choice that had brought me here.

I reached for Cathy's reference guide and paced the office while I read. I scribbled notes and re-stuck Post-it notes, jammed a pen behind my ear, and repeated things aloud as if that would jog my memory. And that was how I spent the few hours I had left, quietly on my own – and not changing the library roster.

* * *

'Okay, I'll admit it.' I pulled the last of the steak from the barbecue and slapped it down on Penny's plate. 'I'm curious.'

All the way home, I could smell the last of the school holiday barbecues. The only way to stop my mouth watering was to have my own cook-up. It was never going to be as elaborate as the ones we had on the beach as kids, around a hastily fashioned driftwood fire where everyone brought a plate, but with a supermarket coleslaw and pasta salad, we had Prosecco tastes on a Passion Pop budget.

Penny popped her last two bottles of beer and slid one across the outdoor table to me. Leaning back, she peered at me curiously, a smile tugging at the corner of her mouth. 'About? Boys? Sex? Women? You should definitely try women.'

'Marcus,' I said. 'What's his story?'

She took a swig and gave her head a delighted shake. 'He doesn't really have one. He's just one of those impossibly lovely people.'

'You're not giving me a lot to run on.' I peered down my nose at her as I tipped my head back. 'He can't be all sunshine, rainbows and kittens.'

'All I know is he keeps to himself a lot. He's not a bragger, he's super passionate about his job, and is delightful to look at.' She peered at me through narrowed eyes and an accusatory look.

I mimicked her look and gave my head a little shake. 'Not really.'

'He's kind of that …' she flourished her hands '… he's a bit of an everyman. Men want to be him; women want to be with him.'

'And I suppose you're of that opinion, too?' I asked.

I'd stayed back at work later than Penny. There were just too many loose ends for me to leave, and I didn't want to risk the dreaded 3 a.m. wake up, eyes pinging open like a dancer at a rave while my brain worked overtime to process the list of what I hadn't done. Just as I was packing up for the evening, blinds pulled low in the office, and lights switched off, a small dusting of women appeared from Marcus's office. I'm sure he was somewhere in the middle of the cloud, his name held aloft on a palanquin.

She shrugged in defence. 'I would not kick him out of bed.'

'You sound like Nanna.'

'And she was a smart lady.' Penny pointed at me with her fork. 'I loved her wardrobe.'

'Anyway.' I shook my head, savouring my steak-melting-in-mouth moment. 'Like I said, just curious.'

'He's definitely gorgeous.'

'More like a painful reminder,' I said, scraping the last of the garlic butter from the tray. 'With his suit and tie and the "I'm such a wonderful businessman" demeanour.'

'No, Ellie.' Her face fell. 'If he was a dick, I would tell you. You know I would.'

I glanced at her quickly, silently.

'Just give him a chance,' she sighed. 'It was your first day and, you being you, you're probably running around with a chip on your shoulder, anyway.'

'What?' I scoffed. 'That's not true.'

'The only way it could be truer would be if you crumbled like that rock-biting creature in *The NeverEnding Story*.' She fixed me with a sardonic look. 'What was his name?'

'Rockbiter.' I rolled my eyes and, though our beloved grandmother would be mortified, spoke with my mouth full. 'What, so be nice to him because he's a smug idiot who thinks people are just there to do his bidding?'

'No, just let people into that gravelly little chest cavity of yours.'

'A, it's not gravelly, that was just a chest infection. And B, I'm not here for that.'

Of all the things I could be accused of, not having a heart was not one of them. It stung a little that it was the first thing Penny thought of. I reached for the pasta salad and dessert spoon, so I could stuff those feelings down with glue-tasting mayonnaise and carbohydrates.

'Then why are you here? It can't be just for my good looks and tropical tastes.'

'It really can be,' I said.

'But it's not, otherwise you would have done more about visiting while you were busy being a rich Melbournian.'

I winced.

Ouch.

That one hurt.

Chapter 4

People seem to have this idea that living by the beach is sun, surf and sand on constant rotation. They were joined by lifesavers with washboard abs and swim caps, ready to save the day at a second's notice. Not so much this morning, though. It was the first day of school, and the weather was putting on a performance matched only by my stomach.

Grey skies rolled in over a fog-covered bay, light drizzle threatening a heavy downpour. If it was anything like the weather of my youth, it'd hang around until about nine o'clock. The sun would then come out, drying up everything in sight, leaving everyone to think they'd perhaps imagined this morning's need for a thick coat. As for me, I ducked under the awning of the local bakery and stepped inside.

It was pure, yeasty warmth. The smell of sticky strawberry iced doughnuts mingled with the burned crusts of a raisin loaf that looked like it was going to be our breakfast for the next week. But, again, there were so many varieties of bread lining the racks now that I wanted to take them all home. I plucked a sample of apple scroll from the plastic box on the counter and let the cinnamon warmth come alive in my mouth.

'That's so good,' I groaned in appreciation.

'Seriously, this place is just amazing,' commented the woman next to me. She was about my age, with rusty-red hair, and the toddler on her hip was preoccupied shoving a Vegemite scroll in his mouth. We exchanged pleasant smiles, until her face dropped. 'Wait ...'

'Yes?' I said slowly. I hoped like hell I wasn't wearing half of the little apple scroll portion.

'Eleanor Manning?' Her smile was broad and bright.

My smile was a little slower to form. I could not place this woman standing in front of me, as many memories as I tried to recall. You'd think redheads would be hard to forget, but this woman did not register at all.

'That's me,' I said. 'I'm sorry, I just can't …'

'Sally Fairburn.' Her only empty hand outstretched in something that might have been excitement. 'I remember you so well. Mick Buckley's Grade Six class.'

Her name triggered all kinds of memories. Sally Fairburn was part of our primary school posse that sat together at lunchtimes. We had our favourite spot picked out, under a teetering pink and grey gumtree in the far corner of the playground. She was one of two Sallys in our year level. Dad had nicknamed them Burnt Sally (Fairburn), and Long Tall Sally (Winters). After she ran into our front door, Dad changed her name to Blind Sally.

Excitement popped my mouth. 'Sally!'

'That's me!' she tittered, moving in for a bone-crushing hug. 'This is wonderful. I heard you'd moved away. Are you just visiting?'

'Nope.' I shook my head. 'Moved back here.'

'Bring your husband with you? Surely, you've got kids now, yeah?'

I shook my head, smiled politely, and ordered a loaf of raisin bread. Ah, I thought, those lovely societal expectations of women in their mid-thirties. 'Just me.'

'Oh.' Sally followed me out of the bakery and onto the sidewalk. Her curly-haired child buried himself in her neck. I didn't blame him, that wind was awful. 'So, what brings you back?'

'I'm actually teaching,' I said. 'Term starts today at our old school, so there's that. I'm really looking forward to it. How about you? I can see you've got your hands full.'

She jiggled her toddler about and smiled wistfully at him like he was the third coming of Christ. 'Well, as for me, three kids. Barrel of laughs and fun. I married Ben Finlay.'

'Really?' I asked. 'Ben, wow. That's a name I haven't heard in a while. Used to play football?'

'Still does.' She clucked her tongue. 'Makes for a busy weekend between the kids' swimming and his sports, but we do what we have to do, right?'

'Speaking of things we have to do.' I drew my sleeve back. 'I really oughta get going. Don't want to be late.'

'Oh, no, no, don't let me hold you up.' Sally rubbed at my upper arm before reaching for her phone. 'I tell you what. Let me get your number. We should catch up. There are so many of us old girls still around. They'd love to see you.'

'Sure, of course, yes, that'd be great,' I enthused. I could see that as a very fun way to spend the afternoon. Memories, a few drinks, and old friends. What could be better?

With little more than a nervous wave to see us off, we swapped numbers, promised each other we'd catch up soon and got on with our mornings. Me, with an extra spring in my step, and I suspect Sally had one, too. Her first text message came through just as I walked into the administration block at school.

'Where'd you disappear to this morning?' I rounded Penny's desk and made a beeline for my pigeonhole. Already on autopilot, my brain was screaming at me for breakfast, if only I could get all my chores done first. 'I came looking for you as I left, but you were already gone.'

'Mission from God.' She unrolled a coffee scroll like a snail, dangling it above her mouth. 'Want some?'

'No, thanks, I've got breakfast right here.' I held my bag aloft. 'Toast.'

'Butter's in the fridge in my pineapple tray!' she called after me. I was already halfway to the staffroom.

With toast dripping with butter and coffee strong enough to perm my hair, I egg-and-spoon raced myself to my office, which was already lit up and waiting for me to jump into the day. My computer whirred away as I sank into my chair and took my first desperate bite of toast.

After the whirlwind that was yesterday, I don't think I'd registered just how much of a mess my office was in. The best thing I could do for myself, I thought, was to clean and start at the top of the list. I was already behind thanks to a lack of PC access for most of yesterday, but with a list to work through, I pulled a chair up to my desk and began.

'Let's do this.' I clapped and rubbed my hands together.

I didn't look up again until I heard the first book being dropped through the returns chute. Those were the magic books that had been found during school holidays. They'd either been buried at the bottom of a backpack along with old permission slips and squashed sandwiches or hidden in the darkness under a bed. If I didn't have to wipe mouldy banana from the insides of *Dear Zoo* again, I'd happily take whichever books were being offered this morning.

Like popcorn in a microwave, the closer we got to nine o'clock, the more books appeared. One at a time, and then all at once. *Clap, clap, clap* went the steel door on the returns chute, and I took that as my cue to get up and head outside for assembly.

Holiday exhausted children were filing into the grounds, uniforms freshly pressed and stain-free. Parents dawdled in behind them. Though they yawned through gossip, their eyes said they were secretly ecstatic that their bundles of joy were now someone else's problem between the hours of nine and three-thirty, and that they could now enjoy their coffee while still hot.

'Eleanor!' Phil had appeared from the admin block, dragging a lectern along behind him like a dead body. He yanked at the cord trailing behind him, and the buzz from the public address system died. 'What do you know about these damn things?'

What did I know about lecterns? I knew that I set them up about four times a week at the city library, in cases of public talks and author visits. Some people just loved to hear themselves speak, but my small collection of autographed books was proof that some people made sense when placed in front of a microphone.

'We got this last term,' he admitted. 'At least I don't look like Letterman delivering a monologue anymore.'

I grinned. Phil was far too nervy to ever be Letterman, but a boy could dream. I plugged in the power, swapped a cable over, and stood back as he tapped at the end of the microphone. The sound of tapping fingers echoed loudly. Success.

'Good morning, everyone,' his voice boomed across the school from a series of speakers dotted around buildings and grounds. Like the Pied Piper, more children raced into the quadrangle. Parents dotted themselves on seats around the edges, and teachers tried to herd their students, though it was quite like watching them try to herd cats.

I stood back on the sidelines and enjoyed the fact I didn't have a designated class of my own.

'Mr Blair, what did you do on your holidays?' a voice came from behind me.

'Well, they weren't really holidays,' Marcus explained. 'I marked all of your assignments, got some new work ready for you, and then I worked for my friend Patrick.'

'The builder?' asked another. A small crowd of students had gathered around him, each of them eager for a sliver of his spotlight. It was a tiny push and pull, give and take of attention as they swarmed him like moths to a lamp, barely feet away from me. After yesterday, he could stay in his corner.

Marcus sat on a bench seat as his audience closed in, some of them jostling for the prime real estate of space either side of him.

'That's him,' Marcus said. 'Good memory.'

'Did you take your dog for a walk?' asked another.

'Daisy went for plenty of walks down by the beach, which meant I had to wash sand out of her coat quite a bit, too.'

'But she loves the beach.'

Marcus chuckled. 'She does love the beach. She loves swimming while I run.'

'Did you get pictures of her in the water?'

'I got a few.' Marcus was quiet for a moment. I didn't dare look at him for fear of being drawn into the conversation. From the cooing that resulted, there were plenty of dog photos being passed around his students, who seemed to multiply in number with each new question that was asked. So did the mothers around him. 'And that's ... yeah, that's a house we were painting, just at the end of the main street ... and, yep, that's my mum making a cake.'

'Did you get a girlfriend over the holidays?'

Marcus laughed. 'They're not like a bag of crisps. I can't just go to the shop and pick one out.'

'That would be easy,' said a boy with sandy hair.

'It would be,' he agreed with a quick sniff. 'But, no, I don't have a girlfriend.'

'What happened to Lady X?'

I snorted. If anyone was going to refer to his girlfriend as Lady X, it was going to be Marcus.

'Lady X moved to Adelaide for work, so that's the end of that.'

'Very sad,' chirped another voice. 'You know, you really should get married, then she can't move away. Unless she's like my dad, but Mum says he's an arse. You have enough suits to get married. You could wear this one, and she would think you're pretty enough to not leave. And your mum can make the cake. My mum makes all my cakes.'

'Good morning, Mr Blair,' a mother chirped as she, and her crowd, began circling his general area.

'Morning.' He nodded politely amidst the teasing laughter of his class.

I bit the inside of my cheek to stop myself from laughing and, despite myself, chanced a look at him. In classic black and white, he could very well have turned up to the church at recess and be married by the first ring of the bell. I was sure any number of the fan club now hovering about his area would line up for the honour.

Weekly school assemblies were a non-negotiable, a rite of passage for teacher and student alike. We mumbled through the national anthem, listened to Phil make rapid-fire announcements and, when my name was announced as a new teacher, a hand from behind propelled me towards the crowd.

When the word 'Dismissed' was finally uttered, it was like jamming a pin in an overfull balloon. Sound rose from the floor, a cacophony of shuffling feet and pent-up voices as bodies got lost in the scramble to stay in class groups. The mystery hand springing me forth into the world? That was Penny.

'You can't run now,' she teased. 'You've been officially introduced.'

'The pet has been named,' I teased. 'And once they've got a name, they're not going back.'

Beside Penny, someone laughed. 'It's good to see you again, Eleanor.'

Sandy hair in a messy bun, and a beard that hadn't been trimmed in weeks? It had to be …

'Jack!' I exclaimed.

'Oh, shit, you haven't been introduced yet, have you?' Penny bounced excitedly.

'No.' I looked at Jack. 'Yesterday was mayhem, and I didn't get around to your classroom.'

'Okay, well, Ellie, Jack, Jack, Ellie.' Penny waved her hands about. 'Jack's going to have a new piano delivered in a few weeks and, yes, he does remember you.'

'You do? You have?' I asked. My ears pricked up. 'A new piano? What brand is it? Can I come and see it? When we've both got a free moment, that is.'

For some people, a new mobile phone or widescreen television gets their go-go-gadget fingers tingling. For me, new pianos evoked those feelings. From the tinkle of shining keys, taut strings under a gloss black hood, to the shy reluctance of new pedals, there was nothing I didn't love about them. I longed for the day I had a place big enough to buy myself a new one.

'Ah … it's a Brodmann upright, and absolutely you can,' he enthused. 'My door is always open. But we should catch up before then. I think we're all doing Friday night drinks, if you're in?'

'Yes! Friday night,' Penny chimed in.

'Okay, that sounds great,' I enthused. 'I'd love to catch up.'

We moved slowly with the tide, me towards my library, Jack towards his side of the school.

'I'll send you the details!' he called. 'It'll be great!'

Chapter 5

Before I made it anywhere near the other end of a Friday night martini glass, I had to wade through the rest of the week. With only a few days' grace before I began taking classes of my own, I didn't have long to get myself in order.

For most of the week, I was pent up in my office. New folders, printouts, an overheated shredder, and an overabundance of spray cleaner and kitchen towel. So far, I'd torn down streamers, football posters, and artwork. A co-worker once remarked to me that a clean desk meant an empty mind, though I was sure that was just an excuse for his desk looking like a junk sale diorama.

I spent evenings working through curriculum and coming up with class plans. Late-night emails were distributed to teachers and, amongst the ones that bounced back telling me to go home, they were approved.

All of this happened in the shadow of catching up with Sally. Now that we'd swapped numbers, the text messages came thick and fast. We swapped stories of school and everything after, laughed at shared memories of boys and high school, and my inbox was soon filling up with photos of her happy family. It tickled me to know that she'd found her spot in the world and was thriving with a bustling household.

By four o'clock Friday afternoon, I'd found my groove. From my stool at the returns counter, I could survey my lands – a little like Simba in *The Lion King*. The courtyard, which earlier had tornadoes of rubbish, was clean. Weeds were gone, pavers swept, and rubbish removed. There were no books wandering about on return trolleys; everything was in its place. I'd discovered my borrowing computer, with the bash of a key and my tongue held right, sent overdue emails to parents. Once upon a time, I'd have been sending letters through the mail, so this was a nice step up in the world. In the corner, my little office was sparkling clean with windows yet to be covered in smeary, snotty fingers.

Everything was coming up Ellie.

Behind me, the library door crept open with a tired yawn.

'Or, maybe not,' I grumbled, spinning on my stool and tucking a flyaway lock of dark hair behind my ear. 'Hello.'

Marcus came close to filling the doorway, at least with his height. He shifted from foot to foot and slid his hands deep into his pockets. 'Hello.'

'Hello,' I echoed. 'Can I help you?'

'I hope so.' Something on my desk caught his attention. 'I just spoke to Grace over in the Prep unit.'

The paper in front of me had been the victim of an hour's mindless doodling. It was covered in musical notes, clefs, quavers, book titles, and my own name a hundred different ways. I reached for it quickly, screwed it up and tossed it into the waste paper basket by my feet. My breath caught nervously.

'Okay.'

'She said we could swap classes depending on what I could give her in return.' He grinned.

'You do realise that this is not life threatening, don't you?' I launched myself from the stool and landed with a little thud on the floor. Marcus followed as I rounded the desk and walked back to my office. His stride was slow, purposeful, and a little too sure of himself. 'Nobody is going to die if you don't get a precious afternoon session. I don't understand what this obsession is. Are you just doing it to upset me? To try and assert some, "I've been here longer than you" type of authority?' I waved my hands about. 'Why can't you just wait the year out?'

'So, what you're saying is that, even though I've met your conditions, you're still not going to help me?'

'What I'm saying is exactly what I said the other day. I've been here barely a week. I would appreciate being allowed to settle in before I go changing things. I'm sure you can last another few weeks on a Friday afternoon.' I reached for my PC, listening to it burp and whir as it woke up. 'And what's so bad about you getting to start your weekend early? I would've thought someone like you would love an early start to the weekend.'

'Right.' He nodded curtly. 'Thank you.'

As I watched him leave, my mobile phone began rattling across the benchtop. It stopped, then started again. Without looking, I picked it up and pressed it to my ear.

'Eleanor speaking.' I tapped a pile of papers against my desk and slipped them into the in-tray. I could worry about them tomorrow.

'Eleanor!' A wine-soaked voice puttered down the line.

My stomach tightened. 'Mum.'

'Don't sound so excited,' she clipped.

'No, it's not that,' I lied, doing a very quick emotional stocktake and chirping up. 'I'm just at work, that's all.'

'How *is* that all going?' she asked. 'Your father told me you'd started a new job.'

'He did?' I asked, surprised. Since when were my parents talking to each other? It was news to me. 'When did he tell you this? What are you, like, pen pals now? He's sending you postcards from the edge?'

'Not quite,' she said, the smile in her voice evident from the next state. 'Facebook.'

'What?' I blurted.

How did it happen that my parents, who barely spoke to each other throughout my childhood, and who refused to be in the same room together, were now having regular catch-ups online? Had I missed something? If they told me they were planning on having dinner next week, I was going to start developing an oxygen sensitivity.

Also, how come I hadn't had a friend request?

'You deleted my request,' Mum deadpanned, though I was sure I hadn't voiced that thought aloud.

I scoffed. 'I did not.'

Then again, maybe I did. Yeah, probably.

Explaining my relationship with my mother makes for prickly skin, especially in a world where we're taught that Mother Is All because, sometimes, she just isn't. The knowledge that she'd packed up and left before I was six months old had always sat in the back of my mind as a warning. We weren't the stuff of Hallmark movies or cheesy greeting cards.

While Dad insisted that I saw her as often as possible when I was younger, which still wasn't very often, it was still a whole lot of awkward. Visiting her often felt like that scene in Austin Powers where he'd got the jeep stuck in the middle of a three-point turn. That she kept me at arm's length and shoved me in the corner with a colouring book or novel while fawning over my stepfather just added to the issues.

'Anyway.' She interrupted my train of thought. 'What do you think?'

'Sorry, about what?' I stuffed my water bottle into my bag, retied my hair, and pulled my office door shut behind me, all with my phone wedged between shoulder and ear.

'Spending some time together, silly,' she laughed, while continuing a conversation with someone named Floss in the background.

'I mean, I can, but can you give me a few weeks to settle in first?' I asked. 'I've barely unpacked my belongings.'

'Okay, do you want to send me details of your flight when you book them?' she asked.

'No,' I laughed. I didn't mean to, it just kind of burst forth in the same way a broken pipe might split asphalt. One minute, everything is quiet; the next, there's a raging torrent springing up from the street. 'I don't quite have the money for a last-minute flight. I could drive up, but it's ten hours either way, so I'd be turning up for dinner and leaving early the next morning. It's doable, but you'd want to be serving me up caviar and Dom Perignon for dinner, followed by five courses with a private chef and a lap dance from Paul Rudd ... or Idris Elba. You know, either one I'd be fine with'

'Who're they? Do you have their numbers? Why don't we do that for your birthday?' she enthused. 'What a great idea, Ella!'

Me and my big mouth. I pinched the bridge of my nose as she prattled on about hiring a yacht for the day. Twelve months ago, when that kind of lifestyle was the norm for me, I would have frothed with delight at that idea. Even with my mother at the helm, I would have considered it. Now, it just felt all kinds of pretentious, like something worse was hiding just below the surface. I walked into the staffroom and made a beeline for the coffee. Hopefully it would clear out the throbbing that was starting to wrap its way around my head.

From the corner of my eye, I caught sight of Jack. He smiled and offered me that little close to the body wave he'd always had. I motioned for the bottle of milk in his hand. Instead of passing it, he poured, and put it back in the refrigerator.

'What was that?' I turned my attention back to my phone call. 'Sorry.'

'Don't you think?' she asked.

'I don't know, what am I thinking?' I asked.

'I said I should come down for the weekend, while your father is still on his trip.'

Ctrl Alt Delete. 'Sorry, say again?'

'I could come down, spend the weekend,' she suggested. 'Go shopping, have lunch.'

'Mum, we haven't seen each other in almost eighteen months,' I said. 'And, can I just remind you that was because I came to you. The last time you were supposed to visit, you forgot and never showed. The last three times, in fact.'

My mother had this habit, and I wondered if it wasn't just a game she quite enjoyed, where she would make plans to visit, and never show up. Her disappearance was always followed up by a quick, apologetic phone call that left me little room to move.

'Oh, honey, I'm sorry,' she cooed. 'Won't happen again, I promise.'

Just like it wasn't going to happen last time, or the time before that. Really, my afternoon would have been easier had I just ignored my phone. Voicemail was the great technological filter. Even another round with Marcus was preferable to this.

'You're going to have to stay in a hotel. We don't have room in the apartment,' I said.

'You know, I haven't been back to that blasted town since you were a baby?' she scoffed as if I was about to jump in and support her.

'What a surprise.' I smiled sarcastically.

Yesterday's lunch box was languishing in the back of the communal fridge, which was kind of an office etiquette red card misdemeanour. Sidelined with side-eye. With nobody looking, I shoved it into my handbag and hoped it hadn't been noticed. I closed the refrigerator door, screwed the lid on my travel cup, and turned to leave. The sound of laughter echoed up the corridor. As I yanked on the door, someone pushed against it, and I ambled straight into a wall of suit.

Everything slowed. The shuffle, the sidestep, the miss, the clash, and the crescendo of realisation. Caught between the two of us, an innocent coffee cup. Only ten seconds earlier, and it would have been full to the brim. Not so much now though.

'Okay, Mum.' I waited for her to take a breath between her words. 'Mum, I have to go, I've just … I need to go. Now. Need to go now. I'm sorry. I promise I'll call soon.'

Stabbing on the red button, I missed the tinny ends of her one-sided conversation. I held my phone out to my side, as if that would keep it safe from any further harm and peered down at my front.

I. Was. Sopping. There was so much liquid that it was dripping from the hem of my shirt and pooling around my feet. A milky brown bloom climbed up across my chest and over the toes of my shoes and, wouldn't you know, there was my five-dollar Target bra making an appearance. At least it was white and fit relatively properly because, right now, I looked like I was starting a one-woman wet T-shirt contest.

'Fuck.' It was all I could muster. I pinched at my shirt and peeled it away from my skin.

'Oh … shit.' Marcus snorted, failing miserably at not laughing.

On what planet was this funny? My shirt was verging on translucent, at least everywhere south of my bra straps. To make matters worse, he'd managed to escape completely, except for a splash on his shoes. When I could focus briefly, it was definitely only on his shoes. I was incandescent with rage, from the acidic pit in my stomach to the bright lights sitting behind my eyes.

'Is this funny to you?' I shrieked. 'Really? You … I have no words for you.'

My words were a starting gun, and he began faffing about, hands searching, darting across the bench to a roll of kitchen towel when it had been discovered that, for once, the cleaners were early and had made off with the dishcloths. He thrust a fistful of paper towards me, his arms bobbing about in suggestion that, just maybe, he'd like to be the one to blot me.

'Don't you touch me.' I held an arm out to stop him moving closer. He placed the towel gingerly in my hand. 'Or I swear to God, you'll never ever have children.'

'Well, that's kind of important to me, so I'll just throw paper at you from here,' he teased. I watched in shock as he began folding a square into a paper plane. Was he serious?

'Why don't you just go away?' I spat. 'Flutter off into a cloud of mothers somewhere. I'm sure they'd be happy to have you.'

'You really are an angry little onion, aren't you?' Marcus turned on his heel and left me, sopping wet in the middle of the staffroom.

Grappling for the kitchen towel as it rolled away, I unravelled another length and began dabbing it against my front. People came and went, curious onlookers joked about there being better ways to score a caffeine hit and, no, I didn't really need any help. Thank you all the same. While it felt like I was there forever, the eyes of the world watching my embarrassing spectacle, it had only been ten minutes or so when the door swung open. Penny stood there looking both confused and worried.

'Ellie?'

I looked up from my shirt, which I'd pulled away from me to better survey the damage. 'Yeah?'

'There's someone here to see you.' The waiver in her voice was not indicative of someone excited for the pub in about seventy-six minutes' time. I, on the other hand, was already doing the mental maths of just how much I could afford to drink.

I groaned. Now what?

* * *

'Eleanor Manning?'

Each step towards the office felt wobblier than the last and, by the time I pushed through the door, I'd imagined every single irrational thing that it could be. My brain was trying to juggle with the idea that my car had be stolen, or Dad having had an accident overseas. I'd have to roll up to a consulate somewhere and bail him out. Or, worse, Mum really wasn't joking about visiting and had been sitting out in reception the entire time. Maybe my grandparents had risen from the dead and were about to serenade me with some 'Thriller' moves of their own. The last thing I had expected was a divorce lawyer.

Stupid, I know.

Looking every bit his serious self, dressed in an overpriced but under-tailored suit, was Bill Napier. He'd been by Dean's side every time there was a deal to be done, hovering downstage with his billowing sleeves and sweat patches. Today was no different.

'Is this a joke?' I snorted. 'Bill, you know who I am.'

He pulled a yellow envelope from his breast pocket. He wore enough rings you'd be mistaken for thinking they were knuckle-dusters. Then again ... 'Your ex-partner is applying for divorce—'

'Hang on, hang on.' I held up a hand to stop him. 'Is this the done thing? We've only been separated nine months. Is this correct?'

'Are you refusing to accept the paperwork?'

'What? No, I'm simply asking a question.' My breathing became shallow, more pointed with their anger. Was this guy serious? I'd done the Googling; twelve months apart and *then* you could apply for a divorce.

Bill placed the envelope on the bench beside me and repeated, 'Eleanor Manning, your ex-partner is applying for divorce, and I am serving you with the divorce application. Your court date is listed for Friday, 9 November 2018.'

Apparently, he was very serious. Like another man I'd recently dealt with, he turned on his heel and walked away.

Chapter 6

'Here, close your eyes. Let me do your eyeliner.' Penny leaned in, the heel of her hand pressed into my cheek. 'We'll make you all beautiful so we can go out and forget all about this week.'

'You know, I'm not actually upset about the divorce. That's not what's upset me.'

Penny stood back and looked down at me. 'She says after draining the hot water because she was too busy in the shower crying.'

Okay, so that part was true. It had been a long week, and what else was a girl supposed to do? I trudged home smelling of old coffee mixed with the tang of deodorant and late-afternoon body odour, and I know of nobody who'd agree that that was in any way appealing. My shoes had felt two sizes too small, I hadn't got through my To Do List, and the divorce papers were a metaphorical weight I couldn't be bothered carrying. So, I did what any overly stressed girl would do – I slipped under the showerhead and had a good old-fashioned cry.

'It felt good,' I said. 'Sometimes you just need to release those tears.'

'I know.' Penny removed her hand and switched to the other eye. 'But, now, we dust ourselves off, we get ourselves fancy, we drink some cocktails, and chase some tail.'

'It just felt like one thing after the other this week,' I said. 'Niggling little things, but I'm sure Bill is what happens when the universe sends someone to laugh at me. She tends to do a lot of that lately.'

'Yeah, well, I wouldn't mind the universe falling on him, to be honest,' she mumbled.

'I just feel like a failure.'

'Ellie, the fact that you are upright and have found gainful employment suggests otherwise. You are smart, you are funny, and you're a wonderful teacher of words.' Penny stood back and admired her work with the make-up brush. 'Fuck, you're so cute. Who are you going home with tonight?'

I snorted. 'Nobody I have to see over the coffee urn on Monday morning.'

'How long has it been?' she asked. 'Am I allowed to ask that?'

'Let me think.' While she faffed about my hair and tossed me a lipstick, I tried to do the mental maths. 'Uh, well, he kind of overshot the mark on his last attempt, so that was over before he even got his pants off.'

She passed a lipstick over her shoulder. 'Are you joking?'

'I wish I was.' I peered into the bathroom mirror. 'All right. Actually, my birthday before last.'

Penny snatched her phone up from the counter and opened an app. 'Sweetie, that's fourteen months, two weeks, five days.'

'Well, then, so it is.'

'Also, we're super late. Let's go.'

* * *

Today was always going to happen, whether I lobbed the grenade first, or he did. There was no point at all being naive about it. Perhaps my anger was more that Idiot Features had got in first, and I was just feeling a wee bit competitive about it all. After all, he was the one who'd done the wrong thing but there I was, being served papers at work like it was me who was the bad guy.

All I wanted to do tonight was have a few cheeky drinks and forget real life for a few hours, make some new friends and maybe catch up with some old ones.

There was one clear-cut memory of the pub that teased itself out from the others as we trounced up the stairs and in through the double doors. It was the last week of high school, and a group of us thought it would be great fun to see out the year with fake IDs, cheap wine, and hangovers. It felt like only yesterday and, here I was again, ready to throw another night the brew fairies' way.

'Isn't this weird?' My eyes zipped around the room, not sure whether I did or didn't want to see any familiar faces.

Penny grabbed at my hand and pulled me up towards the bar. 'Yes, but we're much cooler now.'

A modern foodie flair had replaced the worn yellowing brickwork, Eighties architectural tubular steel, and dart boards. Still, the faces remained generically familiar. The more things change, right?

In an alcove, parents who were silently praying for no injuries or outbursts from their four children. Not quite outside their earshot, a hen's party clucked to life with the appearance of the perennial favourite: the penis straws.

No, don't do it.

The local football team had congregated around the bar, insular worshipping mixed with the scratching of heads and arguing about who did or didn't have the best mark of their recent Grand Final. In the centre of it all, ensconced with back slapping and the odd hoot, was Marcus. Still dressed for work, he sipped from a wine glass and looked my way.

Our eyes met in a slow-motion moment that could have only been choreographed better had Baz Luhrmann turned up with a fish tank and a fancy-dress party. Taking that for the omen it was, I ignored the cotton candy feeling that filled my limbs and ordered a drink. The less I saw of Marcus and his beautiful, but irritatingly smug face tonight, the better.

'Penis face,' I grumbled, hoisting myself onto a sticky bar stool.

'What was that, love?' Mr Bartender, my new best friend, appeared out of nowhere. He looked cool, like he'd seen it all, blue and white check tea towel over his shoulder, and more faded tattoos than a middle-aged interstate truck driver.

'Sorry, a glass of pinot gris, please.' That'll fool him. Ha. 'Actually, make it a lemon meringue martini. I need something to really burn through this week.'

Glass in hand, I pirouetted through the crowd, and was spat out the other side into a beer garden. After today, it was just the tropical oasis I needed. With its overhanging green fronds, large palm in the corner, and synthetic turf, it was a fresh break from the monotony of desks, lost pens and a heaving inbox.

We were a small congregation split amongst standing benches and tiny booths made from recycled packing pallets, and mingling became the adult version of musical chairs. At one point, I got stuck with Glenn, Grade Three teacher, who enjoyed Humphrey Bogart films, and was desperate to get some vegan options on the canteen menu. I wasn't sure our little school was ready for quinoa or tofish, but I wasn't about to knock his enthusiasm either.

Grace was desperate for a husband and, after a failed engagement and an AWOL boyfriend, had her sights sets upon Marcus. Lucky for him, he was still busy inside with his football club. Her reasoning was the very solid, 'He's great with kids and he's hot. What more could I want?'

Patience, a good heart, commitment, amongst other things.

I considered her words for a few sips of a cocktail as we peered into the bar. There he was, all wrinkly eyes and wide smiles, tie gone, and finally looking relaxed amongst friends. Moving around our group, I landed next to Jack, who had a small audience of his own.

'I've been madly waiting for you make your way over here.' He wriggled about in his seat and made room for me between himself and Jane.

'Me?' I joked. 'Never.'

'Yes, you. We were just saying we should play a little game of

Get to Know Eleanor, because I think I'm the only one here besides Penny who actually knows you. And, really, I'm sure that doesn't count because we were like twelve and fourteen at the time and I have a lot of years to catch up on.'

'Wait.' I spun in my seat. 'I thought you were older than that?'

'Thank you so very much.' He did little to hide his disgust. 'I was only ever a few years older than you.'

'Consider my mind blown.'

'I'm so offended.' He sank the last of his wine with a cheeky laugh and a wink. 'Anyway. Ellie, fast facts.'

'Shoot.' I rubbed my hands together and tried to ignore the fact that Marcus was beginning to orbit.

'Favourite drink?'

I picked up my drink, making a display of it for those around the table. 'Lemon meringue martini. At least tonight, anyway.'

'Single? Married? Otherwise?' Jane asked.

'Harem,' I joked, folding my legs underneath me. I waited for the laughter to die down. 'I am single.'

'If you had to pick one meal from the pub tonight, what would it be?' Jack shrugged.

'For quick and dirty, a ploughman's lunch. I mean, if you can't get a platter of cheese, meats and cornichons right, what hope have you got? It makes a perfect picnic, too.' I could slam down some pickle juice right now, I thought.

'And onions.' Marcus's voice cut across the outdoor space as he pulled a chair up opposite me. Grace shuffled aside to let him in but, with the look she was giving him, she was hoping to make room for him in her pants, too.

I said nothing. Everyone else offered up the best confused looks.

'What about a long meal?' Glenn looked glumly at his empty beer. 'Say, if someone were to cook for you.'

I huffed. 'Really? Anything I haven't cooked. I mean, it's been that long since someone cooked a meal for me, I'd probably settle for a Happy Meal and a sundae at this stage. Although, saying that, I do realise that is still fast food, but I'm sure you get the picture.'

On the subject of food, we ordered an assortment of share plates, all picked through the very scientific method of throwing bar nuts at the menu. Oh, and a ploughman's platter. The night wore on, plates stacked higher, and every time Marcus came near me, I moved away, until I couldn't move any further.

Penny, who'd earlier vanished into the throng, resurfaced in my inbox. She was leaving, her message said, with contact details for where she was headed. At least she was being safe, I thought as I scrolled through the length of her message. Still, I wanted to catch her before she vanished into the night. Excusing myself, I left the table, brushing past Marcus on my way through. He reached out, fingers slipping through mine as I placed a hand out to stop him.

When I couldn't find Penny or her mystery man, I called an end to my own night. I'd had enough to drink, was suitably buzzed, and wasn't keen on making a complete tit of myself in front of people I'd barely known a week. Good Vibes Ellie was ready to be tucked into bed. I said my goodbyes to cries of, 'But it's only just gone eleven, stay for one more drink!' before making a beeline for the door.

Stepping out onto the street, I pulled my coat tighter around me and tucked my hands under my arms.

'Eleanor, stop.' Marcus burst out the front door, squeezing between two people, one arm wrangling his coat about his head. 'Wait.'

I shot him a filthy look over my shoulder and kept walking.

'Which way to your place?' His jacket finally slipped over his shoulders with the soft rustle of expensive fabric.

My eyes widened. 'I beg yours?'

'I take it you're walking home?' he asked.

'No, George Jetson was about to pick me up from the taxi

rank.' I swung my arm out and mimicked the noise of the cartoon flying car. 'I was going to go home and have Rosie make me a pot of tea.'

'Smart arse,' he grumbled. 'You've only ingested about half the bar.'

'Oh, and I suppose you're going to suddenly mine your stash of chivalry, are you?' I kept up the quick walk along the main street.

'Actually, I am,' he argued. 'Because I don't think you should be walking home alone.'

'*You* don't want *me* walking home alone?' I stopped on the spot, outside a pie shop that was in the throes of closing for the night, barely a light left on in the place. A teenager moved back and forth with a dirty old mop while a blue-light bug zapper burned brightly above the kitchen door. I turned the buttons on my coat. 'I suppose you think you're doing a community service, too. You're so bloody conceited.'

'Let me get this straight.' He shifted on his feet and shoved a hand in his pocket. 'I've just told you I'd like to walk you home to make sure you get there safely, because God knows where Penny's gone. She obviously cares so much about your welfare that she left you alone in a bar. And you're the one attacking me?'

'Or maybe she understands that a woman in her thirties is more than capable of getting home safely.' I pointed in the general direction of home. 'It's six hundred metres, at the most,' I said, before grumbling, 'maybe a kilometre.'

'It may surprise you, but the places you think are safe are not always so, and a beautiful woman walking home slightly tipsy may very well become a target.'

I glared at him. I didn't know whether to feel patronised or touched by the gesture. Lady Justice was having a hard time weighing up her options, too. I think she was about to shake her Magic 8 Ball.

Reply hazy, try again.

'So, after the day we've both had, if my worry makes me conceited, so be it. Conversely, I have tried no less than six times to talk to you tonight and, on each occasion, you've either turned away, or simply ignored me.'

'You've been keeping count?' I shrieked.

'So, who's conceited now?' Marcus folded his arms across his chest and drummed his fingers. He really was quite attractive. And tall. And pretty.

'Men can get attacked, too, you know,' I sputtered. 'And I've been here for years. I know the ways.'

'So, walk me home instead.'

'Why? You lost your way?' I laughed, snapping my fingers in his face. 'Hold on … did you call me beautiful?'

'I believe I did, yes.'

'Right, then,' I said quietly. 'Thank you.'

'You know, I might even kiss you if you'd stop arguing with me for three minutes.'

'I do not argue with you,' I said. 'Anyway, three minutes is quick.'

'Exhibit A.' He waved a hand towards me. 'I can't even—'

'So, do it.' I almost wanted to backtrack immediately. Almost.

'What?'

'Do it,' I said. 'You're so sure, do it.'

Marcus shook his fists towards the sky and, with one fell swoop, stepped forward, took my face in his hands, and kissed me. As his thumbs drew against my cheekbones, all I could think was, *Oh my God, oh my bloody God!* We were the last two people to succeed at getting along with each other this week, so why were we chasing this so far up the hill I was about to fetch a pail of water?

And why the hell did it feel so unbearably good? Heat bloomed in my chest, sending any and all common sense fluttering towards the sun on a trajectory last seen by Icarus. Let's not forget how well that all ended.

With fingers drawn through my hair, and a tug so gentle it barely registered, my ponytail unravelled and tangled through his fingers.

He drew breath. 'Not bad for someone who's always so wound up.'

'And you're so stuck up.' I kissed him again. This time, I fumbled with the front of his shirt, the thick expensive fabric, the tiny translucent buttons that felt colder than the night air, and the soft silk of this tie. My fingers drew a line up his chest, past his collar, and came to rest at the nape of his neck.

'You wanna just come home with me instead?' he mumbled against my mouth.

'Why, so you can save me from the dragons?'

'Something like that.'

* * *

The Great Penis Drought ended exactly thirty-seven minutes ago.

'Should we perhaps define this?' I asked.

Marcus shifted his weight, rolling over to face me. His breath came in tiny puffs that tickled my cheeks. For a moment, I simply enjoyed looking at him, at the self-satisfied smile that barely registered, at the sleepy eyes, and the arms he folded across his chest. A lock of dark hair flopped down into his eyes. I pushed it back and waited.

'Before I go home and we're both still scratching our heads?' I continued in the face of his silence.

There was no dictionary definition for what had just happened. All right, so maybe there was, and I'm sure the thesaurus would have something to say, too. Sex. Sex had just happened. Very sexy sex. I'd have jumped and run for the bathroom if it weren't for the fact there was a distinct Haven't Seen Use in a While pain tickling my hamstrings.

'I suppose we probably should,' he said, his voice barely a

whisper.

'What do you want to call it?' I asked.

'I'm not entirely sure,' he said.

I tucked hair behind my ear and curled further into the pillow. 'Do you want a relationship from this? Is that what this is?'

'How about we don't call it anything?' He propped himself up on an elbow. 'Just ... I don't know right now. Whatever.'

Whatever? What kind of word is that to use in a situation like this? I detested it. Even my woozy brain, which was plummeting to Sober Land (Icarus, remember?), knew that was bad news. It was the word of choice whenever Dean wanted to dismiss my excitement or devalue me in front of his friends. The worst part about it? It worked every single time.

A beloved author popped in to the library for a quick visit? *Whatever.*

Great day at work today! *Whatever.*

I'm moving out. *Whatever.*

Apparently, I'd just slept with Coastal Edition Dean and, as much physical joy as his naked body may have brought, none of it was worth going through that kind of humiliation again.

I was so, so angry at myself.

'I'm going to have a shower.' Marcus rolled out of bed and strolled across the bedroom, everything on display, as if being intimate with each other were something we did regularly and not just at the end of a drunken night. His body was every inch the footballer, taut muscles, definition, and legs for miles.

'Okay,' I whispered, pulling the duvet up around my chin.

'You all right?' The corner of his mouth drew up into a smirk. 'You don't want to join me?'

I shook my head and, trying to look coolly casual, picked a clump of mascara from my eyelashes. 'No, thank you.'

I watched him disappear behind a glass-doored en suite. Shifting, I tried to reconcile his words with a body whose muscles I hadn't used in far too long, and lady parts that were feeling the aftereffects of a decent seeing to. Finally.

I sat up and took in my surroundings, a room I'd been too preoccupied to look at earlier.

A low-lit bedside lamp gave the room some decent ambiance at least, hiding all the lumps and bumps, and anything else nobody wanted to see. A box of condoms, which had been torn at in desperation, was doing its best impression of an origami flower on the bedside table, and my clothes were strewn from one end of the room to the other, though I was sure my dress was still on the bannister somewhere.

Mixed feelings were something I'd experienced a lot lately, but this was taking the cake and using a blowtorch to light the candles. Earlier, I was oozing confidence and full of those loose-limbed, sated, post-orgasmic feelings. Now, I was panicked. I was a 'whatever' again, and reality was coming home to roost. My head was set to wash, and my stomach was on tumble-dry. This was the dumbest idea in the history of my ideas. I had to work with this man. I had to look him in the eye and act as if we hadn't just had the most incredible toe-curling, back-arching, name-screaming, hair-pulling sex ever.

And he wanted to define it as 'whatever'.

I was a complete goose.

With the safety of Marcus in the shower, I ran. I threw back the sheets, shimmied back into my underwear, slipped on my shoes, and raced down the stairs for my dress. My handbag and coat had been discarded by the front door and, just as the water upstairs stopped running, the front door closed with a gentle click and I disappeared into the night.

Chapter 7

Part of me expected Marcus to come racing out his front door, six-pack on display and towel wrapped around his waist, that finely carved V-shape shown off perfectly. The other part hoped like hell I made it home before he realised what had happened.

Reality had other plans.

I'd barely rounded the corner before I was on my knees in someone's gutter, depositing my dinner and adding a whiff of lemon meringue martini into the local storm-water system. I had to wait for my stomach to stop heaving before I could pick gravel from tender kneecaps and limp home. My walk of shame was complemented by shoes dangling from fingers, and a sweaty sour mess of hair.

None of this was going down in my list of life achievements I was proud of.

I was relieved when I arrived home to find the house empty. It gave me just enough time to shower myself back into human form, and a modicum of privacy to freak out on my own. As my head hit the pillow, I hoped to wake up the next morning and find everything had been some multidimensional Marvel universe style dream.

It didn't. It wasn't. This was not Doctor Strange and his mirror dimension. Or, maybe it could be if I made sure not to tell anyone of my late-night escapades. Hiding from daylight the next morning, I made a very snap decision that I was not telling a soul about my night. What strange magic had been there was not being put up for public consumption. I pulled on some comfortable clothes and shuffled out into the kitchen, and the new morning.

I switched on the kettle and searched for a mug through barely open eyes.

'And a very good morning to you,' Penny said through burbled laughter. She had a frying pan in one hand and a fat old spatula in the other. 'Are you of the genus grease this morning, or the genus carbo-starchy-coma?'

'Both. Both is good.' I slipped onto a stool by the counter and held my head in my hands. Even though I'd showered and double washed myself last night, I could still smell lemon meringue. My stomach lurched.

'Big fat fluffy pancakes?' Penny presented me with a plate stacked high. 'We have not particularly authentic maple syrup, lemon and sugar, or whipped butter.'

'Butter,' I groaned. Something rose in my throat at the idea of going anywhere near lemon. 'And maple syrup. All of it.'

'Alrighty then.'

A leaning tower of pancakes appeared before me, along with butter and syrup, which I poured until I had a small moat on my plate. I shuffled across to the dining table and hugged my coffee cup. I'd have closed my eyes again if it weren't for the fact I got a frame-by-frame replay of my not so best moments from the last twenty-four hours.

'How are you feeling this morning?' Penny stood back from the pan while bacon sizzled and spat at her.

'I feel like I'm never drinking again.' I held my face. While I felt like death, Penny looked like she was enjoying every minute of this. For once, it was me on the wrong end of the bar tab and not her.

'And, where, pray tell, did you disappear to last night?' she asked.

'Uhhhh.' I tucked my napkin under my plate and chewed ultra-slowly. Not even Penny was exempt from my decision not to tell anyone. 'I went for a walk.'

Her brows disappeared beneath her fringe. 'For a walk?'

'I was so drunk,' I tried, fingers fanning out from my temples. 'And I thought the cold air would do me good. All I ended up doing was throwing up in the gutter.'

Her jaw dropped. 'You?'

'Me.' I pouted. 'What a waste of good martini, right?'

'Jesus, Eleanor. If you're not careful, you'll be having random cheap sex.'

Pancake stuck in my throat. I coughed.

'And herein, you are shooketh,' she chuckled. 'Ellie, you crack me up.'

I grinned. 'Glad to help.'

After breakfast, I beat a hasty retreat to bed, where my only companion was going to be Harry Potter and his magic wand. He was going to be far less trouble. Plus, it was my tenth read through of the series, and he was at least a known quantity.

Still, there was only so many magic spells that would keep reality at bay. My hangover tapered off with a thumper of a headache, which was soon replaced by waves of embarrassed realisation. It arrived slowly at first, but then rushed in like a high tide in a monsoon. My life had an egg timer in the top right-hand corner. Less than forty-eight hours until I had to deal with Marcus again.

Penny suggested a day of shopping, but I couldn't process the idea of perhaps running into him on the street. I didn't want that awkward 'How about that, huh?' one-two shuffle on a street corner while neither of us knew what to say. So, I opted for a weekend inside. The couch and a DVD box set were calling my name. I needed to recharge, I argued, and disappeared into a pile of cushions with half the confectionary aisle and another set of What Ifs to be anxious about. I powered through a box of Lindt balls, *balls*, and broke apart a block of Cadbury Fruit and Nut … *nuts*.

Chocolate! Marcus was the chocolate bar I stole from the milk bar when I was fourteen. While the shopkeeper was busy stacking fruit and veg, I slipped a single-serve Cadbury Snack bar into my pocket and raced out the door. Only, this time, I'd been caught. And what did we learn from that episode? There was not thrill in getting away with the crime, and it wasn't ever going to happen again. There, brain. Sorted. Illicit. Illegal. Not happening. Never again.

By the time my alarm went off on Monday morning, bright red and screaming like a banshee, I was well prepared. I'd been awake for hours, pondering what exactly it was I was going to say during the inevitable discussion. I'd rationalised how I was going to get my point across without sounding like a clingy girlfriend. To him, *whatever* may have only been a word. To me, it was a matter of respect. How the ever-perceptive Penny hadn't picked up on my agitation was beyond me.

I kept my head down and thoughts to myself as I walked through the school gates. If I couldn't see the looks in people's eyes, then they didn't know, and I could sleep easier. We slipped into the reception area together, where Penny opened the safe and booted her computer, and I checked my pigeonhole as per my shiny new routine.

My heart thumped in time with my footsteps and my stomach was stuck on spin cycle. They dropped it down a notch as I ventured into an empty tea room. It was one hurdle I'd cleared. It all felt a little like Mario trying to get to the castle to save Princess Peach, except I was the Princess trying to avoid Mario, so maybe that wasn't the best analogy.

I shouldered my office door as it swung open.

'And it's a very good morning to Usain Bolt!'

As it turned out, I was not prepared.

Marcus sat, legs dangling from the desk, bearing coffee and a greasy bag that I took cautiously and with minimal eye contact. Inside the bag, a Florentine – only my favourite biscuit ever. With its sweet chocolate base, crunchy nuts and candied fruit, Penny and I would walk laps of town as teenagers, fuelled only by idle high school gossip and the sugar in these biscuits.

'I thought, seeing as I didn't get my morning after breakfast that I'd improvise,' he continued.

'How'd you know these were my favourite?' I asked.

He shrugged and lifted his feet onto the seat of a chair. 'A little bird told me.'

'A little bird in a tiki dress?' I asked.

'Is that what it is today?' He smirked. 'I can never keep up.'

My gaze shifted from the contents of the bag to him. Panic drummed a beat in my ears.

'Relax, I didn't tell her,' he assured me. 'She certainly seemed completely oblivious to it when I rang for some insider information, so why feed the gossip train?'

'What'd you tell her?' I asked.

He shrugged. 'I told her I wanted to do something nice for you for breakfast. Something about welcoming you into your first proper week on the job.'

I placed his offering beside my computer, twisted my hair up into a bun and shoved a pencil through the middle. Until then, I hadn't noticed I'd left it loose this morning.

'Can I ... I need to know what happened,' he said, hesitant.

Our eye contact was brief. Marcus picked at the edge of my bench, and he swallowed more often than a drowning rat. This wasn't helping me. My heart sank under the weight of guilt and embarrassment, and all the words I'd prepared over the weekend marched out the door two by two. I grappled for them, but they were gone.

I pressed the door closed with a quiet click, keen to sort this out and move on for the day. I crossed my arms, fearing that if I rubbed my hands against my hips one more time I'd tear my skin clean off. Pressing at an invisible spot on my forehead didn't seem to work either. As I paced about, Marcus sat on the edge of my desk and waited patiently.

'I'm not here to argue with you,' he ventured. 'I just want to know what happened. Everything was going great, at least I thought it was. I got out of the shower, and you were gone.'

'You don't think that might have something to do with you at all?' I asked. 'Let's not call it anything? Whatever?'

His head dipped back slightly, frustration lining his face as his words came back to haunt him. He rubbed a hand across his mouth. 'I did say that, didn't I?'

'Yes. Yes, you did.'

'What if I said I wanted more?' He clasped his hands in his lap. 'What if I'd spent all weekend thinking about that night and thought maybe we should do that again, and soon?'

I pursed my lips and I shook my head.

'No?' he asked. 'What, so, you're upset because I said "whatever" and, now, you're upset because I want to take it back?'

'I'm not upset about you wanting to take it back.' I smiled softly. 'I'm upset that I was stupid enough to go home with you in the first place. That I put myself in that position again when I promised myself I wouldn't, that I'd be more careful.'

Eyes wide, his mouth formed a shocked 'O'. 'Christ, okay. There's a spare spot on my back if you want to dig the knife in again?'

'And how do I know you don't try this on with all the girls?' I asked. 'Maybe I'm just flavour of the month.'

'It may surprise you, but our school is not exactly the Baskin Robbins of the dating world.' He stood straighter. 'What happens now?'

'What do you mean what happens now?' I asked. 'You've got a job to do, go and do it.'

'Are you usually this cold?' he asked.

'Cold? How is this a me issue?' I laughed. 'I asked you to define it, and you blew me off with little more than a "whatever". Realistically, it was never going to be more than a one-night stand because we need to work together, and I'm not dragging a relationship around the office like a petulant toddler, but "whatever"? Do you understand how devaluing that is?'

'That's certainly not how I intended it to sound,' he said. 'Not at all. I simply expressing that I didn't think we needed to label anything, that it could just be one fantastic night as it was.'

I glanced up over my shoulder. 'Look, we need to be in class in about five minutes. You need to leave.'

'So that's it?' he asked again. 'I use one wrong word, and I've blown my chance?'

'Do you teach your students to choose their words carefully?' I opened my office door and swept my arm towards the outside world. 'As far as I'm concerned, it didn't happen, and it's not happening again.'

'So, what you're saying is just rewind to four o'clock Friday?'

'Exactly. None of it happened. Whatever, right?'

'All right then.' Marcus backed out of my office slowly. 'Onion.'

'Smug bastard.' I reached for my lesson plans.

So, that didn't exactly play out how I'd hoped. For all the imaginary arguments I'd won over the weekend, I suddenly had about as much bite as sweet tomato relish. But I didn't have time to worry. In fact, I didn't even want to worry about it. The bell had barely rung when Jemima appeared at the door of the library.

'Everybody say good morning to Miss Manning.' Jemima held the door open for her small army as they raced through the door, elbows akimbo, already fragile friendships teetering on the fall of seating arrangements. They sang a sweet greeting and, before I could grab her, she'd vanished. Fair call, I thought.

'All right.' I clapped my hands and looked out at the faces before me. Kids. They were so readable I could tell their level of disinterest a mile off. 'Today, we're going to be reading one of my favourite books. Then, I want you to use the tools in front of you to retell the story of that book back to me.'

They looked bored stiff. Great.

'Miss Manning, are you going to take the roll?'

Fuck.

'Just testing.' I grinned and shook a finger. 'Good pick-up.'

Thankfully, things got better. I remembered roll call at the beginning of classes, worked through retellings with younger students, character profiles with some of the older ones, and word associations with the ones in between. I pushed my return cart around at lunchtime and, on Wednesday, Penny and the Prep teachers (that really should be a band name) took me for lunch at the closest sandwich shop we could find, where I avoided any and all questions about my love life. I did not have one, no matter what secrets the universe was keeping for me.

On my way back, I walked into the library with a fist-sized blueberry muffin in tow to find Phil waiting for me. He looked deep in discussion with Mick, both wearing expressions that told me they were plotting someone's demise; likely mine. I hoped like hell Marcus hadn't said anything. Surely, he wouldn't.

'Eleanor.' Phil held out a hand to stop me before I could disappear too far into my office.

'Phil.' I backtracked cautiously. All I wanted right now was to destroy this muffin and ride the sugar wave out for the afternoon. I peeled back the paper patty case and nibbled as I waited for him to finish mumbling at Mick.

'How's everything going?' he asked. 'All under control? Settling in well?'

I nodded slowly. 'I think so, yes.'

'No problems at all?' he asked. 'Getting along all right with everyone?'

I froze. Throat, meet vomit. Vomit, sit back down. 'Sorry?'

'It's just, I've got you in mind for a project. I was just wondering if there were any issues I wasn't yet aware of.'

I shook my head and glanced at Mick, who offered nothing but a nervous smile. 'No, everyone's been great. Very supportive. Thank you.'

'And you're ready for the Book Fair coming up? That's always a huge day.'

Not really. It was still weeks away. 'Absolutely.'

'Excellent. Good.' Phil rubbed his hands together, surveying the library like he was looking for something out of place, then disappeared with Mick in tow.

I wasn't sure I wanted to know what they were planning.

Chapter 8

If anyone were to ask me to sum up my first two weeks at Apollo Bay Primary School, I'd probably tell them it had been a bag of Allen's Party Mix. Friendships with most colleagues came easily, helped by shared stories of class tantrums and breakdowns over the death of fictional characters. As a book lover, I could sympathise with that far too easily.

We bemoaned workloads that held hands with a lack of funding and, just when I thought I'd climbed to the top of my To Do List, I'd received so many boxes of books for this upcoming book fair that I wished I'd seen them being delivered. Watching them arrive would have looked like that meme with the Amazon truck; oh, look, my book order has arrived!

When it came to Marcus, we had no need to see each other. Like a clip from *Yellow Submarine*, he'd walk in one door, I'd leave from another. I might have thought keeping him out of sight was the key to keeping him out of my mind, but it was only going to last for so long before I had to deal with him, and his class.

On Friday afternoon, with his Grade Six students in tow, he walked into the library. His navy suit and grey tie brought my winning streak to an end. I sighed so heavily my fringe tickled and left me scratching my forehead.

'Good afternoon, Miss Manning.' He grinned so hard, so smugly, that I thought his head might tip back and reveal he was secretly a PEZ dispenser. If he then proceeded to spit out a couple of chill pills, I'd be more than happy to deal with him for the afternoon. Instead, he left nothing more than large handprints on my freshly Windex'd door, because using door handles was so 2005.

'Good afternoon, Mr Blair. So positively wonderful to see your face again.' I smiled coquettishly and turned away.

His class stampeded past him like wild brumbies, dispersing in every direction known to woman and proceeding to tear up the landscape. They were way too boisterous a bunch for a Friday afternoon. I don't ever remember being so intense when I was their age. My friends and I were more likely to be dragging knuckles and yawning out the last of our jam sandwiches but, here they were, raucous and large as life.

'All right, remember what I said.' Marcus strode across the learning zone. 'Let's mix up our reading style a bit and step out of our comfort zones. Max, that means something other than comics for you and, Sarah, get off the Sweet Valley High.'

'Nothing wrong with Sweet Valley High,' I grumbled.

'And I'd like to see a few of you in the non-fiction section. Caroline, I know you'll just *love* to read about French revolutionary history. Napoleon is not just an ice-cream flavour.'

He wasn't even that. What on earth was he teaching these kids? I cringed. 'What?'

'That's it, every corner. Spread on out. That way, when Miss Manning puts all these books back tonight, she gets to familiarise herself with the library, and we do want to help her get acquainted with Mr Dewey and his system.'

I glanced up from the small piles of books forming on the returns trolley. 'I'll have you know I'm very familiar with Mr Dewey and his system. We're old friends, dinner on Friday nights.'

Marcus leaned back against the loans counter, and I wondered if I could slap his elbows from underneath him with a ruler. Funny bones were never comical when on the receiving end of a sharp stick or doorframe.

'A refresher never hurt,' he said.

Hell, I'd worked in libraries for the last ten years. If I knew one thing better my own monthly cycle, it was the Dewey Decimal System. It had got so bad in my previous job that, at one point, I could direct other staff to the aisle number and shelf location.

Looking for a book about Mozart? Somewhere around 780's, aisle twenty on the second floor, right-hand side. I sighed. Oh, for the simple days.

I watched as Marcus ambled around the room, ducking and weaving between children and stacks, congratulating them all on their fine reading choices. 'Concorde plane? Well done, Danny.' '*Tudor History for Children*? Good on you, Emily, you'll love it.' I gave him a filthy look and retreated to my office. The sooner I got rid of him, the better. If only he thought the same. He wasn't done, and followed me straight through the door, his aftershave following him like the slightly appealing smell of lazy Sunday mornings in bed with a man who knew his way around a woman's body.

Urgh.

'Do you have the lesson plans I emailed you?' he asked.

'Yes.' I picked one of the display folders from beside my PC. 'See? I, the capable teacher that I am, are prepared.'

He plucked the folder from my hand and flipped through the contents. 'That was grammatically incorrect, just so you know.'

My eyes widened. 'Sorry, what?'

'You basically just said, "I are prepared".'

'Oh, sod off,' I grumbled.

'Let's not fight in front of the children, hmm?' He smirked. 'Not good for their mental health, is all.'

'What?' I narrowed my eyes at him. 'What the hell are you talking about?'

'Now, do you want me to stay and take this first class? Or have you got things under control?' he asked.

'Of course I'm capable. I just said I was, didn't I? Go away.'

'Ooof! Bitey like cheese.' His tongue rolled about in his cheek pocket. 'Cracker barrel.'

'If anyone's crackers, it's you.'

He stepped out of my office again. 'All right, my learned friends. I'm leaving you with Miss Manning for the afternoon. Please be gentle with her, she is such a delicate soul.'

Marcus turned on his heel and walked away to the sound of scandalised giggling. If I wasn't nervous about taking his class before, I was churning up like a blowhole at high tide by the time he was halfway out of the room.

'We will be fine, you realise?' I called, watching him pull a fruit roll from his pocket.

'Okay then,' he called over his shoulder.

'I'm not kidding.'

'All right.' He stood at the door of the staffroom.

'And I'm not an onion,' I called after him.

I turned to face my students. They broke into a fit of giggles.

When the day was over, I was a whirring mixture of exhausted and enthralled. Unlike their teacher, Marcus's class had been a wonderful experience; bright, engaging, everything a teacher could hope for. It still didn't solve the problems I was having with him and insulting me in front of an entire class probably wasn't the best way to earn my respect. I gave myself a few minutes' peace, gathered up loose papers and pencils from the tables in my learning zone, and decided to tell him how I felt.

But, as I stood in the doorway of his office with the prospect of having to let everything out all too real, my mouth was thick with words I couldn't find, and my heart was shaking my ribs. How was it that he did this to me?

I hated confrontation, having to find the words and then deal with the fallout. The fact I hadn't spoken to my husband since I moved out was proof enough of that. It was only when I changed my mobile number that he stopped calling.

'Miss Manning, to what do I owe this unforeseeable pleasure?' Marcus's words yanked me back into the present.

I shifted from one foot to the other, picking at the debris under my nails until he placed his coffee cup down and sat on the end of his desk. He was looking at me like I was a complete idiot. That, or he was practicing for his next photo shoot.

He sighed heavily. 'Eleanor, you look like you have something to say.'

I had about a billion things I wanted to say, none of them appropriate for a school environment. I was having one of those moments where I was suddenly questioning whether choosing to confront him was the right decision. Perhaps if I simply said good afternoon, went home and slept on it, it would be …

'Do you have a problem with me?' I blurted.

Apparently, my mouth and brain were not concentric. A tiny fire inside me began to crackle and rage.

'A problem with you? Why would I have a problem with you?' he asked.

'Oh, I don't know.' I crossed my arms. 'I've got a few examples to pick from. Do we want to talk about your attitude pertaining to your library session? Or the coffee? The onion comment? Why don't we start with this afternoon's stunt? Or maybe, just maybe, we'll look at this as an ego problem stemming from the fact you got a knock-back.'

'An ego problem? A knock-back? Have you swallowed a *Roget's*?' he asked. 'I have no idea what you're talking about. The coffee was an accident, I did try and explain that to you. If I recall correctly, you bit my head off when I tried to help. Later that night, though …'

'What about your library session? It was my first day here and you put me on the spot in front of everyone,' I argued. 'Do you recall how hard it was for *you* to turn up to an entirely new work environment? Your first day trying to feel your way around? Let alone having to deal with someone like you on top of it.'

'Hardly everyone,' he scoffed. 'Three other colleagues, one of whom I was under the assumption you were already quite familiar with.'

'What's that supposed to mean?' I asked, fingers tapping my arms.

'Nothing!' he laughed. 'It means you're familiar with him. You're the library teacher, don't you know what "familiar" means?'

'I thought you were implying something else,' I grumbled.

'*Should* I have been implying something else?' He fixed me with an accusatory stare. 'I'm not sure that would have been legal at the time you were here. It would pain me greatly to have to tell the authorities.'

'Oh, for God's sake, Marcus!'

'What?' He held a palm up. 'You went there.'

'An angry little onion?' I countered.

'You know, none of this seemed to bother you last weekend.' His mouth twitched and eyes sparkled. It was then that I realised he was enjoying this, and I'd stepped right into his trap. He crossed his legs at his ankles, folded his arms and waited for me to continue.

'What even is an angry little onion?' I shrieked. 'Those little cocktail onions are fun, they're the colours of Christmas, and they're always at parties. They are good things. They're there for a good time. White onions, on the other hand.'

'Do you want me to pay for the dry-cleaning?' he asked.

'You made me eat a jar of onions.'

He laughed. 'I did no such thing.'

'I got a jar on the way home, along with a block of cheese, some dip, crackers and a bottle of wine.' I lifted a lazy hand in his direction. 'Look at you, driving me to drink.'

The left corner of his mouth flinched.

'And, no, the coffee came out.' I looked down at my feet. 'But, thank you.'

'You're welcome.'

'Are you angry at being knocked back? Because it's not going to work,' I said.

'Is that what you think it's about?' he asked. 'You need to

familiarise yourself with the library. I was helping.'

'Ohmygod!' I shouted. 'You are so infuriating! We both know it's not about that. And what's with the bloody suits?'

He brushed his hands down the front of his jacket. 'I don't see any blood on them.'

'Does it help you to teach in a suit? Or is it just a catch and release mechanism?'

'Actually, I think your blue dress last Friday night was the catch and release mechanism, not the suit. I would happily come back for seconds … or is it thirds?' His brow knitted. 'And yes, they do help me in the classroom. It shows that I have some level of self-respect. My students see that and, most of the time, behave accordingly. When I show that I am serious about my job, they become a little more serious about their learning.'

I squinted. 'What?'

'You say that word a lot,' he said. 'What? What? Whatty-what? At least I don't currently look like I'm two leather patches and a monocle away from being Henry Jones Senior.'

I gasped so loud, so hard, I'm surprised I didn't swallow my own tonsils, tongue, and teeth. 'What?'

'And again.' He clicked his tongue and rolled his eyes. I was sure I saw him bite the inside of his cheek. 'You heard.'

'I do not.' I chanced a quick glance down at myself, hoping like hell he wasn't right.

Except, he kind of was. My pant suit was my big purchase straight out of university. It was there to win me jobs and make me look smart. Ten years on, maybe it had dated a little, but it was still a suit, wasn't it? It was no different to what he was wearing, except that it looked very 2005, and wasn't particularly well fitted. My shirt was white, and definitely not see-through – that had been checked thoroughly before I walked out the door this morning. And didn't everyone own that comfy little pair of heels that weren't high enough for a night out, but weren't so low I should be wrapped in pyjamas? It was the professional, but still accessible type of shoe. No? Just me, then. It was about then that it hit me.

I looked like a fifteen-year-old on the first day of their summer retail job. One in which they'd be replaced by another fifteen-year-old just as soon as next summer came around. I cursed under my breath.

'You know, I love how you've bustled your way in here this afternoon, ready to talk about everything except the elephant-sized issue in the corner.'

I scoffed. 'Don't flatter yourself, it's not that big.'

He pouted. 'Well, now, that's just cruel.'

'And you're—'

'I'm what?' He cupped a hand around his ear. 'Go on, say it.'

The words were right there on the tip of my tongue. You're just like him, I was ready to say. You are everything I walked away from, yet here I am chasing after you. From the suits and ties, to the charm laced with backhanded comments. Before I had a chance to turn into a wobbling, choked-up mess, a knock at the door interrupted us.

'Just the two people I wanted to see.' Phil's voice came from some point over my shoulder.

Any conversation that began like that was never going to have an ideal ending. It was exactly the way my redundancy discussion began. *Come on in, Eleanor, just the person I wanted to see. Take a seat.* I braced myself for impact as Phil stepped around me into the room and offered us both an uncertain look. It reminded me of my dad when he'd tell me to clean my bedroom. He never did believe me and would check to make sure I'd put my books back on the shelf, and in order, and that I wasn't hoarding anything under the bed that I'd pick up after lights out. Phil knew something was going on. He had to have known.

'Everything okay in here?' Phil asked. 'I feel like I could cut the tension with a knife.'

For a few brief moments, the room stood still. There was a

quick succession of yeses, nos, and maybes, and I came to the lightning decision that, two weeks in, I wasn't going to upset the apple cart. I could have, but it would be opening a can of worms bigger than I knew how to deal with, and if ever I'd seen a man beg without words, Marcus was doing it right now.

'Everything's great.' I grinned, breaking eye contact in favour of Phil.

'Eleanor and I were just discussing class this afternoon.' Marcus's gaze followed him around the room.

'I take it everything's okay?' Phil walked across the office, carefully inspecting the smallest detail, hands clasped behind his back. 'I've been thinking about the both of you, actually.'

I swallowed. 'You have?'

My brain tripped into overdrive. Someone had heard something or seen us wobble off into the night last Friday. They'd said something to someone else, who'd dobbed on us. Phil would have found out I'd left last Friday with a filthy blouse, and Penny would have crumbled like stale shortbread and told him everything. Or, at least, everything she knew. We'd be hauled into detention for the foreseeable future and, worse, there'd be a hastily scribbled note in my file. Already. I took a deep breath and blew it out slowly. Calm thoughts.

'Yes.' He pulled Roger's chair out and sat between us. 'The senior school end-of-year presentation night is coming up. Have you lot started working on it, Marcus?'

'We were hoping to get onto it this week. We've been incredibly busy.' He swallowed. Hard. 'Just with the curriculum and everything getting back into gear this week.'

'Right,' Phil said slowly. 'Here's the deal. You and Ellie can sort this one out. This year, I want you to take on the yearbook as well. Normally that's something Cathy would have looked after but, seeing as Ellie's only new, I think she could do with a hand. I'm sure between the two of you, you can present something decent.'

'Oh, no.' I shook my head and laughed. Somebody slap me, please. This had to be a joke. 'Is that a good idea?'

'I think it's a great idea.' Phil nodded. 'Marcus, you've been at me all year, telling me you wanted more responsibility and a chance to move up the ladder. Vice principal was it? Ellie, you've just started, so it'll give you a great introduction to the school community. I want weekly updates, preferably in person. On email if you can't find me in this tiny dot of a school.'

'Come to think of it.' Marcus shifted on his feet and turned his attention to me. My stomach did the cha-cha. 'You're right. This is a great idea. We'll get right onto it.'

Phil grinned and disappeared quicker than The Flash on a promise, well before either of us had a chance to argue. Along with a pit of snakes or any kind of Seventies disco on repeat, this was my idea of a nightmare, one that I didn't want to deal with today. My gaze floated from Phil's fast disappearing bald spot back to Marcus. I edged closer to him.

'What?' He shuffled backwards but achieved nothing more than knocking a tin of pens from his own desk.

'Vice principal, huh?'

'Well, you know ...' he mumbled. 'I could.'

I reached out and rubbed the end of his nose.

'What?' He reached up self-consciously. 'What is it?'

'There's something brown on your nose. And it smells. Probably full of corn, too.'

I turned and walked away. As I hit the hallways, anxious energy bubbled up into uncontrollable laughter. The relief of being out of that room helped me float all the way home.

* * *

'Silly question.' I dropped my handbag on the kitchen bench, before searching through the refrigerator for a drink. Penny was out on the deck, tucked into her egg chair with the radio playing low. It wasn't quite beer weather, and cordial was reserved for school nights. A fresh bottle of fizz was strategically hidden behind a bag of lettuce in an attempt to save it for a moment like this. It was the end of the week. It would do nicely.

I grabbed a glass and made for the door. 'What on earth are you drinking?'

'A very virginal Bloody Mary. It's terrible. She might be a virgin, but she's not even a *bit* filthy.' She took another sip while peering up at me. 'What's the question?'

To ask, or not to ask. I bit down on my lip and thought of the consequences. No one ever enjoys being told they look awful, but I needed to know. I didn't want to spend the rest of my days second-glancing myself in the mirror. Plus, I was never going to find a man if I dressed like one of John Lithgow's *Footloose* cronies. Kevin Bacon, yes. Leather elbow patches, no.

'Come on, spit it out.' The straw swung away from her mouth as she spoke. 'Are you okay?'

'Do I dress like Henry Jones Senior?' I asked. 'Like an old man?'

'Well, me lassie.' She attempted the worst Scottish accent I have ever heard. Thank you, *Outlander*. 'If ye happen to know where I can find me a young Indiana Jones, please do send him this way. I'll give him a crusade to remember, possibly in my own temple of doom.'

I took a giant slug of my drink. 'That's a yes, then.'

She winced apologetically, hands weighing up the scales of her response. 'We can fix that though. Your blue dress on the first day was banging. You just need to top up the wardrobe.'

'Banging.' I nodded. Literally. 'Even better.'

'Who told you that?' Penny placed her glass on the table. A ring of condensation quickly formed around it. 'Because I will bippity-boppity-fuck them up.'

'Nobody,' I lied. This was like being a kid all over again. Mum would say something about Dad. Dad would let something slip about Mum, and there I was caught in the middle trying to work

80

out exactly where it was that I stood in all of this. 'I just caught sight of myself in a mirror and thought I looked a little like I should have a wire pushcart for my groceries.'

'Come with me. We'll see if there's anything in my wardrobe for you.' Penny stepped inside. 'And bring me a wine. If I'm going to be your fairy godmother, I'm going to need something with real alcohol in it.'

'All right.'

'And granny carts are the bomb.'

Chapter 9

We didn't get far with the wardrobe catwalk. Music television stole our attention, wine soaked our sobriety, and a pizza delivery boy robbed us of our ability to move after delivering dinner. At one point, I disappeared to my bedroom to charge my phone, and didn't wake up until the next morning.

Months ago, my dad decided to mix things up and head off on a European backpacking adventure. Currently, he was nearing the end of his Camino de Santiago trek. Despite it being considered a Christian pilgrimage, he was in no way a church-goer. He simply liked the idea of the challenge, the living day-to-day, and experiencing new places, even if he did eventually mutter something about his spiritual health.

The idea caught him quickly, and his coffee table was soon littered with pocket guides and language course fliers, maps and internet printouts. Soon enough, I was dropping him at Tullamarine airport with nothing more than a backpack, his passport, hiking boots, and an international SIM card.

When he reached his first stop, Paris, the text messages came thick and fast:

I've just landed.
I'm in the bus.
I got to my room okay.
Start of day one today.
Hostel life sure is something else.
I met some lovely young Cuban girls today.

On day two of his trek, after a text to say he'd checked into a hostel with 'about ten thousand twenty-somethings', he'd discovered social media. Or, perhaps, he's been introduced to it – everyone knows what tour groups are like. Either way, his Facebook became an art gallery of his trip through Italy, France and Spain. From starting with one online friend, me, he quickly amassed a host of people. His newsfeed now looked like a multilingual dictionary and it was beautiful. *See Translation* became the most seen term on his page, and I was thrilled that he was getting out and enjoying the world.

After the fortnight I'd had, I almost regretted not taking him up on his suggestion to go along with him.

Now that I'd moved home, I'd been charged with keeping his yard clean, letterbox empty, and utility bills up-to-date. A quick drive-by before I landed at Penny's confirmed that the grass either desperately needed cutting, or I was about to open a wildlife sanctuary.

Anyone who's been away long enough and come back again will tell you that some of the best things about home are the unique smells, sights, and sounds. Ours was jasmine scented, thanks to a plant that had been creeping up over the carport from as long as I had memories. It greeted me with soft comfort as I stepped up onto the front porch and slipped the key into the screen door. I took another deep breath of the flowers before stepping inside.

I grew up in this house, with its tinkling wind chimes, blistering paint, and Mission Brown coloured everything. It was the colour of the Seventies and Eighties, and it had made its home on every surface, gutter, and downpipe in sight. I remained wholly convinced it was the only paint tint available in Australia at the time. I suppose it matched the overgrown grass and front garden beds which, right now, resembled a child's drawing of a tree; brown and green everywhere, and branches at Edward Scissorhands angles.

But those negatives were easily forgiven. It was a home so full of love and laughter it could have been one of those cheap Live,

Laugh, Love signs from a homeware store. We were blessed to live only a few sandy streets away from the beach and a small community we could go to for anything. I had my own surfboard and, when Dad wasn't busy picking up random jobs and working his backside off, he was doing his best to keep me out of trouble. And as Mum had left when I was a baby, it had only ever been the two of us.

The less that's said about Mum the better.

I switched on the radio and welcomed it drowning out my thoughts.

With cleaning products scattered around the kitchen, I pulled what may have been broccoli from the fridge and tossed it away. That was soon joined by liquified cauliflower, and long-life milk that wasn't as long-life as Dad perhaps thought it would be. I opened windows and enjoyed the fresh breeze chasing its tail through doorways and down halls.

When I finally made it to the backyard and realised the lawn mower wouldn't start, I sent Penny an emergency text: I needed mower fuel and some help.

She tumbled through the door forty minutes later, blurting every swearword known to man. After hoisting a jerry can up onto the dining table, she shoved her hands on her sides with such force I thought she'd give herself a hip displacement and glared at me.

'What?' I laughed.

'I got petrol on my hands,' she complained.

'And?'

'Well, they're all dried out now. I'm the crumpled leaf from that old Vaseline ad, and I can't remember the last time I used Vaseline for *that*. And! And! I think there's some on my shoes. I look like a guy at the pub with sixteen beers and no concept of aim.'

She was right, her glossy black shoes had matte splashes across the toes.

I swallowed down a laugh. 'The Vaseline ad was moisturiser, not petroleum jelly.'

'Yeah … well.' She jerked her head. 'You know what I mean.'

'Do you want to rinse them in the sink?' I asked. 'I need to cut the lawn, and I don't want to be here all day, so thank you for bringing fuel. I do appreciate the immense hurt and anguish you've gone through.'

She snorted. 'Shut up.'

After checking for spiders, snakes, and any other woodland creatures that might want to take up residence in the pair of old boots on the porch, I poured the fuel in the mower and made good on my promise to cut the lawn. Penny helped by sunning herself in a hammock strung between two trees in the front yard, and that was where she stayed until I offered to buy lunch.

'You know, if I rolled myself up in this hammock, the rope pattern would make me look like a pineapple.'

'If you keep swinging like that, you'll probably invert and do exactly that,' I chuckled. 'So, please, be my guest, because that would go straight online.'

'I have a better idea,' she began. 'And it involves lunch.'

* * *

'How was your week?' I passed a hot pie from the bakery counter to Penny, who was busy trying to decide what soft drink to grab from the fridge.

'It was in-sane.' Finally settling on Fanta, she grabbed two bottles and stepped out into the afternoon sun.

The day was bright and breezy in that perfect way that would normally have me sleeping in the passenger's seat of a car. I could easily see myself kicking back on a towel at the beach with a good book, some sunscreen, and an umbrella for shade. It wasn't so hot you'd be off to the nearest hospital with third-degree burns by dinner, it was just nice. The cool pinch on the breeze made it even more acceptable for me to be walking around in an old unbuttoned boiler suit.

'You know, we want parents to pay their school fees.' Penny scuttled along beside me. 'They're a good thing, they help little Karen go to swimming sports, or a cut-price school camp where she'll learn to ask for the manager when her mashed potato is the wrong temperature. I just wish they wouldn't all do it on the same bloody day. And it's not my fault Samuel, the little shit, lost his uniform on the first day. How about you?'

I felt my shoulders sag. 'I'm not sure yet.'

'Really? I thought you loved teaching? Loved being back here?'

'I do.' I threw a leg over a bench seat. 'I love it. I had this great breakthrough with a student during the week, already. He was this little first-grader who was struggling with his words and, I mean, I know I can't provide a panacea, but I think I did a good thing. I got him excited about a book, and he's promised to come and see me on Monday morning and let me know how he went. Whether he does or not is another issue, but it's a start, right?'

'But?' she asked.

I smeared sauce across the lid of my pie. 'It's not the students who are the problem.'

'Yeah,' she said slowly. 'The adults tend to be the bigger assholes.'

'This particular one has been nothing but.'

'Let me do my best John Edward.' Penny placed her drink on the table beside us and waved her hands about, lips puckered, and eyes narrowed. 'I'm getting a word starting with C. Is it caffeine? Ca? Coffee?'

I chuckled. 'You idiot.'

'Talk to me.' Penny leaned forward. 'Surely it's not just the coffee, because this is an awful amount of grief over something that did wash straight out of your blouse.'

'All right.' I wriggled about and got comfortable on the seat, legs crossed in front of me. 'It started the very first day.'

'It did?'

'He wanted me to change the library roster for him and I said no,' I explained. 'He wouldn't let it go. After the coffee, he's taken to antagonising. He slips through the library and makes shitty remarks. He called me an angry little onion in front of his class!'

Throughout all this explanation, I still couldn't bring myself to tell her I'd slept with Marcus. It was constantly on the tip of my tongue, but I just couldn't. I hadn't done anything wrong; I just didn't want to risk her accidentally blurting it out and the entire school finding out.

'A what?' Penny roared with laughter. 'An angry little onion?'

'Yes. I don't even know what that's supposed to mean.' My bottle of soft drink hissed as I cracked the seal. 'Yesterday, he told his class to spread out and find themselves books to read. He made sure they picked from all corners of the library, so I had to spend an extra hour last night trying to sort them and put them back in the stacks.'

'Have you tried just sitting down and, I don't know, talking to him?'

'Talk to him?' I laughed. 'I walked in there last night and asked him what his problem was. We ended up in this row where he told me I dressed like Indiana Jones's dad. Next thing I know, Phil's at the door and telling us we can organise the presentation slash graduation night.'

Penny laughed so hard she coughed. 'He actually said that?'

'So, now, not only do I officially not like him, but I have to organise a soiree with His Highness of the Peacock Feathers.'

'Peacock feathers?' she asked.

'Bloody hell, he has a strut,' I grumbled. 'Please tell me you've seen it?'

'No, he doesn't.'

'He does,' I whined. 'He does, and he's so sure of himself, and so much like Dean, and can't he just go away?'

'Wow. Okay.' Her hands moved like she was trying to pluck words from the air. 'So, there's not a lot I can do about the whole end-of-year thing. It's simple, really. Just talk to Jack about some music, whack some sandwiches on a few plates, crackers and dip, and you bang out a few awards that the teachers give out. Mick's done it so many times I'm surprised he hasn't got an autopilot button somewhere.'

'Of all the people.' I slapped my hands against my legs. 'And I almost had him over a barrel, too, and I let him slip through like a slimy little olive. Pop!'

'What do you mean?'

'I mean that I was just about to unleash when Phil appears like Scotty's beamed him up. And he's all, "Problem?" Marcus just fixes me with this look.' I tried to recreate it, and failed, much to Penny's amusement.

'Hold up, was it the lips parted, head dipped, Puss in Boots eyes?'

'Yes!' I snapped my fingers wildly. 'That is exactly what it was!'

And it was exactly the look he gave me outside the pub, a nanosecond before he kissed me.

Penny laughed loudly, like I'd just told the funniest joke ever. 'He got you. He got you. You are wrapped around his little finger. I'll bet you said nothing.'

I sighed heavily. 'I said nothing.'

She leapt up and performed something that might have been a dance. It was either that, or a fit. I couldn't be sure. I peered out at her from behind barely spread fingers.

'He does it all the time. Boys, honestly. It's so hard to say no to any man who looks like he's about to do naughty things to me.'

I coughed.

Penny peered at me. 'What?'

'I can see it now,' I said. 'It'll be like every high school assignment ever. One person does all the work, while the other sits there and gets fat. It'll end up like that joke where I ask him to be a pallbearer at my funeral, so he can let me down one last time.'

Penny held her mouth shut to stop food spewing out as she laughed. 'Can I say something?'

'You know you can.'

'Your first week or so at any job is balls. Remember that time I worked at that burger joint?'

'The one that closed down after six months because he "couldn't get staff to work weekends"?' I made air quotes while Penny nodded wildly.

'Well, he couldn't get staff because he was an absolute knob. My point is, though, my first week was the worst first week ever. I burned my hand, he screamed at me because I put pickle on a burger when someone had specifically said no pickle, and then told me I was a more than a little bit stupid.'

'You're not stupid,' I sputtered. 'What a dick. I hope you stood up for yourself?'

'I absolutely did. Every time something suspect came out of his mouth, I took him to task. By the time the place shut down, he told me I was one of the best workers he had.'

'Moral of the story is ride it out, right?' I asked.

'I was going more for the "stand up for yourself" mantra. If you do that, then the rough seas will subside. I want you to take a deep breath and enjoy your weekend. You're up-to-date with everything, aren't you?'

'I think so, yeah.'

'So, jump in fresh on Monday, and see what happens.'

One of things I loved the most about Penny was her ability to look at the positive. Flat tyre? Yeah, but look at the scenery. Lost your job? That's okay, a few days off. Husband cheated on you? Let's not deny that it sucks, but you can come live it up by the seaside. I didn't doubt her in this instance, either.

'You're right.' I rubbed at my face. 'You're absolutely right. Let's just write it off as beginner's nerves and start afresh on Monday.'

Penny offered a short nod. 'I just want you to be happy.'

'I am,' I said. 'I really am. I'm here with you, and I know I have a lot of ground to make up there. I want to spend a bit of time getting back to being me. You know, the things I like, and the hobbies I used to have.'

'Knitting,' she gasped. 'If you're getting back into that.' She grappled with her handbag. 'Can you make me something?'

'Sure.' I stood up and brushed crumbs from my chest. 'Knitting isn't really a summer sport, but if you have the pattern.'

She passed me her phone, fingers at the ready to zoom in on a design she was already intimately aware of. 'I saw this online the other night and fell in love.'

I pinched the picture open a bit further. A knee-length hooded jacket in a dusty rose-coloured bobble stitch was screaming out to be made. Hell, I wanted one for myself. 'It's beautiful.'

'You can do that, can't you?' She looked at me hopefully.

'It's been a while, but I'm fairly certain I could. It looks straightforward.' I scrunched my rubbish and stood up to stretch. 'Now, is there anything else we need to do before we go home?'

Chapter 10

One thing I needed but had let slide was finding myself a lawyer. It seemed like a simple enough thing to do, but it was one that I'd been burying my head in the sand over. I hadn't asked around for recommendations, because that meant involving other people and I was enjoying, in my new environment, not having to constantly discuss my situation with those around me. Online forums turned out to be cesspits of reviews and half-truths, so I took the balance of probability, a shot of courage, and made a phone call.

Lawyers' offices were quite like hospitals. Nobody ever really wanted to be there. There was a false happiness inside them; a Klimt print here, a water cooler with crinkly plastic cups there, and ten steps towards an office that would help decide my consciously uncoupled future.

The earliest appointment I could get was late Saturday afternoon, the last slot of the day. I was covered in grass stains and probably smelled like the back end of a spark plug, but I hoped the meeting would be quick.

It was.

I made a decision months ago not to contest anything. It was all part of my proving to the world that I was perfectly fine and capable. What had happened had been more than enough, and I'd be happy if I could settle things quickly and painlessly and lock the door on that chapter of my life. Dean was welcome to the house and everything in it. It was all just *stuff*, and I'd gone so long without any of it already. Deep down, I would have loved my piano, but I walked away with what I had and was already busy living and thriving without him.

Well, thriving if you didn't consider the Marcus situation. If we took the issue of sex away for a moment, we were identical, repelling ends of a magnet. It was *The Good, the Bad and the Ugly* sneering at ten paces.

For the next three weeks, we barely spoke at all, let alone entertained the idea of the presentation night. We were conducting a highly coordinated version of hide and seek. Class handovers on Friday afternoons reminded me of tense custody exchanges, where Dad would stand on one side of some random suburban park, Mum on the other, and never the twain shall meet.

It was all incredibly mature.

Of course, the problem with avoiding problems is that it doesn't exactly help them go away. Oftentimes, it makes them worse – much worse, as we found out the morning we were summoned to Phil's office for a 7.30 debriefing – minus the cocktails.

'I really hope you two have got something to show for the weeks of silence.' Coffee splashed up over the sides of his mug like an overfull bathtub, forming a brown ring on his desk mat. He cursed and shook droplets from his fingers. I didn't want to be the one to tell him all he'd done was spread coffee to his phone. Or wall. 'Something, something, weekly updates. I was sure I was speaking to two humans then, wasn't I?'

Beside me, Marcus wriggled about, pinching at his pants. I shifted nervously and tried to slow the hamster wheel in my mind. We glanced at each other quickly, and at different moments. For the record, sleeping with someone doesn't give you a sudden insight to their facial expressions, because I could not tell what he was thinking at all.

I expelled a heavy breath, the weight of the room catching up with me. 'I'm sorry, it's been completely my fault.'

Phil leaned back and looked at me over the top of his glasses. The only noise in the room was the squeaking of the springs in his chair and the metronomic ticking of a clock. There was a noticeboard next to his desk bursting with family photos, and a shelf above that adorned with award statues.

'Marcus, do you have anything you'd like to add? Perhaps we don't quite need Eleanor to throw herself under the bus this morning? Would you like to help her out from under the wheels?'

Marcus gawped about like a fish out of water for a moment. 'No, no, I just—'

'I've had a lot going on in my life,' I blurted, surprised at my own candour. I certainly hadn't planned on milking excuses from my situation. In fact, I was happily silent about everything. Yet, here I was. 'I've been desperately trying to catch up with where Cathy was with her work, all while getting reacclimatised with the job. It's been a lot busier than I thought, plus trying to organise the Book Fair and …'

'And, and, I thought it might be more helpful to give Miss Manning the space and support she needed to settle in to her job properly before overwhelming her with too much change.'

Now it was my turn to stare. I couldn't believe he was going to try and jump in and score points when at least two-thirds of us in the room knew the real reason for this mess. I wasn't about to sit about while he rolled his tongue about his cheek pocket.

'If you must know,' I sighed, 'I'm in the process of getting a divorce. So, between settling in and getting that sorted, it's all been a bit hectic. I should be free at the end of this week to start working on things. I believe we still have plenty of time.'

'Heaps of time,' Marcus echoed. 'Sorry … a what?'

Phil's head ping-ponged between the two of us.

'I'm getting divorced,' I grumbled. 'Not that it's anyone's business.'

'Are you okay?' Marcus crossed his leg over his knee.

'Like you care,' I bit.

'All right, you two.' Phil flung himself forward and flashed his computer mouse about on its mat. 'We're going to meet next Monday morning at this time, and you're both going to tell me what you've agreed on and locked in a venue. For two geniuses like yourselves, I'm sure it won't be too hard. I want invites sent out by next Thursday. I'd do it myself, but that's beside the point of the exercise, isn't?'

'Last year we used the school gymnasium,' Marcus offered, more of a mumble than anything. 'We could do that again. I can take Eleanor through and show her what we did last year, how everything was set up.'

Phil rested his chin in the palm of his hand and offered a happy sigh. 'At last, a breakthrough.'

'Wednesday right after school good for you?' Marcus asked.

'Me?' I asked.

'Yes, you.'

'I'll see you there.' I stood and left the office.

* * *

'Chairs on desks!' I called. 'Make sure you pick up any rubbish and toss it in the bin on the way out. Does anyone need to borrow anything before the bell?'

Too late.

The end of the day chimed loudly across the library and down corridors, only momentarily drowned out by the scuffling of rubber stops on laminate and the shuffling of shoes out the door.

'Miss Manning, I want to borrow some books!' Harper, who was quiet, but read books like some people ate chocolate, waved a small stack above her head.

'Come on over!' I enthused.

I was already in a hurry. Penny wanted to go out for dinner, Marcus wanted me to meet him in the school gymnasium, and all I wanted to do was go home, return my lawyer's phone call, and see what the issue was. In a moment of weakness, I'd left a message on her answering machine, asking if she could try and secure my piano. Music had once been such a large part of my life and I missed it dearly.

Harper tapped on the desk and angled herself towards the computer screen while we waited for it to load.

'The computer's tired.' Her feet dangled as she leaned further forward.

'Like all of us.' I smiled at her. 'What are you reading this week?'

'I have some *Street Cat Named Bob*.' She presented the cover to me. 'And *The Hundred and One Dalmatians*.'

'I loved that book when I was your age.' I flipped through the illustrations of spotted dogs, delighted when the computer screen finally came to life. 'Do you prefer the cartoon movie, or live action?'

'Definitely the cartoon' she said with a heavy sigh. 'You know, I read it last month. I liked it so much I want to read it again.' She bounced excitedly against the counter as I scanned her school card and her books and sent her on her way for the afternoon. 'Thank you, Miss Manning.'

'You're welcome!' I called to the back of her head as she zipped out the door, backpack bouncing along behind her.

My office phone was already ringing, Mick, Roger, and Tony had already peeled through the library towards the staffroom. Tony had a question about a class set of books, but I didn't have time to stop and chat. I promised I'd see him the next morning, grabbed my bag, threw it over my shoulder, and did the quick-step to the gymnasium.

After yanking at the door, I skipped along the small hallway and past change rooms that hadn't been there in my time. The bounce of a ball got louder as I approached and, stepping out onto the court, I found Marcus shooting hoops on his own.

'Sorry,' I gasped, slightly out of breath. 'I'm not doing this on purpose.'

Marcus passed the ball to me. 'As much as you don't want to talk to me, Manning, we have to do this.'

Manning? Since when had I become my last name?

'I'm not doing this deliberately.' My handbag slipped from my shoulder and I kicked my shoes off. 'I had a class, one of the girls wanted to borrow books. It's not all about you and your ambitions. I said I was sorry.'

Hands on his hips, he watched as I shuffled across the court in my socks, pulling them up with every second step I took. He lunged as I dribbled the ball past him. I ran to the other end of the court where I took a shot. It had been years since sport was something I'd practised regularly, but the instant skip in the heart was exhilarating, if only for the chance to try and show him up. My aim missed, and the ball hit the wall and rolled towards Marcus.

'And another thing,' I continued. 'It's not me ignoring you. You've been ignoring me.'

'Uh-huh.' He waited.

'You waltz on in with your class and barely say a word to me,' I said. 'I have no reason to come to your classroom and interact with you, so it's hardly fair to say this is all me.'

'Really? Because I'm sure I tried to sit with you at lunch yesterday, and you walked away.'

'I was done eating,' I spat. 'And maybe I didn't feel like sitting with you. Maybe I'm still swamped with work.'

'Diddums.' He offered me a look of mock sympathy, complete with pout. 'You know, I tried picturing you as a small child while we were getting chewed out in Phil's office the other morning. I tried to imagine you in there being disciplined for something, but I just couldn't.'

'Really? Because the last time I saw the inside of that room as a kid, I'd lobbed a football through his window.'

Standing on the free throw line, trying to hold his laughter in, he took a shot. It circled the hoop and dropped in. 'Ha!'

'There are precisely two walking, talking Ellie archives at this school. Actually, three or four when you think about it, and you're having trouble picturing me? You're obviously not very good at doing your own homework, Mr Blair.' I scooped up the ball from the floor and began dribbling away from him.

'Really?' He jogged towards me as I rounded the outer edge of the court, slipping past him towards the centre line.

'Correct me if I'm wrong, but I'd only need to ask Patrick about you, wouldn't I? He's your best friend, isn't he? I could ask him out to lunch. We could go on a date.'

'He is,' he deadpanned. 'And you won't.'

I took the shot and, laughing, thrust my hands above my head as the ball slipped straight through the centre of the hoop. 'See, not difficult.'

Marcus snatched the ball up. 'What if I just wanted to ask *you* the questions?'

'Then open your big mouth and ask me.' I reached for the ball, but all he had to do was hold it above his head and it was well and truly out of reach. I jumped once, and barely grazed the bottom of the ball with my fingertips. I could climb him, I thought, but that may have been a bit too close for comfort.

'All right, smart ass. I get the ball in the hole—'

'Don't put balls in holes.' I shook my head.

He grinned. 'I get this in from here, and you answer my questions.'

'Can we just do what we're here to do?' I asked. 'I have a hot date with my cousin tonight.'

'Look at you, living on the edge,' Marcus teased. 'And with your cousin. Kinky librarians.'

I watched him, arms outstretched and ball above his head, as he lined up and took the shot. The ball hit the edge of the backboard and bounced off on an angle. I jogged across the court and scooped it up before sitting on a sideline bench.

'So, in here?' I asked.

He shrugged. 'That's normally what we do. By the time you get parents, ex-wives, husbands, new partners, siblings, the milkman, and grandparents in, it becomes a bit of a tight fit, so it's easier to hold the event in here. We present some awards, do a few speeches, wish the kids well, stuff everyone with cake and send them home.'

'And that's it, is it? All this for, "Okay, let's hold it in here"?'

'Pretty much,' he said.

We sat in silence for a few moments, as close as two people could get without sitting on each other's laps. A grey gymnastics horse, which was doing its best impersonation of an elephant, judged us silently from the corner of the room as the afternoon sun shone a warm yellow through the skylights. As our breathing slowed to normal, Marcus reached for his back pocket and produced a small white card.

'I don't need your business card.' I pushed his hand away. 'I know where to find you.'

'Can you just look at it?' he urged. 'Please?'

This time, I took it and read the name aloud, 'Sasha Sedgeman, divorce and family law.' I offered him a confused look. 'Why are you giving me this?'

'She handled *my* divorce,' he admitted, elbows resting on his knees. 'It was very clean and clear-cut, and I would recommend her in a heartbeat. Not that I hope to ever have to use her again.'

I sank back into the brick wall behind me, cool relief washing over me. Or, maybe it wasn't relief, but maybe something more like connection. Whatever it was, I continued to stare at him for a moment, at the lines and bevels of his face, the slight upturn of the nose, the crinkle of the eyes, and I wondered what was happening behind the eyes that wouldn't meet mine.

Finally, he looked back over his shoulder at me. 'Not that I'd care, right?'

I swallowed down my embarrassment. 'She's great, isn't she?'

'She is.' He was quiet for a moment. 'Are you okay?'

'I think so,' I answered. 'It'll be over soon. Friday is D Day.'

'If you need anything, or have any questions, just ask. It won't go anywhere.' He zipped his mouth and tossed the invisible key. 'Seems to be a bit of a habit for us.'

The elephant trumpeted, and we continued to ignore it. It didn't help that I could feel the warmth of him as he pressed up against my side, or that he was close enough that I could just drop my head on his shoulder and take a quick kip. More than anything, I needed to silence the elephant, and we couldn't go on like this if we had to organise an event.

'I hate the word "whatever",' I admitted.

'You don't say.'

'It was my husband's favourite word. It was humiliating and made me feel like garbage, as if he were telling me that anything I thought didn't matter, especially when he used it around friends.' Admitting that felt like a weight off my shoulders, something that had been fighting for release for weeks.

'I had a feeling there was more to the story than you were letting on,' he said quietly.

'You did?'

He sighed. 'You just had this look in your eyes. You were on the verge of something but were holding back. I am so incredibly sorry. I should have been more careful with my words. It certainly wasn't my intention to upset you.'

'It's fine. It's not your fault.' I shook my head. 'You weren't to know. I should have explained myself properly the other week.'

'And you're right. I have been avoiding you.'

I said nothing.

'At least tell me he didn't leave you because he thought you were boring,' Marcus said quietly. 'Because two boring people organising one of these things is bound to be a mess.'

'Actually, I left him.' I turned the card over in my hands. 'After he slept with my best friend.'

'He's obviously a beacon of originality,' he said. 'I'm sorry.'

'Don't be.' I gave in and placed my head on his shoulder. 'I'm glad I'm here. I think it was the world's way of telling me I needed to shake things up.'

He turned his head briefly towards me. 'That's exactly how I felt.'

In that moment, the room felt so soft, so comforting, that the only thing I could hear was the chirping of birds outside and my heartbeat in my ears. It reminded me of summer afternoons spent bobbing about in a pool, letting the water push me along as I lay on my back.

'You're incredibly boring, and far too dedicated to your job. I can't see us having children while you're so obsessed with teaching. I need somebody fun, Marcus,' he mimicked, spitting the last few words out like a sour lemon.

His words jumped about in my head, Scrabble letters looking for homes, and I was unsure which point to tackle first. In the space of five minutes, and with a little bit of courage, I'd uncovered a very big shared current. Even though Marcus hadn't endeared himself to me initially, it wasn't completely his fault if I hadn't explained myself properly.

'I feel like I need to point out that being a dedicated teacher is imperative in this profession, and a decent indicator of how you are with children,' I said.

'No,' he gasped. 'Surely not?'

'One of our friends was keeping tabs on me to help them organise their rendezvous,' I said. 'Every time I was out for the day, especially on weekends, it was on.'

'That explains the salty, pickled onion vibes.'

My cheek still resting on his shoulder, I laughed. 'That's not what you were saying the other night.'

For once, I think I'd stumped him. He bumbled about, shuffling his feet, twiddling his thumbs, but remaining resolutely silent.

'So, is basketball your thing?' I asked, desperately hoping to sweep any other thoughts aside.

'Nah.' He straightened his leg and rolled his foot about.

'Football is more my thing.'

'Football?' I asked.

'Call it a childhood fantasy come to life.' He smiled shyly.

I groaned. 'That's right, Spring Carnival.'

'I do hope my number one ticket holder will be there with bells on.'

'Cheerleader outfit, pom-poms, and ponytails,' I teased. 'Got a whole routine organised.'

'Now, why weren't you wearing *that* Friday night?' he teased.

I slapped at his chest. 'I'm going home. Tell Phil it's locked in.'

Chapter 11

When I was younger, I was either sitting at my grandparents' piano, or I had my head in a book. I lived for the annual Scholastic Book Fair, that one day of the year when my school turned into a bookstore. It was part of the school's Spring Carnival and, each year, Dad would pack me up with a few small notes so I could wander around with a scrap of paper trying to budget in as many books as I could for my money. As an adult, it gave me life to help other kids chase the rainbow.

Organising this year's event was the best kind of distraction when I was otherwise busy counting down the hours to my divorce. Knowing that the phone call was coming at some stage that day was surprisingly nerve-wracking, so keeping myself wildly busy helped calm that part of my brain right down to a barely audible whisper.

While others were preparing cake stalls, haunted houses, and sausage sizzles, I was wiping down tables, stacking chairs, and making sure the displays were worthy of their own social media accounts. And, yes, I slapped every available hashtag on them, too. As it turned out, chasing the high of the Book Fair was an old habit that died hard – and for some parents, too.

All it took was one, just the one parent, to break the levy. It was the 8.15 a.m. 'Can I just come and browse?' that led to sales, orders, and look-up requests from past catalogues after Little Kimmy flushed her much-loved copy of *The 13-Storey Treehouse*. I wasn't complaining, not by a long stretch. Also, the *Treehouse* books were great.

Classes began filtering through from the first morning bell.

Younger grades first, much the same was as it had happened for me. Get them in early, then get them out to enjoy the carnival atmosphere before the older kids came in and crushed them.

A huge part of the carnival was the interschool friendly football match. Teachers from both our school and the local P-12 College, a new school up in the hills, pitched a team. Locals came to watch for a gold coin donation, and the proceeds were split between the two schools.

'Is this a big deal?' I asked. 'The game, I mean.'

Penny answered with a delighted laugh. She'd rung to confirm my place at the Annual Football Picnic. Did I want to join other teachers and spectators in watching upwards of thirty teachers run around, some of them in short shorts? Late-night memories of Marcus didn't need highlighting or adding to, especially when I was trying to forget all about him, but there were a whole lot of other men to look at. In particular, teachers not from our school, so I promised myself I'd keep my eyes on them instead.

'It's way bigger than we when were in school. When half the town turns out, it ends up being a nice loot for each school. And local takeaways love it because everyone goes out for dinner afterwards. It's the best day of the year, besides end of last term,' she explained.

I chanced a look outside my office and to the students running around the displays. It was almost a *Supermarket Sweep* effort, watching them zip across the library and grab at books like rabid word junkies.

'This year, Marcus is captaining the school team.'

Currently, he was strolling around the library with his class. Like always, he was calm and casual. We'd barely spoken since the revelations of Wednesday night and, even with the chance to big note himself, he hadn't gifted me that piece of information.

'He is, is he?' I asked.

'Uh-huh.' She covered the receiver and mumbled to someone in the background.

'Interesting. Who else is on the team?'

'The usual suspects. He's roped Patrick into playing for the school, too.' Penny swore at something. 'Our landlord Patrick, by the way. I'm so glad you'll get to meet him.'

'Is that strange?' I asked. 'He's not a teacher.'

'Patrick is captain of the local team. Plus, it makes perfect sense when you see the amount of help our lot need to win. Oh! Here he is,' she tittered excitedly. 'Patrick's just arrived.'

I laughed. 'Okay, I need to go.'

'Me, too. Shit, Phil's here.' The dial tone sounded in my ear.

When classes were over for the afternoon, with the start of the football match approaching, I sat back and looked at the aftermath of the Book Fair. My library had turned into a jumble sale. Order forms were strewn across my desks, the cash box looked like it was crawling home from a night on the town, and I wasn't far from feeling like that, either. I was exhausted.

'Ellie!' Phil cruised about the library, inspecting the stock left on tables. 'Successful day?'

'It's been so, so busy,' I said. 'I'm just going to tidy up a bit, reconcile the cash, and head out.'

'Make sure you do. Make time to explore and watch some football.'

'I will.' I nodded.

While I had made my way around the room, upselling to parents and stacking books into recognisable piles, Jack had been performing dramatic readings. He'd moved from Shakespeare for children, to Spot, Blinky Bill and, now, Dr Seuss. He still had a very small audience who hadn't yet made it outside. Each page he turned was met with a trill chirping noise, not unlike Disney audiobooks of the Eighties.

Turn the page when you hear Jack meow like this ...

'Jack, I'm just nipping out for a few minutes.' I gestured wildly to the door, all the while he crawled about on a rug. 'Do you need a drink?'

He meowed at me and thrust an ankle behind his ear. Stunned, I blinked a few times and walked away. In the staffroom, Penny had a handful of teachers circled around a table. Contributions to the picnic were sprawled across the table in front of them. Crackers, cheese, dips, drinks, cakes; you name it, they had it. Had I been asked to contribute? I couldn't remember, but I was suddenly a little panicky about it all. Maybe I could snaffle some leftover cake from a stall outside. Yes, that's exactly what I'd do.

'Ellie!' Penny shrieked.

'Penny!' I copied.

'Kick-off soon. Will you be joining us for some PG-rated bubbles?' She held up a can of soda, condensation rolling down the sides.

'I will be out just as soon as I've finished up in here. Might not be right on time, but I'll be there.' I searched high and low for a clean drinking glass before giving up and rinsing the nearest one.

'I can't wait to see our fearless captain in his tight little shorts,' Grace giggled, packing away a box of water crackers. While she was joined by a chorus of agreement, names of other footballers being bandied about like a pre-match coin toss, I felt something not unlike annoyance poking at me. It took me by surprise, and I wondered if it wasn't just misplaced or misidentified feelings. I refilled my water bottle and slipped out of the room while they continued their conversation.

Slipping past Jack again, and rounding the loans counter, I noticed my office door was closed, though I was sure I'd left it open. I gave it a gentle nudge with my foot and …

'What in the bloody hell fires of Mount Doom?' I failed miserably at keeping my voice down.

There was a half-naked man in my office. He was an incredibly attractive man, with hair tripping over itself like waves rushing the shoreline, shorts around his ankles, and a body Taylor Swift would climb over herself for. He offered me a quick glance over his shoulder.

'Oh, hello.' He smiled, dimples deployed and stubble I wouldn't mind getting a rash from.

This was not Marcus.

I bent over, folding myself almost completely in half until I made eye contact with my handsome new friend. His fluorescent workwear was in a scrunched pile on the floor. 'Excuse me. What are you doing?'

He straightened up and pulled a football guernsey over his head and drew it slowly down a well-defined torso. So pretty. 'Marc said I could get ready in here.'

I closed the door quietly, aware that a highly inquisitive group of mothers were already doing the sideways peer, their Half-Naked Man alert screaming like an air raid siren. Their reflections disappeared from a cabinet door as I pushed the office door closed.

'Did he just?' I puffed. 'Jesus.'

'Not quite, but I *am* a carpenter.' He held out a hand that may very well have just been anywhere. 'I'm Patrick.'

'The infamous Patrick.' I turned away and waited for him to finish dressing.

'You can look, you know. I'm not actually naked.' He stopped. 'And what do you mean by "infamous"?'

'Your reputation precedes you, Mr Nicholls.' I scrambled around my desk looking for the school directory. It had disappeared from beside my computer monitor.

'I would ask you to explain that over a drink, but Marc has already told me to steer clear.'

My lip curled. 'It may surprise the both of you to learn that Marcus isn't the boss of me.'

'Wow, you two really are children.' A snort became a laugh. 'And here I was thinking he was exaggerating.'

Glaring at him, I concentrated on the dial tone in my ear.

'Marcus Blair.' His voice came wrapped in a telltale bathroom echo. And, if that wasn't a dead giveaway, a suspicious tinkle in the background was. Boys.

'Oh my, you are a consummate professional,' I teased. 'Is this your doing?'

'Maybe?' he answered slowly. 'Depends what we're talking about.'

'There's a barely dressed Patrick in my office.'

'I have clothes on.' Patrick scooped his pile of workwear from the floor and proceeded to stuff them into a duffel bag.

Marcus chuckled. 'Tell me, is he waving his bits about and screeching about Excalibur? How it just needs the right lady to—'

'Stop! Stop! Stop!'

'I'll be there in a minute.' The phone died.

Patrick stepped past me and opened the door. 'Listen, I'm not going to make any lame jokes about nailing things, or wood.' A business card flashed in my face. 'But if you ever need a decent erection.'

'Get out.' I pushed him further out the door and made sure to lock it behind me.

Patrick laughed as he walked away. 'I can see why he likes you so much!'

As I watched him disappear down the hallway, I picked up the phone and dialled Penny's number. She was partway through a conversation when she answered.

'I swear, you had better have some alcohol in that picnic basket,' I interrupted.

'Well, there's something in my basket. It's clear and odourless, and it sure does make me feel good, sir, but I'm certain it's just the rehydrating effects of water,' she whispered. 'Get out here already.'

'I'm coming, I'm coming,' I mumbled.

For a moment, silence. In the time between the staffroom and Patrick, the library had emptied out. All sales were done, Jack's audience had scattered, and everyone had moved on to the oval. I was alone for the first time all day and took the opportunity to have five minutes to myself. Me and my box of sweets.

A jawbreaker stuck between my teeth, and it was worth every single one of the fifty cents I paid for it. To be fair, I was surprised they weren't four dollars each owing to inflation, GDP or sugar tax. It was chewy, sweet, and a direct throwback to my childhood, to summer days, and salty beaches. And, man alive, when did I have to stop being a kid? I had a sudden urge to hide under my old Barbie duvet with a Choose Your Own Adventure book and a flashlight.

While I was busy trying to pick toffee out of my teeth, rather unladylike in my methods, I took a moment to check in on my phone. One missed call. It was done. The realisation gave me a solid thump in the chest.

I poked at the dial button and waited.

'Sasha? It's Eleanor Manning.'

'Hey, Ellie,' she began. 'I'm really glad you returned my call. I have some news for you.'

'Hopefully good news?' My stomach did a handstand and the hokey-pokey with my lunch.

I was glad today had been so busy. It meant less space in my brain to think about other things. Namely, divorce things. I couldn't believe it had been a month already since the papers had been delivered. Where had that time gone?

'In the scheme of things, yes. Everything is final,' she continued. 'You're officially a single lady, so you can crank out the Beyoncé on the way home. Unfortunately, I couldn't secure the piano.'

'That's fine.' I thought I'd be upset but, more than anything, I felt relief. I wouldn't have to organise a moving van or turn up on the doorstep and have to have that awkward conversation. The best option was to let sleeping dogs lie, and he had enough fleas for the entire city of Melbourne. I hoped the bites itched.

'Are you sure?' she asked. 'I am really sorry.'

'I am completely fine,' I said. 'It's for the best anyway, I think.'

'I agree.' She was so upbeat that it was hard to be annoyed. If irritation lay anywhere, it was at getting myself in this situation to begin with. 'Unless there's anything else I can do for you, I'll forward my bill to you in the next seven days.'

'No, that's fine,' I said quietly. 'Thank you so much.'

I took a few moments to gather my thoughts, but there was so much going on that I couldn't quite work them out. My eyes watered briefly, but I'd already decided that crying wasn't going to be what this afternoon was about. When my phone beeped with a message from Penny, I locked my cash tin away, closed my office behind me, and headed outside to watch some football.

* * *

Dust trailed behind my chair as I dragged it closer to the group. The famed picnic had been set up across the newspaper-covered surface of two card tables. A bag of crisps was scattered about, the dip had been blessed by a broken cracker, and Jemima had a drinking hat on – complete with two cans of lemonade. I placed my cake offering on the edge of the table.

Penny leaned across to me. 'Ellie, are you okay?'

'Well,' I considered with an exasperated puff, 'I just met Patrick.'

Her face lit up, eyes wide and smile wider. 'Did you love him?'

I grimaced. 'Not sold yet, though I did appreciate the visuals.'

'Oh, Ellie!' Emma squawked over the top of the burgeoning crowd. 'I was going to come see you about ordering a book or two from the fair.'

The last of my toffee and its stringy sugar made it look like Spiderman had taken up residence inside my mouth. I pulled webby threads away and leaned back in her direction. 'Can you please email me about it? I don't mean to be rude. I'll put it through on Monday with the rest of the orders, I'm just worried I'll forget over the —'

'Yes, yes, okay.' Emma suddenly bounced in her chair. 'Well, hello over there.'

A ragtag bunch of teachers, male and female, emerged not from the concrete runs of a well-prepped clubroom, but from the stuffy confines of a poorly ventilated demountable. With no communal uniform to be spoken of, they were a colourful display of individuality. T-shirt designs ranged from Metallica to Ed Sheeran, the sporty Nike and Reebok, and everything in between.

'You know, I feel like this must be how the Very Hungry Caterpillar feels at an all you can eat buffet.' Penny clapped her hands excitedly.

'You what?' I laughed.

'I mean, just look ... there's so many bodies, but only so many eyes,' she explained.

Trailing behind the back of the pack, already deep in discussion and with the loudest cheers awaiting them were Marcus and Patrick.

Boys in football gear were enough to stop traffic on a regular day, but these two, in their local team colours of royal blue and honey yellow, and shorts so tight I doubted both of their reproductive abilities, were enough to spring their female audience forward into mid-summer temperatures. Despite our differences, I wasn't exactly offended by the sight either.

'Do you remember that time I came to stay with you in Melbourne? Way before you were married, and we went to that football match?' Penny watched the crowd of tired-looking teachers walk past.

'When we ended up in a locker room full of towelled men?' I asked. 'Very much so. We lied about your age, and then you disappeared with the ruckman.'

'Yeah, well, with the exception of these two squires, this is not like that time at all.'

I coughed, almost choking on what was left of my toffee. 'Also, nice to see some girls playing.'

'This is not an untruth.' She sipped from her can. 'I mean, Kevin's knees are starting to resemble Thanksgiving turkeys, so we need the girls to come in and take over.'

I bit my lip and looked at her.

To be fair, Kevin had been our physical education teacher back when we were at school, so age was only naturally starting to catch up with him. Emma laughed so hard she fell backwards and landed on the dusty earth below. When none of us got up to help her, she stayed there, still cackling.

I looked at Penny. 'If you do actually have some alcohol, now would be a great time to share.'

When she produced a water bottle from her bag, I could have kissed her. Or, maybe, I should've been horrified. Should I have been? *It was Friday afternoon*, I thought. *I've had a rough day. Bite me.*

'Exactly what is happening here?' Marcus placed a warm hand on my shoulder, a lone finger brushing at the soft space under my ear – the same spot he'd worked out was a favourite in the dead of night. In the light of day, it felt far too intimate and public, even if it meant nothing to anyone around us and, maybe, it meant nothing to him. I replayed my This Will Never Work mantra like a Hail Mary, doused myself in holy water of the vodka, and tried to think of something else other than the crotch hovering far too close to my face.

'We are ladies being ladies, lunching like ladies.' Penny did her best Sharon Stone and batted her eyelids at him. 'And boys, and boys. There are some boys here, too. A luncheon of the people.'

'Yeah, I've seen movies that start like that,' Marcus teased. 'Except, you look like the movie poster for *Up!* and I do mean that in the nicest, happiest, most colourful kind of way.'

I groaned and bit down on a cracker, hoping food would stifle a laugh. It didn't. He wasn't wrong. I thrust my can of tainted soda towards him. 'We're having a picnic.'

'You think this is a picnic?' His mouth pinched as he took a sip. His chin dipped into his chest as he offered me a cheeky smile. 'Sweetheart, you have no idea.'

My cheeks burned the colour of a thousand suns as he jogged off onto the field, knee and shoulder wrapped in medicine tape.

'Sweetheart?' Penny questioned.

I shrugged and, for once, hoped I looked completely daft.

In opposition on the football field, a team so put together and uniformed that it hardly felt like a friendly game at all. Their uniforms were complete and, while our team wandered about like lost ducks, they passed the ball about in drills. Nevertheless, for a gold coin donation, it had brought the locals out in droves. The closer we got to the starting whistle, the less empty space there was around the boundary line, and the more picnic blankets popped up.

With a shrill whistle, and the tiniest bit of silence, feet shuffled and scuffled, dust clouded around feet, the crowd cheered, and the game was underway.

Even with our two minor celebrities, our team was tanking. In fact, they were being slaughtered in a Gerard Butler Roman Empire movie type of way. By the end of the third quarter, and after a half-time performance from the opposition's school band, I gladly volunteered to help clear away the last of the carnival stalls. Everything but the sausage sizzle was closed, and anything had to be better than watching a losing game.

Leftover plants, books and bric-a-brac were packed away in the back of family wagons, though the cake stall remnants were distributed amongststt the few of us not glued to the football. I took my fresh stash of toffees and cupcakes to the library and vowed I'd get at least some of today's paperwork done before going home. Eventually, I gave up trying to think. When someone passed my office, I glanced up and, when a shadow hit my periphery, I jumped in fright.

'Not only did you not bring the pom-poms and short skirt, you'd disappeared by third quarter.' Marcus stood in the doorway, pout and split eyebrow on display.

'You saw that?' I threw him a quick look over my shoulder.

'Of course I saw that,' he sulked.

'I was helping pack up,' I explained. My mouth dried a little, and I couldn't work out if it was the vodka, or the fact I'd been missed. 'Then, I thought I'd come in here to do some work, but it's Friday and I can't be bothered.'

'I notice lots of things.' He sat on the edge of my desk.

'I'm sure there were plenty of others there to cheer you on,' I teased. Standing, I reached up and scratched away a lump of dirt from his brow. 'Look at you, you're a mess. Are you okay?'

'A little sore, if I'm honest.'

I shoved a handful of tissues in his direction, though I ended up being the one blotting at his injury. 'Is this the part where we cut to the romantic scene of me tending your wounds?'

'Are you going to shave my face while sitting seductively on my lap wearing nothing more but matching underwear?' He smirked. I hated that those words pulled at something deep inside.

'That would be far too romantic, and I have no desire to shave you, lest I cut your throat,' I teased, crossing my eyes.

He snorted. 'You're so caring and maternal.'

'I really am,' I said. 'You should see me on babysitting duty.'

'You know, we *did* lose, so I wouldn't mind a teensy bit of consoling.' He was going to trip over that bottom lip if he jutted it out any further. I pushed it back in with a lone finger that lingered longer than it should have.

'You poor darling boy,' I teased. 'If you need consoling, I'm sure I have an old Atari at my dad's.'

'Hilarious.'

I gathered up the last of the scattered books, succeeding only in moving them from one end of the bench to another. What was I even doing? Maybe it was my brain's way of saying the busier I was right now, the less I'd look at the oversized, dirt-covered footballer lounging against my desk.

Marcus sucked a pained breath through his teeth. 'So, I was just going to say that, as much as you hate me …'

'I don't hate you,' I said. 'If that were the case, we certainly wouldn't have had sex.'

Nose wrinkled, he folded his arms across his chest, leaned towards me and whispered, 'It was really, really good sex, too.'

I grinned, but kept my mouth shut. He wasn't wrong.

'Anyway, we should sit down and work out this presentation. It's important to me that we get this right,' he said.

I turned to face him and leaned back against the bench opposite him. 'Why?'

'What's with the smile?' he asked. 'You look like the snake that got the mouse.'

'Why is this event important to you?' I asked. 'Because you think it'll secure you the role of vice principal?'

'I guess it is. I've been a senior teacher here for a few years now. The only person higher than me is Mick, and he has no interest whatsoever. He just wants to ride it on out until retirement. I think I have more to offer. I'm a good teacher with strong community ties and would like to affect positive change.' He paused only long enough to hoist his foot up on my chair. 'I have experience. I can do this. I want to do this, but I won't get there if we keep fucking about and putting things off.'

His words smacked of desperation and caught somewhere at the back of my mind. I remembered that feeling well. Even if I could only relate to it on the level of securing my job here, there was something raw knowing an achievement was so close, but still so far from my grasp.

'Vice principal is a big role, you understand.'

'Yes, Mum.' He made a tender effort to peel back the sticky bandage from his knee.

'Let's say we succeed at this endeavour, and you get the role. Can I hand out the tickets at the coronation?'

He laughed. 'Piss off.'

I flung myself into a theatrical stance reminiscent of a Shakespearean play, eyes closed to the ceiling. 'The king shall stroll through the crowd, crown on his head, ruby red regal cape flowing behind him in a gentle breeze.' I peeled an eye open to find him watching me intently, gloriously happy. 'Staff in hand.'

'Staff in hand?' he mocked. '*Hands*, please.'

'Where it usually is.' I collapsed with laughter. 'Your subjects bowing in your presence.'

'You wish.'

'Oh, come on, they were worshipping you today.'

'I'm not interested in any of them.' He lifted his eyes to mine, only briefly, but long enough to press his meaning across. 'Plus, I'm no good to anyone with a busted knee.'

'Oh?' I said, surprised. 'Mothers aren't your thing?'

'Why? You got womb to rent?'

I picked up the nearest book and slapped his arm with it. My methods may have been more effective had I not been doubled over with laughter.

'Stop it,' I demanded. 'What are you doing here anyway?'

He gestured wildly at his knee. 'Duh, removing my tape.'

So far, that looked to be a painful venture, for him at least. Any wonder; everyone knows to rip plasters off quickly, no matter the size. After watching him picking at the edges and wincing, I crossed the room, snatched the end of the bandage from him, and tore it off in one clean yank. Marcus yelped, bit down on his knuckle, and tried desperately to recoil away from me.

'Christ, remind me never to wax.' He rubbed at his bare knee, a little raw. 'You're awful!'

'To be fair, you probably should have left that on until you got home,' I said. 'Give your knee a bit of support.'

'And you women wax your legs?' he whimpered, rubbing quickly at the spot.

I thrust the waste paper basket in his direction so he could toss the used bandage. 'I can assure you, waxing one's knees is not the painful part.'

He refused to look me in the eye, instead concentrating on

the bald patch on his leg. 'I am not touching that at all.'

'It's not like I'd let you anyway.'

He snorted. 'Now that is just a bald-faced lie.'

Our eyes met. Awkward silence swam into the room, which was beginning to feel increasingly charged with each passing comment. It was a new feeling, and one I wasn't entirely sure what to do with.

'Have dinner with me,' he suggested. 'You don't have to bring anything. I've got a few things I want to run by you.'

'You have?' I swallowed down a confused lump. My plan was to not sleep with him again, so finding myself anywhere near the vicinity of his house was going to be way too much of a temptation. And, if he was still wearing his football gear when I arrived, I could not be held responsible for my own actions. This was not a good idea.

There, I said it. And wasn't the first step admitting you were powerless? Powerless to the itty-bitty shorts and tight guernsey and go the hell away. No.

'I figure we can grab some wine, go through last year's programme, work out how closely we'll follow that.'

I stuffed some homework of my own into my bag. 'You know, I don't think that's a good idea.'

'What do you suggest, then? We don't have a lot of time left.'

'My divorce went through today,' I spoke slowly, feeling a flutter of annoyance bloom. 'I just … I think I'd like to be alone tonight.'

Marcus was silent for a moment, his expression softening. 'Manning, I—'

I shook my head. 'Sorry, I don't mean to sound difficult.'

'No, it's fine. Really, it's fine. I shouldn't have pushed.' He moved towards the door. 'I'm glad it's all sorted, enjoy your night.'

The library door swung closed behind him, leaving me standing there feeling adrift. I hated myself for using that as an excuse again. I was supposed to be getting on with things, not burrowing away in the past.

Chapter 12

Whether I'd received my divorce papers three weeks or three months ago, the build-up to this moment had been almost a year in the making. When the key hit the lock and barrels dropped to reveal I'd come home to an empty house, it was almost a physical representation of how I felt.

Almost.

Walking through town this afternoon, sea breeze at my back and seagulls swooping overhead, I realised I wasn't feeling anything. I wasn't a kitchen sink vortex of happy, joyous, or ecstatic, nor was I sad, mournful, or regretful. What I was, was thirty-six years old and single. That's not considered old by any stretch, but I was well aware of a flashing railway crossing in the back of my mind. Its ringing bells would occasionally alert me to a coal tender that would scream down the tracks with my biological clock its only cargo.

The idea of celebrating my new life status wasn't exactly appealing and, when Penny arrived home with a bunch of flowers and a bottle of wine for me, we made like all good thirty-something girls on a Friday night. It was home-delivered pizza, comfortable old pyjamas, and a well-worn copy of *Bridget Jones' Diary* while we giggled our way through a blow-by-blow replay of the football match.

When I woke the next morning, buried under a pile of pillows and cocooned in my navy duvet, I felt a renewed energy floating through the air. The breeze coming through my window was crisp and carried a hint of freshly cut grass. It was the perfect combination to make me want to get out into the world.

Looking around my room, I pawed at my bedside table until I grasped the edge of my phone. Everything was still a bit too beige, too bland and, really, there wasn't much in here except my bed, bedside tables, and a chest of drawers, all of them a pinkish shade of beech. Today felt like the right day to make some fresh changes, buy a few small pieces that announced my name to the world. Or, at least, to the confines of my room.

'Pen?' I stepped out into the kitchen.

'In the laundry,' she called. 'Do you need anything washed?'

'Maybe, yeah,' I mumbled to myself.

'How are you feeling?'

I shrugged. 'Good, I think.'

'I'm sorry I didn't ask yesterday.'

Honestly, I hadn't expected her to. Before my own experience, divorce was one of those awkward subjects that stilted conversations. No one was ever quite sure of what to say for fear of causing offence or upsetting the situation. I mean, what do you actually say? I thought it was best to offer a quick greeting and wait for those affected to bring up the topic. At least, that's how I felt and, honestly, it was time to move on, so the less airplay it got, the better.

I waved a dismissive hand. 'Really it's okay. No need to make a fuss. Listen, is that old antique shop still around?'

'That one on the bend of the main street?' She peered around the doorframe. 'Yeah.'

'I might head on down there for a bit of a look, see if I can't find a few nice pieces for my room.'

'Only one rule.' She held a finger up.

'Sure.'

'Bring me back something tropical.'

I smiled. 'I can do that.'

* * *

The weather was warm for early November, in a way that made for sticky flyaway hair. The air had a sweet salty tang that beckoned you to swim in the ocean. Sounds of passing traffic were caressed with lapping at the shore, directly across the road and behind nascent dunes that edged a children's playground. It was so relaxing I could have torn off my clothes and floated about in the bay all day if it weren't for public nudity laws and morals. Penny was right – I should have done this twelve months ago.

Sand had reclaimed its place in the bottom of my shoes as if I'd never been gone. I paused briefly outside the café for a quick shoe shake, and a deep breath of the yeasty scent of fresh bread. A Dalmatian watched me as I peered into the window at a queue that threatened to spill out onto the street.

I looked at the dog. 'I think I'm going to stay out here with you for a few minutes.'

She didn't reply, but stretched her front legs out, almost supplicant in hope of a scratch. When I obliged with a scratch behind the ear, she shuffled in between my legs and placed her head on my thigh, because she was not loving this at all. Was there a better way to wait for coffee than to have a snuggly dog? I couldn't be sure who was enjoying it more.

'White with two sugars, right? More, depending on how salty you're feeling?'

I wasn't so much annoyed as I was slightly nervous at the sight of Marcus as he stepped out onto the sidewalk. Dodging a torrent of people flowing past, he made his way over to us with a wry smile and a small limp. Immediately, the dog's tail began flickering like a metronome. If she kept going, I suspected she'd make like a helicopter and take off into the sky. Offering me a coffee, he turned his attention to his dog. 'Can't leave you alone for a second, can I, Daisy?'

'What a gorgeous name,' I cooed. 'And you are so very pretty.'

Daisy was so impressed that she yawned.

'She's very affectionate.' I wiped a slobbered-on hand against my jeans and took the heavy cup, my fingers brushing against Marcus's at the switchover. He was warm. Solid. 'Thank you, by the way. I wasn't expecting you … how did you know I was out here?'

'See those windows? I could see you through them, thought I'd save you the trouble.'

'Do you want some money?' I asked.

'No, I don't want some money. It's a coffee, please accept it with my compliments.'

'Your compliments?' I chortled. 'Do you come with one of those little packing slips, too? With compliments.'

'You know, I could just take that back and you can get in the queue?' He thumbed towards the door. 'The far queue.'

'The far queue,' I mouthed back at him. 'Anyway, why are you hobbling? Old age? Arthritis? Weight of the world on your shoulders?'

'Because I am an old man who needs to understand he's no longer twenty.' He took a sip. 'Or so said my doctor last night.'

'Football?' I asked. 'It's hard work being a hero.'

'It really is.' He wrestled with reattaching the Daisy's leash. 'But it's a cross I must bear.'

Laughing, I asked, 'So … what are you up to today?'

'Not a whole lot. I thought I'd start by taking Daisy for a walk along the beach.'

'How very romantic.'

'Oh, I know.' He held in a laugh. 'But then I thought we might also go home, do some marking, work on the yearbook.'

'Fancy.'

'What about you?' he asked.

'I was just heading to the old antique shop up … that way.' I did the Retail Worker Point. It meant somewhere over there, in that general area, but I won't be showing you the way.

'Oh, yeah.' Marcus nodded along sarcastically, even peering off in the same random direction. 'Over there. That's the way we're headed, actually.'

'Should I just walk with you then?' I suggested. 'It'd be rude not to after such an exquisite coffee.'

'Not just the coffee.' He pointed. 'After all, who else is going to save you from dragons?'

'You best lead the way, now you put it like that.'

Marcus crooked an elbow and waited for me to slip my arm through his. He gave it a playful wriggle when he saw me hesitate. 'Come on. If we're going to do this morning stroll, we have to do it properly.'

'Since when are you worried about doing things properly?' I teased, finally taking him up on his offer.

'You know.' Marcus leaned in. 'This makes me feel rather posh with my dog and a lady on my arm.'

'Calm down, Roger Radcliffe.'

'Hey, I understand that reference.' He elbowed me as I laughed, my head dipping almost instinctively into his shoulder. 'Anita.'

'So, football and childhood fantasies?' I asked, hoping to fill some of the silence as we walked alongside each other.

'Yeah. I'd never really played until I moved here and made friends with Patrick. I take every opportunity to remind him of that every single time I hurt my knee.' He glanced down at Daisy, who was making eyes at a light pole. Like all good dog parents, he stood, and waited for the sensation to pass. 'What about you? What do I find in your gym bag?'

'Knitting needles.' I leaned in to him. 'But it's not exactly a summer sport.'

'Knitting?' I wasn't sure if that was the sound of surprise, disgust, or the confused love child of both. 'Really?'

'Truly,' I said.

'At least I know you'd get along well with my grandmother.'

I snorted and came to a stop outside the antique store. In the front window, a butter tray, a Charles and Di commemorative plate, some faded *Woman's Weekly* magazines, and an art deco style radio that looked promising.

The antique store, with its old-world signage had been around for as long as I had memories. It had changed hands over time, but it was still the same dusty old place full of items collected from old estates, records and books, trinkets and bric-a-brac. Occasionally, you'd stumble across a great furniture find, like Dad's old rocking chair. It cost him thirty dollars, twenty-five years ago, and was still in perfectly good working order.

'Here we are.' Marcus pivoted as Daisy used us as her personal figure eight workout.

'We are here,' I said. 'Here is where we are.'

I looked back along the street we'd just walked up. Watching people at tables, and waiters delivering lunches gave me a few moments of thinking time. What did I do now? Marcus tried pulling Daisy to a stop. When I turned to face him, he was already watching me.

'Do you want to come in with me?' I asked. 'Unless, you know, you've got more exciting things to do.'

'Oh … uh … I'm not sure I can bring the mutt in with me.'

I stepped up into the doorway and called out to anyone who might answer.

'Excuse me,' I called. 'Can we please bring our dog inside? She gets terrible separation anxiety.'

'You hear that?' Marcus whispered loudly. 'I think you've got a fan.'

A dachshund did a power slide around the corner of some shelves, its black and brown stomach too close to floorboards that were being scratched up by tiny toenails as it rushed to greet us. 'I guess that's a yes.'

The brilliance of junk shops lies in the random nature of them. Sure, the clothing was usually displayed in the one spot, but you could be guaranteed to find candle holders beside plates, toasters near cassette decks, and vinyl sitting in warm windows. It was perfect marketing when you had no choice but to dig through everything to find the gold.

'You know, it's unusual seeing you without a suit and tie on.' I watched Marcus through a partition in a glass shelving unit.

He was quiet for a moment, mulling over his thoughts. 'Really? I'm sure you've seen me naked.'

I worried my lip. 'I meant in regular clothes. Jeans, T-shirt. It's a little jarring after all the formality.'

'I guess you're right. I mean, it's not every day you come to school dressed like teen rock star.'

'I am not dressed like that!' I gasped.

'Manning, you're two steps away from the seventh circle of eyeliner hell.'

I pulled out my phone and switched the camera to selfie mode. It was an eternal wait for the screen to illuminate and learn that my make-up hadn't turned me into a bipedal panda. Slipping my phone back into my pocket, I breathed a sigh of relief. 'Wait. How do you know about eyeliner?'

His mouth twitched. 'I have a mother, and a sister who's heavily entrenched in theatre.'

'Theatre? Really?' I asked, turning over a coffee mug. Since when was a Seventies orange glazed cup worth twenty dollars? 'How'd you end up in teaching?'

'Firstly, I can't act. Secondly, I had a shit time in school. I was the fat kid with Coke bottle glasses and bar piano teeth. Mum will tell you it wasn't *that* bad, but it certainly felt like it in the eye of the storm. Initially, I wanted to be a carpenter, but ended up in a teaching degree when I realised, or maybe someone suggested to me, that a lot of shitty behaviour could and should be nipped in the bud early.'

'I'm fascinated by this milk bottle glasses kid.' I picked through a box of sheet music. There was nothing more recent than Rodgers & Hammerstein. 'You look so put together. It makes me wonder where he is, the milk bottle kid, that is.'

'He's still here.' He smiled softly, his eyes meeting mine. 'He just wears contacts now.'

'And suits.'

Marcus turned a book over to read the blurb. 'He's got *much* better taste in clothes now.'

Below us, Daisy waited around patiently. A sniff here, a chew of her feet there, and a quiet trot when we moved to the next stall, stand, or table. It felt weirdly comfortable, the three of us in here, digging through shelves and taking turns scratching the dog.

'If it's any consolation, I always wanted to work in our school, in the library,' I said. 'You can be guaranteed I'm an exhilarating person.'

'Really? Why? I mean, it's a brilliant community, but why? Of all the places you could go in the world.'

'I always felt at home in there, and not because I grew up here, either. Or maybe it is. I'm sure there's some psychological reason for that, and I'm not convinced I want to pay someone to delve into it. Of course, Cathy was there for the long haul, and I was busy being a smug married, but life is life, and things fell into place in the end, didn't they?'

'Is the plan to hang out until retirement?' he asked. 'Or are we a wayside stop on the way to something better?'

'I've had something better, and it's not always the best option.' I handed him a floral teacup, delighting at the slide of my fingers across the palm of his hand. 'But maybe I'll stop somewhere in the middle to have some kids. What about you?'

'Me? I'm not sure my body is built for childbirth,' he admitted. 'But if I were any cluckier, I'd be trying to hatch Creme Eggs.'

I sniggered and moved along to the next shelf. Was that kind of admission considered flirting? It had been so long, I couldn't be sure, but the idea of him with children was far more appealing than it should have been. I'd spotted him tucked into a corner of the library the other day, consoling an upset student at lunch, and I was a little jealous at how easy dealing with children seemed for him.

'I don't think it's a secret that I want Phil's job,' he continued.

'Do you think that's the most useful role for you?' I looked up. 'I feel like your passion lies in the downtrodden kids, and it can be hard to enact great change from behind a desk.'

'Honestly, I'm not even sure,' he conceded. 'I guess that's all part of the challenge.'

'That's fair,' I said.

'All kids are ever looking for is acceptance and friendship, but some of them are just plain assholes. I mean, I'm sure it's a product of their upbringing, but I don't think I have to explain that to you.'

'No, you don't.' I dug through a box of baubles. 'What does your Christmas tree look like?'

'Right now?' He moved in beside me and peered over my shoulder into the box of decorations in front of us. 'Currently wrapped in plastic and in the garage. During the month of December, it's a decidedly scruffy looking thing. You?'

'I don't currently own a Christmas tree, but last year's tree was quite fabulous. I walked into a department store and bought the window display.'

'Why would you do that?' he asked.

'Because I liked it.'

'Just like that, you said, "Give it to me," and they did?'

I shrugged. 'Turns out it was cursed, anyway. More fool me.'

'It sounds like there's a story there.'

'Depends on if you want to hear it.'

'I would be lying if I said I wasn't mildly curious.'

Standing huddled together in a mothball-scented corner of old clothing, I took a deep breath and set the scene for my story. It was a balmy Saturday afternoon just before Christmas last year. Presents wrapped in gold ribbon sat patiently under an ornately decorated tree, and our sitting room was full of colleagues and important clients. It could have been the perfect day to secure some important business deals.

It was true that the tree had come from the front window of a department store. Despite Dean's stronghold on the bank accounts, if something was going to paint him in a positive light, he was on it like ants at a picnic. The tree was deep green leaves, pastels, fake feathers, and tiny lights that blinked soft yellow in a dark room. It took centre stage in our sitting room, opposite my baby grand piano.

My piano was my pride and joy, a celebratory gift from my husband on my thirtieth birthday. Polished to the point that reflections slid from its surface, it was played only ever when I had the house to myself. The evening's request for a public performance had been muted by Dean, who declared it out of tune. It wasn't; I'd only had the tuning forks out earlier that week.

He'd whizzed through the kitchen, quickly grabbed a fresh bottle of whiskey and a pinot noir, pressed a kiss into my forehead, and offered rare praise. Dinner looked good, he'd said, and I looked better. It was unusual, but I was happy to take it. Who didn't love praise from their husband? Perhaps the Christmas spirit was working in mysterious ways, even if it was Scottish and aged twenty-five years.

An anecdote about a lost laptop on our recent travels brought the sound of laughter from the next room. And, while Dean stood in the corner of the room, suit and tie still in place from work, and a tumbler full of whiskey, his phone sat abandoned on the kitchen counter. When it vibrated, I picked it up.

My best friend, Sian, who was leggy, blonde, and cover model gorgeous, was sitting in the lounge with her husband Raph. The message was from her. '*Wish we were alone x*'.

'Then what?' Marcus stopped, turning over the price tag on an old coat.

'I went back into the sitting room where everyone was.' I scratched at my forehead. 'And the thing with Dean's friends is they always thought I was a little stupid. As if working in a library meant I wasn't capable of much more than reading books and cooking meals. They never said it to my face, but I just knew. You know when people sort of alter the way they speak to you and how they interact with you, like *Charlotte's Web* was the best I could do? Anyway, one of them asked me if I'd read anything good lately.'

A rollicking laughter burbled up from the deep, Marcus's eyes wide with delight. 'No.'

'Yes,' I chortled. 'I mean, my heart was absolutely hammering in my chest, and I could feel the drops of sweat forming, but I thought bugger it. It was happening, and there was no way for me to win after reading those messages. So, I told them I'd recently been reading the ballad of the philandering husband and proceeded to read out the text messages between the two of them. The idiot hadn't changed the passcode on his phone.'

'How was that received?'

'I moved out about an hour later,' I said nonchalantly.

'Okay, well, mine is hardly that dramatic. All I got was a Saturday evening discussion where Alice sat me down after dinner and told me that I had become increasingly boring and obsessed with my job, and perhaps it was time we looked at separating.'

My nose wrinkled like a foul odour had wafted through the room. 'How had you suddenly become boring?'

'I don't know.' He shrugged a lone shoulder. 'I mean, look, we'd always had this agreement that, if one of us were unhappy, we'd have to come to the table and lay everything out and decide what to do from there. But, she just kind of skipped that part and went straight for the, "It's over" speech.'

'I'm sorry.'

'It's fine.' He shook his head and stepped away. 'Apparently, I was always marking work or talking work or learning for work, and she'd run out of patience. I tried explaining we weren't in university anymore, so weekends weren't exactly for beer bongs and pizza, but then she launched into the second part of her speech that alluded to how I probably wouldn't be the best father if I were so preoccupied with work.'

'Marcus, that's completely ridiculous.'

'Yeah, well, whatever, right?' he grumbled.

Whatever. That bloody word again. I pursed my lips and felt my brows twitch.

'I guess the good thing about your situation is that it wasn't your fault,' he said.

I scoffed. 'I'm not entirely sure that's correct. I had to have done something to send him running.'

'No, I don't think that's true,' he argued. Daisy tugged on her lead, sniffing about at the dachshund that had joined us. 'His cheating had nothing to do with you. He was obviously looking for something, something he hadn't given you the opportunity to provide. He hadn't asked for it, he just took it from someone else. You're not responsible for that. Me, on the other hand, I am a bore who thinks nothing more of spending a Saturday afternoon marking assessments and rereading *Harry Potter* for the forty-seventh time just so I can keep up with class discussions every year.'

'How is that boring?' I asked. 'That's your job. We all know there's a mountain of unpaid overtime in this profession. It's the nature of the education department which, unfortunately, we don't have a lot of control over. Yet, we run headfirst into this job because we believe in something bigger. This stupid bloody presentation, for instance. A lot of that will be weekend and evening work. Marking papers is part and parcel, taking an active interest in your job is not boring, it's dedication and, I'm sorry, I've seen you with those kids, you are damn good at what you do. Never apologise for that.'

Marcus stood silently at the end of the next table, watching me. His face was soft with something I couldn't yet put my finger on, but it tugged at me, nonetheless.

'What?' I asked.

A relaxed smile pulled at his mouth. 'Thank you.'

* * *

In the end, all I walked out of the shop with was a small armful of novels and some old sheet music. There was every chance Dad had some of these pieces at home, but I'd lost most of my music, so was keen to start building up my collection again. It would come in handy when I eventually replaced the piano.

Stepping out onto the sidewalk again was an awkward *Sliding Doors* moment. A will they or won't they continue the conversation over hot coffee and soothing cake? Marcus watched silently while I tucked my life back into the pocket of my jeans. I'd been sans handbag today, and it was a nice light feeling, but made it slightly annoying to Jenga-balance everything on the walk home.

'What are you doing this afternoon?' I asked.

'Now that I've finished procrastinating?' he asked, scratching at the back of his head. 'I've got a heap of marking, surprise, surprise, that I need to get rid of so I can start final report writing.'

The devil on my shoulder was screaming at me, accessorised with megaphone and spittle, to go and help him. Offer him some assistance. It couldn't be too hard, there was always an answer sheet to work from. When it came to the angel, though, she was very happy to remind me of what happened last time I made it to his front door, then asked if I was prepared for the possibility of that again. I wasn't sure I was, so I sided with her.

'Do me a favour, will you?' Daisy wound herself around Marcus. 'Stop blaming yourself. It's not your fault.'

'Only if you promise to do the same,' I said.

'I promise you, I'm okay. It's been a few years now, so I'm looking forward to the next chapter,' he said. 'Oh, God, dog, stop. Sit. Just sit. Two more minutes.'

'I'll let you go, but if you need any help, just call me, okay?' I stammered, tongue wrapping around tonsils and mouth drier than a beach in summer. 'With marking and stuff like that. It's been a while, but I'm sure I've still got it.'

Wait. What? My heart skipped as my breath caught. I wasn't sure if I automatically regretted saying that, or if I was more worried about the answer.

'I might just do that.' He smiled, arm outstretched as Daisy pulled him towards the corner. 'Thanks.'

Chapter 13

Crawling around on my hands and knees, arm buried elbow deep in wool, was not how I expected to spend my Sunday, but knitting felt like a great way to reconnect with the Eleanor of old, to wake her up gently, so I packed Penny into the passenger seat of my car and brought her along with me. Right now, I was revelling in the joy of picking through different ply yarns, flipping through pattern books, and realising I wasn't sure exactly what gauge needles I had anymore.

'You're quiet today, Ellie,' Penny said, arms laden with the balls of yarn I'd already tossed in her direction.

Talking to Marcus yesterday had given me so much food for thought that I'd kept my mouth shut out of fear of talking with my mouth full. His words spent most of yesterday afternoon tumbling around in my head, arranging and rearranging themselves until sleep finally gave my brain a chance to unwind and relax for the night.

Right now, wool was keeping my mind busy. If all I had to think about today was matching dye lots – and that stuff was imperative unless you wanted your latest cast-on to look like a rainbow – then I was going to be happy. If the suggestion in Penny's voice was anything to go by, though, I was not done digesting. I slipped back onto my haunches, a lock of hair flopping down onto my face. I tucked it back behind my ear and peered up at her.

'I am?'

'I'd say so, yes.' She took another skein from me, rubbed the soft fibres across her face, sighed, and added it to her swaddle …

pile. 'You wolfed breakfast without saying a word, asked to go shopping, and said nothing the entire way here.'

The drive to the wool mills, which was run from an old farmstead deep in the Otways, had taken forty-five minutes end-to-end and, to be fair, we were listening to a podcast the entire way there. A very good true crime podcast that we'd both been engrossed in. So, there was that.

'Sorry?' I said, more of a question than anything. Was I meant to be apologising?

'You don't need to apologise.' She smiled sadly, like you would at a toddler who'd done something cute, but a little bit wrong at the same time. 'I'm just worried about you, that's all.'

'Oh.' That was a no, then.

'You haven't even spoken about what you got up to yesterday, let alone how you're feeling about ... everything,' she continued. 'All I know is you went to the antique shop and came home with two books and your mouth sewn shut. Did something happen?'

I shoved my hand back into the cube shelving unit. 'I ran into Marcus.'

'Oh,' she pipped, a cheeky smile spreading slowly. 'Well, that's interesting.'

'It was,' I confirmed. 'He gave me a lot to think about.'

I pushed myself up to my feet, bouncing as I straightened out and plonked the last ball in her arms. I wanted to share his insights with her, and what they had meant to me, but putting exactly what that was into words right now was the hard part. Reaching for a burnt-orange wool, I held it up to my cheek.

'Does it work?' I asked. 'The colour, I mean.'

Penny shook her head. 'Blue is more your colour. Brings out your eyes.'

'Really?' I asked, not entirely sure she wasn't making this up on the spot. 'Blue?'

'A nice dark navy,' she continued. 'Or green. Emerald-green.'

I traipsed across to the next lot of shelving, all of them dusty, all accentuated at the end by spinning stands of pattern books, Cleckheaton for yards. Penny picked up a 4-ply baby book and flicked through it quietly, wool abandoned on the shelf next to her.

'I'm glad you ran into him, actually. He was worried about you,' Penny continued. The shop assistant, who'd otherwise been hovering about, handed her a shopping basket. 'He was asking after you on Friday night. A few of us caught up for post-game drinks. He said he'd seen you in the office and you'd just kind of switched off on him. I suspect it triggered some memories for him.'

Confusion was swiftly replaced by a feeling of deep regret. I'd only spent my first month in the job absolutely loathing him. I'd gone out of my way to find fault and, yet, he was the only person so far who'd been able to offer advice from the perspective of hindsight and first-hand experience.

'Don't say that.' My bottom lip, which had been doing so well lately, began to falter. 'He's been far lovelier than I deserve.'

'It's not that you don't deserve it,' she argued. 'It's just that, this time, it sounds like you dialled down the sarcasm and listened … and heard.'

I looked at her, hand outstretched waiting for another ball of wool. Even though she currently looked like a watercolour painting, and the lump in my throat was creeping up, I really did feel okay. I was just in the middle of an epiphany, one that was almost twelve months in the making. No big deal.

'It wasn't my fault,' I said, voice strangled with tears.

I'd spent so long inside my own head, analysing and overanalysing everything that had gone wrong, trying to ascertain at what point exactly did Dean decide a new girlfriend would be a good idea. Was it the fact that I didn't resign from my job when he suggested I should just stay home? We had enough money, he reasoned. Or was it when one of his colleagues alluded to doing exactly the same, with zero trouble getting away with it. After all, it was nothing more than risk versus reward, wasn't it?

And, boy, did he love high risk. He was an investment banker, for crying out loud. He spent big, returned bigger, jumped from planes, and held business meetings in the casino. Our home was obscenely large for two people, and any suggestion we might fill those rooms with smaller people was met with, 'I don't fucking think so.'

Standing on the outside looking in, it was an obese little world – and one that saw me increasingly incompatible with it the more it expanded. Fine fittings, expensive cars, and high-end fashion was how we lived. Was it any surprise then that my life fell apart the way it did? Everyone knew what was happening, everyone was in on the joke, except me.

But, whatever Dean's reason, it was mine no longer. That simple realisation made it feel as if a weight had been lifted. It gave me a little more oil in my joints, and air under my wings and, even though I was now crying, I felt free of everything.

Penny shook her head, a soft smile on her face. 'No, it's not.'

I wiped at my eyes and laughed. 'I don't even know why I'm crying. This is so silly.'

'I'd say you've had yourself a breakthrough.' From out of nowhere, the shop assistant was standing next to Penny. She had a Bea Arthur-ness about her, with shoulder pads propped high and a handmade cardigan. I could get behind that. 'I'm Carol.'

'Carol, this is my cousin and my good friend, Eleanor. She finally got herself a divorce this week. We're celebrating.'

'As someone who's been there and done that, three times, that does call for a celebration.' Carol rested a hand on Penny's shoulder. 'Let me get the teapot.'

'I'm just ... I'm a bit worried about her.' Penny fell into step as she chased Carol into the rear of the shop, as though they'd been friends since the dawn of time.

Ladies and gentlemen, behind pantry door number two: the intervention.

While they were gone, I patted tears away from damp eyes and pulled myself together. Public crying was not my usual thing, and I didn't want to start now. I made sure I had everything I needed, just in case of an emergency exit. I counted off yarn, needles, markers and a pattern book or three. I'd make something from them eventually.

They returned with a floral tea tray which landed on the sales counter with the chatter of porcelain teeth. Biscuits were presented on a dishwasher-warped plastic plate, and tea was being poured from a Wedgewood pot.

Our new friend, Carol, had overhead everything and, instead of getting on the blower to her friends and relatives, decided that she needed to hear the full story. Maybe she was bored. It didn't help that her shop was emptier than a schoolyard on curriculum day. I think even the spiders had shuffled off somewhere else.

'And, can I just say?' Crumbs burst forth from Penny's mouth. She'd scored an early biscuit and a toilet trip while chewing Carol's ear off in the kitchen. 'If this guy at the coffee shop doesn't start getting my name right, I'm going to jump the counter and tattoo it onto his forehead with a compass and a Crayola.'

Our only stop on the way here had been the café, the same old same old, where Penny's name had come out as Sally today.

'Well, that's a bit violent.' Carol grimaced. 'You could at least start by throwing the coffee back at him.'

Because third-degree burns were such a non-violent option, too. No wonder these two got along so well.

'To be fair, stabbing someone with a compass is more her style.' I'd seen Penny fight in school and, just as she was now, there was nothing subtle about her. I plucked an Iced Vo-Vo from the plate and shoved it almost whole into my mouth. I was both hungry and ready for some emotional eating, which was no doubt a winning combination. 'This is incredible.'

'Now.' Carol shuffled about on her chair, the cat lining up the bird, and fixed me with a very serious look. 'Tell me everything.'

Where I tried to hold back some of the finer details, Penny filled the gaps like a foreman going over blueprints on a worksite. For the next few hours, the three of us discussed my marriage, Carol's marriages (she loved wedding cake, her words), Penny's love of the random man, and all the bastardised things in between. Carol's ears really pricked up when I hit the subject of Marcus, of the push and pull, and how his wisdom yesterday was the reason for today's episode.

'I mean, I always knew deep down, somewhere, that this wasn't my fault. You can't just go out and rob a bank and say, "Yeah, but my brother made me do it," right?' I looked to my companions for support.

I picked up the teapot and drained the last dregs of our second pot of Earl Grey. Cup number three was going to make for an interesting drive home. Coffee was fine, I could hold an Olympic swimming pool of coffee, but tea? Forget about it.

Penny and Carol nodded in agreement.

'At any point, any point at all, my husband could have sat me down, told me he wasn't happy, asked to work through a solution,' I continued. The last dregs of any teapot were dusty, and I coughed a little at the last mouthful.

'And that's where it stops being your fault.' Carol dunked her biscuit. 'Maybe there was an aspect he wasn't happy with. Who knows? But the fact he circumvented all common sense and just followed his pants down the road. Well, then, it stops being your problem, your fault, your anything.'

It seemed like an easy conclusion to come to, and I supposed she was just adding another colourful layer to the box of theories that had been presented to me by various women in the last year. Unlike the others, some of whom had suggested I had obviously done something wrong, this was one to hang on to.

'I think it was just the added male perspective that Marcus offered, not that I need a *man* to validate my feelings.' I swallowed. 'All right, the human perspective. The shared experience.

It was nice to connect on that, to know that I wasn't alone, and to discuss things in terms of the aftereffect, and the blame. Because there's always so much blame, often misplaced.' I looked at the two women before me, one who looked like she'd heard and seen it all before. The other, still a little green around the relationship gills, looked like I was good research on What Not to Do.

Carol folded her arms across the counter and leaned in. 'Is there any chance you reacted so strongly to this guy because you have feelings for him?'

'Eww, no.' That idea presented a teensy-weensy chasm of confusion, which threatened to get bigger if I pulled at the thread. Instead, I scoffed and offered a tear-strangled laugh. 'No, not feelings, no. A new appreciation, yes. I certainly am grateful for the words he offered and for the clarity that they've given me. It's especially important—'

'You think he's pretty,' Penny sang.

'What?' My eyebrows disappeared up under my fringe. 'Nooooooo.'

'Yes.' She plucked the blue yarn from the shopping basket at my feet and held it up against my face. 'This shade works particularly well with your embarrassment. Very cute.'

I snatched the ball from her and waved it about like a presentation stick. 'I'm just saying that perhaps I underestimated him as a *human*.'

'Man.'

'And that I could be nicer to him.' I dug my heels in, tossing another shovel full of dirt over my shoulder.

'With a penis.' Penny spat the 'p' across the room like a piece of gum.

I coughed. If only she knew half of it.

Penny lit up. 'Here, Carol, do you want to see what he looks like?'

Before I had a chance to protest, Penny had whipped her phone from her pocket and was scrolling wildly through a bunch of photos – don't mind that naked man … or that one – before the social life spinning wheel landed on a shot of Marcus. She'd captured him at the same pub we'd been in the night we went home together. He was leaning back in his chair, suit still on, but with tie nowhere to be seen, shirt unbuttoned just so, ankle crossed over a knee, and arm slung casually over the back of his chair.

'That was his birthday last year,' she explained. 'There were lots of drinks, lots of laughs and, then, he went home *alone*.'

Carol pinched the screen and zoomed in on his face. 'My, he does look to be someone who takes himself very seriously.'

Penny tapped at her chin and turned to me. 'I wonder who that could possibly remind me of.'

'Shut up, you.' I gave her arm a playful tap. 'I do not.'

The three of us peered at the screen, which had taken the place of Baby Jesus in a manger. It was both a marvel to behold, and it was holding up a mirror to my life. In its reflection, Penny with her thinking cap on. Carol, her lips downturned in a look that screamed she'd be straight on him if only she were thirty years younger. At the end, there was me, and I wasn't sure who I was looking at this morning.

Was it the man who called me an angry little onion? The man who delighted in my scandalised upset at being compared to a seventy-something Scottish man? The same person who'd just about carried me home over his shoulder before making a limp-limbed mess out of me? Or was it the sweet but vulnerable boy who'd stood beside me yesterday and poured his heart out like he knew me, all to make me feel a little less alone in the world. I looked away quickly, as if checking the dye lots on the wool was going to provide an adequate distraction.

It didn't.

Confusion had a new home, and it was the junction box of my heart and brain, clinging to a vertebra like King Kong on the Empire State Building. With the way I felt right now, I had one of two choices: I could climb back down the building, careful not to misstep on the way; or, I could throw myself off the ledge and see if anyone would catch my fall. As I dithered about a decision, King Kong didn't so much beat at his chest, but formed a clumsy love heart with his fingers and thumbs and crossed his eyes.

Later that afternoon, while spooning out the insides from an apple slice, I decided to climb down carefully, step away quietly, and do nothing more than take his advice for what it was: the gentle words of someone who'd been there, done that, and had the T-shirt to prove it.

It was a great place to be.

Chapter 14

Unlike our Hollywood primate friend, a woman doesn't always need to beat her chest to make an impact. Sometimes, all she really needs is a quick step, sensible shoes, and a sense of humour.

Sunday afternoon found Penny and I in a second-hand clothing shop. I did my part in reviving my wardrobe with a large bundle of half-price dresses, shoes and embroidered cardigans. I catwalked through the shop, past the change rooms, and waited for Penny's thumbs up because, as eccentric as she was, she knew her clothes.

When I remarked that a faux fur stole on the window mannequin reminded me of a Twenties screen siren, the idea of an Oscars theme for our presentation night took seed. Over the course of the weekend, I watered it with ideas, and it bloomed into a lovely little flower that had me taking notes on my phone and jotting emails to myself before my tiny moments of brilliance disappeared into the void.

Penny was still pitching random ideas that would, could, maybe slot into the night as we walked through the school grounds on Monday morning. We'd already talked about red carpets and photographers while I'd been casting-on her knitted coat the night before but, by this morning, she'd moved on to flash mobs and choreographed dancing.

'I'm picturing a very climactic *Footloose* type of scene.' Penny waved a hand in front of her. 'Chintz, glittery things, statuettes ... Kevin Bacon.'

'If you could manage Kevin Bacon, I would approve the budget personally.'

Penny snickered. 'I should think I could teach him to dance.'

'What are you two giggling about?' Marcus called from somewhere behind us.

I turned to find him dragging his trolley case behind him, the flaps of his jacket billowing in the breeze as he scampered to catch up with us. Judging by the slight wince he wore every second step, his knee still wasn't one hundred per cent.

'Nothing!' I called. 'Well, nothing you need to know about, anyway.'

'Really?' He came to a stop and gave me a questioning look. 'Where are you heading to then?'

'Nowhere,' I said slowly, pointing towards the office. 'To get a coffee.'

'But you don't like that coffee, you've said as much yourself. Why don't you come to my office? I'll make you a nice coffee and we can workshop my ideas for this presentation night.' When I said nothing, he continued, 'Come on, I'll even put those little chocolate sprinkles on the top for you.'

'You have ideas?' I asked, taking another step backwards. 'What ideas?'

He shrugged. 'I may have come up with a few good options yesterday. I'm going to speak to Phil about them this morning.'

'Oh, are you?' I stepped again. 'And what if I have ideas?'

'Do you though?' He moved closer again. 'I seem to recall we didn't make it that far on Saturday.'

'I have heaps,' I lied. I only had one. 'Very good, fantastic ideas.'

His nose scrunched. 'Mine are better.'

'They really aren't.'

'Bet you they are,' he challenged.

Apparently, his quest for ladder climbing brought out his competitive streak. And mine.

'Hold my bag.' I shoved my things at Penny and left her standing there dumbfounded as I raced towards the main office.

'Wait!' Marcus dropped his case by Penny's feet and followed me up towards the building. 'That's not fair!'

'Hey! Hey! Hey!' Penny shouted after us. 'I'm not Freddie fucking Mercury, you know!'

I'd never been much of a runner unless there was a book sale, but if Claire Dearing could do it in heels with a Tyrannosaurus Rex hot on her tail, surely, I could manage it in a pair of five-dollar boat shoes. I leapt up the step into the office and threw back the door before Marcus had managed to hobble across the quadrangle. Phil was already waiting in his office and, judging by the bemused look on his face, had a stopwatch hidden under his desk.

'The Oscars,' I puffed, hands on knees. 'I really think we should do an Oscars theme.'

'You do, do you?' He grinned.

The door burst open again, knocking me on the backside and propelling me two steps forward. Marcus stumbled breathlessly into the room, also coming to rest with his hands on his knees. I'd call it the look of someone who hadn't seen football training recently. A bead of sweat trickled at his temple.

'Heroes and villains,' he coughed. 'Christ, Manning.'

'Ellie Manning, actually.' I rocked on the spot. 'I neither hold, nor want lofty religious ambitions.'

'You two have obviously spent a lot of time together formulating a single plan,' Phil teased.

'Well, you know.' Marcus straightened up and threw an arm around my left shoulder while his spare hand patted my right. I did my best to ignore the warm sensation that wrapped itself around my heart, stomach and mind. 'I did tell Miss Manning that hers was indeed a wonderful idea. I just wanted to put forward a better, more suitable alternative.'

Keeping my hands clasped in front of me, I drew back to look at Marcus, an expression of utter disbelief on my face. Phil's face told me he wasn't believing a word of it either. Inside the room, deathly silence was counted out by the ticking of a wall clock.

Outside, Penny grumbled at her computer, and basketballs bounced across the quadrangle.

'What was yours again?' Marcus offered me a pained look, hand now clutched at his side.

'The Oscars,' I deadpanned.

'Oh,' he breathed, waggling a finger at me. 'Right. We did discuss that. I remember.'

Phil's chair squeaked as he leaned back, threading his fingers across his stomach. For someone who was in his office at eight o'clock on a Monday morning, he was remarkably chirpy. A slow smile crept across his face, and his eyes shifted between Marcus, who looked like he hadn't slept, and me.

'I love it,' he said. 'The Oscars theme, that is. How far ahead are you with planning?'

'Oh, you know,' Marcus began, 'It was a very hasty weekend meeting, and it was hard to—'

Phil turned his attention to me. 'Eleanor?'

'Honestly? Not far.' I shook my head. 'But, now that we have a theme, we should be good to start working on things. I dropped Jack an email about the music yesterday evening. We'll workshop some ideas around the rest of the night but, basically, I want the kids to walk away feeling like they've achieved something special which, in essence, is the Oscars.'

I couldn't read the look on Marcus's face at all. He seemed stolid compared to only moments earlier. Was he dying a slow, painful death, or was he impressed? All I knew was he wasn't exactly about to orgasm.

I pivoted to face him and folded my arms across my chest. 'What do you think, Marcus?'

He bumbled about a bit, before tapping me on the shoulder. 'I'll ... yeah ... I'll iron the tux.'

* * *

'I cannot believe you threw me under the bus in there.' Marcus scurried after me as I walked through reception, through the swinging door to the staffroom, past the refrigerator where he snatched up a bottle of milk, and straight into my office.

As it turned out, the look in Phil's office was his severely put-out look. I suspected then that he wasn't used to having his ideas vetoed as often as they had been lately. The idea tickled me.

'Bus?' I tried pouting but laughed instead. 'I don't see a bus around here.'

Still clutching as his right side, a chuckle bubbled up. 'You are terrible, Manning.'

'I am,' I said. 'I am absolutely horrible.'

'After everything we went through,' he sighed heavily, using the glass doors of one of my cabinets to adjust his tie. I won't lie, it was quite a sight.

'Everything we went through?' I sputtered. Now was not the time or place to begin *this* line of enquiry. 'I thought we'd—'

'The coffee, the onions, the deep and meaningful on that fateful night. Our shopping expedition.' He scratched at a piece of tape on the bench. 'I come in this morning prepared to make you a special coffee to save you from drinking that god-awful cheap shit they seem to want to feed us, just to see if I can't come to an agreement. But, no.'

I rolled my eyes.

'I can't even get a look in. I feel so cheap. So dirty. And you've moved on to Jack already? What does he have that I don't, huh? Is it the scruffy beard? Because they don't really do it for me; too itchy. Plus, I don't think a man-bun would help the aesthetic I'm trying to achieve.'

'You are such a giant cock,' I mumbled, pushing him out of the way and reaching for my course folder. 'And you can calm the jealousy down. All I did was send him an email. He hasn't got back to me yet because it was the weekend, which are those two days between Friday and Monday where some people don't work. And, if you must know, I'm not interested in him like that.'

'Well *that* is a compliment for the ages,' he said with a delighted chuckle. 'I thought it was certainly adequate to the task, but nothing extraordinary.'

I hid behind my folder, hoping to stop a hysterical laugh spewing forth, but succeeded only in bringing out his own deep-seated chuckle.

'Go away.' I shoved playfully at his shoulder. 'I can't even look at you, you're such a grub.'

'Well.' He sank against my desk, arms folded. 'If I can be frank—'

I nodded. 'Okay, Frank.'

'All right.' He looked away momentarily, a wistful smile on his face. 'I need to admit something to you.'

'You do?' I asked, feeling my throat close in on itself. I swallowed and hoped to whichever God was in charge that he wasn't about to say something he could never take back.

'It's a brilliant idea.'

I blew out a heavy held breath as I felt relief wash over me. 'Thank you.'

Was that a pin dropping? Or the mechanisms of my brain grinding to a halt? My chest expanded with a held breath, and the silence was so loud I could hear blood rushing about my ears like a conch shell.

'Anyway, I wanted you to know that, despite, well, *whatever*, I'm looking forward to seeing how this pans out,' he said nervously.

Every time I thought he might be eroding some of my crisp candy coating, he'd go ahead and do something like call me Manning instead of Eleanor, or use that bloody word, 'whatever'. It only served to deflate an otherwise lovely moment. I wondered, then, if it were wise to say something about Saturday, or had that just been a whatever moment for him, too?

'Good thing, too, because I'm planning on working you hard,'

I bit.

Marcus winced. 'Poor choice of words, don't you think?'

I stabbed his chest with a single finger from each hand, drumming a little beat into the front of his crisp white shirt. 'Maybe, but he picked *my* idea, not yours.'

'Oh, la-dee-da,' he mocked, grabbing at my hands and holding them still. 'Because you're not competitive at all.'

'Nope.' I grinned. 'And I'll see you tomorrow afternoon to get the invites sorted. I've got a tonne of paperwork to do today, and some classes – not yours, by the way.'

'Oh, I know,' he said. 'And, on that note, I know where I'm not wanted.'

'Wait.' That one word took me by surprise, pulling me to a quick bounce. I felt like I was crossing a rope bridge over a wild sea, dainty footing and flowing dress being threatened with the idea of a deep dive should it all go belly up.

'Hmm?' Marcus grabbed at the doorframe on his way out.

'Before you go,' I began.

'Yes.' A smile spread slowly.

'Thank you.'

He tilted his head. 'For what?'

'For Saturday. For the things you said. You might have thought it didn't mean anything, but it …' My voice drifted as I twirled a pen through my fingers. I lifted my eyes to his, large green and welcomingly soft. 'Well, it's helped a lot.'

'Manning, you've gotta start being kinder to yourself.' He swung from the doorframe. 'You're strong, you're capable. Go forth and conquer. It's your time now.'

'Thank you,' I said. 'And it's Eleanor, in case you were confused.'

Marcus winked, tapped on the door and left.

After the excitement of the last few days, I was glad for simple things, like the whirring of my computer as it booted slowly. Even better was the feeling that, when it finally awoke, there was nothing life threatening or urgent in my inbox, nor were there any requests to chip in for yet another office birthday present.

Surveying the damage left from the Book Fair, it was clear that the first few moments of my morning were going to be spent cleaning if I had any chance of holding a class in the library. I decided to skip Monday morning assembly to focus on doing just that. I could hear everything through the PA system, so I wouldn't miss anything important.

I unfolded a flattened box and, one by one, dealt with the piles of books I'd abandoned on Friday afternoon. I packed them and stacked them, filling out returns paperwork, and booking a courier. All the while listening to the echo of announcements from the sanctuary of my office. I peered out the window at Marcus, who was standing about thumbing at his phone. As he turned the screen to a small crowd of students, he was showing off pictures of Daisy again.

I wanted to punch myself in the face, because the first thought that flashed through my mind was what a proud father he'd be if he ever got the opportunity.

Christ, Manning!

Chapter 15

Despite what my biological clock might tell me with each passing month, I was in no hurry to have children of my own. If ever I got too worried about it, I reminded myself I was lucky enough to be a teacher with plenty of kids to call me 'Mum' when they momentarily forgot they were at school and not at home.

Teaching was a brilliant eye-opener, particularly for anyone who'd ever considered what it might mean to have twenty-five children at once. Sometimes, I likened my days to an out-of-control McDonald's birthday party, minus the Happy Meals and ice-cream cake, but with the whirlwind kids, playground fights and vomit.

Yet, for all its frustrations, there was a wonder in teaching the younger classes. They were fresh minds in the early stages of discovering the magic of language and handwriting. Their first year of school was as much a learning curve as it was a shock; for me, and for them. While wading through phonetics and word families, rhyming books and alphabet-based crafts, there were huge breakthroughs almost daily. It was an amazing feeling to see a child walk away with a tiny puffed chest and the knowledge that something, somewhere had just unlocked for them.

Nobody took on this job for the accolades, but it was doubly nice when parents acknowledged and appreciated our efforts, even if it meant being held up while trying to deal with courier drivers and on the way to a meeting. Moments like those were gentle reminders of why I'd chosen this profession in the first place.

As I watched a parent walk away from one such interruption,

I felt a lovely sense of achievement. Things were heading in the right direction. It had taken me a few long, hard weeks but, there I was, persevering and doing the job. Names of students were becoming quicker to recall and, if borrowing reports were anything to go by, I was having an upswing in library visitors. Before I had a chance to get too caught up in my thoughts, I was interrupted by the crunch of gravelly footsteps approaching from behind.

'Eleanor, before you race off for the night.' Jack lumbered towards me, guitar case under one arm, and a bundle of papers in the other.

'I'll be here for a while yet, Jack, you should know that.'

'Life of a teacher.' He tossed his head back with a dramatic sigh. His hands grappled wildly as the case slipped to the ground. 'Anyway, Dad tells me you used to be a dab hand with the piano.'

'Does he just?' I watched as Mick scuttled past, finger pressed to his lips.

'Are you still?' Jack turned his attention back to me.

'It's been a while,' I admitted. 'But I'd hope it's like riding a bike. Why?'

'Okay, so, as you know, we got a piano delivered recently. I thought that it would be a nice thing to have in time for the presentation night, look at the school, new equipment, etcetera and so forth, but I can't get anyone out to tune it before the night.'

'After moving them, they generally need to rest for at least a fortnight before tuning,' I explained. 'Even then, you're talking about moving it to and from the gymnasium.'

'Right.' His top lip curled. 'So, what you're saying is that it's not quite doable?'

'What if we used the old piano? We can shift it into the gym tonight,' I said. 'I can tune it next week and check it just before the night. At least then you don't need to worry about the new one moving about and shifting again. I can still do all the tuning, that's not a problem. I'm sure I still have my toolkit.'

He pouted. 'I was really hoping to use the new piano.'

'I know you were,' I soothed. 'But this will be easier.'

'It will be, won't it?'

'Do you want to move it now, get it over and done with?' I asked. 'I've got a few minutes spare before a meeting.'

'I can't.' He winced apologetically. 'I've got to get going, band practice. You should come along one night, listen to us play.'

'Maybe,' I drawled. 'Anyway, I need to go do a few other things before this meeting. I'll see you tomorrow?'

Without much more to add, Jack scuttled over to his car, a clapped-out hatchback that looked like it would circle a roundabout in some sort of British comedy skit, sweets rolling about the dashboard and scented tree that erred on the wrong side of ashtray. Smiling as I waved him off, I checked the time and made my way inside.

* * *

'Hello.' I popped my head inside the classroom.

'Oh, look, it's Miss Manning.' Marcus, looking genuinely pleased to have me in his space, replacing the cap on his whiteboard marker with a flourish. 'What can my lovely class do for you today?'

With his tie loosened slightly and jacket hanging from the back of a chair, it was an altogether casual man that presented this afternoon. His eyes were tired but still bright as he waved me inside. I walked towards the back of the room and awaited further instruction. There were still four students in class with him, books open, pens in hand. I must admit, as a student, I loved being in the school after-hours. There was something about empty halls and classrooms that felt a little naughty.

'Haven't we finished for the day?' I asked. 'It's after three-thirty, and I'm sure I heard the bell ring?'

'Most people have, yes, but we are the extra learners. We're working just a little bit harder to get ready for high school next year.'

I pointed somewhere in the direction I'd just come from. 'I've just popped in to talk about end of year. Shall I come back tomorrow?'

'No,' he said. 'I think you might like to join us for the last ten minutes. What do you guys think?'

Instead of answering, I was greeted with a chorus of giggles. They were same giggles that told me Marcus and I would be starring in our own playground romance by recess tomorrow. I could play this game. With a smile, I dragged out a chair in the corner of the room and sat. Arranging my belongings around me, my phone, some papers, and the pen I pulled from my ponytail, I threaded my fingers across my front and waited for him to continue.

'Ready, Mr Blair.'

'How are your maths skills, Miss Manning?' Marcus rolled the marker between his fingers like an old coin trick. 'Good?'

'I think they're okay,' I said. 'Is that what we're doing?'

'Five points for you!' He pointed at me. 'We're working on multiplication. Is there anyone in here who's still not quite sure about the longer method? It's okay if you're not, this is exactly why we're here and I certainly won't judge you because it's my job to help you.'

A lone hand went up, a sheepish-looking boy. 'I'm still not sure.'

'Tom, I promise you, it's fine. I remember how much I struggled with this at school.' Marcus sat on the edge of his desk. 'Are you getting lost with carrying numbers over?'

Tom nodded. It tore at me that he looked on the verge of tears all over a maths problem. Equations that had been written across the whiteboard were solved using a single method but, in my experience, sometimes learning isn't a one-size fits all approach.

I thrust my hand in the air and waited. The look of sheer delight on Marcus's face was worth more than oxygen.

'Miss Manning?' he asked.

'Have you tried the Japanese visual method?' I asked. 'Perhaps our friends could benefit from a different perspective?'

'Can't say we have.' Marcus shook his head slowly as he spoke and tossed his marker at me. 'Let's see it.'

'Are you sure?'

'Absolutely.' He shrugged. 'After all, it takes a village.'

I took a deep breath and stepped up to the whiteboard. Marcus took my seat amongstst the students, crossed his legs at the knees, folded his arms, and waited. This felt entirely different to standing in front of a class and talking about books. I wasn't a maths teacher, and, for a fluttering moment, I doubted I could do it. But, as with most things that had popped up in the last year, I was going to roll with it.

The further I got into explaining the method of intersecting lines and simple addition, the more comfortable I began to feel. The sceptical look Marcus wore washed away, slowly replaced by something akin to surprise when Tom thrust his hand into the air, shuffled to the front of the class, and created his own problem to solve. When he walked out of the room minutes later with a smile on his face and the loose air of accomplishment, there were high-fives for everyone.

'It looks like you'll be coming to teach my class more often.' Marcus nudged me into his office.

I blew out a heavy breath and stretched up, hands way above my head. 'I don't think so. What even was that? What did I walk in on?'

'Like I said, that was our extras class,' he explained. 'Maths on Tuesday and reading and writing on Thursday nights. The kids who need a little help get an extra class.'

'Since when?' I asked. 'I didn't know this was a thing.'

'It's absolutely a thing.' In the corner, the coffee machine hissed as he switched it on. 'For me, anyway. I just hate the idea that they won't otherwise get to high school fully prepared, and the last thing I want on my conscience is one of them getting left behind when they get there. It's my job to make sure they're ready, so here we are. Selfishly, I refuse to do Monday nights because, ewww, Mondays. Tuesdays and Thursdays fit with football training during the season, so it works.'

'I'd hardly call any of this selfish.' I looked up as he handed me a coffee. 'I think what you're doing is wonderfully selfless.'

'Says the one who snapped the puzzle together for Tom in the closing five minutes.' Marcus sat at his desk and motioned for me to join him. 'He's been struggling for weeks, and in you strut.'

I blew against my fingernails and buffed them against my shirt collar. 'I'm just that good.'

We cleared a small space on his desk. A computer keyboard was relegated to a precarious balancing act atop of the monitor, and papers were jammed haphazardly into an in-tray as I pulled out a small notebook I'd been keeping about our project. I'd dot-pointed potential suppliers, rough prices, and any more ideas that had ballooned up in the process. I watched as Marcus studied my handwriting for a moment, his eyes drifting carefully across the page.

'You do realise you're doing a fantastic job of upstaging me lately?' he asked.

My cheeks prickled. 'Does that bother you?'

'No,' he said. 'On the contrary, I quite like it.'

We looked at each other, eyes searching faces. The silence sat heavily on my chest and, for a moment, I wondered if this was the tipping point, the moment when something was going to change. My ebony-keyed heart had been tinkling away, trying to get the tune right since the weekend. Every time I saw him, my mind disappeared back to his bedroom. Mix that with his words, and I had to remind myself why opening that door again was a bad idea.

'Right.' I reached down into my bag for my phone. 'Let's do this.'

'Do you want a biscuit?' He wheeled himself to the opposite side of the room. 'I'll get biscuits. They'll be good. Hopefully, Mick hasn't eaten them all.'

'He does love his sweets,' I said, suddenly, slightly, irrationally annoyed at the awkwardness. Could we not just get on with this?

There was a knock at the door. My head shot up to see who'd interrupted, and Marcus looked like he'd been caught, quite literally, with his hand in the biscuit barrel, eyes headlight wide and lips parted.

'Hello, Marc.' Grace flitted about by the door. She looked ethereal in a long skirt and crisp shirt. Her normally limp hair had been replaced by soft curls, which suited her perfectly.

I wasn't sure, but I thought I heard Marcus wheeze. 'Hello, Grace.'

'Have you—' she waved an awkward hand in the direct of his classroom '—got a minute or two? Sorry, Eleanor.'

'Don't mind me,' I dismissed.

'Are you sure? Just something really quickly.' She pinched her thumb and forefinger together and looked at me an apology that was as real as her eyelashes.

Marcus followed her from the room.

From my squat seat at the desk, I did my best to look like I wasn't spending the entire time watching Grace fall about him. If he spoke, she giggled and rubbed at his arm, she twirled dark hair through her fingers like a cheerleader with a baton and threw a sneaky look my way when Marcus hung his head in embarrassment. What began as mild annoyance turned into something incandescent when she tugged at his tie. I tipped my belongings into my bag, shoved my pen back in my hair and walked out.

'I'm sorry to interrupt.' I pressed a hand onto Marcus's forearm. 'I have to get going.'

'Oh, no, no.' He shook his head. 'Five minutes, just give me five more minutes.'

'It's okay, really. I can see this is important, and you both look like you have a lot to talk about. Let's just do this another time.' My brows slid up towards my hairline. 'It's okay.'

'What about tomorrow?' he asked.

'Can't do tomorrow, sorry.' Looking at my phone, another missed call from Mum. 'Talk soon.'

Shifting on his feet, Marcus pressed his lips into a thin white line. 'Eleanor.'

'Marcus,' I answered.

'Five minutes,' he stressed.

Grace fixed me with a look of victory. The corners of her mouth turned up and her eyes squinted into a false smile.

'I have another appointment,' I said, before turning and walking away.

Walking away hadn't just ended our conversation, it also stopped Grace in her tracks. I wasn't sure that had been my intention. I had no right to. Then again, maybe it had been. Could I not just have someone commit to a group activity and see it through properly? Did he have to run off and flirt with anyone who offered? Maybe I was just being a prude.

'Manning, wait.' Marcus skipped along behind me, stopping short when he found me tugging on the library door.

Yep, still locked.

'What do you want, Marcus?' My jaw twitched. 'Huh?'

'What do I want?' he asked incredulously. 'Are you kidding me right now?'

'No.' I gave my head a quick shake, lips downturned. 'Don't think I am.'

'What the hell was that back there?' His arm swung out in the direction of his classroom. Grace slipped out of the classroom, her heels echoing off the brick walls of the hallway.

'I don't know.' I folded my arms across my chest. 'Why don't you tell me what that was back there.'

'It … it was nothing,' he stammered. 'She just … wanted a chat is all.'

'So, just a chat about the weather then? Could've waited, don't you think?'

He rolled his eyes.

'Oh, for pity's sake, don't roll your eyes at me.' I raised my voice. 'I'm not blind, Marcus.'

'What did Jack want?' he spat. 'I saw you out there with him before in the car park. What did he want?'

'This is not about me. This is about you.'

'How is it about me, Manning?' he asked.

'Why is it so hard for you to use my name?' I asked. 'I'm not one of your football buddies, I'm not wearing a guernsey around everywhere, so why can't you just use my name? It's Eleanor, in case you forgot.'

'So you keep saying.'

'Then use it!' I raised my voice again.

'You know what? Why don't we talk about what this is really about?' he asked.

'And what do you think this is really about?' I mocked.

'You're jealous.' He shoved his hands in his pockets and rocked on the balls of his feet. 'You are jealous that she has the guts to ask me out on a date, and you do not.'

'This may surprise you to realise, but not all women want to date you. I, for one, happen to fall into that category.' I dug around in my handbag, double-checking I had everything, and avoiding his eyes at the same time, because even I wasn't sure if that was the truth.

He chortled. 'Is that so?'

'Yes, actually, that is so.' I began to walk away.

'I'll go out with her then.'

I shrugged petulantly. 'Okay.'

'Fine,' he said.

'Fine.' I threw a wave over my shoulder.

'It is fine,' he called after me.

'Fine!' I shouted.

* * *

I'd just about ground my teeth down to nubs by the time I'd walked home. My heart rate still hadn't returned to normal when I strode up the driveway to find a Nicholls Construction pick-up truck had parked me in, and freshly cut lawns.

The sweet tang of red wine pasta sauce with a hint of garlic wafted from our kitchen. It transported me back to cold winter nights, fogged windows, hot baths, fluffy pyjamas, and cartoons on the television before dinner. I almost forgot about Marcus and Grace when I registered a clothing rack and sewing items in the lounge room, and Penny's mum in the kitchen.

Dad's eldest sister, Aunty Gwen had been one of many amazing women in life. Not only had she raised Penny and her siblings, she was on hand to pick up my crumbs whenever the need had arisen. To be fair, that had been quite often. Nobody ever heard her complain because, to her, family was life. It was sobering to realise just how much I'd missed her.

As well as being the heart of every home, the kitchen was Gwen's natural environment. Right now, her home environment was ours. A pasta maker had been attached to the corner of the bench, a dust storm of flour was spread across a workspace, and wire racks heaved under the weight of cupcakes, pancakes, and a suspiciously molasses looking cake.

'Hello, Aunty.' I lifted my bag onto the kitchen counter and dropped my keys into a disused fruit bowl.

The oven door slammed shut as Gwen sprang to life and wrapped me in a warm, life-affirming hug. Any wonder Penny was so good at them. 'Hello, gorgeous girl. I've so been looking forward to seeing you!'

'Same, same. How are you? Are you well?' I pulled back and

held her shoulders as I took her in again. She reflected my cousin back to me, only a little older, a little shorter, with greyer hair, and a murder of crow's-feet from laughing so often.

'I'm great.' She bopped about the kitchen like a much older, wiser Penny. 'I hope you don't mind cannelloni with a meat sauce?'

'Are you kidding?' I filled a glass with water. 'I could smell it all the way up the street, there's no way you're tearing me away from it.'

'Good.' She smiled. 'Because, after that, we have Guinness chocolate mud cake and double cream.'

'And on that note—' I slipped up onto a stool '—Penny is officially evicted.'

'You girls.' Gwen clucked her tongue. 'Speaking of your cousin, she's just ducked back home to grab something for me. Patrick is in the backyard. He's just fixing a few things on Penny's list. I can't be sure exactly what. And those dresses in the lounge are for you to try on.'

'For me?' I squeaked. 'I thought Penny had placed another order.'

'Well, she did, but for you.' Gwen pushed me into the lounge, towards the rack. 'They'll probably need some finer alterations, but they'll only take a day or so.'

'You are … really?'

'Really.' Gwen turned back to the stove. 'Go on, try them on.'

When I'd mentioned to Penny that I'd love some new dresses, I was in no way expecting to come home one night to find a new personal wardrobe waiting for me. But here I was, with Gwen stepping me through the features of each dress. From the Hepburn inspired black number, to the emerald green copy, the grey linen tunic, a satin-lined floral print with hidden pockets, and everything in between, it looked like Penny had gone through a list of my favourite colours, and Gwen had magically picked out the perfectly styled patterns. I was more than a little bit in love with what was presented.

'And this?' I pulled out a dark grey wool blend coat from the end of the rack.

'That matches this here.' Gwen plucked out a similarly coloured A-line dress. 'This one, too, I suppose. Honestly, I was worried they'd be a bit too formal for everyday use.'

'No!' I waved an excited hand. 'These will be great for work. Please, don't think like that. They're not casual, but they're not so formal I should be in a high-rise office. They're perfect. I grabbed a few pieces from the vintage shop recently, but they haven't quite been working for me.'

'I've got a pair of trousers here. They're very Katharine Hepburn, but you're welcome to try them on.'

There was no way I was going to knock that back; everybody knew Katharine Hepburn was a style icon. I sighed happily as I held the garment out in front of me, high-waisted, wide-legged, and pleated. They were …

'Astounding. Thank you so much. You don't have to do all this for me. It's been an age since I've seen you.'

'Don't be silly, it's my pleasure.' She wrapped a reassuring arm around my shoulder. 'After all, life throws all kinds of things at us. Sometimes, new clothes help shed old skins.'

Now, there was some quality life advice if ever I'd heard it.

'Let's wait for Penny,' I suggested. 'Should we? We should.'

Gwen wrinkled her nose and gave me a shrug.

We didn't. Within minutes, I was being pinned into a gorgeous lavender shift and racing to the nearest mirror to glimpse my changing reflection. I hated being that walking, talking, makeover cliché but, with each new dress, more pieces of the new me were falling into place. When Penny finally arrived, cradling a few bottles of wine and a fresh bread stick, she appeared flustered and a little lost.

'Can you please, please tell my father that it is absolutely not okay to walk around the house naked. I learned way too much about my creation today.' She shook her head over and over, disappearing into the kitchen. 'Where's Patrick? Maybe he'll be naked, that'll cleanse my eyes.' Penny returned. 'And ohmigod that dress is gorgeous. Do you love it?'

'I do.' I flattened the material against my front. 'I feel very spoilt.'

'I keep telling Mum she needs to turn this into a business.' Penny appeared in the doorway. 'We could go to markets with our little Thermos of coffee and some sandwiches, sell some dresses.'

'You really should.' I looked at Gwen. 'Think of all the custom orders.'

She frowned and gave her head an embarrassed shake. 'I'm really very happy just doing this. Look how good you look.'

'Mum!' Penny disappeared again.

Much to her disgust, Patrick had no need to get naked in our backyard, no matter how covered in dirt he was, or how many suggestions Penny made. He'd checked the hot water service, pottered around the backyard, fixed fence palings, and restrung the clothes line, all before mowing the lawn. I had to wonder whether he was avoiding going home, or just making work for himself. I mean, it wasn't as if this was something we paid for on top of the rent. At least I hoped it wasn't.

'Just waiting for a dinner invite, actually.' Patrick appeared in the kitchen, sliding the side door shut behind him. 'It smells amazing and I figure if I hang around long enough, you'll feed me.'

'Lordy wordy,' Penny laughed. 'Are you kidding? Of course you're staying for dinner. Do you want to take a shower? You stink.'

'Can I?' he asked. 'And hello, Eleanor.'

'Patrick.' I smirked. 'Good to see you wearing some pants today.'

'In case you forgot, you actually own this house.' Penny looked at him like he was stupid. 'Honestly.'

'Whether I do or not doesn't preclude me from using manners, does it?' he asked.

Penny spun him around and pushed him towards the bathroom. 'Just go and wash. There are clean towels in the cupboard.'

At first, I found the landlord and tenant friendship strange, because hell hath no fury like a Penny without a hot shower or a broken fence paling, but I was starting to come around to it. The more time I spent with Patrick, it was becoming easier to see exactly why she held him on a tiny pedestal.

With Patrick tucked away in the bathroom, I returned to the safety of the lounge, where I was being pinned in and out, measured, and spun about like an Adjustoform. We dithered on the decision of whether to keep the skirt of one above or below the knee and, in the end, above the knee won out. Gwen shuffled about on the floor, measuring tape around her neck and pins in her mouth, mumbling about how much she loved the fabric, which was satin backed and felt altogether sexy.

'I love this one so much.' I pinched at loose emerald-green fabric around my middle, hoping we could remove another inch or so. Then again, it was extra space for a food baby.

'It suits you so much.' Penny folded herself into the recliner and held her phone in my direction. 'I'm totally Facebook-ing this.'

'Next time I get married, you're making the dress.'

'It makes me happy to hear you say that.' Gwen rested back on her feet and clapped her hands. 'Go look in the mirror.'

As I passed the front door, I spotted a familiar four-legged friend sitting outside on the landing. My stomach wibbled. She tossed her head back excitedly and barked as I approached.

'Daisy, are you lost?' I teased as I stepped out onto the landing. She wriggled backwards, yipped and did an excited little dance with her back legs, and tried to bury her head in my crotch. It was a dog thing, I got that much, but with a dress covered in pins, I did my best to push her away. 'Or are you walking your dad?'

'She is ... that's exactly what she's doing,' Marcus said, bemused. He waited at the bottom of the stairs, his arm strained with the tension of a retractable lead. Seeing him stabbed at something soft and spongy. I'd lost my cool at him earlier, yet, here he was, and I didn't know whether to feel relieved that he wasn't on a date or confused that he was here instead. What I did know was that I felt sad for how I'd behaved earlier, and it sat on my chest like a ... well, like a Daisy. A big heavy dog that was excited but not sure what to do with itself.

'Hello.'

Marcus shifted on his feet. 'Hey.'

'How are you?' I asked.

'I'm okay.' He stuffed his spare hand in his pocket and leaned against the railing at the bottom of the stairs. 'What are you up to? Are you busy?'

'Oh.' I flapped my hands at my sides, jerking away just as quickly when I hit a rogue pin. 'Just a wee wardrobe malfunction.'

Marcus blew out his cheeks and climbed the first step. 'I can assure you, that does not look like a malfunction at all.'

'Looks like you've had an accident.' I drew a finger across my neck. 'Tie's gone.'

'You know how it goes.' He fiddled with a button. 'Once I get changed, it's all over for the night. I have to get her out for a walk before that, so then we both get some exercise.'

I continued to look at him, my brain playing hopscotch with all the alternative endings to this conversation. Coming in for dinner? Going out for dinner? Let me race inside and get changed? My heart tumbled and fluttered about. I took a steadying breath and waited.

'Is that yours?' He pointed to my car.

I nodded. 'It is, yeah.'

'Nice.'

'Thank you.'

Wringing my hands, I looked at the street around us, taking in the darkened sky and white glow of street lamps, the whiff of damp sea breeze, wheelie bins on kerbs, and a discarded bicycle on the lawn across the road. Headlights swung around the bend, and Daisy's ears pricked at the sound of a dog barking somewhere in the distance.

'Why are you here?' I asked, as if we didn't know.

'Uh, I wanted to talk to you about this afternoon. I owe you a massive apology.' He looked down and frowned, mining the depths of his mind for his next words. 'I do need to pull my socks up and be more involved. And I wondered if you had a bit of time now to sit down and get this thing sorted. By that, I mean really get things moving. Let's get the invites out and step out everything we need to do, because we don't seem to be communicating particularly well. I think that's where we're going wrong.'

'It's not just communication that's important,' I said. 'I need commitment, too. This won't work without it. It's the three Cs: communication, commitment, consistency.'

'I understand that.' He lifted a lazy hand to point at the door behind me. 'That's why I'm here.'

'You can't just flit about with other women while we're trying to achieve something.'

'I don't want other women.' He climbed two more steps. 'You know that.'

'You're either in or you're out. People have let me down in the past and, honestly, I don't want to go through that again.'

'Can I say I'll do my best not to do that?' he said.

From the corner of my eye, I saw the blinds shift. We both turned towards the disturbance at the same time, laughter threatening to break the surface tension as our spies ducked in an uncoordinated retreat. The blinds swung in their absence.

'They've been watching the entire time,' Marcus said with a huff.

'Who's they?'

'All three of them. Patrick, Penny, and … someone else.'

I rolled my eyes as I watched him take another step forward. He was close enough now that I could lean down the next step and kiss him – if I wanted to. Instead, I reached out and folded over a wayward lapel that danced in the breeze. 'I can't very well send you away now they know you're here, can I?'

'Technically you could,' he whispered, his eyes searching mine. 'But you're right, it would be terribly rude.'

'In that case,' I said. 'Have you eaten? Would you like to stay for dinner?'

'You're so romantic, Eleanor,' he whispered, a twinkle in his eye as he stepped past me and opened the front door. 'My only plan tonight is to be here, and I'm staying until we get it right.'

Chapter 16

I woke with a start, back aching, cheek smeared with drool, and buried under Penny's crochet blanket. On the coffee table, my phone buzzed and blared out the opening bars of Tchaikovsky's 1812 Overture Op.49 and, despite how energetic that may sound, it in no way inspired movement. Wiping at my mouth, I reached out to grab it before it woke Penny as well. A thank you note sat under my phone, in Marcus's handwriting. He was officially the first thing I thought about today.

'Good morning, sleepy head.'

Penny was wide awake and chirpy, as only she could be. She slid across the kitchen floor in her socks and flicked on the kettle. I looked at her through bleary eyes and a head that told me I should have skipped that last red wine.

'What'd I miss?' I asked.

'Well.' Penny mused slowly, dumping two mugs on the counter. 'Do you remember Patrick leaving?'

I drummed my fingers against my chin. Last night had been a balancing act, I remembered that much. When I wasn't running about being pinned in and out of dresses, careful not to rip seams or fall out and expose myself, I was dashing between the lounge and kitchen to help Marcus piece together our group project.

Creating the invites had been a simple exercise of drag and drop formatting in a mailing list program. We pored over whether we'd included all the important information, along with the school colours and contact information. After all the gnashing of teeth and arguing yesterday afternoon, it had turned out to be a simple affair that we managed between mains and dessert, and all with a crumpled notepad and pen.

When the last dress had been tried on, and I'd been stabbed with one final pin, I changed into a fire-engine-red onesie and shuffled my way about the house making coffee and eating more cake, much to the bemusement of Patrick. There'd been more than one reference to the backside flap and whether it was useful for anything. When he looked to Marcus for support, he looked up blankly, oblivious to the world around him. We'd pulled him from the abyss.

He'd been paying no attention, preferring to keep our conversation on course. We volleyed ideas back and forth, listing things we still needed to organise. Marcus jotted notes while I threw suggestions at him. From catering and seat hire, to splitting up remaining responsibilities into something that looked fair and even. I'd even managed to finally air my suggestion for gift bags for the students. We could include a school mug, their certificates, and a voucher for Thatcher's Books. It was a tiny congratulations and thank you for their hard work throughout the year.

'Patrick drove your mum home?' I asked, scrolling aimlessly through my phone. 'About thirty seconds after he wolfed down a slice of cake.'

'Correct.'

'I need a shower.' Stretching out, I crossed to the counter and took a hurried gulp of coffee. 'I'm going to be so late this morning and I feel like a wreck.'

'You and Marcus were working exceptionally hard last night,' she said, a tiny accusatory hint in her voice. Her eyes, set firmly on her own phone, barely met mine. What was she getting at with that? 'I didn't hear anything other than work, work, chairs, tables, invites, food.'

'It was productive.' I held my mug to my mouth. 'I'm glad. We've got a plan. I feel lighter knowing that, like a blockage has moved, except the whole drinking on a school night thing.'

'You sure that's not fibre?'

'Quite sure.' I offered a sarcastic grin. 'Simply some things coming together.'

Penny smiled. 'I have a question for you.'

'Shoot.'

'What's his favourite film?' she asked.

'How should I know?' I called from where I was gathering up some clothes in my bedroom.

'His favourite book?' she continued.

I poked my head out of the doorway. 'Where are these questions coming from?'

'Just curious,' she said around a mouthful of cereal.

'The only thing I can tell you is that he needs to leave the tie at home more often.' I dashed towards the bathroom while my words volleyed about the kitchen.

'That's quite the statement coming from you.'

'Yeah, well, he has this nice collarbone thing going on.'

She sniggered. 'I can't say I pay a lot of attention to a man's … collarbone.'

'No, neither do I,' I said. 'I guess it was just because he doesn't normally get about without a tie, so, you know, easily noticeable.'

'Uh-huh,' she said. 'You've got five minutes, and I'm helping myself to the shower.'

'No, you won't.' I closed the bathroom door behind me.

* * *

I burst through the doors of the staffroom, which was its usually busy arterial self, reeking of burned toast, coffee and not enough sleep. Teachers came and went, students knocked on the door with questions and complaints, and there I was desperately trying to snaffle breakfast in the five minutes I had remaining. It had been one mad rush after the other, culminating in the decision to skip my morning trip to the café.

When my toast sprang forth like an Olympic diver, I grabbed

at it like I was going for gold, regardless of burning fingers, a trail of crumbs, and a not especially clean plate that had been donated by Jack. To my left, Glenn washed dirty dishes and moaned to no one in particular about climate change.

'Eleanor, can I ask you a question?' Grace sashayed up beside me, winding her ponytail around her hand. She was one of those people who always had impossibly beautiful hair, always perfectly clean and shiny, and not a strand out of place. Most mornings, I opted for an up-do simply to prevent me looking like a troll doll.

I surveyed the room quickly and, amongst the many impromptu morning meetings, found her teaching group as they had been the day I first arrived. They were huddled together on the couch except, this time, they were merely pretending to be busy on their phones.

'Absolutely.' I dug my knife into the butter and ignored the fluttering in my stomach that told me to run. If I knew anything about my day yesterday, it was that there was only one way this conversation was going to go.

'Have I done something to offend you?' She shifted her weight from foot to foot and fixed me with this look that I could only describe as feigned innocence. It was the look that said, *I know that you know, but let's pretend.* She tipped her head slightly, as if to prompt my answer.

I gave her my best surprised face. 'No.'

'Are you sure?' She squinted. I half expected the tips of her ears to tinge a shade of cut-grass green. 'Because last night I was getting this whole vibe that maybe I was treading on toes, and I'd so hate for your toes to get squashed.'

'No.' I bit down on the first heavenly, melted butter and strawberry jam toast. 'No toes are getting squashed. I wear very comfy, closed-toed shoes.'

The side door swung open with a tired yawn, and Marcus appeared over my shoulder. He looked like he had something to say, something urgent, but our present company put a quick hold to that.

'Good morning, Marc,' Grace cooed, her attention instantly diverted to where he was by the fridge

'Hey.' He returned, pinching my elbow gently. 'Good morning, Eleanor.'

'Marcus.'

I turned back to my plate to find it had vanished. So had Marcus, who was scarpering towards my library with nothing more than a wave and a boyish smile, one that I'd seen over again on much younger classes. It was the cheeky recognition of knowing right from wrong, and not caring either way. I tossed my butter and jam back in the refrigerator and gave chase.

'That's hardly fair,' I complained to the back of his jacket. 'Cake isn't enough, you have to steal breakfasts, too?'

'You're right. I'm awful. I should tell her I spent last night with you.' In my office, he turned and inspected what was left of the toast. 'Nice jam.'

'It was in the discount section,' I deadpanned. 'Feel free to tell her though, it's your death warrant.'

'Really? Judging by those eyes, I suspect it might be yours. Good thing I bought you a solid breakfast for your last meal.' He presented me with a lukewarm coffee and crinkly plastic tub of fruit and yoghurt that had been waiting beside my PC.

'You bought me breakfast?' I asked, surprised. 'Why?'

He shrugged, though there was a twinkle in his eye. 'Just as a thank you for last night.'

'You didn't have to do that,' I said, genuinely touched by the gesture. 'Honestly, I'm glad we got things sorted so thank *you* for coming past.'

'You don't have to thank me,' he said. 'It was Daisy who wanted to see you.'

'Naturally.' I waved the idea away and shuffled through a few invoices that needed my signature. 'Blame the dog.'

I cupped my hands around the coffee and sat beside him on the desk, pivoting slightly to look at him, at the curve of his nose and the slight stubble that told me he'd also slept in. 'I'm glad you came,' I said. 'It was nice to have a full lively house.'

'It was great, once you stopped arguing with me.' Marcus scratched at his upper lip. 'Which I think was about thirty seconds before the snoring began.'

'I was not arguing with you,' I baulked. 'And I do not snore.'

'No, no, silly me, of course not. You were just road-blocking everything.'

'I was not!' I threw my head back. 'You know, you are unbelievable.'

'Oh, no, no, you're right. Again.'

My eyebrows reached for the ceiling.

'You were just expressing an alternative approach,' he said with a laugh, folding his arms across his chest.

'Correct.' I nodded once. 'I'm allowed to have a different opinion.'

'Quite a lot of alternative approaches.'

'Do you complain this much about everything?' I asked, wondering if he hadn't just decided to take up annoying me as his newest off-season sport.

'My toast was cold.'

'It was *my* toast.' I peeled the lid from the salad and popped a piece of pineapple in my mouth. 'Mine.'

Marcus dug about my fruit salad with his fingers and stole a plump strawberry I'd already spied and hoped to save. 'Shall we go and speak to Phil about our plans?'

'You know what? Let me go through your email, I'll add some notes, we'll reconvene and send it through.'

'Sure thing.' His fingers dove for another piece of fruit. This time, I gave in, handing him the fork and holding the container out for him to have it. With another piece of pineapple held aloft like a prize, he made his way to the door. 'Let's get it out by lunch, then we can move along.'

'Good, good.' I nodded, snatching the fork back from him. 'Hey, I have a question for you.'

'Shoot.'

'What's your favourite movie?' It had been all I'd been able to think about as he stood there in my office. The seed had been planted, and now I wanted to know what made him tick.

'My favourite movie?' His brow knitted, like he couldn't quite work out what I was saying.

'Yeah. One that you've memorised and can quote.'

Chewing on his bottom lip, he peered up at the ceiling, made a bit of a noise, and drew his eyes back to mine. '*Raiders of the Lost Ark*. My eight-month-old niece isn't a huge fan though, so it's plenty of *Tangled* repeats whenever she comes to visit.'

'You have a niece?' I asked. I may have been more surprised to learn this, except for the fact that Penny had already reminded me that Marcus and I spoke about nothing but work. This information was fresh and, again, presented a new layer – one that I quickly found that I liked.

Before I had a chance to ask anything further, Marcus had pulled his phone from his pocket and was scrolling through to an extensive photo collection. Photos whizzed past, eventually slowing and landing on one particular shot, much like a prize wheel in a bingo hall. Marcus was curled up on the couch with a toddler nestled under his chin.

'She's so sweet,' I cooed. 'I bet you use that photo to pick up all the time.'

He smirked. 'Probably why I've never shown you, then.'

'Ha!'

'Have a good day.' He wrestled his phone back from me and slipped out the door. 'Eleanor.'

* * *

It had only taken us weeks to get ourselves aligned, but it was so nice to have a plan. I could properly compartmentalise things, instead of having bits of catering overlapping invites, which straddled the music, and mixed up in a cauldron of who knows what else we may not have thought of.

Phil loved the email we sent through just before the end of lunch, where we'd been huddled in my office checking and double-checking before hitting 'send'. All our further plans for the night – the red carpet, the gift bags and a photographer – were enthusiastically approved.

For the rest of the week, my inbox pinged at regular intervals as RSVPs began mounting up. Every time I thought I could sneak a look at my computer between classes, hoping for an eBay dispatch notice for a pile of books I'd bought, there'd be another email completely unrelated waiting for me. Regardless of whether my education lay firmly in information technology, and that the invites were merely a mess of drag and drop options, I was excited to see such enthusiastic responses.

Then, of course, there was Glenn: were we going to have vegan options in our catering? We should consider, he wrote, that some of our guests would like the option.

I read his email again, just to be sure. I wasn't entirely sure he was supposed to be at the event, and nobody had come back with a remotely similar request. So, were we going to be catering to him? I couldn't afford not to after reading his email, lest I open myself up to debate about not treating everyone equally. I made a note amongstst the scribble in my diary. Looking at the ever-growing list, which I think read: tree nuts, regular nuts, sugar, potatoes, shellfish, cow's milk, eggs, soy, and dairy, I sighed and may have admitted that maybe Glenn was on to something. If nothing else, a vegan menu might work if only to avoid allergens.

That realisation led me to scrolling dozens of recipe websites in search of the perfect cake recipes, loaves of bread, and sandwich fillings. On its own, it looked like a mammoth task, keeping everything and everyone catered for. I hoped the school canteen could cater to our needs but, being no dietary expert (my level was nothing short of eat everything in sight, either), I hadn't counted on the idea that they no longer baked everything on site. While we provided an allergy-free canteen, some of the products that were brought in weren't guaranteed to be from a nut-free, gluten-free, allergy friendly production space.

'Have you seen these emails?' I paced the length of Marcus's office at lunchtime. He sat hunched over his laptop, typing with single fingers, which was the last thing I expected to ever see from him. 'What are you doing?'

'Making notes,' he said. 'And, yes, I've seen them.'

Our last few days had been perfectly coordinated, and I put that squarely down to our night of planning. If we'd organised a quick lunchtime catch-up, he was ready and waiting before me. If one of us was listed to call a supplier, it happened. For the first time in weeks, I was comfortable with the way things were coming together.

'What do you think?' I asked.

'I don't think Phil's budget will stretch to serving shellfish in the first place,' he teased.

'Marcus!'

'What-us?' Frustrated, he ran his fingers through his hair. 'If the canteen can't guarantee it, the caterers can organise it. We've got enough going on without worrying about the intricacies of the food. Just take the list to them. It'll be fine.'

'Are we still going tonight?' I asked. 'To the caterers, I mean?'

'Commitment, consistency, communication,' he recounted with a pointed finger. 'So, yes, of course we're still going.'

'Oh boy,' I groaned. 'You're wheeling that out at every opportunity, aren't you?'

He shucked on his jacket and pinched my cheek. 'You better believe it.'

'And we can't take forever.'

'Have you got plans?' he asked.

'Penny seems to think I should go on a blind date.'

'You?' he said, a hint of amusement in his voice.

I stopped and looked at him. 'Is that so unbelievable?'

'Fair enough.' He shrugged. 'So, tell me about this blind date. What do you know about him?'

'I know nothing about him.' I stepped past as Marcus held a door open for me. 'But he better not be an idiot.'

Chapter 17

Blind dates weren't exactly a new concept to me, though I was reluctant when Penny first broached the topic on Thursday night. I'd suffered through a handful of them in the past twelve months, but I'd been wracking my brains trying to work out who on earth she thought she could set me up with.

Awfully, I wondered if there was anyone left in town that she hadn't been involved with? Since I'd been here, it seemed like she had a different date each weekend, but I immediately shook that thought from my head. Firstly, because it wasn't any of my business, really. Secondly, because she was trying to do the right thing. My only job was to simply embrace the fact and enjoy the night.

I was home five minutes, only long enough to pour myself a long cool drink, before I found myself bundled into the bathroom, Penny armed with a make-up brush and reminding me I was on a time deadline. I was more than capable of getting myself ready, but recent experience had proven she was far more talented at this make-up malarkey than me. Plus, I just really loved having someone else brush my hair. It was truly one of life's simple pleasures.

'Tell me, is he lovely?' I asked, looking at her in the mirror's reflection.

She sighed gently. 'He's a total gentleman.'

'That's a good start,' I said. 'Good family?'

'Strong family ties. He would bend over backwards for them. Loves his mum.'

Considering my relationship with my own mother, the thought tightened around my chest, then embraced me like a warm hug.

'Good. That's good.'

'Classically handsome, funny, sweet. Just about everything you need.' Penny dabbed at my face. 'I think, once you scratch the surface, you'll find you have quite a lot in common with him.'

* * *

My instructions were to head straight for table two, a cosy booth with high-back leather seats and an ocean view, and to be there at six o'clock on the dot. No earlier, and absolutely no later, otherwise I might just ruin the entire surprise. Oh, and I was to face away from the door to avoid peeking at any of the oncoming man traffic.

When I arrived, at one minute to six, I peeled off my new coat, folded it far more carefully than I would any older piece of clothing, and slipped into the booth. From where I sat, my only male view was the barman, and a man in a tuxedo who was sitting at the bar with his back to the world. Was that my date?

My stomach wobbled about like jelly and sent shivers up my throat and along my jawline.

'Sorry I'm late, I wasn't expecting to—' Marcus slipped into the booth opposite me.

We froze, thrown by the mutual discovery. He broke first, a nervous glance towards the door and around the rest of the pub, no doubt wondering if he was indeed in the right spot. I watched as he glanced across at the table number, his eyes lifting to mine when he realised he was indeed in the right spot.

If it weren't for the fact he was sans his roller case, I'd have thought he'd come straight from work. Or, maybe he'd just left it behind. He was still dressed as he had been all day, the royal blue suit, crisp white shirt (seriously, who had shirts that white?) and a silvery grey tie.

He frowned, confused. 'Eleanor?'

'That's my name, yes.'

'Patrick told me to meet him in this booth at six o'clock.'

I shook my head in quick, confused jerks. No, that wasn't what was supposed to happen. Over at the bar, the tuxedoed man slipped from his chair and wandered over to us. Sucking lazily on a straw, he had a swagger Clint Eastwood would be proud of. Right now, it was beginning to look like neither of us were lost, and we were exactly where we were supposed to be.

'Patrick?' I squawked, clapping in delight. He looked fantastic! A little awkward and completely out of his natural environment of khaki shorts and fluorescent polo shirts, but it was just so … refreshing to see him like this.

'Relax, it's perfectly harmless fizzy water,' Patrick announced. 'Maybe a pinch of lemon.'

'No, no, no,' I bumbled, waggling a lazy finger between the two men. 'But … you? And him?'

'And that's my suit!' Marcus almost fell about himself laughing. 'Oh, you utter cock!'

'See, here's the thing.' Patrick turned his attention to me, tossing a thumb in Marcus's direction. 'I kinda mighta told Buggalugs here I had a hot date tonight, so he let me borrow some of his fancy pants clothes. Joke's on him though, because I'm not wearing any underwear. Hence the funny walk.'

'This is so wild,' I chortled. 'You do look smashing though, don't let anyone tell you any different.'

'Don't scrub up so bad, do I?' He smiled proudly, brushing himself down. 'Might keep it.'

'For Olivia?' Marcus teased. 'How is she, by the way? Does she know you're out and about dressed like the pre-school version of Magic Mike?'

'I was reliably informed today that she does not like sausage but is indeed rather fond of the occasional eggplant.' He flipped his notepad over and tapped at it with a pen. Watching him, I was tempted to tell Patrick he'd be a successful waiter should the building game ever dry up. 'I'm not sure what I'm meant to do with that information, but there you have it.'

My eyes met Marcus's. He did his best to hold back laughter.

After inspecting his notepad for a few more moments, Patrick jammed the pen in his breast pocket and opened his hand to us. 'Right, so, first order of the night is for you two to give me your phones.'

'I'm not giving you my phone!' I laughed delightedly. 'No way.'

'Don't worry, I won't go looking for the porn. I'm only going to give yours to Penny.' He pointed to my cousin who, leaning into my line of sight, sat at the far end of the bar. She gave the tittering overjoyed wave everyone's grandma had at family gatherings before tipping her drink back up to her mouth. Patrick turned his attention to Marcus. 'And I'll drop yours in your letterbox. Or over the fence. I'll ask Daisy if she needs a new chew toy.'

Reluctantly, we handed our gadgets over, though I wasn't convinced this was the best idea ever. We both offered warnings about hacking and personal information. Some of the conversations I had with Penny weren't suitable for public consumption and, if they didn't cause outrage, they'd probably be cause to have us committed. The only response was rolled eyes and a comment about technology addiction. In exchange, Patrick handed us each an envelope. Mine was lemon yellow, Marcus's a coffee brown.

'Also, I've taken the liberty of ordering you some drinks. Straight whiskey for you, Marc, because you seem to think you're refined. And you look like you might be a gin and tonic girl. I'm told lemon martinis are apparently off limits.'

I wrinkled my nose, though I can only imagine how he found that out. 'Probably not the best idea, no.'

'Followed by a bottle of pinot noir, because I at least know you two lushes both enjoy a tipple of red.'

Marcus offered me a gentle smile.

'So, here's your mission, should you choose to accept it. You have thirty seconds to decide if you're in or if you're out. Speak now or forever hold your peace.' He paused. 'I could do the wedding celebrant thing, couldn't I? Quite good at this.'

Marcus relaxed in his seat and placed his envelope on the table before him. 'I'm in.'

'Manning?' Patrick flinched, clutching a hand to his chest. 'Sorry, sorry, so sorry, Eleanor.'

Marcus covered his mouth, but he couldn't hide the crinkled eyes of mocking laughter. It pulled, hard, at what, I wasn't sure, but I knew I didn't want to be anywhere else.

'Me, too,' I said. 'I'm in.'

'Oh, the romance of it all,' Patrick deadpanned. 'Now, there are no rules tonight except those contained in your envelopes. Wait until we've both left the building and away from all sharp cutlery before you open them.'

'This all sounds rather elaborate for a—' Marcus formed air quotes '—blind date.'

'Yeah, well, if you make it through tonight without mentioning school, the library, presentation night, or anything at all to do with work, Toby behind the bar has got scratch and sniff stickers. Neither of you will get them, because that circumvents the whole no school thing, but he just has some. I suspect he uses them in place of markers for that strawberry-scented high.'

'Jesus.' I laughed, glancing over at the bar. The barman was engrossed in a news broadcast on the telly behind the bar

'Nope, just a carpenter.' Patrick tucked his notepad away in his back pocket. 'No more questions?'

Marcus and I checked each other. 'No,' we said in unison.

'Correct answer.' Patrick grinned. 'Have a wonderful, two-derful night.'

Patrick left us staring blankly at each other as he stepped outside, stopping only to blow us a kiss as he scuttled by our window on his way down the street. Penny slugged down the last of her drink, dropped from her stool and raced out the door behind him with nothing more than an excited wave. Marcus held his envelope up between us, his name written in an elaborate font.

'Do you want to go home?' he asked, bottle-green eyes peering at me over the artificial latte horizon. 'I won't be offended if you do.'

For all my nerves leading up to tonight, seeing Marcus arrive had been a genuinely pleasant surprise. Not simply because he was a known quantity, but because I was becoming increasingly curious about this man I worked with.

I shook my head. 'No. Do you?'

He gave his head a quick shake. His expression told me he was almost a little despondent that I'd asked. It was reassuring to know he wanted to be here, too.

'Let's do this at the same time, shall we?' He sat poised with a thumb under the lip of his envelope.

'All right,' I said, knife in hand and ready to tear open my own envelope. 'Let's.'

It was a quick countdown from three as we tore at the paper. Confusion over the contents followed. I pressed my envelope in at the edges and tried to make out what I was looking at. Marcus pulled a bundle of cards from his envelope.

'Okay,' he said slowly. 'It looks like we have a question and answer game. My cards are numbered. I start at two.'

My stack, which was wrapped in a handwritten note, began at one.

'Ladies first,' I teased. Dangling the letter in the air between us, I asked, 'I'll read it out, shall I?'

A waiter presented our drinks, wiped down the table, and disappeared.

'I'm ready.' Marcus held his glass out to me. 'Cheers?'

We clinked glasses, and I took the first refreshing sip of what turned out to be strawberry gin and tonic. It was subtly perfect and made me think that maybe I'd give the red wine a miss after all.

'All right,' I announced. 'It says, "Hey Kids! Guess who? It's us, your fairy godparents! So, dinner was fun the other night, wasn't it? We really enjoyed listening to you two bicker, squabble, and talk shop ALL NIGHT. Seriously, it was fascinating, so much so that we decided you both need a break. Eat dinner, talk about something other than work. Those cards? They're conversation cues. Great idea, right? The rules are simple: you must read each card aloud and in order (trust us, it'll be worth it), and you can't skip anything. If you're tempted to talk shop, you need to make a five-dollar donation to charity. Now, go forth and enjoy your night. Have a drink or two and look after each other."'

We looked at each other for one quiet moment in the chaos of a pub on a Friday night, the slow-motion centre of a lightning-fast world.

'We weren't that bad, were we?' Marcus asked, not quite ready to believe the accusation.

I winced apologetically. 'I think we were. Penny said as much the next morning.'

'Right, okay, all right.' He clasped his hands and rested them on the table. 'So, you're number one?'

'I am number one,' I confirmed with a coy smile. 'Shall we?'

'Let's.'

I tapped my pile of cards of the table and cleared my throat. '"Marcus",' I began, covering my mouth with genuine embarrassment. My eyes had already skipped a few words ahead. I couldn't back out of this now and making something up just felt insincere. '"I told Penny the other night how much I enjoyed seeing you without a tie, that I thought you had a nice neck."'

'You what?' He roared with laughter, unconsciously reaching for his throat, tugging his tie. 'You didn't?'

'I am neither confirming, nor denying that.' My entire being burned up, and I felt light and bubbly, like I was floating out of orbit. I returned to the card in front of me. '"Could you please remove your tie and unfasten the top two buttons of your shirt?"'

Without argument, and with a look of smug satisfaction, he complied. 'Can't very well leave you wanting, can I?'

'It would be terribly unfair if you did.'

'Is that the last of the card?' He folded the fabric gently and pushed it into his pocket. When I nodded, he picked his next one up. The same rush of embarrassment flooded his face as he stumbled over the start. 'All right. It says, "Eleanor, it's no secret I find you ridiculously attractive. I've told Patrick as much, more times than he's sawn wood."'

I squeaked. Completely involuntarily. 'Is that a euphemism?'

'It's Patrick, so probably.'

'"But the pen in the hair? It's gotta go."'

I reached around the back of my head and tugged out the offending item. 'You know, I don't even know it's there half the time. I even went home and got changed for tonight and, still, pen in hair. It's just a me thing.'

'At least I know you'll always have one on you.'

I smiled and looked down at the pile in front of me, the next question open and waiting. All it needed was a voice. After gentle goading, I spat it out.

'Okay.' I shuffled and crossed my legs. '"When are you the most yourself?"'

'That's a great question.' Marcus plucked the card from my grasp and looked at it. 'Most myself? I think, yes, in my kitchen, or my home, either, or surrounded by family. I can be a complete buffoon in my tracksuit pants.'

'Are they grey?' I asked.

'What? The tracksuit pants?' he asked. 'They might be.'

'Good.' I bit my lip with a smile. 'Continue.'

'That's it. Just at home, surrounded by family. Maybe with the barbecue going. My little niece and my sister, my parents, cousins if they're ever about. We just have a really lovely time. It's nice to be adults and make it through as friends. So, I think that's the best place to catch me.' He stopped. 'How about you?'

'I think I would be most myself with one or two close friends. Maybe even just my dad and me, sitting about and discussing books, or music, or travel, watching a numbingly dumb film, that kind of thing.'

'Sounds way more intellectual than me.'

'Hardly.' I grabbed for the straw with my mouth. 'What's your next question?'

'Here we go. Next is—' Marcus gave a disbelieving scoff and shook his head '—"Patrick is sexy. Discuss".'

I tried hiding behind my stack of cards as I laughed loudly. 'I can see where Patrick might get that idea from.'

'Oh, you do, do you?' Marcus leaned back into the wall and rested his arm along the top of the booth. 'Well, go on then. Discuss.'

'No, no, no.' My ears, cheeks, neck were burning up. I clapped my hands to my cheeks to try and cool them. It didn't help, and I felt noticeably guilty that I might have offended Marcus. 'I don't personally find him sexy.'

'Cute?' Marcus tried.

'Eh.' I waggled a hand.

'You know, this is great. "How was your date, Marcus? Oh, wonderful. She really likes *you*."'

I leaned forward and rested my chin in the palm of my hand. 'I said I can see how Patrick might get that idea. He's a tradie, he gets around in his shorts all the time, he has a lovely physique.'

'You realise this is not helping?' He pivoted on the spot, catching a glimpse of a group of tradesmen who circled a pool table. 'See? Look at that. You like that?'

'Tradies are a popular lady trope,' I blurted. 'They're just not mine.'

'Back-pedal, back-pedal,' he teased. 'What's your trope, then?'

'You mean what do I look for?'

He lifted a lazy shoulder. 'If that's how you want to interpret it.'

'Kindness.' I counted on my finger. 'Intelligence—'

'Okay, so Patrick's out. Good to know.'

I laughed. 'That's not very kind.'

'You're right, I'm awful. Stop it, Marcus.' He peered at me over the lip of his glass. 'What else?'

'I don't know so much anymore,' I said. 'I had what I thought was what I wanted, and it turned out to be a giant mess. I guess what's important now is, like I said, kindness, support and space to grow, and family.'

'I like that answer very much.' Marcus pushed his glass across the table. 'What's the next card say?'

'Hang on, what about you?' I asked. 'What are you looking for?'

'I think you covered it really well.' The corner of his mouth lifted gently. 'Perfectly.'

I tapped my pile of cards against the table as Marcus drum-rolled his fingers. 'Okay, next, "What's your favourite time of day?"'

'Three thirty-five p.m,' he said with a wry laugh. 'God it feels so good.'

'Really?' I asked. 'I would've said the first five minutes in bed. Sheets are cold, I'm not yet asleep, but I can just curl up in the silence and let my brain stop.'

'Also a good time.' Marcus poked the air. 'But the simple act of standing in an empty classroom, knowing I don't have to work for the next seventeen hours is great.'

'Friday nights at yours must be lit.'

'You know it.' Marcus flipped the next card. 'Oh, this is a good one. "Well done on making it this far, make sure you order food, this is supposed to be fun."'

That was the cue for toilet breaks, more drinks, and some good food to soak up all our alcohol. I looked up in time to witness Marcus slide back into the booth, adjust his jacket, and crack the twist-top on our fresh bottle of wine.

'Now, I hardly think this will be as fancy as the tipples we just enjoyed, but hopefully it passes muster.' He propped his head up with a closed fist and smiled happily to himself.

'I'm sure it'll be fine.' I was of the adage that after two glasses, it all blended into one anyway. That's not just me, is it?

Blend it did; the conversations, the jokes, the seemingly mundane observations as the pub moved around us like a time-lapse video. We picked up on shared university lecturers and student hangouts, one or two common friends who'd managed to slip through the cracks, and how a small town was so much better to work in than a big city. It was agreed that the community was closer, life was a little slower, and a bit more family friendly, something the both of us thought important.

Dinner appeared somewhere in the middle, pizza with stringy cheese, hot chips, and even more wine. Is there anything as good as pizza when you've admittedly had a little too much to drink? I think not. It disappeared over a conversation about what there actually was to do around here on a Saturday night, except for the local cinema.

I stuffed a few chips in my mouth and picked up the pile of cards again. A small grin tugged at my mouth. 'Want another question?' I asked.

'Sure.' Marcus brushed his hands against his pants. 'What've you got?'

'"Marcus, on our next date, it's your turn to cook. What are you making me?"'

'Oh. We're having another date? Good to know.' He reached across, seeking my permission with a quick look, before relieving me of some of my dinner. 'I would make you a roast chicken, with potatoes, pumpkin, broccolini not broccoli, pan gravy. For dessert we might have chocolate cake.'

'Are you making the chocolate cake?'

'Unless I'm feeling lazy. In which case, I might try and swing a Lucy Williams special.'

'Oh, fancy.' I couldn't help but smile. 'Name dropper.'

'Impressed?'

'Totally,' I teased. 'But I'd rather you baked.'

'You look lovely tonight, by the way.'

'Thank you.' I made a point of not looking at him as heat bloomed in my chest. Instead, I poured out two glasses of wine. 'I figured this would work better than my seventy-something Scottish history professor look.'

'I really should apologise for that.' Marcus wriggled in his seat and looked suddenly uneasy. 'I feel that, if I could explain something to you, that comment might make a bit more sense.'

'I'm all ears.'

'I was a bit worried the other night when I arrived, and you were covered in pins.'

'Why? Because you thought I might stab you?'

'No, I can deal with a little pinprick occasionally.' The hollows of his cheeks sunk as he sucked on something in his mouth. 'It was the homemade clothes that scared me.'

I laughed. 'Trust me, you weren't the only one. It's a new hobby for Aunty Gwen, so …'

'Do you remember me telling you my sister was into theatre?'

'I do.'

'Right. Well. My mother also got heavily involved. It was like *Dance Moms* for the Nineties. She was right in there with rehearsals and set design and, eventually, costuming.'

'Oh, no.' I covered my mouth and laughed. Anyone who'd lived through school productions and rock eisteddfods knew that, sometimes, it was best to leave the costuming to the professionals.

'See, you know where this is going.' Marcus waggled a finger at me. 'You know.'

'She went and bought herself a Singer, didn't she?'

'Not only that, she turned our house into a sweatshop.'

I roared with laughter, a protective hand the only thing stopping a little bit of dinner shooting forth across the table.

'My sister was probably fourteen or fifteen at the time, so I was nine or ten; something like that.' Marcus clutched at his elbows. 'Soo, Mum decided she didn't need to buy real clothes anymore, because she knew how to make them. And, so, little Marcus was sent to school in pants befitting a *Sesame Street* extra. There was one pair in particular that were rusty orange corduroy, and they flared out like jodhpurs. They were fucking awful. I spent a large portion of my childhood and teen years being bullied over my clothes.'

'She seriously didn't buy you clothes?'

'Not while she was busy making them. I mean, it was all well and good to sew up a Mr Mistoffelees over the weekend, but I wasn't exactly chomping at the bit to go to school dressed like him.'

'Stop talking,' I wheezed. 'Please. I'm going to wet my pants.'

'And let's not forget the time my sister, Jessie, woke me up in full costume. I thought I'd stepped right into a nightmare.'

'No!' I coughed through the laughter. 'No, no, no.'

'It was my sixteenth birthday the night before, and I might have gone out and got a bit drunk. So, there I was, having a sleep in, being very hungover and feeling awfully sorry for myself, and I feel a knock on my shoulder. I peel open one eye, and my life has suddenly turned into a B-grade horror movie. Here I am thinking I've lost my mind completely and am stuck in a nightmare with this human cat hybrid trying to climb into bed with me, meowing noises and all.'

I couldn't speak, couldn't breathe for the laughter. 'Photos? Please, for all that is holy, please let there be photos.'

'There is one Polaroid in existence,' he confirmed, taking what was left of my chips. It didn't matter. I was having far too much fun to care, and I could always order more. Drinks, combined with how I was feeling right now, the sheer joy of revelling in his stories, made me want to stay all night. 'I look for all intents and purposes like I'm trying to climb the wall.'

'That is way too perfect. I want to see that photo.'

'I'm sure I can wrangle a copy for you.' He reached for his pocket. 'See, I would text my mum, but I can't because my phone is gone.'

'Is she still in theatre?' I dug through the box. 'Your sister, I mean?'

'A little.' He nodded. 'She's got the kids, so it's more behind the scenes stuff now. Mum's given up the clothes making, thank God.'

'Is that why you're always in suits?' I asked.

'I guess it is, yeah,' he said. 'I remember one particular day at school that was just revolting. I was being called all kinds of names, and I just wanted to crawl into a hole. You know, you're a twelve, thirteen, fourteen-year-old boy, and your image is kind of important, but you're just getting rallied constantly because your mum thinks she's more Versace than Picasso when it comes to sewing and, so, I promised myself that the moment I could buy my own clothes, I would buy decent, fitted clothes.'

I watched him over the top of my glass, lips wrapped around the edge and fixing him with a look.

'I guess what I'm trying to say is that I had no right to criticise your clothing choices.'

'No, but you weren't wrong, either,' I said. 'And, to be fair, I bit first, so it was in the spirit of the game.'

It was around that time our cue cards were forgotten, and our conversation disappeared into the depths of family, their further quirks and misdemeanours. We were enjoying our night so much or, at least, I was, that time ran away, and we were soon being bundled out the door by bleary-eyed barmen who wanted nothing more than their own beds.

We stepped out into an almost silent street. Car parks were mostly empty, and the only thing making a noise was the occasional seagull out over the bay. My breath puffed in front of my face.

'Can I ask something before you go?' Marcus held my jacket out for me.

I slipped my arms through my coat and began fastening buttons. 'Tonight has been the night of questions, so I think that's only fair.'

'Did you know this was going to happen tonight?' He did the late-night pat-down, the double-check to make sure we weren't doing a mad dash back to the pub for lost items in the morning.

'I knew that I was going on a blind date,' I said. 'But I didn't know it was with you.'

'Oh, right.' He rubbed his mouth. 'Because blind dates don't strike me as an Eleanor thing.'

'Don't they?' I smiled. 'I've been on blind dates before. In fact, I've been on a few in the last year, it's just that I have a few more stipulations now.'

'And what are they?'

I smiled gently, revelling in his face under the light of the street lamp. He looked altogether different now compared to the start of the night, gentler, more striking. Beautiful, even, and the weight of that sat heavily in my stomach. 'My only requests were that he be kind, gentle, a family man, and undeniably handsome.'

Marcus laughed nervously. 'Looks like you were shit out of luck tonight.'

'On the contrary.' I stepped away. 'I got exactly what I asked for.'

His expression changed almost instantly, a relaxed happiness replacing uncertainty. 'Okay.'

'Okay?' I ducked into his line of sight.

'Eleanor, can I walk you home?'

For a brief moment, we were silent. A cheeky, knowing laughter took over, the connotations of that question far heavier than usual.

'I'll be okay, but thank you,' I said, laughing. 'I'll text you when I get home.'

'All right.' He brushed his hand over his mouth. 'Would you like to do this again, maybe?'

'There's no maybe,' I said. 'I'd love to.'

Marcus's eyes widened. 'Tomorrow?'

'I can't tomorrow. I'm having lunch with an old school friend, but I would definitely like to do this again. Tonight was nothing short of …' My voice trailed off, my shoulders rose, and I made a noise I hoped came across as blissful.

It did.

Marcus smiled proudly. 'Let's talk soon, then?'

'We will,' I said.

We stepped into each other at the same time, not a misstep, but an understanding of what may be to come. Without another word, Marcus leaned down, his nose brushing against my cheek as he kissed me. Warm breaths puffed against my ear and I stood there, fixed to the spot. As he pulled away, I felt his nose draw against mine, and all I could think of was just how much I wanted him to kiss me in the moment.

'Goodnight, Eleanor,' he whispered.

'Goodnight.'

Walking away, there was that little flutter again. Somewhere under the ribs, but above my stomach, something that let me know my night had not panned out exactly as expected. It had been better, wonderful, and made me think that the possibilities were endless. The realisation was one-quarter thrilling, one-quarter curiosity, and two-quarters running for the hills, back to the safe harbour of singledom. At the corner of the street, far away enough to be considered breathing room, I stopped and looked back at the street behind me. The street was empty, Marcus long gone.

At home, I walked through the door to find Penny on the couch with a box of tissues and a packet of sweet biscuits. I poured myself a cold drink and sat gingerly in my favourite recliner.

'Hola.' She didn't waiver from the television.

'Hello,' I said. 'What are you doing?'

'Watching *Dawson's Creek*.' She shoved another biscuit in her mouth. 'It's amazing. The Flash is about to Hulk out, and Dawson thinks he's Dr Phil. This guy has got more red flags than a beach in summer.'

'You what now?' I laughed. 'The Flash?'

'Dawson's dad was The Flash in another life.' She looked at me as if this were common knowledge. 'Keep up.'

'Oh, right.'

'And?' She leaned out over the side of the couch and fixed me with an expectant look. She was never any good at waiting for news. I was surprised it had taken her this long to ask.

'And what?' I smiled, pulling my skirt out over my knees.

'That smile says it all.'

'Does it?' I asked.

'It does.' She sunk back into the chair. 'Good night?'

'It was lovely,' I confirmed. 'Thank you for your fine organising. I'll have to thank Patrick the next time I see him.'

'And?' she teased.

'And what?' I took a sip.

'Did you kiss him?'

I laughed. 'No, no I didn't.'

In a grump, she picked up her phone, fingers dancing across the screen. 'Bugger it. I owe Patrick fifty dollars.'

I laughed and turned in for the night. 'I promise, you'll be the first to know when I do.'

Chapter 18

He was the last thing I thought of as I drifted off to sleep, and the first when I woke the next morning. But, unlike normal, I wasn't so much thinking about how infernally infuriating he was. Instead, I was staring at a crack in the ceiling and wondering whether something, anything, would work with Marcus.

Reaching across, I angled my alarm clock towards me. Plenty of time. Sally, who I was still having long and late conversations with via text, had organised lunch for midday. Nervous excitement tickled at the idea that I could have said yes to a breakfast date after all. Would that have made me look a little too eager? Did that even matter anymore? I tampered down the idea like the final embers of a campfire and distracted myself with social media instead.

My inbox bulged with messages and friend requests from a small circle of old friends who'd realised I was home. Memories came decorated with LOLs and smiley faces, and I lay about in bed laughing quietly at some of the anecdotes that popped up. *Wait, you're working at our old school?* asked one. *Who's still there?* asked another. *Can't wait to see you!* Sally exclaimed through the thrumming dots on the chat app. *It's been so long*, commented Claire. They all looked so different to the girls I remembered. No doubt I did, too.

Time did that, and I hadn't seen any of them since I left Apollo Bay in favour of the bright lights of Melbourne and university. Life in general and the natural attrition of friendships meant that they'd all but dropped off my radar.

Even so, when Saturday lunch was first suggested, I'll admit I was sceptical about wanting to see everyone. Chat groups were nice, but we'd all moved on. What could I possibly have in common with these women that didn't revolve around old memories? Would there be anything? They all looked like they'd settled down happily with their families. Social media accounts were full of weekend football games, pony clubs, or school artwork. While I was sure I taught some of these kids, I didn't have any of my own, and nobody had pulled me up after Monday morning assembly to say hello. Our entire ethos would be markedly different from that of the fifteen-year-olds who often made my dad cringe in horror.

Still, maybe it was as simple as carving fresh friendships. As I gargled mouthwash, I though about last night and my not-so-blind date with Marcus. It had taught me that my initial judgement of him had been so far removed from the reality of him, of the overweight boy with jodhpur pants and poorly stitched outfits. The best thing I could do, for me and for everyone, would be to take another leap of faith and just turn up, be present, and enjoy the olive branch of adulthood.

'Eleanor!' Sally greeted me at her front door, a child on her hip and one hidden behind her legs.

Growing up, Sally had come from a farming family and had always lived on the outskirts of town, a twenty-minute walk past the last bus stop. On hot days, when a group of us lumbered up the hill, it felt like the worst thing ever. Her bronze ringlets were always hidden underneath a battered Akubra, her boots always covered in either dust or dung from an assortment of horses, cows, sheep, or pigs that her family kept.

Two years ago, she gave all that up for the suburbs, a weatherboard home with floor-to-ceiling windows, and a beach view from her spot in the green hills.

I followed her along the entrance and into the kitchen, through the piles of children's toys, narrowly avoiding being mown down by a rogue ride-on train, complete with light and sound effects.

'It's only you and me today,' she explained with a roll of her eyes. 'I tried getting some of the other girls together, and they were all keen, but you know what it's like with kids. It's swimming, or little athletics, or pony club, or gastro.'

'Don't worry, I'm sure we'll be fine.' I smiled though I felt a pang of disappointment.

'I know, I know.' She placed her child down, who scampered off into the next room. 'You'll have to excuse the mess. Ben's out at work today, and I really can't be bothered to worry about the small stuff. Let's just get outside in the sunshine.'

'I … yeah, the mess isn't a problem,' I started. 'You should see the classroom after some of those little whirlwinds go through.'

'You're probably used to it, right? What, with the school and everything. How is that going?'

I was lost in that weird headspace of trying to take in new surroundings, the silver glint around oversized mirrors and sparkling of chandelier-like light fittings, cataloguing items and paying attention to the layout, while also trying to listen to everything Sally was saying. Work was great, I told her. Kids are great, love my job. Truly, I did.

As I followed her through the kitchen and towards the outdoor area, I felt perfectly comfortable and relaxed. Conversation came easily. My worries had been unfounded. I'd made the right decision coming here today.

'You must be seeing a lot of our kids now,' she joked. 'That must be weird?'

'Honestly, I haven't seen anyone I know or remember yet,' I said. If I had, they'd been doing a great job of avoiding me.

'I'm just trying to think.' She frowned a little, screwed her face up in thought. 'No, I think most of them go to the new school. The prep to twelve college on the hill?'

That explained that.

Pushing open a set of French doors, we stepped out onto a back veranda that could have swallowed our apartment for breakfast. Café blinds lined the vast space, ready to protect us from squalls that drifted in from the ocean. Pink and white peonies burst excitedly against the grey of the recycled door turned table, and a bottle of champagne had already been popped in anticipation of my arrival. It was one throw rug away from a home decorating magazine, one of those rooms you only wished you had so you could curl up in the corner of a comfortable sofa with a book and cup of hot cocoa.

'This is so beautiful,' I said with a wistful sigh. Another child caught in the peripherals of my vision as they climbed the stairs towards us.

'Thank you.' She smiled. 'Ben's put a lot of work in since we moved back into town. Figured if we were going to downsize, we'd do it properly.'

'Naturally.' I took the glass of fizz she offered. 'Cheers.'

Sally tapped her glass to mine. 'To old friends.'

'Not quite so old,' I joked, taking a seat at the table, right by a tray that had been laden with shaved meats, cheeses, dips and crackers.

'Right?' she cackled. 'So, come on, fill me in. Tell me where Ellie's been hiding all this time?'

The questions spewed forth like tennis balls from a launcher. Overwhelming at first, I caught the ones I could answer, dodged the ones I couldn't, and gave the Twitter-condensed version that said I was okay, living with my cousin, working here, presently single. The usual.

I think we were both grateful for the ice-breaker that was the nibbles tray. It gave us some time to sit, eat, and consider being in each other's space again while we made small talk that, so far, wasn't venturing too far past children. Where that was concerned, I felt a little awkward, like I was sitting on the cusp of a joke that I didn't quite get. As many children as I taught, it was no substitute for motherhood.

'Do you remember that afternoon we sat around by the old

gum talking about where we wanted to be in twenty years' time?' Sally waited for me to agree, but I shook my head slowly. 'I remember it vividly. I wanted to be a scientist. The closest I ever got to a petri dish was the IVF clinic.' She snorted her laughter. 'Claire wanted to be an astronaut.'

Claire was short and dark-haired. If you didn't know her, she came across as very serious and studious. If you did know her, you knew she was behind a lot of the trouble we got ourselves into. It was Claire who, in our final year of high school, tossed glitter into a portable air conditioner during art class and let chickens loose in the corridor.

'Oh, Claire,' I sighed wistfully. 'She popped up in my messages over the weekend. Is she well?'

'She's great.' Sally nodded emphatically. 'I'm going to try and organise this a bit better next time so more of us can come along.'

'Let me know,' I said. 'I'll help where I can.'

'And, Eleanor, you played the piano, I think. You were a total rock star.'

'I'm not sure about rock star,' I said, a little embarrassed. 'I while away my hours in a library now.'

Her eyes widened excitedly. 'Actually, as the teacher, you might have an idea on how to solve this one.'

'Sure.' I clapped my hands in my lap. 'What's up?'

'Our eldest, his reading isn't the best. How do you suggest I approach that?'

I scratched at my upper lip. 'Does he read at home? That's really the best way to start.'

'Oh, no,' she said. 'I meant when I speak to the teacher. I mean, I'm paying taxes to pay their wages. He should be able to read.'

'You don't read with him at home though?' I asked.

She snorted. 'I've got three kids; I never have the time.'

I grinned so tightly I thought my jaw might cramp. It wasn't the first time I'd heard these types of comments, not by a long shot, but they still grated. I'd also learned long ago that you couldn't argue with some people about their children's education, so I stayed shtum.

And I was glad that I did because, not long after, conversation returned to normal, non-teachery things, and I could sit back and enjoy the afternoon without the worry about getting myself into a *SmackDown* style argument about children's literacy. Sally availed me of condensed versions of everybody's histories, at least the people we could jointly remember and, when the subject of teachers came up, naturally, we chatted about Mick. And Marcus, who I wished was here to discuss the reading issue.

'You know, I thought about sending the kids there.' Sally chewed thoughtfully on a cracker. 'I just couldn't, you know? The college on the hill will see them through until the end of high school. They won't have to move, they'll have all the same friends, it'll be great.'

'That's fair,' I said, wrangling a small child who'd climbed onto my lap.

I was curious about the college on the hill. When I'd been searching for jobs, a class teacher role was available, but I was enamoured with the idea of our school library. It certainly looked like a great school, much better funded than ours, and Sally was happy to talk me through teachers and their quirks, and what she loved about the school. But she was also quick to remind me there was something missing.

'But you've got Marcus and, no word of a lie, I considered sending the kids to your school just for the eye candy.' She tipped her head back. 'Oh, boy-o.'

Wrinkling my nose, I asked, 'How, how, how does everyone know about Marcus?'

'Football.' She rolled her eyes. 'Ben plays with the team occasionally. Well, he mostly trains, but pulls on a jumper when he's not injured.'

'Ah, makes sense.' I shoved a chunk of cheese in my mouth. 'Marcus injured his knee during the last match.'

'Is he nice?'

'He's lovely,' I said, finding myself echoing my cousin.

'You know, I love my husband dearly.' She waggled her wedding ring in my face. 'And he loves me. Check out the size of that rock, that's love. But if I got myself a hall pass, I'd be on it like white on sugar. So would a lot of the women around here.'

Deflation. That's what that feeling was, and it had been creeping up like a slow leak for the last few minutes. I'd started the day so full of hope, thinking that something might have been possible with Marcus and, then, it was gone instantly, and all in a few clipped sentences.

I didn't want this. I didn't want to listen to her talk about him as if he were a prize to be caught. If I did end up with him, that chatter would only move to the back rooms and private conversations. Would it morph into flirting and end with a misplaced text message like last time? I wasn't prepared to put myself through all of that again. And the real struggle in all of this is that Marcus is exactly how Penny described him. He was lovely, sweet, and gentle, but that was precisely what I loved about Dean to begin with, too.

What a complete mess.

Chapter 19

One of my favourite childhood memories was the smell of the lemon tree in our backyard. The yearly harvest that began in November kept our home smelling citrus fresh right through summer and well into early autumn, when a crackling wood fire would begin to take over. Our tree had been planted when the house was first built, ten years before we moved in, which meant it was well established by the time I was looking for trees to climb. Even now, it clocked in at over three metres tall.

The next morning, with nothing else to do and a massive case of the Can't Be Bothereds, I walked around to Dad's. I checked the letterbox, ran the mower over the grass, opened some windows and let the fresh air in, grabbed an old laundry basket, and began scaling the heights of the old tree.

Clearing the tree had been something that had always fallen to me to do, and why wouldn't it? It was the perfect extracurricular activity for a little wild-haired tearaway child with energy to spare. I dumped an old laundry basket by the trunk and, with my hand wrapped firmly around a branch, I took my first tentative steps up into the tree.

I'd barely settled onto one of the thicker branches when my phone buzzed. I pulled it from my pocket, not so silently reminding myself I couldn't afford to drop it from a great height.

Just wanted to let you know that I really enjoyed Friday night.

I looked at the message sitting hopefully on the screen in front of me, crying out for a response. From the moment I left our blind date, my thoughts had been performing their own Newton's Cradle in my mind. On Friday night I was swinging wide in the surprising thrill of Marcus's company and, had he called the next morning, I'd have jumped at the notion of a breakfast date.

After lunch with Sally, I felt an unmistakable ache for what she had – the family, the children, the happy, comfortable home. Regret sat on my lap in the form of a four-year-old, intent on explaining the finer details of her favourite book to me. I wanted that, and I'd wanted it for many years before yesterday, so why had I waited so long? Was Marcus the answer to that question? A large part of me wanted to believe that he was, but after listening to Sally speak about him yesterday, I was more concerned with history repeating itself. Brave, bold Ellie had retreated into the centre of her thoughts again.

I had a great night, too, I replied.

It was true. I wasn't going to lie and tell him it was awful. Anyone who'd listened to or seen us fall about in fits of laughter could have confirmed as much anyway. I slipped my phone back into my pocket. It vibrated again almost immediately.

Are you busy?

Lost in thought, I continued to stare at the screen until it blacked out again. In my right hand, absentmindedly, I felt the telltale give of another lemon coming clean from the tree. I watched it fall into the washing basket below me. It lumped and rolled into an empty space.

Steadying myself on the next branch, I decided to return his message with a call, otherwise I might have found myself spending far longer in this tree than I wanted to. I pressed my phone to my ear and waited.

'Hello.' There was an undeniable smile in his voice as he answered. It served to do nothing more than turn me into a watery mess. The tug-of-war between my head and my heart had officially begun.

'Good morning,' I replied. 'How are you?'

'Well … a little bit of this, a little bit of that.'

'What's wrong?' I asked.

'Are we allowed to talk shop?' he asked. 'I mean, we aren't in the pub, so it's a free-for-all now, right?'

'Of course we're allowed to,' I answered with a chuckle. 'I've been reliably informed that it's what we do.'

'Right. Good to know,' he started. 'The thing is, I've just piled up all my work this morning and, well, there's a bit more than I anticipated.'

'Have you been lazy, Mr Blair?' I teased, another lemon tumbling below me.

'I ... you know, that sounds a little too kinky for so early in the morning,' he admitted, the fluster evident through his bumbling.

'It's almost lunch, isn't it?' I asked. 'About eleven o'clock?'

'Maybe, yeah,' he admitted quietly. 'Anyway, between all this marking I've been putting off, and the bundle of shit the boys handed me yesterday for the yearbook, I feel a bit ... flooded.'

Not so long ago, I'd told him to reach out for help if he needed it, though I wondered if he was a little reluctant to come straight out and ask for it. I wanted to see him. I wanted him to prove that my reluctance was ridiculous and that I had nothing to worry about, that he was different.

'Would you like some help?' I blurted.

'Yeah.' He cleared his throat. 'Yes. Please. I would like some help. If you're not busy, that is.'

'I'll make you a deal.' I plucked at another lemon, rustling a bunch of limbs and leaves.

'Wait, where exactly are you?' he asked.

'That's the thing,' I said. 'I'm currently up a lemon tree.'

'You? Up a lemon tree?' He laughed. 'Please tell me I'm not hearing things.'

'You're not,' I said. 'I'm at my dad's, and the tree is full of fruit. Don't worry, he's not home, he's away. But, if you'd like to come and help carry this oh so heavy tub of lemons I couldn't possibly handle on my own, I'd be ever so grateful.'

'And where am I carrying the lemons to?'

'See, that all depends.' I moved about gingerly, listening for the heave and give in the old branches. 'Do you know anyone who could use a few kilos of Apollo Bay's finest citrus? Possibly watered by my dad, no doubt watered by uncles and friends, and countless men.'

'Chances are, my grandmother would probably Hansel and Gretel me if she knew I had access to them and passed up the opportunity.'

I clapped my hand over my mouth and giggled. The mental image of him having his ear twisted by an old lady, who I imagined was far smaller than him and hunched over, was immediately hilarious and one I'd love to see.

'That settles it, then,' I said. 'I'll text you the address, you come and get them.'

'And then?' he asked.

'And then we work,' I pipped. 'Simple.'

'Well ... okay. If you're sure.'

'Hurry up, before I change my mind,' I said. 'Won't somebody please think of your promotion?'

'All right, all right, I'll be there soon.'

By the time I heard the rattle of the old side gate, and the familiar shuffle that could have only been Marcus, my basket was heaving with fruit. He approached the tree cautiously, looking back at the house on more than one occasion.

'Are you still up there?' he asked.

'You'll have to come around the back.' I tossed a piece of fruit through the foliage, and it landed just to his right.

He picked up the offending missile. 'You know, that's not a statement one hears very often.'

I laughed, a little embarrassed, and slightly pained at how easy this all was with him. 'Okay.'

I listened as Marcus circled the tree, coming in to land just behind me. I dropped more fruit, glancing up around me to see exactly how much was left. Not a lot, and perhaps I could leave them, but I shuffled another branch higher.

'Are you sure this is safe?' he called. 'What are you? Two, three metres up?'

'About that,' I answered. 'I'd have used the ladder, but there's a huge ass spider on it, and I ain't got time for that.'

'Right, so … one spider precludes the ladder, but you'll climb into an entire tree full of insects and God knows what else and maybe fall out?'

'Correct.' I aimed for his head but missed. The best part was, he didn't even flinch.

'So, this is home?' he asked.

'Home, sweet home.' I turned to look at the house and wondered exactly how it looked to him. Did it live up or down to expectation? I plucked at two last lemons and began the wary climb down.

'You know, I have walked, jogged, and run past this place so many times.' He held out a steadying hand as I reached the ground. 'I feel like we should have met a long time ago.'

The thought jolted me as my eyes met his. He wasn't wrong. This town was small enough that there was every chance we had bumped into each other before. Maybe he'd driven past as I stood in the driveway with Dad, or he'd sat at a table next to me in a café on a rare trip home. I'd just been too busy running around with my eyes shut to notice him.

I allowed myself a moment, only a quick one, to think about how different my life could have been if he had been around earlier, if we had had our meet-cute by the counter in the café and got talking about teaching and kids. Even Daisy and her bizarre love of me would have been enough to get me talking. I pushed that right out of my mind just as quickly when I realised the thoughts were sitting heavily on my heart and mind. Nothing could change the past, so there was no use dwelling on it.

'Well.' I shoved my hands on my hips. 'I just have to lock up and we can go?'

'I ... yes, let's do that.' He looked around his feet. 'Want me to bring the tub?'

'Sure.' I stopped with a jolt and snapped my fingers. 'Come to think of it, if you give me a few moments, I think I still have my old yearbook here somewhere.'

'I was so close to asking.' Marcus pinched his fingers together, delighted by my admission. 'So close.' Catching a look over my shoulder as he followed, I watched his arms flex and strain under the weight of the laundry basket. The handles flared out under the weight and, I, well I was just delighted by the show. I offered up a teasing smirk as I held the back door open.

'Honey, I'm home.' He winked, stepping past me.

'Welcome.' I followed him inside.

'Well, this is lovely.' Marcus moved quickly through the galley kitchen and into the lounge.

'You're being very polite,' I teased.

'No, I'm not being polite. It feels really homely in here,' he said. 'A lot of creature comforts, stuff you've owned for a hundred years that's completely worn in.'

Rinsing a mug in the sink, I stopped and smiled. 'I like that description.'

'There are lots of photos of you and your dad.'

'Yes.'

'Can I ask about your mum, or is that off topic?' He'd stopped walking around.

'She lives in Sydney,' I said. 'She left when I was a baby. I don't see a lot of her.'

'Is that a bad thing?'

'I don't really know any different.' I offered with a tiny shrug as I stood between both rooms. 'I'm not sure if that's because she doesn't know how to mother, or if there's maybe another underlying problem, but I've always had a strange relationship with her. If I'm honest, I wish that was different, but it is what it is.'

'And your dad just picked up the slack?' he asked.

'He did.' I approached him by the sideboard where Dad kept an assortment of photos in various mismatched, sometimes handmade, frames. 'Let's go find my old school stuff.'

My old yearbook had always been buried in a cheap translucent plastic box under my bed in my old bedroom. It was one of those boxes with castor wheels that fall off too easily and handles that snap if pushed too hard. I knelt beside my bed and dragged it out into the sunlight for the first time in years.

It landed on my bed with a heavy, dusty thud.

'I feel like this room hasn't seen change in a while.' Marcus leaned into the doorframe, arms folded across this chest and legs crossed at the ankles. 'It's almost like eighteen-year-old Eleanor moved out, and it's just been waiting for you to return.'

'I always jokingly call it the museum.' I flipped through the first few items. There were certificates and old textbooks, report cards and photo albums or random teenage things that I held up with a modicum of embarrassment. 'I keep telling him to change the room, make it a library, or a theatre room. I mean, you can see, this house is tiny. Two bedrooms, one bathroom. You'd think he'd be excited for the extra space, but it's always, "It's there if you need it."'

'And, yet, you moved in with Penny.' He handed back a certificate I'd thrust in his hand.

'Would you like to try and sneak past him in the dead of night?' I held my yearbook aloft like a trophy. Marcus snatched it up just as quickly.

'No.' He flipped through the first few pages. 'I can't say I'd enjoy that honour. Then again, I never really did a lot of that as a teenager, so maybe I could relive my lost youth?'

'Much easier to sneak a boy past Penny.'

'Oh look.' His groan was tinged with laughter. 'Is this you?'

'This is me.' I leaned into the page where he was pointing.

There I was, in all my childhood glory, hair in pigtails and covered in mud on school camp. 'Do you like the early Nineties cut and paste job?'

The entire yearbook looked like someone had cut people from old photographs and glued them to a sheet before adding headings and running the whole thing through the photocopier no less than fifty times. But that was also why I loved it so much. Simpler times and, really, this was the pinnacle of student publishing, especially if you were singled out to contribute one of the carefully drawn headings.

When he'd finished laughing at photos of me, but more so at the ones of Mick, he placed the book on the counter by the door.

'Somehow, I don't think it'd sail today with our super integrated cloud storage Photoshop land, would it?' He looked for my approval. 'Someone would be asking why there wasn't a hashtag, filter applied.'

'That's true.' I collected a few lemons for myself and tucked them into the fruit bowl in the pantry. I checked and double-checked windows and door locks, then looked to Marcus, who was standing about awkwardly, now with my yearbook held against his chest 'Shall we head to yours now?'

* * *

Last time I'd been inside Marcus's home, I hadn't seen a lot. Realistically, it was a blurred, distracted race up the stairs that had been punctuated only by the ridges of wallpaper under my fingertips, and a getaway that didn't stop to take in the sights.

After being greeted by Daisy at the door, I was ushered past a wall full of family photos and through to a kitchen of stainless-steel appliances and stone benchtops, downlights and a coffee machine. While Marcus busied himself with drinks, I sifted through one of four piles of work on the kitchen table. Workbooks balanced precariously atop each other while dog-eared pieces of paper were sorted by topic. No wonder he felt overwhelmed.

'I'll take these?' I offered, holding up a pile of maths sheets.

'Please.' He checked me over his shoulder. 'I'll be there in just a second.'

I moved into the lounge, onto a deep-seated sofa that was comfortable enough to induce sleep and waited. Marcus dropped down next to me on the sofa, laptop propped open and ready to start work. I was fascinated by how different our approaches were. I'd claimed nothing but a red pen as my tool, while he had a word processor and some fandangle looking project management file open. Oh, and a red pen.

Daisy padded across the room lazily and dropped herself by our feet. She was more than happy that we'd stopped by the café on the way home and bought her one of their dog biscuits.

'Okay.' Marcus picked up a pair of glasses from the side table and pushed them up the bridge of his nose. They were black and thick-rimmed, though they didn't strike me as the milk bottles he'd told me he wore as a boy. In fact, I'd never seen these before, ever. 'What do you want to mark first? Each pile has the answer sheet at the top.'

'Hang on.' I held up a finger. 'I've never seen this Marcus before.'

He rolled his eyes. 'Go on, have a laugh.'

'Laugh? I don't want to laugh.' Pivoting and climbing to my knees, I held his head still, silently revelling in the warmth of his skin against mine, the stubble that grazed my fingers. Stubble was an awful, awful weakness, and here I was holding him like a long-lost toy. As his eyes searched my face, and I tried to keep my focus solely on the frames of his glasses, my brain went straight back to the bedroom. I swallowed. 'I like them.'

'You do?' he asked, surprise rippling his answer.

'They suit you.' Still, my eyes danced about his face.

'No, they don't,' he argued. 'They're far too chunky.'

'Yes, they really do,' I countered, drawing a finger across the top of the frame. 'They're strong, they match your face. I thought you said the other night, in the pub, that you'd had laser surgery?'

'I suspect it was less laser and more Thor's Bifröst,' he said. 'Didn't entirely fix the problem, but it's better than nothing, and I forgot to buy more contacts last night. Can we move on?'

'As you wish, boss,' I teased, to muted laughter.

'That's VP to you.' He winked.

Chuckling, I set the papers between us and, while I worked my way through the pile I'd selected, Marcus began piecing together the yearbook. Between checking on grammar, or handwriting he couldn't decipher (to be fair, some of it looked like hieroglyphs), we said little to each other. I was happy for the white noise of the television in the background, and Daisy eventually rolled to her side and stretched out fast asleep. I chewed through two piles of papers before we spoke again.

'Eleanor?'

I held my finger in place, stuffed my pen in my mouth, and looked up. 'Hmmm?'

'You seem a little distant today,' Marcus remarked. 'Is everything okay?'

I frowned. 'Hey?'

'I don't know, I just feel like you're a little out of sorts this afternoon? Since we got here, really. It's as if you're here, but you're not? We're not really talking, are we?'

It hadn't struck me that anything had been wrong per se, but he was right. I had been quiet. *We* had been quiet. Especially when comparing this afternoon to Friday night. I hoped it didn't mean we were lost without cue cards. No, I thought, we'd been chatting on text and this morning in the backyard. Surely, we were just working quietly?

'You know, I had lunch with an old friend yesterday, and she just said a few things that are bugging me.'

'Like what?'

'So, I met up with Sally. We were friends as kids but, you know, you move away and things change and people change and suddenly they're not in your life anymore.'

'Uh-huh.' He kept tapping away at his laptop as he spoke.

'Everything was going well until she asked me advice on how to get her kid reading more. I assumed she meant could I give her some tips to help at home, and I start reeling off these great age-appropriate books.'

Marcus worried his lip and removed his glasses. 'This sounds like that one parent–teacher interview I get every half-year.'

I grimaced. 'She stopped me and said, "That's not quite what I meant." She wanted me to help her word a discussion with her teacher. She's of the opinion that her taxes pay our wages, so we should be the go-to for everything her child is learning.'

'I hate those conversations. I mean, we've got, what, twenty-five kids at a time to teach. It's not like we can do intensive one-on-ones with all of them. You've always got your bell curve of kids. Some of them don't need a lot of help, because they just get it. Most of them sit in the middle and chug along, but there's always one that turns up at parent–teacher interviews telling me they pay my wages and what the hell am I doing with my time because Little Jimmy, who's not exceptionally bright, is apparently suddenly the smartest kid in the room and would just excel if I did my job properly.'

'See! This is what I don't get.' I discarded my marking and wriggled on the couch, much to Daisy's disgust. If I were honest with myself, I was certain that wasn't my biggest worry from yesterday, but I also wasn't sure I wanted to air what it was that was really bothering me. 'Why is it my problem that you're not interested in your child's education enough to be able to do something at home?'

'You can't be everything to everyone,' he said. 'And, look, I know I do those extra classes. It's not out of the goodness of my heart, it is literally so that I can avoid shit like that. I don't have to and perhaps I shouldn't have to, but …' His voice trailed off.

'It just makes me rage.'

'Yep.' He nodded slowly, lips pursed. 'But you need to remember you aren't a panacea, either. You can only do what you can do with the limited time you have.'

I sighed. 'You're right. You're absolutely right. It's just …'

'Ignorance?' he tried.

'I guess so, yes.'

'I have an idea.'

I lifted my eyes to his. 'What's that?'

'I still have a little way to go on this document.' He turned his laptop to face me, as if to prove the point.

'Do you want to swap?' I asked. 'I'd be glad for the break. Mix it up a bit.'

'Definitely, we're absolutely doing that.' He shoved his laptop aside. 'But I was thinking, why don't you stay for dinner? If I start now, I can make that roast chicken I talked about the other night.'

Urgh. The eggshell moment that was, one way or the other, setting itself up to be the sequel to our blind date. It was something we'd discussed and, yes, one of our cue cards definitely said he was cooking 'next time'. He looked at me expectantly. I hoped I didn't look like I was full of dread but, after yesterday, I'd decided I wasn't sure on anything. Surely it wasn't fair of me to stay and eat dinner when I was feeling like this?

'It's a no, isn't it?' he asked, finally.

I let out a held breath. 'Not tonight,' I said, going on to reason, 'it's Sunday—'

'School night.' He nodded. 'You're right.'

'I'm sorry, I'm so sorry,' I pleaded. In a heartbeat, I'd gone from comfortably quiet to ditheringly awkward and falling over myself to apologise. My stomach churned, and it felt like my vision had shrunk to a tiny window that included only him.

'Eleanor—' he held his palm out '—stop apologising. It's fine.'

'I don't feel like it's fine.' A lump threatened to cut off my throat.

'It really is, it's okay. I don't want to rush this. It's okay.' He stood, brushing his lap off. 'Do you want a coffee? Water? Wine? Soda?'

I shook my head. 'No. Thank you.'

Our words hung heavy in the open, threatening to spill into conversation every time we tried to discuss work. We did swap, and I took over the helm of the yearbook while Marcus finished his marking, but everything felt riddled with charge, as if any minor offence would result in something akin to lightning.

After finishing the last page of the book, sometime around six o'clock that night, I stretched my fingers up towards the sky and yawned. 'I think I'm going to head home.'

'Are you sure I can't just whip something up?'

I shook my head and checked my pockets. I still had everything I arrived with. 'It's fine, really. I don't want you to go to any trouble.'

Instead of arguing, he simply said, 'Okay, no worries.'

'So, yearbook is done.' I counted off on my fingers. 'What I have, anyway. Are you caught up with your marking?'

'I've got about six sheets left.'

'Brilliant.' I smiled softly. 'Tomorrow, I have to meet Jack to tune the piano and see how he's going with the music component of the night.'

'You with your hidden talents.' He whirled his finger about. 'Would you like me there? Or is that a stupid question?'

'Well, I can't very well do this without my wingman,' I said. 'I don't have a class last period though, so I'll try to head over about three o'clock? Hopefully the gymnasium will be empty.'

Marcus followed me towards the front door, edging closer as I came to a stop. 'Thank you for today. I appreciate your help.'

'You're always welcome.' I rubbed his forearm. 'See you in the morning?'

'I'll bring the coffee.'

'You've got yourself a deal.' I reached up on my tiptoes and kissed his cheek, breathing in the intoxicating smell of a warm, solid male. This was not doing my resolve any favours, but it felt like a nice way to close out the afternoon.

Chapter 20

My love affair with the piano began when I was just five years old with 'Twinkle, Twinkle, Little Star'. Long before I'd mastered the art of shoelaces, maths, or dressing myself properly, music managed to capture my attention. It was a blisteringly warm day, so drenched in humidity that each breath felt like a lungful of warm water, and I'd been left with my grandparents while Dad went off to one of his random jobs. It was there, in their lounge room, with curtains drawn and fan set to arctic, that I sat on the green velvet piano stool next to my grandfather and bashed out the first unknowing sounds on rickety old ivories.

Immediately, I was hooked. I was making that noise? Me? From that moment on, every visit had me glued to that piano. Like all kids, I wanted just a little more. One more scale, one more song, please just one more anything, and it wasn't long before I was keeping my grandparents captive with impromptu concerts. If Penny happened to be around, which she quite often was, I'd have a dancer to accompany me.

Nursery rhymes soon became pop songs and, somewhere around the last gasping breaths of high school, they gave way to the works of composers whose own last gasping breaths happened hundreds of years earlier. Tchaikovsky's *Sleeping Beauty* Suite was my favourite piece of music. Ever. Playing it became my favourite way to relax and unwind. If ever I needed white noise to fall asleep to, it was in an iPod playlist all its own.

Amongst Dad's changing jobs, and my trips interstate to visit Mum, the piano felt like one of the few constants in my life. Along with books, it gave me a single point of reference to focus on. Wherever I was, or wherever I was going, I could always return home to it. For that, I loved it even more. I pushed myself to learn everything I could about it and, as I got older and my grandparents less mobile, professional lessons supplemented holes in my knowledge.

And, yet, despite all this, I never considered becoming a music teacher, even when playing in my university's symphony orchestra. Music had always felt like something I did just for me and, while sharing that love with others made perfect sense, I didn't feel that way during university.

Throughout auditions and public performances against the backdrop of some of Melbourne's most beautiful recital halls, suggestions from friends and family, I stuck steadfastly to my plans of becoming a library teacher. Three unsuccessful attempts to join the Melbourne Symphony Orchestra only confirmed that I'd made the right decision on that matter. That didn't mean I let my skills stagnate though.

While living in Melbourne, in a university share house with four other girls, I picked up the dirtiest, oldest upright piano known to man for the cost of covering a week's worth of shifts at a local pub. Being a money poor student, I taught myself another trick: tuning my piano. Between shifts at the student bar and a retail job that saw me pushed further out the door with each candle added to my birthday cake, the thirty dollars the tuning kit had cost me ended up saving me hundreds in the long run. Throw in some YouTube videos, and I had a new feather in my cap, just call me Johan Sebastian. All Bach, no bite.

My new trick came in handy. Not only did it earn me a place with other students from the music stream, but I picked up the odd tuning job here and there. I charged minimal amounts, but every little bit helped and, most of the time, I was already hanging out with friends when the request came. It was through these new friends that I met Dean.

When we first met, backstage at a recital centre, Dean loved nothing more than long nights listening to me play, with a bottle of wine and a box of pizza. But, as we both left school and moved into the big world of business, life changed. He became busier, his job more demanding, and his patience for anything outside work grew considerably smaller.

My music, something that had once brought us together, became a force of tension. If I played, he said stop. If I continued, we fought. That alone should have rung alarm bells for me to leave, but I didn't. Instead, my music became something I indulged in less and less until, eventually, it had stopped being part of my life altogether.

Looking back now, it seemed like such an easy loss to prevent. At the time, bobbing about in the middle of the storm, it didn't feel like that at all.

So, I won't pretend I wasn't secretly thrilled when Jack asked me to tune the school pianos. It tickled at a nervous energy that both brought me back to something I loved and terrified me at the same time. What if I'd forgot everything? What if I made a complete fool of myself? Yet, despite these worries, I was chomping at the bit for our Monday afternoon catch-up.

That's how I found myself walking into the school gym right on the 3.30 bell. I hadn't managed to get there earlier as I'd originally planned, even though my last class had been let out a few minutes early. I ignored my returns trolley emptied and a fresh delivery of books in favour of scurrying through the school yards like a thief in the night. I was like a kid in a candy store; only one thing on my mind.

Five minutes, that's all I wanted. A few moments where I could feel my way around the instrument again, try and get a feel for the intricacies of this one and maybe, just maybe, I might be able to pull a rabbit from my hat and play something. I tugged the heavy fire door open and peered around the basketball court. The storage room was locked, and Kevin had already disappeared for the night.

And there it was. If this had been a film moment, there'd be a break in the clouds, a ray of light shining through the ceiling, angels chanting, and a harpist floating above the top of screen somewhere. Except it wasn't. It was simply a piano under an old black bed sheet. At least it wasn't a fitted sheet; they're bad enough to fold, let alone get one off a piano.

Pulling the sheet back, I untucked the stool from where it had been nestled underneath the key bed and sat down. The yellowing varnish was worn across the front board and fallboard, the surface scuffed where feet had missed pedals, but it was still beautiful. I took a shaking breath and struck Middle C.

I listened carefully as the first fuzzy note of a poorly tuned piano rang out. The school gym wasn't the best room acoustically, but it was perfectly suited to an end-of-year production, so I wasn't going to get picky about things I couldn't control. It would work perfectly, and everyone would go home happy. As if on autopilot, my fingers began traipsing along scales and familiar chords, music humming and vibrating through my heart.

A few frustrating missteps were soon drowned out by the fluidity of song and the crescendo of realisation. It had been almost eighteen months since I'd had a chance to play, yet it came back to me quickly, easily, as if it were a physical part of me that I could never shake. My fingers danced across the old keys with renewed confidence, from 'Clair de Lune' which, at the right note, swung into the more difficult *Sleeping Beauty* Suite.

I was playing, lost in what a beautiful, fulfilling feeling it was. A well that had been left to dry was trickling with water once again. I paused at a wrong note, listening to the hum again as I rearranged fingers and tapped out a beat, only to find it drowned out by a slow clap.

Marcus was sat on the sideline benches, as we had been on that afternoon weeks ago where we could barely form full sentences at each other.

'Don't stop on my behalf.' He held out his hands. 'In fact, I want you to keep playing. I love your fancy music.'

With a smirk, I broke out the first few bars of 'Chopsticks' as he crossed the court, laughter wrinkling the corners of his eyes.

'That's what I'm talking about.'

I wriggled across to give him room on the stool beside me. 'How was your day? I don't think I've seen you around.'

'I know. I feel awful. We've been forced apart by the powers-that-be today.' He pressed a hand against his chest and offered his best downtrodden face. 'However, had I known this was on offer, I would've run to listen.'

'You know, if you were as clever as you say you are, there are videos of me on YouTube.' I wriggled into his side, possibly to get a better reach of the keyboard, though maybe it was more likely just for the physical contact that was at once both familiar and thrilling enough to curl toes. From the corner of my eye, I could see Marcus move about; hands in his lap, hung loose to his side, and then on the rear of the seat behind me. I didn't flinch as an arm landed around my shoulders and pulled me closer. 'Has anyone ever told you how smooth you are?'

'Just call me chunky peanut butter,' he mumbled, pressing his mouth into my shoulder, not quite allowing himself to kiss me. 'And, yes, I did know, because someone directed me to them.'

'I wonder who that might have been.' I smiled.

'I'll never reveal my sources,' he said, voice tinted with laughter. 'You are astonishing though, but even that word doesn't feel like enough.'

'It's more than enough,' I said, dropping my hands into my lap. 'It still feels a little rusty, a few bits here and there, but it feels great.'

'*You* are enough.'

'Thank you.'

A crashing stumble through the door was followed by scattered papers and a bumbling Jack, who stopped us in our tracks. Marcus shuffled away from me, though I was sure Jack hadn't seen anything. He was too busy gathering up all that he'd fallen through the door with, papers seesawing their way through the air. We watched, waiting for him to approach.

'Was that you, Ellie?' He crossed the basketball court quickly. 'Playing, I mean? I could hear you on the way across.'

'It certainly wasn't me.' Marcus grinned.

'Wow, okay.' He blew his cheeks out. 'Amazing.'

'I just wanted to get an idea of how much work needed doing,' I said.

'How long do you think this is going to take?' Jack dragged a chair up beside me. He unwound his bun, threading his fingers through hair that was far more luscious and conditioned than my own, before piling it all atop his head again. I made a mental note to ask what brand of conditioner he used. 'And Philbie will pay you, right?'

'Normally, that depends on what condition the instrument in. It could be two hours, could be six.' I got up from the stool and pulled my tools from my handbag. 'Thankfully, this one doesn't seem too bad. And, no, he's not paying. It's fine, really. It's nice to be back around the big old things.'

After my quick play, I was sure this would be an easy enough job. With my leather tool pouch spread about the floor like a surgeon's rainbow, I unfasted the case and pulled it away. It tired and yawned, telling me it had been an age since she'd found herself naked in front of anyone. That made two of us, I thought, placing the case on the ground beside us. Well, maybe more her than me.

'Could be all week.' I waved the tuning lever in his face.

With his elbows on his knees and chin in his hands, Jack watched quietly. His interest wobbled between fascinated and questioning as I pushed wedge mutes between strings and fiddled with a chromatic tuning app. Life had become so much easier since the world of apps exploded. I managed to get through the entire octave from Middle C before either of my colleagues spoke.

'You know, I should know how to do this, but I just don't,' Jack said. 'It's mesmerising.'

'It's simple, really. Listen for the warbles between the strings, we want that little messy vibration to clear up. I could probably teach you.' I pinched my fingers together as I worked on the next string. 'Can you hear that?'

'It's so crisp when it's in tune.' He stopped still, his eyes focused tightly on the felt striking the string. 'Should I be worried about my job right now?'

I scoffed. 'Hardly.'

'Are you classically trained?' he asked.

'Does it matter?' Marcus bit, and quickly.

We both turned to look at Jack, his eyes darting nervously between the two of us. I won't pretend I didn't enjoy the show of unity. It was nice to know someone had my back when it counted, especially considering this was a question I'd come up against often. I'd seen my share of disbelieving faces when trying to get into recital groups.

'I'm not trained classically, or as a music teacher, Jack,' I assured him, leaning back on the stool. 'You can relax. It's just a hobby that kept me occupied throughout university. Kept me out of trouble.'

Marcus snorted. 'A hobby if you consider the MSO a garage band.'

'What?' Jack asked. 'You played for the MSO?'

I shook my head. 'Auditioned, didn't quite make the cut.'

'And, as usual, she's being far too modest about her skills.'

I swivelled, glaring at Marcus.

'YouTube.' Marcus talked around me and gave Jack two thumbs up. 'You'll find a great video of her, a few actually. I mean, she is fully clothed, but she's playing with a symphony orchestra and it is off the charts good.'

'Stop it,' I hissed.

'What? You should share that. You're good. You're better than good, and who gives a fuck if you're not specially, classically, formally trained. Does it matter? I've got half a mind to buy this piano from the school and pay you to play for me. I'll sit there in the evenings with my smoking jacket, eating my chocolate biscuits and drinking. Daisy will have her biscuits, too, and you can play for us each night. I'll throw coins in your hat.'

'Or, even better, I could teach you,' I teased. 'Then you can serenade yourself. It'll be the gift that keeps giving.'

Marcus shrugged a shoulder. 'Works for me.'

'I hate to interrupt whatever's going on here.' Jack's head bobbed about anxiously. 'But I need to be somewhere shortly. Shall we work through what we have before it gets too late?'

Set against the backdrop of sharpening piano strings, and my occasional cursing, Jack talked us through each of the classes, the songs he'd picked for them to perform, and where they were at in terms of preparation. He'd made crude videos on his phone and, after sitting through each of them, assured us they were going to be as ready as they could be on the night. In the end, he spent less than thirty minutes with us before disappearing under some pretence of an appointment.

I watched the door swing shut behind him and focused my attention back on Marcus, who was already watching me.

'What?' I asked.

'Show me how to play something.'

'Like what?'

'I don't know.' He shrugged. 'Something easy.'

'Okay.' I held my right hand out over the keys. 'Put your hand on mine.'

Carefully, almost painfully slowly, Marcus slipped his fingers along mine. His palm, warm and surprisingly heavy, sat atop of mine. The innocence of the gesture didn't translate to how I felt in the moment. A crackling fire raged through my belly and up into my chest cavity, and the first prickles of heat rolled up my neck.

'You ready?' I searched his eyes, big, beautiful, and bottle-green, trying to work out what was going on inside that brain of his.

'Yes.' His tongue darted out across his top lip, retreating quickly. 'What are we playing?'

'"Twinkle, Twinkle, Little Star".'

Chapter 21

I never did finish tuning the piano. It was far too big a job, though I promised myself I'd come back at lunchtime the next day to pick up where I left off. I left a mute wedge between a set of strings, because there was no way in hell I'd remember where I was up to without a lot of guesswork, covered everything up, and went home for the night.

I'd hoped Penny was home so I could tell her about my excitement at having a piano to myself, uninterrupted for a good period of time. I was effervescent with the knowledge that my skills hadn't just packed up and left me, and I was already yearning for more. But she was nowhere to be seen.

That was fine. Her absence gave me time to plan, think, and work out where I'd stick a piano should I manage to find one at a reasonable, don't earn much money, price. Walking around the house with a bowl of mac and cheese, I tried to find a spare space in the apartment.

Size was an issue. I'd always known this place was small, but maybe I could push my bed up against a wall. It would look very sullen teenager, but it could work. Another option was to clear a corner of the lounge, but I wasn't sure Penny would be keen on that. Everything in that room, as cramped as it was, had its place, and I feared a piano might be too much of an ask. One final thought: there was always the garage.

Strip lighting buzzed at the flick of a switch. It was cold, and probably a little damp, so not ideal, but if it were only temporary and I began looking for my own place, it could work. I didn't want to count Dad's home as an option, because I wanted something for me, to take with me, that I could access whenever the feeling arose.

For now, it looked like I might have to shelve the idea, at least until I found my own place to live. Although, if I were honest with myself, Marcus's suggestion that he buy it and I teach him to play it wasn't the worst idea ever. It just meant dealing with things that had been fizzing away in the background like a papier-mâché volcano set up for a science fair.

I decided it was best not to bring it up with Penny until such time as I had a solid plan. She didn't get home until the early hours of the morning anyway. By that time, I was busy sleeping, dreaming about how soon I could get back to the gymnasium, and back to the music.

* * *

'Marc, I've gotta ask, what's with the suits?' Kevin asked loudly enough that I was sure even Phil would be able to hear in his office through doors and brick walls. It was certainly designed to get everyone's attention.

Kevin had followed me into the staffroom and Marcus, who was standing by the sink trying to knot a tie he couldn't seem to get right, was his first order of business. 'You look like you've got a stick up your arse. It's not as if we're in a corporate office. I mean, unless you're trying to impress someone.'

Not a bad observation, coming from someone who looked like he hadn't seen the inside of a department store since Cyndi Lauper was singing about girls wanting to have fun.

Kevin waggled his eyes at me in a way that said he obviously expected some level of loyalty-based support. It didn't go unnoticed, but it did go unanswered as silence ate the room alive. If the air was more evidently dead, I'd have thought we'd simply slipped off into the vacuum of space. With nothing to say, people simply stopped and stared. Toast began to burn, and Gemma whipped her hand away from the urn, an overflowing cup sending boiling water over her fingers. Jack covered his mouth in a vague attempt to stem laughter.

The worst part? Not one single person stood up in defence of Marcus. There hadn't even been a muted rumbling. Remembering all the times I'd wished I'd had someone in my corner, I knew I had to say something, anything.

'Kevin, we've known each other a long time, so correct me if I'm wrong.' I cleared my throat and turned towards him. 'But does this school not have an anti-bullying policy? Do you know where I can find a copy to read.'

Kevin's mouth flopped about like a fish out of water, but no sounds came out.

'Ellie, it's fine,' Marcus mumbled from the corner of his mouth. 'Really.'

'No, actually, it's not,' I argued, with pointy finger for added effect. 'I'm sure I had to read and sign an anti-bullying policy when I accepted this job, and I sure as hell know I read it when I was planning my classes. And I absolutely *have* had to refer to it to deal with students recently. Now, if we are supposed to teach students to treat others with respect, how are we to do this if the adults themselves are jumping on each other for something as simple as how they're dressed? And what does it matter to you, Kevin? He looks *good*. He's well presented, neat and tidy. There's nothing wrong with putting in a bit of effort.'

A teaspoon clattered against a table. I looked around the room, at the slack-jawed faces watching on, and all I could think was, why the hell was I the only person airing this?

'It was just a joke,' Kevin mumbled.

'Why?' I asked. 'Because someone called you out on it?'

Kevin mumbled an apology and offered his hand to Marcus, who shook it without so much as a word of acceptance. Idle chatter filled the air slowly, washing over the moment like it had never existed. With Marcus still standing there, I offered him a faint smile, poured milk in my coffee and walked away.

In my office, I stared blankly at the computer monitor. For the life of me, I couldn't work out what I wanted to do first. Everything felt a little too jumbled, like the very last of my nerves had been trodden on. I settled for checking emails and waiting for my wobbling stomach to subside.

There was a gentle knock at the door. I swivelled my chair to find Marcus. A slow smile curled the corners of his mouth.

'Can I come in?'

'Always.' I waved him inside.

Pressing the door shut with a dull click, he fished around in his pocket, producing two Creme Eggs. 'My hero.'

'Please.' I stood to meet him. 'He asked for it.'

'Come here.' Marcus settled on the edge of my desk. He grappled for my hip, catching his finger in a belt loop and pulling me between his legs. 'Eleanor.'

'What?' I looked at him.

'Thank you for what you just did.'

'It just makes me so angry,' I said with a deep sigh as I fiddled with his tie. 'Him and Jack. They're both people I'd looked up to when I was younger and they've both, in the space of a day, turned out to be complete idiots. It's disappointing, I guess.'

I lined the thin end of his tie up with his ribs, crossed the thick end over, wrapped it under, over, and slipped it through before tightening the knot. The entire time, Marcus watched me quietly.

'Do I want to know how you know how to do that?' he asked.

'My grandfather taught me,' I explained. 'My dad is a little useless at doing formal well. Grandy knew this and was well aware my dad had a lot of job interviews. So, he decided to teach me.'

'Not your dad?'

'Yeah, Dad could be a bit stubborn in the face of helpful advice.' I tried to move away from him but was stopped by two warm hands on my hips drawing me back into him. Now, he was so close I could feel his thighs against mine, his long, deep breaths tickling the tip of my nose. 'Anyway, I would go to my grandparents every weekend. Grandy taught me how to knot ties and play the piano.'

'I think I like Grandy.'

'He was a great man,' I said. 'Found his own son infernally frustrating, but I understand that. Dad was young when he had me. Or when he and Mum did, anyway.'

'How young is young?'

'The edge of seventeen,' I joked.

'Jesus, they took that far too literally, didn't they?'

'A little, yeah,' I said.

'What about you and me?' he asked. 'You think we're too young, or too old?'

'For what?' I asked.

'You and me.'

'Huh?'

'Let's do it.'

My brows shot up under my fringe. 'Is that schoolyard speak for sex, or are you getting at something else?'

Lips downturned, he shrugged. 'I'll take that option, too, but I was talking about going on a date.'

'A date?'

'A proper date. None of this hanging out to work, or other people pushing us together. You and me, of our own volition. We'll go and get dinner somewhere, maybe catch a movie.'

'Big words,' I teased.

'I know, I apologise. I understand they're difficult for you,' he fired back as I laughed. 'Come on, what do you say?'

I sighed heavily.

'That's not good,' Marcus said. 'Sighing is rarely positive.'

'No, that wasn't a bad noise,' I said. 'I'm trying to put what I'm feeling into words.'

'All right,' he said slowly. 'Did you not enjoy Friday?'

'I ... Friday was incredible,' I blew a raspberry as I stumbled over my words. 'Spending time with you recently has been a joy.'

His smile, which had been so full of hope, faltered. 'But?'

I threw my head back. 'I don't know!'

'Eleanor, I adore you. You've shaken my little world up, and I love it. Look at me, I've walked into work without a tie on. I'm wearing glasses because I still haven't picked up my contacts. I'm running late for the second day in a row, and the best part is I don't even care. For the first time in years I feel truly relaxed and at ease with who I am and what I'm doing because of you. You get it. You get *me*.'

'Well, you should care.'

'You think this doesn't scare the absolute hell out of me, too?' he asked. 'And can you please look at me?'

I lifted my eyes to meet his. Recently, he'd brought about entirely new feelings. It was the laughter of Friday, combined with the relaxation of Sunday, quiet hours spent on his couch, and all the thoughts I was having trouble reining in. This feeling? This was new. This was wanted. So why couldn't I just leap off the edge and let it be?

'For all the things we've talked about, you could still walk through the door in five or ten years' time and decide, you know what, Alice was right. You're a complete bore, and I'm done.'

'That's not true,' I argued. 'Because if you're a bore, what does that make me?'

'But it *is* true.' He folded his arms across his chest. 'I could still be teaching, or I could be vice principal, and I could be buried under marking or paperwork, but I still want to try. We at least owe ourselves that much.'

'Marcus, this is such a huge thing. We both know that this won't be little, we've all but set the course for the SS *Commitment*.' I shrugged. 'I just ... I don't even know.'

'So, let's stop skirting around the edges, stop talking about it in parables and what-ifs, and start ... I don't know, something.'

'Please don't push me into an answer.'

'No, no, no, I'm not pushing.' His hand moved from where he'd been holding the edge of my desk, landing on my hip. He squeezed gently, thumb brushing softly against the fabric of my dress. 'I'm not going to force you into a decision. I won't ask again. Instead, I'll wait for you to come to me.'

'What if it goes horribly wrong?' I watched as he slipped off the desk and walked towards the door.

Marcus doubled back and tapped at the window near the door. 'And what if it goes spectacularly right, Eleanor?'

I watched as he walked away, joining the flow of foot traffic that was moving through the library, as if we hadn't just had a conversation that took an altogether awkward turn. The answer to all of this was simple. I knew what I wanted to do, but I felt like a bungee jumper in those last precious seconds before leaping into freefall. While my stomach churned with horrific nervousness, my heart danced a jig at the excitement to come.

* * *

Late spring rain lashed at the windows, turning the outside world and its swaying gum trees into a Turner watercolour. I sipped slowly from a piping hot tea, strong and sweet with only a hint of milk, and listened as Penny regaled me with stories from her latest dating disasters. Rufus from the football team had turned into a dud, Elliot from who knows where was allergic to her perfume, and Chelsea, well, she had more issues than a *Cosmopolitan* magazine. Penny had been desperately unattached ever since.

'As if that's not bad enough, Danny has just sent a thanks, but no thanks, text.' If her bottom lip fell any further, she was going to give herself pash rash. 'I think I'm having a crisis of confidence, Ellie.'

Wrapped in an oversized, doughnut embroidered bathrobe,

she curled in on herself again and tried to wrap a fraying crocheted blanket tighter around her shoulders. It was a rainbow of fruit colours and, usually, it matched her personality to a T. Today, her heart was washing away with the outside downpour.

Judging by the bowls that surrounded her, she'd not only eaten her way through all the food groups today, but also the entire contents of the pantry. Right now, she was shovelling handfuls of popcorn into her face like an excavator in a sandpit. This was Penny's upset look.

'It's okay to be single though,' I tested. 'I'm single.'

'Oh, no, of course. I mean, no offence to you.'

'None taken.' I took another warming sip and tightened my grip on my mug.

Of all the seasons, and of all the weather, this was my favourite. Give me a heavy downpour, a bit of thunder and lightning for good measure, a quality book and a hot drink, and I could happily while away the hours. Penny was more the happy, chirpy, summer sun and sea breeze type of girl. As it was, she'd thrown herself headfirst into a box set of *The OC* with a side order of Oreos and Doritos, and I was sure she was about to snort a few lines of Cadbury.

'Maybe I need to settle down,' she said. 'Find that one person, you know?'

Placing my mug on the side table, I folded myself up in an armchair. I felt my way around my knitting stash and pulled up what was still the beginnings of Penny's jacket. I hadn't yet made it past the end of the seed stitch border, but I was already in love with it. I dropped the bundle in my lap, wound the yarn around my fingers and looked up at her.

'Do you still believe in a happily ever after?' she asked. 'After everything, and please be honest.'

'Yes.' It might have sounded simple, but it was an honest answer. If I didn't believe in that, what hope did I have? I certainly didn't want to live out my life a single woman with no family of my own. Sure, spinsters made nice coin back in the day, and I probably could now, but I didn't want that to be it.

'Really?'

Wind howled around the eaves and corners and, somewhere in the distance, a branch cracked.

I shrugged, slipped a needle through a loop and wound the wool around. 'Sure. Honestly, I think I was blinded by some inflated idea of success and wealth and living this high adventure life with the cars and big houses and all the trimmings. But that's not real life. This here is real life, the small friendship groups, the families, smiling as you see each other cross the road to the beach, and meeting each other's kids. I made a wrong decision and, you know, I look back on him now not so much with regret but knowing that things could have been a lot different had I used better judgement.'

'You don't regret him?' she asked. 'Even after everything?'

I winced. 'Not really. Because everything I've learned has brought me here, hasn't it? I mean, I could regret it and wish I'd done things sooner, but life has a way of sorting things out.'

She reached out and grabbed a bowl of sour jellies. 'So, you're saying I should just ride it out?'

'You know, I think I remember someone saying the same thing to me recently,' I teased. 'If you are serious about settling down, maybe you need to be a bit pickier about who you spend time with. Sure, kiss the frogs, but not the entire pond. All you end up doing is swallowing a heap of rank water.'

She smiled. 'Pond water. Yuck.'

'You do realise that these types of thoughts were all the basis of your cue card game?'

She blinked at me.

'Think about what and who you're looking for in life. Do you want a family, or just the two of you? What qualities would he have? And are his ideas compatible with yours? In the end, it'll work out. I mean, if I had moved down here to teach years ago instead of getting married, I probably wouldn't have the life, the fun, and the friends I have now.'

'You have friends?' she teased.

'Please,' I scoffed. 'Millions of friends.'

'Who?' She folded her arms over, chin tipped towards the ceiling. It was all very Gary Coleman. 'Come on, spill?'

'Everyone at school,' I lied.

'Marcus,' she teased.

I rolled over the arm of the couch and reached for the teapot. 'Don't.'

'Why are you not with him?'

'I'm not done talking about you.' I pushed my knitting back up the needle and placed it carefully in my lap. 'Are you open to going on a blind date? Seeing as you so graciously sent me on one.'

Penny scrunched her nose. 'I can't really say no, can I?'

'You can always say no,' I said.

'You know what else I'm pissy about?' she asked.

'What else are you pissy about?' I crossed my legs at the knees, now prepared to be here for the long run.

'I'm so sick of that school. I'm sick of the whiny teachers, I'm sick of the Graces, I'm sick of the gossip. Most of all, I'm just sick of being the dummy on the phone. I need more.'

'Could you talk to Phil about taking on another role within the school?' I asked.

'Eleanor, I'd need to be qualified for anything other than that. Even the school nurse needs a certificate now. It's not like back in our day when mums would take turns administering Betadine and Band-Aids.'

'So, get qualified?' I said. 'Grab life, go get yourself a qualification. Live in Melbourne for twelve months. Hell, take my car. I've barely used it since I arrived.'

'I'm not like you,' she sulked. 'I can't just up and leave. I have neither the brains, the car, nor the licence.'

'Hold up a second. Firstly, you are wonderfully bright. You have a brain in your head. Secondly, you don't drive?' I asked, shocked.

'Ah, no.' She shook her head, eyes wide.

'In that case.' I tossed my knitting back in the basket next to my chair. 'Here's what we're going to do.'

Penny rolled her eyes and threw herself down onto the couch.

'No, listen to me.' I leaned forward and pointed a matriarchal finger at her. 'Over the summer, you're going to learn to drive. We're going to wind on up the Great Ocean Road until you can do handbrake turns past the caravans and slow folk. We're going to book a cockroach-infested hotel and spend nights in Melbourne to get your driving hours up, and then you're going to get your licence. You're going to spend the Christmas holidays thinking about what it is you really want from this life. As much as I love working with you, if you aren't happy at that school, there's no point in you being there. Of everyone you know, I can tell you exactly what it's like to rot your brain in a job where your talent is lost. And, you know what, if you decide to pack up and leave town at the end of summer, then so be it.'

'God, you sound like some internet motivational speaker with pretty pictures and oversized quotes.'

'Well, if the teaching gig ever dries up.' I gave a half-hearted shrug.

Penny looked at me. 'It's just ... well, you seem to have everything so together.'

'I really don't.'

'But you do, Ellie. You've turned up at this school and you have owned that job from the minute you stepped into that library. You've created this little world where girls are looking at you like you're this beacon of brain power, and there's talk about a book club next year. You've got parents thanking you because you've made a difference in their child's life. You had all this shit thrown at you last year, and you've just dug yourself out and bloomed. It's wonderful, but I am a little jealous.'

'Don't be jealous,' I said. 'Honestly, my life feels like a shambles. My dad is about to return from his holiday, which I'm worried is going to be a bit of a mess. It's almost as if he's reverted back to being a teenager and I'm the one looking after him. Meanwhile, I'm stuck in a cycle of will she or won't she turn up with my mother. And, while I'm very comfortable with my choice to return here, and the work I've done since, I still can't bring myself to go on a date with Marcus, who was just about begging me for one this morning.'

'Why, Ellie?' she complained. 'Everyone can see how well it'll work. Why do you think Patrick and I did what we did? We could see it a mile off, all the little touches, the looks, the snuggling into each other and murmured conversations. Even when all you were doing was work, there was still something there. Normally, Patrick would walk away from trying to set people up, but even he saw it.'

I groaned. 'I just don't know if I'm ready to go through all of that again. There's meeting family and friends and being trotted out as the new girlfriend. And let's not forget that it'll all be happening with the extra bonus of being in the spotlight of the school community.'

'There are women in that school who've been trying to pin him down since the minute he arrived, and he has not once taken the bait. You? You walk in, and you've got him wrapped around *all* your fingers, not just the little one.'

'I like him,' I admitted. 'I do, I do ... but, argh, I don't know.'

'I know you do,' she said. 'But, and I say this with the loveliest of hearts and best of intentions, you are treating this place like it's some sort of punishment.'

I baulked. 'You just told me how good I was doing.'

'At work, sure, because you're as bad as he is when it comes to being focused on work. But, most of the time, you just come home at night and you read books, or you watch telly, or you're busy with something for school, or you go to bed and do God knows what.'

'Sleep,' I deadpanned. 'I sleep. I rest. And you know I'm a homebody.'

'What do you dream about at night, Ellie?' she asked.

'Sorry?'

'It's a question. What do you dream about at night?'

'Why?' I asked. 'This has nothing to do with what we're talking about.'

'Just answer me.' She thrust a packet of biscuits at me.

I took a small handful and picked a raisin from the back of a Venetian. 'I had a dream the other night about Chris Pratt.'

'Me, too,' she gasped. 'What happened in yours?'

'We were digging up dinosaur bones,' I said. 'We were in the desert with all those little brushes they use. It was dusty, dry, and warm, and he was all, "What a good job," and I said, "We're so good at this." It wasn't particularly sexy, but it kind of was, if you know what I mean?'

A disbelieving look turned into a burbling laugh, which turned into roaring laughter. Eventually, she calmed down, flicked some crumbs from her blanket and turned to me again.

'Well, mine involved Chris Pratt and bones ... in a roundabout way.' She smiled wickedly. 'Same, same, but different.'

'Christ, I *do* need to get out more,' I grumbled. 'The height of my erotic night was finding a T. Rex fibular.'

'Yes, you do.' The packet of biscuits landed on the table with a cellophane crunch, and she turned back to me with wide eyes. 'Look, I love that you're getting back to Ellie. Helping Jack with the piano is lovely, and I love the knitting. It's a wondrous thing to be able to create something with your bare hands. But it's not going to nourish you in the way that other humans will. Men, in particular. And I'm not talking specifically about penis, either. Men and women are different. We are equal, but we are different, and their thoughts and perspectives, while sometimes baffling, do enrich us.'

I blinked at her. What a little nugget of wisdom she was turning out to be.

'God, you're using bottom shelf psychology on me,' I grumbled.

'Well, I'm short. I can only reach the bottom shelf.' She offered a playful wink and a smile. 'And, I mean, I feel like that blind date kind of changed your mind about him?'

'It was a great, great night.'

'And?' she pressed.

'And nothing.' I shrugged. 'It was a lot of fun. We laughed, we talked, we ate dinner. The cue cards were a riot. We haven't finished them, actually.'

'See, you have to go finish the cards. You like him, he adores you. You've just said you're keen, so why not go out with him? I don't say this because you owe him anything, but you owe yourself something. You owe it to yourself to be happy, so why deny that?'

'You're right,' I said.

'You know it.' She bounced, suddenly perking up. 'And what is it that *you* want from life? If I'm being asked to think about that, then so should you.'

'It's totally syrupy, but I want the white picket fence, two-point-four kids, and the tall, dark and handsome husband who comes home each night to spend time with all of us.' As I threw that idea into the universe, I could picture only one person in that fantasy. It hit me like a sucker punch, and I took a deep, gasping breath.

'It's him, isn't it?' Penny clutched her hands to her heart. 'That's your tall, dark, and handsome.'

'Okay, all right. It is,' I admitted. 'Just once. Once can't hurt.'

'That's my girl.' She smiled. 'Where do you think you'll go?'

'He said it was up to me. He'd wait for me to decide, and we'd go from there.'

'Off you go and pick something, then. Just don't go getting

married until I've learned to drive; I'm going to hold you to that promise.'

'Pinky swear, cross my heart.' I drew my fingers across my chest. 'You're going to get some wings.'

Chapter 22

No matter how much I gnashed my teeth and pulled out excuses as to why I shouldn't, couldn't, wouldn't go on a date with Marcus, Penny's reasoning returned serve and kicked my doubts to the kerb. The inescapable truth was she was right.

I had always been *that* girl. The one who excelled at school, who did the extra assignments for bonus credit, who spent her nights reading and afternoons memorising musical scales. I moved into an all-girl share house for university because boys were only a distraction to education, instead preferring to keep to myself and wads of lecture notes in the library.

Rehearsals for the symphony orchestra were as wild as I got, and I married the first idiot who seemed to have his shit together. Newsflash: he did not. When I grabbed at life's calculator and added it all up, playing it safe had resulted in nothing more than a sobbing afternoon in a lawyer's office and a stick jammed so far up my own arse I could have beaten the Paddle Pop Lion at his own game.

As I wandered about the school yard at lunchtime, narrowly avoiding a football to the back of my head, I drank the last pulpy dregs of an orange juice and considered my options. I didn't especially think of myself as a hermit. I'd been social since the end of Dean. I'd shifted house twice and been on dates my housemates had insisted on organising, even if they had been sorely misguided.

Regan from finance was a fiscal bore, Sam from advertising had nothing to offer, and Eddie from legal was so tied up in his own red tape that he couldn't see sunlight. I'd partied through late nights in a high-rise apartment and raced down aisles of supermarkets when I thought I'd seen my mother-in-law. I'd watched the sun come up over St Kilda Pier, and had made up for all the weekends when, as a university student, I didn't go anywhere near the iconic Corner Hotel. I was fun.

But, if that was true, why did I consider staying home in my pyjamas, getting ready for another round of high-speed knitting to be the height of fashion? The only entertainment at hand would have involved watching a movie the free-to-air channel had already played four times this year. Even Penny was booked solid for a weekend away, only days after her crisis of confidence had exploded.

'Bugger you.' I tossed my empty bottle in the recycling bin. With the ping of a solid ball bouncing from a demountable, a soccer game hurtled past me in a cloud of dust and moved back out onto the oval.

'Live a little,' I grumbled to nobody but myself as I slipped around behind Jack's music room. I picked up some trash and tossed it in the bin on my way past.

'Get out there.' I walked a gravel path between classrooms and past a small pocket of girls playing clapping games with each other.

I pulled up outside the main school building, hand pressed against the door. 'One date, that's all.'

I paused. 'You owe him that much.'

I yanked the door open, stepped into the hallway and walked towards Marcus and his classroom. 'Screw that. You owe *yourself*.'

Me. I deserved this.

I peered into his office, which was empty, but hadn't noticed I'd walked straight past him in the process. Standing by the whiteboard in his classroom, he whistled. With his jacket hanging limp over his chair, he looked resplendent in just his shirt and tie. I decided that I liked the less is more approach. The Marcus Stripped Bare, even.

I smiled. 'There you are.'

'To what do I owe this pleasure?' He clapped shut the book that had, until then, been spread out across his palm.

'What are you doing tonight?' I asked. 'Say, about six o'clock?'

'I'm quite sure that's dinnertime,' he said, pretending to be completely clueless. 'Why?'

'There's a book launch at Thatcher's Books. I was going to go, and I thought you might like to come with me. If you fancy, I could book a table for dinner afterwards.'

'Come to think of it, I might wash my hair instead.' He returned to his whiteboard where he'd been previously writing out maths equations.

I screwed up my nose and continued to watch him.

'I'm kidding,' he urged. 'Want me to pick you up, or meet you there?'

'Meet me there,' I said. 'I might get in early for some personal shopping.'

'This is good.' He smiled proudly, pointing a marker at me. The tips of his fingers were ink-stained. 'This is very good. I'll see you tonight.'

'Make sure you wash your hands, won't you?' I called over my shoulder as I stepped into the hallway. 'It's difficult to get ink out of clothes.'

I could still hear his laughter as I pushed open the library door, this time with a little more spring in my step. All I had to do was make sure tonight went well. I was nervous, excited, terrified, a true bag of mixed sweets, but I was looking forward to it.

* * *

Thatcher's Books was a beautifully quiet second-hand bookshop at the far end of the main street. It had been there as long as I could remember, with its homely Edwardian design and weatherboards, a second storey that had always remained a mystery, and tiny cottage garden that looked like it had seen better days. Dad and I had spent many afternoons digging about in the books that seemed to be stacked in every corner and on every surface.

A coffee cart had set up business under the twinkling festoon lights of the carport, selling anything from hot chocolate and coffee, to fresh fruit and raw vegan slices. If Dad were here, and not just at the other end of my phone, he'd be ripping apart his wallet like he'd just won the lotto.

If health food didn't take your fancy, there was a chalkboard informing everyone of champagne inside. Anyone care to guess where I was headed?

It seemed even Thatcher's Books was moving along with the times. Old Mrs Thatcher had been replaced by her granddaughter, Olivia, someone I vaguely remembered from my teen years. I was sure I'd met her once or twice. Her face was familiar, but I felt like she was more of a summer holiday kid. Come the start of the new school term, she'd disappear back towards Melbourne with most other tourists. She was trim and blonde and, as of the minute I stepped into the store, was sucking on a luminescent green smoothie.

Looking around, I wondered why I hadn't been back to this store yet. I may have loved the look of Sally's home, but this place was my calling. Rooms were lined with period fittings that merged with floor-to-ceiling bookshelves. A few newer ones were dark wood lined with brass rails and ladders that I could guarantee had been used to re-enact the library scene from *Beauty and the Beast* when the store was closed. If they hadn't, it was a terribly wasted opportunity.

'Are you okay?' Dad's voice interrupted my thoughts. 'You're a little quiet today.'

Currently in Bordeaux, he'd finished his trek and was reaching the closing stages of his trip. He'd called to update me on his adventures instead of sending countless messages, which I could never be unhappy about. I loved hearing from him. It was such a thrill to know he was out in the world he'd wanted to see as a teenager. We could text each other all day, but it wasn't the same as hearing his tittering laugh echo down the line.

'I'm sorry, I've just popped into Thatcher's. Remember shopping here?' I searched the front rooms for the children's section.

'I remember I always had trouble getting you out of there.' What sounded like a kettle whistled in the background. 'How's everything else going? You know, legally?'

'Everything's perfectly fine,' I said. 'You can say the word, you know. It's all good.'

'Divorce.' He cleared his throat. 'Your divorce. How is that all?'

'All done, all sorted. Onwards and upwards,' I said. 'Really, it's fine. I feel great.'

'Good, good,' he said. It sounded like he'd breathed a sigh of relief. 'So, Thatcher's huh?'

'I'm just here for a book launch,' I said. 'It's a non-fiction piece about children's literacy.'

'That sounds perfectly up your alley,' he said. 'Are you there with someone?'

'I might be.' I smiled.

'Oh, boy, I know that tone anywhere,' he teased. 'Is it a proper date?'

'Uh, yes, yes, it is.'

Listening to someone else put it into words tickled me. It was my first legitimate date. And I'd put in enough effort for it, too. It was a waxing, preening, washing, and cleaning expedition from the minute I arrived home from work to the second I stepped out the door. Make-up was applied, removed, applied again. There was the catwalk dress-up to see which of my clean outfits got the thumbs up from Penny and, in the end, ran with the emerald-green A-line and a pair of heels. Now, just the thought of tonight sent a warm thrill up my spine.

I pulled a copy of a childhood favourite from the shelf.

'Remember reading *Charlotte's Web*?'

Flipping through the first yellowing pages, I reminisced at the voices Dad would use as he read it aloud, pointing out all the illustrations, and lamenting Templeton the rat. The fact I had left my old copy behind when I left Dean tore at me. A lump grew in my throat. I decided there and then I would take it home. I couldn't leave without it.

'Only seventy-five thousand times,' he said. 'You used to love it, all tucked up in your bed in your little pink pyjamas, but I haven't read it in years.'

Oh, that sweet, sweet memory. I wiped at my eyes. 'I've just found a copy.'

'There you go, then, it's a sign from the literary gods.' While he tinkered with something in the background, I tucked my new book under my arm and moved into the next room. 'You know, I'm thinking about hiking Machu Picchu in the next twelve months. This trip has just been magic.'

'Really?' I stopped on the spot.

'You should come with me.'

I hadn't travelled since my honeymoon and, even then, it had been first class, round-the-world, complimentary champagne and caviar at each stop. Given my recent penchant for getting back to my roots, this didn't sound like the world's worst idea. Tall mountains, fresh air, and ruins of lost civilisations. It sounded properly tempting.

'You know what, I should.' Ironically, I'd landed in the travel section. 'So, am I looking for books about Peru?'

'Sure,' he said. 'Or just anything that looks fun, really. Maybe I could get myself a job at Disneyland. Probably only as a cleaner but, hey, it's something, right?'

'Look at you planning things already, and you're not back for another few weeks yet,' I said. 'I am looking forward to seeing you though.'

'When I get back, we're going to have a big cook-up. I'm going to show you a heap of recipes I picked up over here. Lots of local, traditional stuff. You can guarantee it won't taste the same, but let's say we'll give it a go anyway.'

'Don't say that,' I admonished him. 'I'm sure it'll be fine.'

'Maybe you can bring your friend with you,' he tried.

'You're so cheeky,' I teased. 'Maybe. I'll ask him. He's just arrived.'

Marcus had stepped through the door with the face of a lost man. Dressed down in slacks and a knit jumper, he still looked better than any other man in the room. His eyes darted around until they landed on me, where they wrinkled up into a tight, but wide smile. I'd come to learn that was his happily satisfied face. *Here you are, I've found you.*

'I better stop monopolising you, then, let you get on with it.'

'You don't have to.' My own smile grew as Marcus approached. 'I'll just tell him to wait. He'll get over it.'

Marcus's brow knitted and mouth popped open in mock disgust, though he still had hint of a smile. He pointed at the rows of chairs lined up in the room. With a nod and a thumbs up, he left me alone to finish up my call.

'Is your mother still coming to visit this weekend?' he asked.

'She says she is,' I said. 'She sent me a text message a few days ago to say the trip was still on and that she'd email me through the boarding pass when she gets it.'

'Yeah, well …' he sighed. 'I'll reserve my judgement until tomorrow then, shall I?'

'Dad,' I grumbled. 'Let's just see what happens?'

'I'll try and call you in the next few days,' Dad said. 'See how it all goes.'

'You don't have to,' I assured him. 'Seriously, just go and enjoy your trip. I'll make sure everything's ready for you when you get back.'

'All right. I'll see you soon,' he said. 'I love you. Enjoy your night.'

'I love you, too. Bye, bye ... bye.'

I held up a finger to my date. *One moment*, it said, and shuffled across to the sales counter to pay for my find. If Olivia did recognise me, she didn't let on, and I didn't push the point. As I made my way back across the store to Marcus, the anxiety began with a tightly held breath that burst forth into a slight pant. It was followed by tingles, a faint pins-and-needles type feeling that started in the tips of my fingers and travelled along the palm of my hand, wrists and up to my inside elbow until it had wrapped itself around my heart, lungs, ribs, in a show of nervous solidarity.

'Hello.' I dropped into the seat next to him, placing my bag and purchase on the ground.

'This is a nice surprise.' Marcus surveyed the room. 'When does this begin?'

I pushed my sleeve back. 'A few minutes. Do you want to talk to Olivia about getting book vouchers for the gift bags?'

'No work tonight,' he said. 'Just us.'

The corner of my mouth curved upwards. 'I like that.'

It wasn't as if Olivia had time to stop and chat to us anyway. Looking back at her, she was currently busy entertaining the author, who stood amidst a crowd of eager supporters and autograph hunters up by the sales counter. I glanced around briefly before turning my attention back to Marcus.

'I'd have thought there'd be more teachers here,' I commented.

He made a noise that didn't agree or disagree with my sentiments.

'Is this okay?' I asked.

'Is what okay?'

'Tonight,' I said. 'Being here.'

'I did say your choice.'

'Okay,' I said, breathlessly. 'Dinner afterwards?'

'I do hope you've booked,' he said mockingly. 'The restaurants around here are sure to be teeming on a weeknight.'

I gave his leg a playful tap. 'How were your extras today?'

'Ah.' He crossed his ankle over his knee and gave me a satisfied smile. 'They asked when Miss Manning was coming back to help.'

'Aww, that's sweet.'

'You know, it could be something you and I do next year?' he said. 'I think we could do great things.'

'How so?' I asked.

'Maybe … perhaps … something along the lines of expanding the programme?'

It was in that moment that I decided maybe this wasn't the best idea for a date. Did we really want to sit here and listen to someone rail on us about teaching literacy to children? I knew I'd likely jump to my own defence if I heard something derogatory about my profession. Like most people, I'm happy to learn, but I didn't feel like being lectured to, especially if someone was about to tell a captive audience we weren't doing enough.

I leaned in to Marcus. 'What are the odds you want to get out of here?'

He leaned into my ear. 'Let's go.'

We scrambled quickly, hoping to avoid the disapproving gaze of anyone who'd seen me sneak a glass of champagne earlier. Stepping out of the store and into the mild evening, turning my head towards the sea breeze, Marcus found a spot underneath a street lamp and began digging around in his back pocket. 'Firstly, that was going to be ridiculous. Did you read the blurb?'

I cringed. 'I did.'

'I do plenty of work in the classroom and at home. I don't need to be pontificated to, although I can understand why you'd want to go.'

'Let us never speak of it again.' I laughed nervously, hoping I hadn't completely scotched the night.

'Good, glad we agree,' he said. 'Secondly, how hungry are you?'

'Is this a trick question?' I asked. 'I'm always hungry.'

'The rest of my cue cards.' He held up the bent envelope with a jiggle. 'I'll be honest, I cheated and read some of them already.

How do you feel about grabbing a slap-up burger somewhere and finishing them off?'

Peering into my handbag, I pulled out my envelope. 'I'm game.'

'All right.' He smiled, holding his hand out to me. 'Shall we?'

My hand found his and I gladly followed him into town.

* * *

'Eat in, or takeaway?'

Ensconced in the warmth of the newest burger joint in town, with its gingham tablecloths, low lighting, and All-American edge, Marcus's attention was focused on a table just inside the door. Or, moreover, on the two students sat with their parents, and the scandalised giggling that erupted as we walked through the door.

'I think we'll takeaway, thank you.' I leaned in to speak to the front of house staff, my fingers still firmly entwined with Marcus's.

At that was how we ended up walking the mean streets of Apollo Bay, our arms laden with paper bags of food, tomato dropping out the back end of our burgers, laughing at what was left of our little question and answer game. I'm not sure even our friends thought we'd get so much mileage out of what they thought was a joke.

Honestly, I wish I'd thought of it.

'But, you know, I don't think ... hang on.' I dropped an empty bag in a bin and wiped sauce from the side of my hand. We were at the base of Marriner's Lookout, a point just towards the edge of town. I was weighed down enough by food, I wasn't carrying garbage uphill as well.

'You think what?' Marcus prompted. 'Go on.'

I sucked on my straw and frowned. 'I can't remember.'

'You can't remember? We were just talking about the one thing you love. You know, if someone were to touch you.'

'That was the question?' I played.

'Yes.' He followed me as I began the steep climb up the hill.

'You know the answer to that already,' I called. 'And if you need me to answer that again …'

'No, no, no, of course not.' He trudged heavily behind me. 'Did we decide to climb this hill?'

'Yes.'

'No, we didn't,' he argued, out of breath. 'I don't teach sport.'

Arriving at the top of the lookout, we had the rolling deep green hills of the Otway Ranges behind us. Waterfalls and skywalks hidden from view. After such a lively dinner, our trip up the hill had been remarkably quiet, peppered only by the sound of passing cars and the late-night wash of the beach. Ahead of us, a coastline that appeared to have been pinched by the hand of God was dotted with white-foamed inky ocean, Monopoly-sized houses and liquorice strap roadways shone under street lights.

'Let's switch it up then.'

'You know—' I leaned into Marcus, who offered me the last of our fries '—I don't think I've been up here since I was a teenager.'

'It's an entirely different perspective up here, don't you think?' he asked. 'I bring Daisy out here when she's being particularly active. The walk alone wears her out, so she sleeps beautifully.'

'I know the feeling,' I joked.

'That must be why she's taken to you so easily.' He slurped the last of his milkshake.

'What do you see?' I tipped my head in the direction of the town lights. 'When you look down there, what does it look like to you?'

'I spy, with my malfunctioning eyes … work and leisure, my present and my future. I can see the beach I run along with my football team, I can see the cafés that make great coffee, and the ones that make not so great coffee, and I can see my ridiculous hound flashing her bits around. I mean, honestly, the rate she lollygags around, you'd think she were posing for doggy *Playboy*.'

I giggled. 'Doggy *Playboy*?'

'Sure.' He nodded. 'What about you? What do you see?'

'I can see the jetty my father and I used to sit on while we ate fresh mussels and oysters when he'd come back from a day on a fishing trawler.'

'Your dad's a fisherman?'

'Occasionally.' A smile teased my lips. 'I can see summers spent in a tin can boat with Penny's father getting burned rotten. I can see gravel-filled knees as I learned to ride my bike downhill. I can see the terracotta-tiled roof of my grandparents' home where I was taught to play the piano. There's also the school I always wanted to work in. For the first time in my life I can say I've made at least one of my dreams come true. I can see first kisses and last dates, winter storms and lightning rolling across the bay, and sticky summer days with melting ice creams, running under garden sprinklers, and overworked air conditioners.'

'Now, see, I say something as simplistic as school and beach and café, and you come back with this winding narrative full of light and colour.'

'And yet you've got Grace all over you,' I teased. 'Go figure.'

Marcus leaned into my neck and sniffed audibly. 'What *is* that perfume you're wearing? I fear it smells of something close to jealousy.'

I retreated slightly and offered him a look of disgust. 'I am *so* not jealous of her.'

He narrowed his eyes and pinched his fingers. 'Come on, not just a teensy bit?'

'How can I possibly be jealous of someone who's so vapid she makes a helium balloon look like Albert Fucking Einstein?'

There was a pin drop of silence, a momentary vacuum in which the world fell still, and we stole surprised looks at each other before roaring with laughter.

Marcus leaned forward and clutched at his knees, his shoulders jiggling about. 'Do you reckon that was on his birth certificate? Albert Fucking Einstein.'

'If it's not, it should be.' I reached into my bag and checked the time.

I wasn't checking the time because I wanted to go home. On the contrary, I was hoping I still had a nice chunk of time to kill, which may have been the irony of the night. Previously, when Penny and I had discussed the merits of a weeknight date, there was one resounding plus. If things went pear-shaped, and we were suddenly and totally incompatible, I could call it a night, citing work in the morning. And so could he.

But the more time we spent together, the more I wanted to be here. I could sit and listen to him talk all night. Not just our questions, but about anything that came to mind. The words he spoke were nuanced and thought out and, as we stood in comfortable silence, I wondered if he wasn't the reason I moved home. Some power in the universe somewhere knew I needed him in my life, and I was becoming increasingly comfortable with the idea. Before us, lights across town began to blink out.

'Do you think they're trying to tell us something?' Marcus looked at me.

'Probably that my bladder is full and they're about to lock the public toilets,' I joked, not entirely sure I should put my thoughts out into the world quite yet.

'Shall we go home, then?'

'Do we have to?' I asked. Okay, so maybe I would.

Something in his face softened. 'No, we don't have to.'

Instead, we cosied up in the nearest cake shop and took whatever they had to offer, which wasn't much given it was late. But it didn't matter. It bought us some more time to mull over a few thoughts, pull out one or two cue cards, and pretend like we didn't have to or didn't want to be anywhere else.

It was only when the owner began placing chairs on tables and dragging out a mop bucket that we called time on our night. Not that it stopped us nattering like a couple of old ladies on a park bench as we gathered our belongings and walked out the door. Something had happened tonight, a switch had been flicked, and we now had more to say to each other than I'd ever thought possible, only to arrive on my doorstep and stand about awkwardly.

Our words had up and vanished. Instead, we took turns glancing around the street, at grass that glowed like neon under headlights, and moths that swam about street lights.

'I'm, ah, going to go inside.' I pointed back towards the apartment, which was currently sitting in darkness. I wondered if Penny was home at all.

'Eleanor, I have enjoyed every minute of tonight.' Marcus scratched at the back of his neck.

'Me, too.' I shifted my weight to my other foot, and the movement tripped the security light on the porch.

Marcus rocked gently on his feet. 'I could always offer you a nightcap? We could go back to mine and ...'

'I would.' I smirked. 'But, it's a school night.'

'Oh my God, you just went there. You used that excuse.'

'It's my Draw Four card,' I sniggered.

'All right, all right. I'm going home.'

'Thank you for tonight,' I said. 'I enjoyed skipping out of the bookshop for you.'

'And I enjoyed encouraging you.'

Watching as he stepped backwards down the street and into the night, I felt flat. Defeated wasn't the word, because there had been nothing taken from me, but there was something missing. How did I know? The moment he turned around, it was unmistakable quiver in my stomach that propelled me forward, down the road and after him.

Was I a loud lumbering mess? I had no idea. I could feel and think of nothing other than what I wanted to do right here and now, and I was going to do it before I lost the nerve. Reaching him, I tugged at his hand, turned him to face me, and kissed him. Hesitation gave way to the relaxed touch of his hands slipping to rest on my hips, where they burned against the cold night air. He tasted of warm cinnamon and coffee, and everything I wanted more of.

Marcus broke first. 'Wow.'

'Sorry, I just got sick of waiting.'

'I wasn't sure.' He shook his head. 'I didn't know … you were in, you were out … I couldn't tell if that was what you wanted.'

I nodded and kissed him again.

'I did tell you I was a late bloomer.' His smile was soft and warm, and he kissed me again before disappearing into the night. Again.

Chapter 23

Avalon Airport was a tin shed, blink and you'll miss it single-runway complex between Melbourne and Geelong. As I approached it, crossing a narrow bridge over the freeway, I was greeted with the wheaten hues of what was once an old cattle farm.

Even though it felt like I'd spent weeks waiting for today to arrive, the last few days had scrolled past in a blur of heightened colours, stolen kisses, lunch dates, and late-night texts. It was exactly my luck that, having finally put the wheels in motion with Marcus, he would be busy the rest of the week. If he wasn't working with his extra classes, he'd agreed to help Patrick with after-hours work just to clear up a backlog.

That left me with little more than a handful of photos taken inside a shed somewhere, face masks and safety gear on. We talked the subject of Mum's visit to death. Over again, Marcus assured me everything was going to be fine, the lead-up was always so much worse than the event, it was just that I was anxious and, like always, wanted to make a good impression. Those text messages seemed to be the only things keeping me sane right now. Sort of.

My brain was scrambled, so much so that I returned to my car twice just to check I'd locked it. Once through security and inside the terminal, I made my way to the gate, grabbed a coffee and chocolate bar, thumbed through books in the newsagent, and stood about checking the flight tracker on my phone. The plane hadn't moved. My foot tapped in time with a beat only it could hear. I wished it would stop.

A Melbourne to Sydney flight was an hour on a good day, and I'd arrived about ten minutes after the scheduled departure time. Call it nerves, call it excitement, call it Eleanor hates being late for anything. Whatever the reason, I was there. When the arrivals board read *Delayed*, I popped to the loos, scrolled social media, and availed myself of a sandwich and bag of crisps.

The worst part about waiting for someone was the uninhibited time left to think. At the top of my mind this morning was our date earlier in the week. A butterfly cage had been well and truly unleashed in my stomach, and each thought made my stomach jump excitedly, my heart twist, thrilled by the prospect of what awaited at the end of those kisses.

Barging their way into my headspace were thoughts of my mother. I was cautiously optimistic that she'd arrive, even if I had been in this situation a handful of times before, even if she'd never booked her flights to begin with. Things had been going so well lately, with my job, the house move, with Marcus, that today would have been the perfect culmination of all these great things. I checked my inbox to be sure I hadn't simply imagined seeing her boarding pass.

It was still there in all its orange and white glory with big black letters.

I took a shaky breath and checked the arrivals screen again; thirty minutes to go. People began milling about, each of them awaiting their *Love, Actually* moment, and all I could do was stare at my phone screen. Five minutes before the plane was due, I bought two fresh coffees and biscuits. What better way to bond than over a hot drink and food? When the plane finally landed, time slowed to a crawl and my heart took its place at the Royal Edinburgh Military Tattoo.

Flight attendants checked the gate, opened the doors, and drew walkie-talkies to their mouths with muttered instructions. The influx began slowly, a businesswoman here, a mother wrangling her child there, a family of four, and then the teeming bell curve of the crowd. I peered up, over, and around hats and hairdos, waiting for the telltale blonde bob to appear. When the crowd began to thin again, leaving one last wheelchair bound passenger being helped through the door, the crushing realisation began seeping in.

My foot stopped tapping and a new weight fell on my shoulders.

She wasn't here. She hadn't got on the plane. Again.

I was ten years old again, only this time I wasn't waiting in a Melbourne park for birthday cake. My memory of that day was still etched vividly; the helium balloons tied around my wrist and party hat on, only to be told hours later that the plane was 'broken'. A few scurrying minutes later, the airport gate was empty again and the doors drawn shut and I stood there, still clutching two coffees. I swallowed down a lump and looked for the nearest exit in a room that was fast closing in on me.

How are you supposed to react when you feel both let down and completely bloody stupid for believing something might have worked out differently? There was only so much I could steel myself against in preparation for these moments. Every time I thought something was going to change, that she was going to show up and make an effort, I was left sitting alone in an airport car park. I'd come so close, only to be pushed away again. The only thing I had to be grateful for right now was that at least it was Avalon, and not Tullamarine, another hour up the freeway. There is a silver lining in everything, after all.

For a few confused moments, I sat in my car trying to work out what to do. There was nothing to do but go home. With coffees in cup holders, my phone connected to the charger, and parking ticket between my teeth, I turned the ignition over began the drive home. Guilt trickled in to slowly erode my anger. What if something had gone wrong? I couldn't be angry about that, could I? By the time I was halfway home, I pulled over on a turnout to call her.

Under the dappled light that filtered through the canopy of ferns and tall trees, I listened as the phone rang out. I tried again, with the same result. I sent a text message. As expected, there was no answer. For a moment, I contemplated making another call and, as I unlocked my phone again, it rang. Shocked, I dropped it in the footwell and knocked over an empty coffee cup. I yanked my seatbelt off and grabbed about the floor for it.

'Mum?' I'd answered in such a rush that I hadn't seen the number.

'Oh no.' It was Marcus. He groaned and cursed under his breath. 'Really?'

So far, I'd managed to keep the tears at bay. I'd been too exhausted, too confused, too … everything. I hadn't slept well last night, tossing and turning and cycling through what might happen. It was one hell of a build-up, only to be dropped from a great height. But now, in the privacy of my car, my lip trembled, eyes blurred, and my throat tightened.

'Hello.' I tried for upbeat Ellie, but think I overshot the mark. 'How are you?'

'She didn't show, did she?' he asked.

'That would be a big fat no.' I wiped at my eyes.

'Are you okay?'

'I think so?' I squeaked. 'I don't know. It's not as if it's the first time she's done this. It's so bloody ridiculous. I should have expected this. Tell me I should have expected this.'

'No, you shouldn't have expected this. You should have expected her to be an adult and keep her promise.' He stopped. 'Where are you? You're not driving, are you?'

A log truck hurled past at an unsafe speed, my car rattling in the downwind force. Its tail-lights disappeared in a cloud of burs as it wound around the gully, never to be seen again.

'I'm currently in the national forest, somewhere between Winchelsea and home, hoping like hell I don't get crushed by a log truck.' I watched another car go past. 'But, no, I'm not driving.

Not right now, anyway. I've pulled into a turnout.'

'If it's not them, it'll be grey nomads in their caravans holding everyone up like a conga line.'

I scoffed. 'I know.'

'Look, you probably want to get home, so I'll let you go. Do you want me to let you go? Or do you want to talk some more?'

'I'm going to get going, head home.'

'Can I call you later?' he asked.

'I'd like that.'

'All right. I'll give you a bit of time to get home, settle down, and then I'll check in,' he said. 'Drive carefully, okay?'

'Yes, Dad.'

'Nah, not into the Daddy kink, sorry,' he teased. 'Talk soon.'

Forty minutes after his phone call, and now swinging somewhere between a longing ache and raging anger, I pulled up in my driveway. With Penny away at a hen's weekend, all I had planned now was an afternoon in my pyjamas with a whole lot of comfort movies, and probably food, too. I tossed the empty coffee cups in the recycling bin and thumped my way up the stairs. Busy digging about in my handbag, I completely missed Marcus sitting on the top step, picnic basket at the ready.

I clutched at the bannister and tripped over laughing. 'Oh, shit, you scared me.'

'I'm not *that* ugly.' He feigned disgust. 'Please.'

'You're right, how awful of me.'

'You okay?' He tilted his head towards me as I stepped past him and unlocked the front door.

I shook my head. 'You want to come in?'

'Yes, yes I do.' He climbed to his feet.

I dithered about in silence for a few minutes, dumping my handbag inside my bedroom door, opening the sliding door for a kick of fresh air, and boiling the kettle. The whole time, Marcus stood patiently by the bench, arms wrapped around his wicker basket.

'What's in the basket?' I placed two mugs on the bench.

'Remember I said to you that you had no idea what a picnic was?'

I smiled as I measured out coffee into each mug. 'I might.'

'Well, I thought today was as good a day as any to have a picnic. We could go down to the beach, roll out a blanket, and feast.' He lifted the lid. 'We've got coronation chicken sandwiches, passion fruit macaroons, crisps in the event that's all too fancy for you, homemade hummus.'

'Is it homemade because you made it?'

He gave his head a quick shake. 'The pizza shop did.'

'Cheese?' I picked up half a wheel of Brie.

'There's cheese, crackers, dips and, the pièce de résistance, a lemon myrtle and poppy-seed cake from Lucy Williams.'

'You ... a Lucy Williams?'

Everyone knew both how pricey a Lucy Williams cake was. Also, the café she ran with her husband, celebrity chef Oliver Murray, was ninety minutes away, so Marcus must've been made of magic to have picked one up between our phone call and now. I peered into the basket to find the barely iced beauty in its cardboard box.

'How?' I looked up at Marcus.

'Patrick is pretty much her best friend.' He stopped. 'Or she's his. Either way.'

'Patrick?' I said, surprised. 'And Lucy?'

'They've known each other since they were teenagers. I've done a bit of work for Patrick at their café, so ...'

'My, you do get around,' I teased.

'So, what do you say?' Marcus waved his hands like a game show compere. 'Shall I spirit you away to the tropical sands of the local beach?'

'Would you be offended if I said I didn't feel up to going out today?' I asked. 'I think I'm just going to put my pyjamas on and watch a movie.'

'I am one hundred per cent behind that theory.'

'You sure?'

'Of course I'm sure. Honestly, I just wanted to make sure you were okay. I know today was a big deal for you, so staying in is perfectly okay if that's what you need.'

'Thank you.' I leaned over the counter and kissed him.

I'd have moved away if he hadn't pulled me into him, wrapping his arms tightly around my shoulders. He was pure warmth, his heart thudding lightly in his chest. Closing my eyes, breathing him in, I sank into him and just waited for the moment to pass. I wasn't sure I wanted it to.

'I'm going to get changed.' I mumbled into his wool jumper. 'Something a little less formal.'

Marcus smoothed a hand over my head and pressed a kiss against my hair. 'Need a hand?'

'No.' I walk away, closing the bedroom door behind me.

'Just being polite and offering,' he added.

Wrapping myself up in a blanket, I shuffled over to the couch, offloading control of the remote. I promised myself I was going to watch a little television, raid the picnic basket and enjoy my company. How could I not? It was such a juxtaposition to have one person who should be there not show up and, yet, another who didn't owe me a thing show up without so much as a request. My resolve to stay awake lasted until I decided to use Marcus for a couch, resting my head on his leg, snuggling in to the rear of the couch. I was out cold.

I woke when Marcus tried to shuffle off to the bathroom carefully. He was never going to succeed, but I loved that he at least tried with gentle hands and soft movements. When he returned, he placed the picnic basket on the floor by the coffee table and sat back down. I reclaimed my place on his leg.

'You look funny from this angle.' I reached up, poking and prodding at his face.

Cupping a hand over my cheek, he said, 'Newsflash, I look funny from every angle.'

Smiling, I pinched the end of his nose. 'I don't believe it.'

'This is a common occurrence, isn't it?'

'Very.' I checked myself. 'Well, only as common as every time I'm expecting her. It's not an every weekend thing.'

'I feel like I should say something, and I don't want you to take this the wrong way, but I need to ask you something.'

'Go for it.'

'Why do you let her do it?'

'I don't let her do it.' A disbelieving laugh bubbled to the surface as I sat up. 'You think I want her to do this?'

'No, no, no.' His shoulders sank. 'Sorry, I didn't mean it as if to say you encourage it. I just mean that you give her the opportunity to hurt you. You agree to her coming down even though, deep down, you know she won't turn up.'

'You're saying I should tell her not to bother?' I said.

'Well, I mean, she keeps hurting you, doesn't she? This hurts. And please don't say it doesn't, because I can see it all over your face.' He drew his fingers through my hair. 'You walked in here and the first thing you did was nap. It's mentally exhausting.'

I pressed my lips into a thin line and took a breath. 'I've spent the last twenty-five years trying to work out why she doesn't want me.'

'I can't answer that for you, I wish I could, but I just think that this is toxic behaviour. Actually, I don't want to say toxic, because I don't know, but it pulls you in and spits you out just as quickly. Why agree to her requests? Why give her the chance to hurt you?'

'I deserve better.'

'Absolutely you do.' Marcus shifted, almost cocooning me between him and the sofa. 'If it were me, and she were to call again, I wouldn't engage. No, you can't visit, don't tell me you're coming if you're only planning on not showing. It's childish and ridiculous, and I can't wrap my head around why she does this. It makes no sense.'

'I just want her to engage with me as an adult. Isn't that what mothers are supposed to do?'

'Have you discussed this with her?' he asked. 'I know my mum gets a little funny if I try and bring stuff up, but she eventually comes around.'

I had tried, a few times, more so in the last few years, but I could never get a straight answer. There was always an excuse for cancelled flights, from her husband's work or other commitments she'd forgot about, but she would never address the problem directly. It was as if she were scared to put something out into the world. Whatever her reason, I was no wiser. The one time I pushed, she shouted and hung up the phone.

Like every other time this happened, I didn't want to spend a lot of time dwelling on it either. It was a recipe for doom and gloom and, well, I didn't want to. I wanted to enjoy that fact that, instead, I was here with Marcus. After all, I'd spent all week looking forward to some alone time with him. I leaned forward and peered into the basket. So. Much. Tasty. Food.

'Tell me something,' Marcus said.

'Sure.'

'What did you have planned today? Were you going to do something special or were you going to sit around here all day?' he asked.

'Well, I had bought tickets for the P-12 College school play.'

'Which is?'

I smiled.

'Please don't say *Cats*.'

I meowed.

* * *

That was how we found ourselves sitting in the middle of a darkened school theatre watching a play I was sure both of us had seen more than once before. We'd gobbled down the contents of the picnic basket as an early dinner, though the cake had escaped under the pretence of dessert later tonight.

A perfectly wonderful buzz filled stalls before performances, it was a nervous energy for both the audience and performers, and for entirely different reasons. Once upon a time, it was something I'd done regularly. I'd put on a nice dress, collect our front row tickets and a glass of bubbly, and wait for the stalls to open. Tonight was more relaxed. I didn't feel like I was under any obligation to be here.

'Will this give you flashbacks?' I leaned into Marcus as he placed his coat across my knees.

'It is entirely possible.' He kissed my cheek. 'I'll just have to hang on to you for good luck.'

A slippery jolt ran through me as his fingers grazed the top of my knee. I wasn't sure if the goose bumps that raced along my arms were from the air conditioners, or him. Who am I kidding? It was definitely him. Squeezing gently, he looked to me for approval as he let go and slipped his hand under the hem of my dress and up the length of my thigh. White hot electricity chased the fingerprints I was sure he was leaving, through my core, and tugged at the base of my belly in an almost silent room.

'You can't do that now.' I brushed his hand away and tried to stifle a laugh.

'Why not?'

'We've got hours of this to get through before you can do anything about that,' I whispered.

'Is that so?'

'That is so.'

'We could leave now?' In the darkened room, seconds before the stage lights burned to life, I saw him crook an eyebrow.

'This was your idea.'

'And so is this.' He kissed me again.

'You do realise my place is closer?'

'Oh, I know.' I smiled.

* * *

Where I'd expected to find a body beside me the next morning, I found nothing more than a warm shadow and ruffled sheets. I was alone. The only consolation to that being the knowledge that there'd be little chance Marcus had bolted from his own home.

We'd all but run home from the theatre, taking a short cut through an empty block of land and knee-high grass to tumble through the front door and up the staircase, just as we had the first time I'd gone home with him. But that was where the similarities ended.

The first time we'd slept together had been crude and frantic. We were in such a rush to get to the result that we hadn't thought to pad out the middle and enjoy ourselves. This time, as he moved above me, he did so slowly and with care. We touched, explored, and revelled in the feel of each other's skin, fingers intertwined, and mumbled nuances of instruction to each other. More than anything, we laughed.

It was that same laughter that dragged me from my thoughts to the activity happening downstairs. A dog's too long toenails scratched excitedly across floor tiles as the front door opened.

'What on earth are you dancing about?' Marcus asked Daisy through laughter. 'Where's Ellie?'

Daisy, who'd slept downstairs all night, appeared at the bedroom door first. Marcus, dressed down in tracksuit pants and an old T-shirt, appeared next, a weighted plastic bag in one hand, a tray of coffee in the other.

'I didn't have anything much in the cupboards, so I thought I'd just grab a few things from the bakery.' He held up a plastic shopping bag.

I sat up, pulling the duvet around me. 'A few things?'

He shrugged. 'I wasn't sure what to get, really.'

It was a lazy morning in the Blair household. We set ourselves up outside on the rear deck. Kicking back under the warmth of the sun, I'd found myself some drawstring shorts and an old T-shirt to wear. With breakfast, a seemingly never-ending coffee, and Marcus by my side, it felt like my troubles were all but distant memories. For today at least, but I hoped that it would last longer.

Chapter 24

'Okay, so what have we got?' Phil took the coffee offered from Marcus and pulled up a chair at Roger's desk.

'So, firstly, the yearbook should be delivered by the end of this week,' Marcus said. 'Eleanor finished that last Wednesday night. I sent it off for printing first thing Thursday. Yes, that sounds about right.'

'That's right.' I turned from where I was sat at his desk, scrolling through emails from suppliers. 'You were working with Patrick, so I finished it off.'

Phil wrinkled his nose like a sour odour had wafted into the room. 'Things are going well then, I take it?'

They were. Well, if he were referring to what was happening behind closed doors. After breakfast yesterday, we'd retreated to spend a large chunk of Sunday in bed, not caring for anything else. We emerged to eat and shower, and that was about as far as we got. But he wasn't, and if we thought we were going to float away on a sexual cloud of strewn seats and torn foil, we were sorely mistaken. It was Monday, we were back at work, and reality was ready to bite.

The three of us had met early Monday morning in Marcus's office to discuss where we were. Up until that moment, things had been going well. I opened the newest email, caught sight of the first two sentences, and groaned in annoyance.

'And that's the screen printers out,' I said. 'They can't print our backdrop, have refunded our money, and that's the end of that.'

Marcus hovered over the back of my seat. 'I'll look for someone else at lunch.'

I craned my neck to peer back at him. 'My first class isn't in this morning. I'll do it.'

'Are you sure?' he asked.

Whether I was sure or not, we didn't have many options, as Google would tell me later that morning. Our next best hope told us they possibly couldn't deliver the item in time, but we were welcome to pick up from their warehouse in Ballarat, which was only a five-hour round trip away and one that I'd have to do in business hours. I blew a raspberry at the screen as I read those words, then told them I would do it anyway.

There, that problem was solved.

That was, until Wednesday, when our caterer decided they wouldn't be able to supply food on the night. A family emergency, they explained, and they'd be one baker short for the next fortnight. It would leave them barely enough staff to cover the shop, and certainly not enough to help us.

I stepped out of the café feeling like Murphy's law was sprinkling his luck across our week, perhaps even hoping to become a theme. It felt like nothing was going right and, as we walked back towards the school, Marcus was silent beside me, his fingers jabbing at the screen of his phone.

'Oliver Murray,' I blurted.

'What about him?' he asked.

'You know him,' I said. 'You can ask him to cater. Or Lucy, at least.'

'I can't ask him that,' Marcus exclaimed. 'That guy has got so much going on besides our silly little night.'

'It's not silly and it's not little,' I argued. 'It's important.'

'I'm sorry.' Marcus sighed. 'I know it's important, but I really don't think that he would agree.'

'Have you asked him?' I urged. 'Have you rung and asked him?'

'We just walked out of there.' He threw his arm back towards the café. 'So, no, I haven't.'

'Are you going to ring him?'

'No, no I'm not. I hardly know him. I've barely got a good morning from him while I was hanging off scaffolding outside his restaurant, so I can't just call and ask him to do something cut-price out of the goodness of his heart. He's out of our league, Eleanor.'

'Only because you won't try,' I snapped. 'Give me his number.'

'I don't have his number.'

'Then ask Patrick.' I stood on the spot. 'I'll ask Patrick.'

'I'm not asking Patrick for his number, and neither are you.'

'No?' I asked.

'No.' Marcus shook his head defiantly. 'There'll be somewhere else around here that can do it.'

'You know, you drive me insane,' I blurted, turning on my heel and continuing the walk back to the school. I passed another café, and a table full of school mums who sat silent throughout. No doubt we'd just handed them the news headlines of the day.

'I do, do I?' He followed me. 'Well, let me tell you a thing …'

'No, you're not telling me a thing, because I'm going back to work.'

'Eleanor.'

I looked over my shoulder at him. 'No-anor.'

'Honestly,' he grumbled. 'You're impossible.'

'I'm not being impossible, Marcus, I just want things to go right.'

'You're right, I know,' he said. 'Look, we've got the yearbooks arriving tomorrow. Surely they'll be fine.'

* * *

Our yearbooks arrived on Thursday afternoon in the middle of a class. They were wheeled in unceremoniously on a trolley cart by a delivery girl in shorts, tattered boots and a fluorescent shirt. Neatly packaged and screaming for attention, the most I could do with a library full of students was sign for them and hope everything was okay.

At the end of the day, I closed the office door and drew the blinds. I wanted to see that they were all in order before I went showing them off to anybody else, including Marcus. Over on the other desk, all the things that had gone right this week. There were gift bags, mugs, book vouchers from Thatcher's, and a box full of cards that were almost ready to go into the bags. I cut at the adhesive with a knife and opened the box.

The smell of fresh print wafted from the box as I pulled out the first of the books. Glossy and colourful and everything they should be, I pored through the contents, looked at the photos of students and their mini-profiles. I recognised most of them and loved that their young voices shone through their words. I feel like we'd captured them perfectly.

The photos from school camps and excursions were big and bold. Tiny anecdotes and swathes of creative writing sat beside lists of favourite books made me feel like maybe I'd had an impact, however small, in the time I'd spent in the classroom with them. They were so beautifully put together.

I shifted as the edge of the desk dug into my hip, and flipped through to the back, to the final few pages, dedicated blank spaces for everyone to sign. There was a page set aside to highlight the organisers and our inspiration for the night.

'We hope you enjoy our Oscar's theme tonight. Put together by Marcus Blair, we wanted to ...' my voice drifted off, disappearing into a disbelieving ether.

I had to read the same sentence half a dozen times before it sank in. When it did, it hit me like, well, like a book in the face. I'd been all but erased from the night. All my work, my effort, all of it credited to someone else. It smacked of everything I'd walked away from in the past, and everything I promised myself I'd stay away from as I rebuilt my life. My heart squeezed and my throat became tight. Then came the anger. I picked up a box of the books and walked it down to Marcus's office.

'Hey, Eleanor.' Mick glanced across as me as I walked in the room.

'Hey, you.' I offered a contrived smile. 'Gentlemen, can I please have Marcus to myself for a few minutes?'

Tony snorted, Roger gave him a playful tap on the shoulder, and Mick shuffled out quietly with a questioning look. With his glasses on, tie off, and top two shirt buttons undone, Marcus looked well on his way to winding down for the night. Everything in his world was seemingly going right.

I rolled Roger's chair across the floor and sat near him. 'What are you up to?'

'Just starting to compile end-of-year reports.' He rubbed his eye, then cursed the new fingerprint smeared across the lens of his glasses. 'What's going on with you?'

I held the box aloft. 'The yearbooks.'

'Oh! Exciting.' He reached for the box. 'How are you, anyway?'

I was not going to cry. I wasn't. I bit the inside of my cheek and swallowed down a lump. This was not the place for tears, I reminded myself. All I needed to do was impart my thoughts and leave. I was an adult. I could do this. I'd been through worse. This was a mosquito bite, not a sword's gash.

'Eleanor?' He looked at me briefly. 'You okay?'

I nodded. 'Just keep reading.'

'It's come up well, don't you think?'

'Sure.'

'Sure? What's that supposed to mean?' He flicked through the rest of the book quickly. As his eyes settled on the last page, his frown began deepening. When the realisation hit, his shoulders slumped as he rubbed his mouth. 'Shit.'

'Do you remember the other night when you asked me why I was so slow to date you?'

He let out a long, slow groan. 'Don't make that correlation, Eleanor.'

'But this smacks of someone who is all about the spotlight being on them. They're so busy trying to gather their kudos, to keep their fan club happy, that everyone else pales in comparison.' I stabbed a finger at the page. 'Organised by Marcus ... no word of anyone else who had anything to do with it.'

'You know that's not true,' he said, shoulders sinking lower with each word.

'But it is true. It's there in black and white, and it's been there since the moment I walked into this school,' I said. 'And it's not even about the accolades or the spotlight. I don't want to be singled out as the most amazing person ever, because I'm not. It's about the simple acknowledgement of me as a woman, as a human being who has contributed something.'

'I don't know what to say.'

'I spent years in someone else's shadow, bending and twisting and being forgotten, and I always hoped that, in the end, it would be okay, that someone would notice me, that he would turn around and realise I was worthy of the spotlight occasionally. But it became all about him, about the sycophants he surrounded himself with, about the women, about how beautiful he apparently was. This feels no different,' I squeaked. 'And it hurts because I should have seen it coming but didn't.' Standing, I pushed Mick's chair back across the room. Outside the office, our colleagues were waiting to re-enter the room. 'And I can't even get five minutes of peace to put my own case forward, because people are constantly leering at us.'

Marcus looked out at the boys, then back to me. 'Can you just ... no ... this isn't right.'

I wiped my eyes. 'No, it's not. But it's all yours now. You want the fanfare, then it's all yours, but please don't ask me for anything more.'

'Eleanor, wait, please.' He reached for me as I made to leave. 'Let's just sit down and let me work out what's happened, because you should be in here. You should. I swear I put you in there.'

'I want to make it clear that I think you are an amazing teacher and I have seen you do the greatest things, but I can't continue to mould myself or stand in anyone's shadow. I deserve to be seen.'

'Absolutely, I agree.' He leapt from his chair. 'Eleanor, come on, this has to be a mistake. I can fix this.'

'It is a mistake.' I yanked the door open with just a smidge more anger than I'd anticipated. 'I'm just not sure whose.'

Chapter 25

The fallout was more in line with an EMP bomb than a nuclear weapon. There were no big screaming matches, no overly wrought declarations, and no death and destruction. It was eerily quiet. I said what I had needed to, and I walked away. I was at least proud that it hadn't devolved into some tear stained, torn-shirt epitaph. What I had was something more like embarrassed sadness.

After the silence came the static. An energy that buzzed its way through a narrow field of view but began to underline actions. It was Mick coming to check on me the next morning under the pretence of a simple question, only to end up asking if I was okay and could he do anything to help. It was Roger bringing me cake after recess to tell me what a good job I'd done, and that he was proud of me for standing up for myself.

It was the heads that tipped into each other with salacious gossip when I entered the staffroom at lunch. I hoped I was simply imagining it, but I couldn't be sure. Either way, it was enough to send me in search of a quiet café to eat in.

Penny, who'd spent last night in a rage over my love life, called as I sat in a café in the main street. With an empty first period after lunch, I took the opportunity to sneak off school grounds and enjoy some time alone. It was refreshing to be amongstst the clutter, to listen to the mundane din of everyday life that kept the two elderly ladies beside me cackling with delight.

I was reluctant to answer but did anyway.

'Hey, you,' she chirped.

'Hello.' I hunched over my plate. 'What's happening?'

'Not much, are you around?' she asked. 'I want to tell you

something.'

'I'm off site,' I said. 'Just grabbing lunch in peace.'

'Oh, right,' she said. 'Well, I have a bit of gossip.'

I shielded my eyes and pinched at the bridge of my nose. I was certain I didn't want to hear this. 'All right.'

'There's a blazing row happening in Phil's office right now.'

I concentrated on the salad in front of me, on the tiny green chunks of broccoli, the blood-red cranberries, the whites of the almonds, and the burned onion sauce I wiped from the side of my mouth. Penny's words rattled around inside my head like bitter lemon, and the realisation alone made me want to both laugh and cry at the situation. This wasn't how it was meant to be.

'Look, I really don't want to know,' I grumbled. 'Let's just get on with things, hmm?'

'I mean, I say blazing, but there's only Phil and Marcus in there, and I haven't heard a peep from Marcus.'

'Penny, stop. This is so wrong,' I blurted. 'Whatever has happened, or is happening, please don't make him a spectacle. It's not right.'

'I just thought you'd want to know, that's all.'

'No, I don't want to know,' I bit. 'I'm fed up. I'm exhausted. I don't want to hear about it. And singling him out isn't fun, and it sure as shit isn't entertainment. It hurts. This is not a nice situation to be in right now. Try and think about how other people are feeling. Please?'

'Right.' Penny cleared her throat. 'Well, you have a good afternoon.'

'We'll get dinner tonight and talk about it,' I suggested. 'But I have to deal with him shortly, and I don't want … you know.'

'Yeah, I know.' She heaved a sigh. 'I'm sorry.'

'I'll see you after work. We'll go straight to the pizza place from there and grab an early dinner.'

All it took was the sight of Gemma and Jemima walking

through the café door, and I was ready to leave. They didn't outwardly say anything; they didn't have to. It was the shared look, the heads dipped towards each other so that nobody else could hear their conversation. I got the rest of my lunch to go. As much as I'd hoped for some time alone, maybe the best place for that was my office.

But, like most things this week, I was wrong about that, too. When I arrived, Phil was inspecting the diary I kept by my PC.

'Can I help you?' I asked. Sure, there was nothing more than work-related scribble in the book, but it still felt a tad invasive to have him reading it.

'Firstly, I need you to know that I'm not here to side with anyone. My priority is the school, and to see that everything is done appropriately.'

'It's fine, Phil.' I flicked through my class notes until I came upon this week's lesson plan. 'Please.'

'I guess I just wanted to check that what's happening won't have a knock-on effect with the project?'

I shook my head. 'No, everything is set to go.' I gestured to the piles of goodies in the corner that were merely waiting to be put into gift bags. 'All we need is for the night to get here. The rest is fine.'

'I don't need a buffer?'

'No,' I said, more than a little hurt at the insinuation. 'We are all adults here, aren't we?'

'Good to know.' Phil dug into one of the three spare boxes of yearbooks. 'I spoke to him about this mess at lunch.'

'I know you did.'

He snorted. 'Gee, I wonder who passed that on.'

'I told her I didn't want to hear it. It's bad enough without people adding their opinions to it all.'

'He's going to speak to you this afternoon about it.' Phil leaned back against a shelving unit. 'I guess I'm just concerned that this is going to fall apart now, the whole thing will be a mess because you won't be able to complete the job.'

'Excuse me?' I stood ramrod straight, my attention momentarily drawn outside my office. Marcus had arrived with his class. 'None of this is my doing, and I won't deny that I am upset about all of this, but now *my* work ethic is being questioned? I didn't do this, he did.' I pointed to Marcus. 'He removed my name, he did. So, why isn't he being questioned about whether he can do his job? I thought you said you weren't taking sides?'

'I can assure you—'

'Don't assure me,' I said, shaking my head with derisive laughter. 'Just let me do my job, Phil. You've got nothing to worry about.'

I yanked on the office door and stepped out into the library. 'Marcus.' I smiled. 'How are you this afternoon?'

He bumbled around for a moment before swallowing hard. 'Good, thank you, Miss Manning. Just dropping my class off for their lesson.'

'Excellent, thank you.' I ushered them all in and to their seats.

'Do you think we might … have you got five minutes?'

'Not right now,' I said. 'But after class today, absolutely yes.' I turned to Phil and grinned. He pushed off the shelving unit and left the office with a barely noticeable shake of the head.

* * *

Entertaining Marcus's class that afternoon was an exercise in self-control, and not because there was anything wrong with the kids. As Phil left, we spoke briefly, in clipped sentences and tones harsher than we were used to. Combine that with restless students approaching both the end of the day and the year, and I was grateful to see the back of them as the final bell rang.

Determined to not stay any later than I had to, I tossed my own homework in my bag and raced out towards the front gate. The sooner I got away from today, the better. Tomorrow would be a better time to talk to Marcus. It was the weekend, I would have had the night to calm down, and we could probably work it out with coffee. If only he hadn't had other ideas.

'Eleanor, wait.' He scurried up behind me, clambering for my hand. 'Stop.'

I turned to face him. He looked exhausted, and I wondered how he'd become a stranger so quickly; literally overnight.

'How are you?' he asked. 'Are you okay?'

I nodded, scared that if I opened my mouth, I might let it all out and completely set fire to anything that might have been salvageable.

This was the type of discussion I hated; the clipped words, the stilted sentences and awkward looks off into the distance while we feigned the notion that we had some idea what we were doing. It felt altogether unfamiliar after the last few weeks. As he reached for my hand again, all I could think of was a recent night at the beach, my fingers threaded through his as we danced in icy shallow waters like ... idiots. We were idiots. Moreover, I was the idiot.

My handbag slipped and I hoisted it higher. 'I'm fine.'

'Can I talk to you?' He closed his eyes for a moment, his head dipped in defeat. 'Actually, you know what? I *need* to talk to you.'

The telltale scuffle of Penny's walk approaching from behind. It was a one-two shuffle of quick feet through the gravel. There was nothing wrong with her gait, it's just how she was, but it gave her away. Her mum was always telling her off for wearing out the soles of her shoes.

'I'm just going to go to the pizza shop and get us a table.' She flattened her hands against Marcus's ears.

'It's okay, I won't follow,' he said. 'I just want to explain to Eleanor what's happened, and then I'll go away.'

Penny left, uncharacteristically quietly, but I was grateful for the lack of scene she could have otherwise made. We watched and waited, wanting to be sure she was out of earshot.

'I guess, firstly, I am sorry. I know that, on the surface, this looks bad.' He paused. 'In fact, it looks really bad, but I've spent hours trying to work out what happened.'

'And did you?' I asked.

'I did.'

'And?'

'You know when you're working on a document and the file name is like final, second final, very final, final, the end dot doc, do not add to this anymore? Well, I had a file named final one and final two. When I uploaded, I clicked the wrong file, so the wrong file was printed. The one you finished off was sent to the printer last night. It was an honest, stupid mistake, and I'm so sorry you think I don't value you, because I do, but what's done is done.'

'Thank you.'

'So, what, that's it? Thank you?' he asked.

'What would you rather?' I asked.

'Don't you think we should talk about us and sort out what's really going on?'

'Sort what out?' I asked. 'Didn't you just explain what had happened?'

'Well, yes, but us. I want to see if we can salvage something from us, from you and me.'

'Marcus, I adore you, but I'm not entirely sure we can,' I said. 'I think this week has proven why this isn't a good idea.'

'Come on, Eleanor,' he complained. 'It was a mistake.'

'How is this suddenly my fault? I told myself I didn't want to get involved with you because I knew something stupid like this would happen. I didn't want my life to be this all over again, a rolling series of being pushed into the background all over again. Coming here was supposed to be a new start and, one day, finding someone who is happy for me to stand beside them, not behind them. All of this? It's ridiculous. It's always been about you, about the great Marcus Blair. Marcus designed the night, Marcus cared so much he checked his work before submitting it. And, now,

Eleanor has the world coming down on her like she's the one who can't do her job.'

'Surely you know me better than that.'

'Do I?' I grumbled.

'All right then,' he grumbled. 'Whatever, right?'

Shaking my head, I turned and walked away. *I didn't mean it, it's not like me, I'm not like them, but I'll draw out 'whatever' when I want a reaction.* He didn't follow, nor did he call out, though I'd have been surprised if I could hear it over the tidal wave of blood rushing through my ears. I bit down on my lip and didn't stop until I reached Penny, who was waiting for me in the back corner of a pizza place.

She looked up from the menu as I slipped into the high-backed, sticky red booth. The gingham pattern was about as solid as food after a bender, and the table was sticky enough that one could possibly consider a Friday afternoon arm wax a special menu item.

'Wow, you look rabid.' She frowned her concern.

'I feel rabid.' I blew my cheeks out, all the while wondering if I had really done the right thing.

'I ordered drinks.'

'Great.' I grinned tightly.

'Want to talk?'

'Nope,' I said, giving my head a tight shake. 'All over talking about it. What's happening with you?'

For about the one hundredth time since I'd moved here, Penny started on about the barista at the café and how he'd spelled her name wrong. This morning, she'd been relegated to a Percy. She was so incensed she'd taken a photo of the offending cup. With my current state of mind, I couldn't help but laugh at the irony of it all.

'Have you ever thought of, I don't know, standing up for yourself?' I asked.

'What?'

'If it's so bloody offensive, say something. Stop sitting there going around in circles about, "Oh, I'm not Jenny, or Perry, Percy, or Jerry." You have the right to be seen, to be heard. Go and say something. I'm so sick of it.' I sighed heavily and tucked the menu behind the parmesan cheese. 'At least he knows you have a name.'

'You're sick of it?' she laughed. 'God, listen to yourself. You've got a man who is literally throwing himself at your feet. He is grovelling, Eleanor, and do you know what it's like to sit in that blasted staffroom and listen to women whinge about how awful you're being to him.'

'I have the right to be seen!' I argued, stabbing the table with a finger. 'That's why I'm in this situation right now, because I stood up for myself. I said, "This is not right." I'm not going through the same shit again as I went through with Dean. Not again.'

'Yes, yes you do. Nobody is arguing that. Nobody is saying that is wrong, but it was a mistake, and mistakes happen. To err is human. So, he uploaded the wrong file, so what? He fixed it. He has gone out of his way to pay for it himself, that's how much it means to him. He hasn't slept with anyone else; he hasn't murdered a baby; he has made a mistake.'

'And if it meant that much to him, he would have been more careful to begin with.'

'Yeah, and if he means so much to you that you're this upset by it all, you wouldn't be treating him the way your mother treats you.'

I cocked an angry brow. 'What did you just say?'

'You heard. You have this push me, pull me play going on with him. You draw him in, but don't get too close, because Eleanor can't possibly open herself up to new experiences. The first marriage went to shit therefore you've made the automatic assumption that every other relationship ever will.'

'That's rich, coming from someone who tosses men in the trash the minute she's done with them,' I scoffed. 'I'm surprised you don't make like a barn spider and eat their corpses when you're done.'

'You don't need to get all defensive. Or rude. Your mother does the same thing with you. She draws you in every time, she doesn't even have to promise you anything. All she has to do is allude to her coming to visit, and you're just about frothing. And we all have to sit around consoling you when she spits you out. You go back for more because you hope that, one day, it'll change, and she'll realise how amazing you are. Newsflash, it won't change, and that's her loss. She's been doing it forever. Everybody knows how many trips down here she cancelled when you were a kid. All the trips no one ever told you about. It's not even a secret anymore. But, Eleanor, you don't have to be like that, because God knows continually spitting *that* man out is not a good idea.'

My jaw dropped, and I flubbed about looking for a response. 'What do you mean all the trips she cancelled? I always went to her.'

'My point exactly.' Penny jabbed my forearm with a finger. 'Have you ever considered that maybe you're so bloody offended by all of this because you actually care so much about him? That all of this angst is because what you actually *want* is his approval? And, you're right, it might not be about the spotlight, but maybe it's about him acknowledging you as an equal, and someone he's impressed by? Someone he loves as much as you love him.'

I sat in silence, too stumped by her outburst to form anything coherent. I adored him, yes. I'd even said as much myself. But love? No, it was far too soon for anything like that, surely. As I sat there trying to weigh up either option, Penny drank the last of her coffee and produced a set of L-plates.

'Also, I think we should get out of town for the weekend.' She grinned. 'Skip the pizza.'

'Why?' I asked. 'Tonight? Now?'

'I think a bit of time away will help put things in perspective,' she explained. 'We're going to go home, you're going to pack an overnight bag for tonight and tomorrow, and we're going to spend some time in Melbourne.'

'We are?'

'Yes,' she said, matter-of-factly. 'And I'm driving.'

Chapter 26

'No, no, no, I can't do this.' Penny yanked on the handbrake and threw her seatbelt off.

'Can't do what?' I asked. 'It's a laneway. You'll be fine.'

'That's right, it's a laneway, look how tight it is!' she shrieked. 'The walls might come in on me. What if I take out the side of the car?'

'It's insured,' I said with a laugh. 'We'll get it repaired.'

'No, no, no, no, no.'

Before I knew what she was doing, Penny had abandoned the car, standing in front of a heavily graffitied brick wall. It would have been a proper social media worthy shot had she not been completely freaking out. The last five minutes of a four-hour road trip abandoned in an uncharacteristic show of nerves.

In fairness, the alley was exceedingly narrow, like a lot of Melbourne's backstreets, but she'd been so confident until now. I was sure she'd make it.

'It's all right.' I watched her clip up her seatbelt. 'You did amazingly.'

'I did?'

'Of course.'

It was a far cry from the Penny who'd stood over me while we hastily packed bags and ran out the door. The same girl who flirted madly with the concierge as we checked into a Collins Street hotel in the centre of Melbourne. Having not been back since I'd moved, it felt a little jarring, the twinkling lights of the city, the names in neon, and the unrelenting flow of traffic, both pedestrian and vehicular. What once was so familiar and common all felt a bit garish.

From the window of our room, I looked out on the street below. Orange street lights glistened from windows and wet bitumen and loved-up couples held each other up as they lumbered down the street towards warm restaurants.

The hotel itself was opulent but offbeat in a way that only Penny could be, and I congratulated her on an inspired choice. Chandeliers swung low towards the horizon of marble floors and our room, which was muted browns and beiges offset with red, had a clawfoot bath and chrome as far as the eye could see.

'Where to first?' I asked, turning from the window to find Penny asleep atop her bed.

It was just ticking over 10.30 in the evening, and there was no doubt the stress of driving had exhausted her, so bed sounded like the perfect place to be.

With nowhere else to be tonight, I took my time in the shower and, in the relative silence of the hotel en suite, mulled over the afternoon that had been. When Penny had first suggested heading to Melbourne, I'd been sceptical, but had hoped that a different environment would indeed help me think of something else.

It didn't. Taking the spare bed, I slipped under the covers and hoped for the best. I was still awake at two o'clock, back in the bathroom at three o'clock, and only just drifting off at four o'clock. It would have been a fair comment to say I was crabby when room service woke me up with breakfast the next morning.

'Sorry, you were flaked, and I just wanted to get you breakfast.' Penny offered me an apologetic look, and a slice of toast.

'It's fine, I promise.' I placed my hand over hers. 'Thank you.'

'What do you think we should do today?' she asked.

'I have no idea.' I slumped back in my chair.

'I couldn't find any concert tickets that we'd like, so I skipped that option.'

I yawned. 'No trouble. Let's just wander about the city, eat, drink, be merry.'

'Are you okay?' she asked.

Nodding, I bit down on my toast. 'I'm just tired. That, and I have a lot on my mind.'

'How do you feel about Marcus?'

Yes, he'd made a mistake. Yes, he'd apologised for it. But last night had become a lowlight reel of everything I'd experienced since I'd arrived at the school. The cloud of women who gathered around him at morning assembly, changing direction like a flock of birds if he so much as moved somewhere different. The phone numbers pressed into his palm, and the comments from Sally at our afternoon tea. She was supposed to be happily married, but would just as easily 'go there'?

And how was it that I was suddenly called into question over my work ethic? Had he been questioned at all? I felt like somehow the blame for whatever this was was all being pointed at me. I needed a distraction. Something to think about other than this. I wound myself in so many knots that, if I were hair, someone would just cut me off and throw me in the bin.

'I feel like I want something other than him to think about.' I grinned.

While I'd been asleep, Penny had been scrolling through all the things she wanted to do today. Using a notepad and pen she'd found on the bureau, there were restaurants, parks and contemporary art museums jotted into a list.

We were soon walking the streets of Melbourne, up past Carlton Gardens and into Lygon Street for an intense coffee and cake hit, boutique clothing stores, and a bookstore I'd always favoured when I'd lived here.

Rattling trams took us back into the centre of the city, to shopping centres and blinking theatres. We melded with crowds, in and out of alleyways, and crossing busy intersections. Lunch happened when we stumbled upon a crepe van in Federation Square and, when it came to what we were going to do tonight, a jazz club in Flinders Lane caught our attention.

Back at the hotel room, we plumped and preened and changed into new outfits. Until now, I'd avoided thinking about my problems. Maybe that wasn't the best idea ever, but it was nice to have a break. But, as I got changed, it made me think of how different my life was now.

The bright lights of the city had been swapped for the star-drenched sky of the coast. Nights out were now nights in, and loud parties were now a dog racing across a beach or winding herself between legs. I didn't miss having to get so dressed up to go out anywhere.

Stepping into the darkened club was like stepping into a new world. It was dark and smoky, brick walls, hidden alcoves, purple lights and ratty seats. In contrast, there were intimate booths and roped off areas, and tables in front of a stage that was currently occupied by a solo saxophonist.

Penny leaned into me. 'This is … different.'

'Drink?' I asked.

We were either early, or this club was incredibly unpopular. The bartender assured us the night would kick along closer to seven. He suggested we pick the best seat in the house, relax with a drink or two and enjoy the place before the chaos that late nights normally brought.

So, that's exactly what we did. We ordered share plates and more drinks, and enjoyed the music, which was presently Ella Fitzgerald. Eventually, we settled into a comfortable silence with each other. We'd spent all day talking, and it felt like the topics well had finally dried up.

Two men walked by in suits, each of them rather attractive. I couldn't quite catch their conversation but, judging by the suits and ties, there was every chance it would have been work related. Penny caught the eye of one and followed him up to the bar.

No sooner had she moved, and her seat was filled by the second man. He was tall and dark, possibly a Don Draper impersonator. He dropped his briefcase and coat by his feet and smiled at me.

'Hello.'

I grinned tightly. 'Hello.'

'I'm John.' He leaned over and offered his hand. 'How are you?'

'Fine.' I looked over his shoulder, making sure I could still focus on Penny. 'Thank you. Yourself?'

'Good. I just … I've been over at the bar for a while and noticed you. You're gorgeous. Can I buy you a drink?'

I held up my current drink. 'I'm good, thank you.'

'Do you mind if I get one for myself?'

'Go for it.'

When he returned, John launched into his elevator pitch. Early forties, lawyer, recently single. His girlfriend, who he adored for her fierce nature and crazy intellect, had moved home. Where was home for her? Geelong, which was an hour away, almost halfway between Melbourne and Apollo Bay. They'd broken up because the guy couldn't stump the hour drive to his girlfriend's new home.

'It's not so much the drive,' he explained when I questioned. 'My work hours are all over the place at the moment. She's just thrown herself headfirst into this big family project. Speaking of which, she was absolutely desperate for a family of her own, which I could never understand.'

'You couldn't?' I asked.

'I mean, of course I could, but I didn't want to be pegged down.'

'Is having a happy life and supportive family akin to being pegged down though?' I asked. 'Surely she was supportive of your job?'

'Far too forgiving of it, actually. Look, it was quite a casual affair if I have to be honest.'

'Honesty is a virtue.' I tipped my glass at him, sarcastic smile the best I could offer. 'Anyway, tell me about your job.'

'Oh.' He huffed heavily. 'Law. It's a busy game.'

'No doubt.' I caught the eye of the bartender. 'Criminal?'

'No. Civil.' He snorted. 'Much easier to get money out of businessmen than criminals. Plus, there's the ethical issue of whether I want to stand up in court and defend a murderer.'

Between the bartender bringing me a new drink and a text from Penny, I got the inside scoop on John's latest courtroom conquests. The hours he'd billed for the month, and how he was so efficient he was booked solid for the next twelve months. His boss loved him, of course, bringing in a heap of profit for the coffers.

He was exceedingly dull. Men in suits, huh? All of them different, none of them alike …

The music had picked up now, and the club was fast filling with weekend revellers. None of them looked like John, who was fresh from work, briefcase by his feet like an obedient hound.

'Sorry, what?'

John shook his head. 'I'm sorry. I'm talking too much about my job. What is it you do?'

I crossed my legs over at the knees. 'I guess the first thing you should know about me is that my name is Eleanor.'

His jaw dropped. 'Shit. I'm so sorry, I hadn't …'

'No, it's fine.' I waved a hand. 'And I'm a teacher.'

'What's that old saying?' He smiled gently.

Here it comes.

'If you can't do, teach?' he continued.

I didn't like this. I didn't even like John. Not that there was anything terribly wrong with him per se. Then again, I couldn't find many redeeming features, either. Silence scratched and spun out like a needle on a turntable, right at the moment a side of vinyl had finished. Pivoting in my seat, I turned my attention to the band, who were now playing Miles Davis.

This was all so completely backwards. Here was a man complaining about a girlfriend who'd moved home to fulfil a life's ambition. It would be exactly the response I'd get from Dean, too, if ever I'd tried that. Yet, when I drew out a few notes on a piano, I had Marcus right beside me. Not only was he championing me, he wanted to be part of it as well, wanted to learn.

Where other people had told me not to sweat my divorce, that things were going to be okay, he'd known they weren't quite the words everyone needed to hear. He'd been where I had and had the insight and clarity of distance that allowed him to walk me through new ideas and different perspectives. As much as others had tried to help and do the right thing, he still knew.

Yes, he'd stumbled and fallen, but so had I. There was no question, I knew I had. I'd been so caught up in worrying about hurt and anger and repeating the past that I'd done just about that. Only, I'd managed to push him away before he'd had a chance to jump.

I wanted to go home. To Marcus. To tell him how much of an idiot I'd been. Penny had been right about everything. The push and pull was entirely me. For all the squabbles, the serious and sarcastic, Marcus had always shot straight back up, a bop bag in the boxing ring of life. What had I done other than what I'd known? I'd thrown down my tools and walked away. Like it or not, I was my genes.

Perhaps talking to my mother would give me a little insight into why this was happening.

'You know, I think you should make the journey to see your girlfriend.' I placed my empty glass on the table. 'It's only an hour. If you love her, an hour is nothing. Or maybe don't, if it's all about what *you* want in this life.' John's eyes followed me as I stood up. 'And, you know, I've just realised I need to do the same.'

When I told Penny I was going back to the hotel, she packed up immediately and followed. She didn't need to, I assured her, but she insisted. Like John, her companion wasn't great either. Like me, her weekend hadn't been the dazzling lights and parade she'd been hoping for and, so, we shivered our way back towards Collins Street.

'Too many sleazy guys,' she grumbled. 'We really do breed them differently back home.'

'Have you ever thought about dating Patrick?' I asked.

'What?' She threw me a repulsed look. 'No, no thanks.'

'Really?' I looked at her.

'Trust me, I tried. It wasn't long after he separated from his wife. He shut it down quicker than a KFC without chicken.' She gave her hand a quick wave. 'And, honestly, the guy is such a perfectionist. He needs someone who'll burrow right into his brain and gnaw away at him. In a good way, of course.'

I snorted. 'Really?'

'"I don't mix business and pleasure, Pasta, and I'm all out of wanting pleasure at the moment," he said,' she mimicked him. 'And we've never spoken of it since. Also, he calls me Pasta, so there's that. I'm not exactly an air-filled tube. I mean, I adore him, great guy, hot as fuck, but no.'

'I really think you should talk to the barista who gets your name wrong. I mean, you have a great reason to go in and introduce yourself, tell him your name.'

'I do, don't I?' she asked. 'Do you really think that's why he gets my name wrong?'

'Yep.' I nodded, swinging from the hanging handgrip of the tram. 'And if I'm wrong and he doesn't want a date, at least he has to get your name right.'

'I might do that. Tomorrow. I think he's working.'

'You know his timetable because?'

'He's a little cute.' She scrunched herself up. 'He is, isn't he?'

'If you say so.'

'If I say so,' she baulked. 'Come on, you think Marcus is cute and he looks like … I don't know.'

'So does everyone, apparently,' I said with a laugh.

'Not my type.' She pointed. 'Just so you know, he's safe around me.'

'No?' I asked. 'I'm sure you told me how beautiful he was.'

'I told you he was lovely. As for the rest of him, he's so tall I'd need a chiropractor on call.' She dug about in her bag. 'Never mind the rest of him.'

We fell about laughing as the tram rattled into our stop. Once inside the hotel, Penny took a detour by the bar while I went upstairs to make my phone call. Changed into my ratty old pyjamas, I made a coffee for courage, pulled my mobile out and dialled.

I hadn't given too much thought to what I was going to say. I just wanted to talk, see if I couldn't just get a dialogue going. Nothing more than a friendly dialogue and, maybe, if I asked her advice, she might have something profound to say.

I wasn't expecting her to answer. I really wasn't.

'Hello?' Her voice, tired and small came down the line.

'Hey, Mum,' I said. I went for bright and happy, and hoped it got a response.

'Eleanor,' she chirped. 'It's a little late.'

'It is, I apologise,' I said. 'But I just … I really needed to talk to you.'

'Me?' she asked.

'Yes. I want your opinion.' Well, I got there quickly, didn't I? I swallowed down my nerves and waited for a response.

'My opinion?'

'Uh-huh.'

'On what?' She clattered around in the background, telling Barry I was on the phone. He sounded as surprised as anyone. 'Barry says hello.'

'Hello, Baz.'

'She said hello,' she relayed. 'What did you want advice on?'

'A boy.'

'Really?'

'Are you ready for a story?' I asked. 'This one's a doozy.'

'I'm just a little shocked that you'd call me,' she started. 'Of all people.'

'We don't really talk much though, do we?' I started. 'And I figured this might be a good place to start.'

'Oh, okay,' she said. 'Well that ... that's lovely. Let me find a chair. I'm ready.'

I poured out everything I could think of, rewinding right back to my divorce and all the reasons behind that. Everything that had gone wrong. I talked about the utter thrill of coming across Marcus, and the complete pendulum swing that he'd provided, and how I was wholly petrified of history repeating. I elaborated on the things I loved about him: his work ethic, his way with children, and how he was quiet but solid, and cheeky in an underhanded kind of way, the way that I enjoyed so much.

'You always did have a wicked little glint in your eye,' Mum added. 'I can see why you'd take to him.'

I laughed. Oh, boy, my mum made me laugh, and it was amazing. 'Thanks, I think.'

'Even as a small child, I could see that much. It's one of those things that drew me to your father. You just knew you were going to trip yourself up over him, but I couldn't help it.'

The mere mention of my father, and hearing her speak of him so positively, blurred my vision and tightened my throat.

'I guess what I'm asking is: do you think I should?' I managed a few strangled words before I wiped my eyes on the sleeve of my pyjamas.

On paper, it looked completely ridiculous to go to my mother for advice. I know this much. But I also felt it would at least be the ice-breaker we needed to dig deeper. If Penny was right, and God knows she probably was, then I had to build that trust. It was the elongated silence on the other end of the line that scared me now more than anything.

'I think that you should, even though you're scared,' she said, chuckling. 'Listen to me. I ran at the first opportunity, and here I am telling you to give him the chance to prove you wrong. If you run now, you might be right in that moment, sure, you won't get hurt, but you may just miss out on some wonderful moments.'

'Is that what happened with you and Barry?'

'I was so worried about him,' she whispered. 'He seemed perfect. Too pure to be pink, really.'

I laughed loudly.

'And, I mean, this was the point before his loud chewing annoyed me, and his snoring made me want to chisel out my eardrums but, in those early days, I was so scared I was going to screw everything up. Just like I did with your father, but Barry told me I had to take a leap of faith, and I did.'

'Do you regret Dad?'

'Oh, no,' she said wistfully. 'I adored your father. He was gorgeous, caring, and such a free creative spirit. What girl doesn't find that attractive? Plus, I have you, in whatever strange way we have each other.'

'Can I ask why you never show up?' I asked. 'Because, honestly, I look forward to it, and it never comes to fruition. It's so disappointing. It hurts.'

'Oh, Ellie,' she said with a quiet sob. 'It's just so hard to know what I'm doing. I was so young when you were born. I was seventeen. I was still a child myself.'

Deep breaths, I told myself. Deep, deep breaths. My immediate reaction would be to fly off the handle. Why not turn up if she loves me so much? Why not just get on the damn plane and make the effort? Like everyone, I guessed she had her reasons.

'Having me was a brave thing to do,' I tried. 'Considering the alternatives. I probably wouldn't have made the same choice at that age.'

She laughed softly. 'Your father was very keen to meet you. I don't know what happened, it was like someone flipped a switch in him. He took to the parenting lark like the sun takes to the sky, but I just could never quite work out what I was doing. I felt like I was going in circles, wrong turn after wrong turn and, one day, I just decided I couldn't do it anymore.'

'Just like that?' I asked. 'There wasn't an inciting incident?'

'Your father lost another job.'

'He is a bit of a floater,' I admitted. 'To his credit, he makes it work. I think he likes the variety. Change is as good as a holiday, right?'

'Don't you think he takes it to the extreme though?'

'I don't know.' I shrugged. 'I always had everything I needed. He did his best, and I can't ask any more of that.'

'That man sent me more mail than the gas company,' she joked. 'I've got boxes upon boxes of photos of you here. I just … I'm sorry, Eleanor. I'm so sorry I wasn't there.'

I held the receiver away from my ear and let myself sob openly, just long enough to let it out, but not too long that she'd think I'd dropped dead of shock, either. It was, at last, a breakthrough, and one I'd spent such a large part of my life waiting for. I know that words didn't fix things instantly, they don't. Actions not words were the thing but, gosh, it was a great starting point. I cleared my throat and grabbed the tissue box from beside the bed.

'Here's what I'd like to do.' I wiped at my eyes and hugged my knees. 'I need to sort things out with Marc.'

'Please, please do.'

'After that, we're on holidays in a week's time. What if I bring him up to Sydney around Christmas? Would you like to have lunch with us?' I asked. 'No pressure, we'll just grab something at Darling Harbour. I don't have to come to your house, you don't have to come to mine. Let's meet in the middle and go from there.'

'Your cousin Emmy is coming home this Christmas, too, if you'd like to catch up with her.'

'That sounds perfect. I've been keeping up with her adventures on social media, but I haven't seen her since we were teenagers.'

'I'm sure she'd love to see you,' Mum said.

'What about you? Would you love to see me?'

'Eleanor, I would love to,' she said, her voice strained. 'I've just always been so scared.'

'I don't want you to be scared.' Even as I said them, the words choked me. 'Surely we can come together as adults and work something out?'

'You've always seemed to have everything together, and I thought that maybe you didn't need me.'

'Of course I need you,' I squeaked. 'But we both have to work on it.'

Just like I had to work on it with Marcus. Give and take, but in a good way. Look at me, solving my own problems.

Mum and I nattered on the phone for another hour. Through shared stories about my father and fits of laughter, she gave me a clarity that, surprisingly, hadn't come from anyone else. Somewhere deep down, I was sure she still loved him.

Penny had been right when she summed it up, but my mother clarified the finer details. She was scared of getting hurt, or being rejected, and so was I, just with different people in our lives. It took me by surprise, and, in the end, she wouldn't let me off the phone until I promised I was going to try and sort things out with Marcus.

She needn't have worried, I told her, I wanted to fix this.

Chapter 27

Bright red numbers shone from the alarm clock like they were laughing at me. Of course they were. I could have really used some sleep, but it was five o'clock in the morning and I was watching the world from the tenth floor of a hotel room.

Today, I was going to change everything. Hopefully, that meant making things right, but I was also steeling myself for the fact that Marcus could turn around with a big 'No' in neon lights. If that were the case, I'd have to be okay with that, too. After all, that was his prerogative. I would just have to swallow my pride and own my mistake. But that alternative was not a future I wanted to live in.

Penny returned from the hotel bar to find me a happily crying mess. Talking to Mum had created a whirlwind of emotions, mostly good. When she sent me a message, thanking me for calling, I howled all over again.

After a solid breakfast at a hole-in-the-wall coffee shop, we checked out of the hotel and made our way home. We buzzed along with Penny in the driver's seat while I played navigator and DJ. And, when we arrived home, I tossed my bag inside and got changed quickly.

If all else went pear-shaped today, I needed comfort, something only a soft old pair of jeans and band T-shirt could provide. Even my underwear was a favourite pair normally relegated to home use or period week. Definitely no sexy lingerie for me today.

Walking up the street towards his home, it became increasingly clear that Marcus was not home alone, and that there was every chance he was having a party. Cars cradled gutters and the faint sound of a too-loud stereo danced up from behind his fence, followed by the faint waft of barbecue. My stomach growled.

Beautiful roses were in full bloom, and I was more than a little jealous of the perfectly sculpted lawn. We still had the same faded Santa Stop Here sign in the front yard, only now he was joined by weeds.

A voice in my head told me more than once that I should come back later. Everyone would be gone, and we'd be able to sit down and have a decent chat over a glass of wine. It would be easier that way, but the impulsivity of desperation told me to do this now. It told me to strike while the iron was hot and get everything off my chest. After all, nothing good ever comes from dwelling on things, and I know I'd done way too much of that lately.

I stepped up to the door, listening to the laughter coming from somewhere behind it, and rang the doorbell.

'That is so like you, Marc!' A voice got louder as it approached the door.

I still had time to leave. I could turn and make a run for it. I'd be at the corner before those footsteps got any closer. I didn't move. My feet, or my stubborn nature, had me glued to the spot. The door opened just a smidgen, enough to identify a broad smile and twinkling eyes that had looked back at me previously, only not from her.

'Hello!' The door shot wide open. 'I'm Jessica.'

Like her brother, she was tall, lean, and beautiful. She wore hip-huggers and an old sweatshirt with her hair in a functional ponytail.

I offered her my hand. 'I'm Eleanor.'

'Oh! It's you!' She bounced excitedly.

'It's funny you say that.' I scratched at my top lip. 'You're Mr Mistoffelees?'

'Are you kidding?' She threw her head back and laughed. 'He's already told you that?'

'He has.' I smiled. 'I'm still waiting to see the photo.'

'In that case, come on in. Marc's just out the back.' She stood aside. 'And I'll send the photo to you.'

Somewhere in the distance, a sliding door opened. Daisy yipped, and charged at me in an uncoordinated bum-rush of arms and legs. Her tongue flailed about as she leapt and shuffled and shoved her head between my legs until she got the under the chin scratch she was after. I looked at Jessica and shrugged.

'Come in.' She waved again. 'We're all just, you know, everywhere.'

It felt like each time I stepped inside his home, I saw a different layer to Marcus. My first visit had introduced me to Marcus the lover, fierce, strong, and quietly confident in what he was doing. I'd also met Marcus the teacher, who some may call a bore and who I would call the consummate professional. Today, I was meeting Marcus the family man.

That version was loud, boisterous, and surrounded by masses of people. His home was full of light and laughter, people and food. Dirty dishes were stacking up in and by the sink, and half-eaten trays of sandwiches, cakes, and sweets littered the kitchen table. Jessica introduced me quickly to their grandmother and, in my nervousness, I forgot her name almost immediately. I also managed to say the word 'fuck', because why wouldn't I?

We looked out towards the backyard, Marcus with a months-old child in his arms. Slowly, as he worked his way around the circle that surrounded him, his eyes switched focus and landed on us standing inside the kitchen. He smiled in a way that told me he understood, that everything was going to be okay, and walked towards us.

For the first time in days, my shoulders relaxed and my breathing got a little deeper.

'Oh.' She leaned into my shoulder. 'That's my Janie. He's slightly in love with her. In fact, I think they're a little obsessed with each other.'

My ovaries stumbled about in a Punch and Judy routine with my uterus. All I hoped was that common sense prevailed, at least for this afternoon, because I did not need any of that quite yet. I drew my bottom lip in and rolled it about between my teeth. Hell, I hadn't even apologised to him yet, and my body was already cataloguing its next life step.

Calm the farm, Eleanor!

'She's gorgeous,' I said quietly.

'And she hasn't quite worked out how to say Marc yet. She calls him Barc. God help me when she gets to the letter F.'

'Oh!' I snickered. 'I shouldn't laugh, but that'll be great.'

As he stepped inside, the noise level dropped dramatically. It was a recital hall in the last terse moments before a performance. There were hushed voices, instruments at the ready, brains switched on, sheet music stands upright and in a locked position. When the moment was right, and after a random tingle from a triangle, all the players assembled and took their places. A conductor stepped up.

'I'd always hoped to perform in front of people again,' I joked, waving a quick hello to all the new faces who'd adjourned in the kitchen. 'I just didn't expect it would be like this.'

'I thought maybe you could start with a small crowd.' Marcus smirked, finger and thumb pinched together. Regardless of the fact nobody knew what we were talking about, though I suspected it would only have been more obvious if I'd worn a sandwich board, our audience still tittered about excitedly.

At a glance, my knuckles were white as my fingers twisted around each other. 'Okay, so, firstly, I was wrong.'

Every single man in the room laughed. It wasn't just a polite, 'We aren't sure what's happening laugh', but the laugh of men who'd been married long enough to know better. Instead of joining them, Marcus simply smiled politely and waited for me to continue. He pushed Janie's hand away as she stuck an entire first in his mouth.

'When I moved here, I was determined that this was going to be a fresh start. Life was going to be new and fun and exciting, and I was going to make my way in this amazing new job while, somehow, managing to keep to myself. I was determined not to make the same mistakes I had made in the past. Except, I think I may have done exactly that.' I swallowed despite a Sahara dry mouth.

'I like her,' said an elderly voice somewhere to my left.

'Yeah, me, too.' Marcus took another step towards me and offloaded Janie, who was so happy about the idea she thrust herself backwards in a stiff arch and mewled at her mother.

'You see, I had this idea of what I wanted and who could and couldn't provide that, and I was going to stick to that. It was almost like this checklist of no suits, no ties, no egos, no … everything that I had known. I didn't want the popular guy, the one who made heads turn when he walked in a room.'

'I hardly do that.' Marcus scratched at the back of his neck.

'He really doesn't,' Jessica chimed in.

'You really do. The problem with that, as you know, was that I wasn't opening myself up to new people or experiences. Guilt by association, I suppose you'd call it.'

'Do you—' Marcus pointed to somewhere that could have been the staircase, or the ceiling cavity. 'Look, you know how much this lot loves theatre. They live for drama. Do you want to go somewhere private and finish this?'

'Here is good.' I gave my head a quick shake. 'I've been letting past experiences dictate the future. I don't want to continue like that. I can see how it's affected me, and us. I'll be honest, figuring this out did take a few deep and meaningfuls with other people but, you know, I got there in the end.'

His smile deepened. 'You rang your mum?'

'I did.' I took a deep breath. 'That was interesting.'

'How was that?'

'As much as I'd hate to admit, I guess the apple didn't fall far from the tree.'

'Yes it does. Don't discount yourself.'

I smiled gently, my increasingly snotty nose making me sound all backed up. 'What I was doing to you is what she was doing to me, and I don't want to do that. I don't want to be like that. I want to break that cycle.'

'Cycle?' he teased with a wrinkle of the nose. 'Did you bring your bike with you?'

'See, the funny thing is, it's a tandem,' I joked. 'I hope you don't mind. I mean, if you want to get back in the saddle with me, I'd really like that.'

'I ...' He nodded. 'I think I can get behind that. I mean, you will let me sit up the front and pilot, won't you?'

'Occasionally,' I teased. 'Can't always be about you.'

'Come here.' He took me by the hand and pulled me into the empty lounge room at the front of the house. When muted, scandalised laughter began, Marcus turned back to his family. 'Like I was going to do this part in front of you, you pack of vultures.'

The sliding door closed with a heavy thud, barely muting the laughter on the other side. For a quiet moment, we did nothing but look at each other.

'I missed you,' I whispered.

He didn't answer. Instead, he pulled me into him and kissed me. Though we'd only had the briefest time apart, we kissed like I'd just come back from a months-long overseas sabbatical. Marcus was always a confident kisser but this, this was something new. This said neither of us were leaving, ever again. Pulling back, I cupped his face and took him in all over again.

'I love you.'

Marcus tipped his head and narrowed his eyes. 'Is that food poisoning speaking?'

'I haven't eaten anything you've cooked yet,' I teased, kissing him again.

'So, are you planning on staying, or are you making like Usain Bolt again?' he asked.

'I think I'll stay this time.'

'You picked a great time to do this, didn't you?' A smile teased his mouth. 'Because, now, you have to meet not just my parents, but everybody.' He swept his arm out with a flourish. 'All of them, even the crazy ones who are here because no option.'

I took his hand in both of mine. 'If there's that many of them, we better get started.'

'Whatever happens next—' he pressed a kiss into my temple '—I love you, too.'

With little more than a wink and a smile, Marcus pushed the door open, and pulled me into the next chapter of my life. It was bright and beautiful, and I was looking forward to everything that came with it.

Chapter 28

'So, I have a little bit of personal news that I wanted to share.'

Marcus's statement was echoed by the shuffling of feet and the occasional clearing of a throat. Our end-of-year presentation had arrived, finally. The new yearbooks were delivered an hour before the start of the ceremony and were perfectly printed. Cakes and sandwiches jostled for pride of place on a table at the back of the gym, and I sat comfortably on the sidelines with a handful of other teachers as Marcus gave the closing speech of the night.

'Last night, I was offered the role of vice principal.' He fiddled with the papers in front of him and waited while polite clapping died off. 'This morning, I declined the role on the basis that I am not ready.'

Low-level chatter began to rise, proportionate with the lump in my throat. Penny reached across and grabbed for my hand. This was all news to me, and I was a little confused as to why I hadn't heard about this sooner. Or maybe I shouldn't have been.

'I believe that I'm at least a half-decent teacher, and I do hope some of you might agree with that. However, organising tonight should have been something of a breeze for me, a last hurrah before that next stepping stone.' He looked out at the room. 'I failed.'

Ever wondered what the correct protocol was in moments like this? As it turned out, most people went along with stunned silence. Phil stood to his side, hands clasped in front of him, a look of uncertainty on his face. Roger, Tony and Mick all peered down the end of the aisle to me where I sat with my head bowed, heart racing, and mouth drier than the back end of a dehydrator.

'Most of tonight was organised by Eleanor, Miss Manning as most of you know her. There are people who will argue that she was tossed in the deep end when tasked with planning this evening. It's only her first term with us here. But I also know that, if you ask her, she might disagree with my assessment.' He looked at me.

No, no, that was quite the deep end that I didn't want, but I made do because that's what I do.

'So, there we were. Two idiots who'd barely met and, if I can be frank—'

'Okay, Frank,' I chuckled. My laughter was joined by the voices behind me.

'It's fair to say we barely liked each other. We clashed. A lot. Yet, the more I got to know Eleanor, the more I got to know myself, which has been a sobering but welcome experience. Where I sat back and slacked off on some points, sometimes a little too much, and made life difficult, Eleanor was hard at work not only learning the ropes of her new job, but also giving me quite the schooling of my own, too. The invites you got? She did most of them. Tonight's incredible theme and the gift bags? All her idea. We shared the task of the yearbook, but I failed dismally when I uploaded the wrong file, which has caused a frenzied last-minute reprint. As it turned out, my priorities were somewhat out of order, and I let her down. For that, I apologise.'

Though his eyes were a little wider, Phil was not reacting at all.

'What happens now, I hear you ask? Well, I expect I'll be in my classroom next year with a new bunch of students, preparing them for high school. After a few focused discussions, I'll also be working with Eleanor to expand a learning programme I've been running with my class this year. I won't waste any more time with a lengthy explanation, because I know we're all itching to get out of here, but I just wanted to highlight a few things that needed to be said.' Marcus cleared his throat. 'Oh, and Eleanor's a very talented pianist, too.'

Childish giggling rose from the body of students and spread to the adults.

'You boys,' he chided. 'I said pianist. Perhaps someone can talk her into playing at some stage tonight.' He gathered up his things. 'Anyway, I won't single her out any further because I know the consequences of that, too. There's every chance she'll sneak into my house tonight, ply my dog with treats, then murder me in my sleep. But I do want you all to know who pulled ninety per cent of tonight together, and I want you to please make sure you thank her as you leave. And thank you for coming along tonight. I hope you've enjoyed looking back on the year that has been.'

* * *

'You know, you didn't have to do that.' I followed Marcus into his house. Daisy barely lifted an eyelid to us this time. I think that meant she was sick of me. Already.

'Eleanor, you pulled most of tonight together.'

I wasn't sure I agreed. Over the course of the last few months, we'd shared the load evenly enough. When one of us stumbled, the other offered a helping hand, even with the yearbook problems considered. I'd collected the gift vouchers from Thatcher's and put together the gift bags containing congratulatory cards and certificates along with the vouchers. Marcus had come through with the catering, though I suspected there was some low-level begging where Lucy Williams and Oliver Murray were concerned. Though, it had earned him massive brownie points when people discovered who was behind the delicious spread of food we ate.

'So, you *have* been offered the job?' I asked.

'I'm not taking it,' he said over his shoulder.

'Look, without getting into the semantics of men continually being allowed to fail upwards in this world, I don't think anything that's happened recently is a reflection on you as a teacher.' I traipsed up the stairs, stripping off as I went. After the rush of the last few months, I was exhausted. I was so looking forward to waking up tomorrow and have nothing to organise, no parents to talk around, and nowhere to be but in bed.

Marcus followed me into the shower. 'In English, please.'

'You are still a brilliant teacher, and you have everything to offer.' I squirted a blob of shampoo into his hand. God, how domesticated was this? 'None of this was ever about your teaching ability. It was you and me and all that entailed. I think you would be crazy to turn it down.'

'Maybe I need another year to get myself settled.'

'Oh.' I smiled. 'Settled, okay.'

'See how things go with my girlfriend.'

'Uh-huh.'

'Work out what we both want from the future.'

'You dick,' I teased. 'I want you to be happy and fulfilled in your professional life.'

'Eleanor, stop.' He smiled gently. 'It's okay. I'll get there.'

'What have you got planned for the weekend?' I asked.

'I am looking forward to doing nothing this weekend.' Marcus moved me aside so he could rinse his hair. 'I could get used to that kind of life.'

'It was a lot, wasn't it?'

'It was,' he agreed. 'What are you doing? Are you seeing Penny?'

Ah, Penny. While I was busy begging Marcus for another chance, she'd fronted up to the café and demanded to know why her name was always wrong on her order. Freddie, our favourite local barista, had been trying to work up the courage to ask her on a date for months. When he couldn't, he hoped that spelling her name wrong or making cute drawings on her cups might be enough to impress her. So, when she walked in expecting to tell him off, she'd walked out with a date.

At last, it was nice to be right about something.

I was thrilled for her. She looked genuinely happy and settled for the first time in months. It had only been two dates (in the last week), and he'd sent her flowers to work – with another variation of her name attached, of course. It was utterly gorgeous, and I was so keen to see how things were going to end up for them. Because, sometimes, when you know, you know.

And one thing I knew was that Marcus and I were onto a good thing.

With Dad extending his trip to celebrate New Year's Eve in London, Marcus and I were headed to Sydney over Christmas. I was sure I asked him one thousand times over if he was okay with being away from family during the festive season, but the fact he bought the airline tickets and presented them to me along with a hotel booking was answer enough.

Mum and I talked a lot. I'd even taken the lead from Penny and Patrick and explained the cue card game to Mum. I even sent her my own version, things I'd always wanted to know. Our phone calls never stayed on topic, but that was the entire point.

* * *

'Have you got everything?' I slipped my arm around Marcus as the ferry cut its way into Darling Harbour.

He looked down at me. 'Look at you, getting all anxious. I've got everything. Have *you* got everything?'

I had everything I could think that I'd need, my handbag, photos, and a small gift bag for Mum. After she mentioned having boxes of photos of me, I decided she at least could put them in an album, so I bought her a photo album. It was completely daggy, but practical.

The ferry bumped and swayed as we docked, and the water around us fizzed like a shaken soda, which I thought was a fantastic representation of me right now. Stepping off onto the wharf, Marcus watched me as we walked along in the sunshine, which was sizzling in a way that only summer in Australia could.

'What are you looking at?' I asked.

'You.'

'Why?' I continued.

'Because I like looking at beautiful things.'

I glanced at him, rolling my eyes playfully. 'Please.'

'Thank you,' he teased. 'Hey, so, just a thought.'

'You? Thoughts?'

'Rarity, I know.' He slipped his arm around my shoulder and pulled me into his side. 'Anyway, I'm going to go and slip off down a side street here for a few minutes.'

'Why?' My stomach flip-flopped into uncertainty.

'To give you a bit of time with your mother, just the two of you,' he said. 'I thought that would be obvious.'

'No, no, no.' I looked up at him. 'I want you to come with me.'

'I just figure you could both do with a few minutes to get used to each other's company again before I bombard it.'

'Are you sure?' I asked. 'Because I don't mind you being there. I did ask you to come with me after all.'

'Maybe I'm just here for the hotel.'

'In fairness, it's a very nice hotel,' I said.

Each morning, we woke to sunlit views of the Sydney Harbour Bridge and marvelled at the amount of early morning traffic we didn't have to sit through as we ate breakfast. Now, it looked like all those people in their cars had descended on Darling Harbour and were looking for lunch. Marcus was adamant that he was going to look around for a few moments on his own. With a quick kiss on the cheek, he slipped off into the next street, leaving me to look for my mother.

I took a deep breath, which did nothing for my nerves, and kept walking.

As the restaurant came into view, with its outdoor tables and market umbrellas, I crossed my fingers that all of this hadn't been in vain. I was sure she'd be there. My eyes searched each table, nervously scanning for a figure that resembled me. I caught a family with the stroller, a grumpy older couple who complained about seating, corporate high-rollers who still loved a cheeky lunch special, and the overworked waitress trying to keep them all happy.

Then, at the very last table, underneath an oversized sunhat, was my mum. She was here. The next few moments passed in a wobbly blur of excitement. My limbs felt heavy, and I wasn't sure I could even feel my legs, but one foot in front of the other squeezed me past tables and patrons towards her.

'Hello, you,' I greeted her with a laugh.

She stood, slowly at first, and then leapt towards me, wrapped her arms around my shoulders, squeezing like I might vanish if she drew another breath. I was surprised to find I'd forgot how close in height we were. 'Eleanor.'

'That's me.' I smiled broadly. 'Shall we do this?'

'Let's do this.' She wiped at her eyes. 'I'm so glad you're here.'

Acknowledgements

And here we are at book three. By now, I'm sure that each book is sent to teach me something different. The lesson from this book is that things take time. I know that this one certainly has.

Rewriting, coming at old characters from a different angle has been an interesting experience, and certainly a challenging one. As a result, this book is a little fatter than the last two. It seems that these two characters had a lot to say.

Now that it's finally done, I owe some big thankyous to a lot of people:

I can't start this without both apologising and thanking HQDigital. In particular, my editor Charlotte. I'm sure there were times I was lucky I lived outside the UK. Thank you for your patience while I tried turning this book into something a little less messy. Thank you for your guidance and suggestions. This book is so much better for your touch.

Shane, you're probably in every book, but you deserve to be. Thanks for putting up with me, period. Author spouses get lumped with a lot of stuff (housework) while us writers are busy doing writerly things. At least I can bake, right?

Erin & Michael, I think I've known you both way longer than anyone else outside my own family. Thanks for being awesome, thanks for explaining Game of Thrones to me, and thank you for making me laugh until I went my pants. Erin, our trips to Le Plazeur are the stuff of memes, and I'm sure our discussions are where half my characters' sidekicks come from.

To the Savvy Authors – thank you for all your advice, support, and massive knowledge bank.

Tracy Fenton and the team at TBC – thank you for keeping

my Kindle full and for running an amazing review group. Your support of authors is invaluable.

Dymocks Waurn Ponds and the Bookshop at Queenscliff, thank you for being champions of local authors and for allowing me to pester you. I promise I'll try and turn up to more book club meetings – and not just for the wine, either.

This book was basically a call-back to my childhood and a school library I always wanted to work in, so thanks to all the teachers I've had before. Some of you I still see, some of you I wish I did.

As always, thank you to anyone who's bought and reviewed my books. Every time you buy or leave a review, I get an extra power up, Super Mario-style, so thank you.

If you loved *Lessons in Love* then turn the page for an exclusive extract from *An Impossible Thing Called Love*

Chapter 1

Hogmanay, 2010

Flames danced towards the night sky, slowly snaking their way along the cobblestoned street like a slow-moving river of fire. At the front of the procession, Viking warriors chanted to the steady rhythm of a beating drum, blending with the sound of bagpipes.

It all sounded so medieval, but it wasn't anything like that – not by half. Positioned near St Giles Cathedral on Edinburgh's famous Royal Mile, our tour group huddled tightly near the end of the spiralling mass of people taking part in the traditional Torchlight Procession.

Tonight officially kicked off Hogmanay, one of the most spectacular – and exciting – ways to ring in the New Year. And I was there to experience it all.

An icy wind sprang up, causing the flames of our torches to wobble excitedly. I tugged my jacket tighter, warding off the chill that blasted my face, and pulled my beanie further over my dark brown hair. Somewhere nearby, a bagpipe started another frenzied rendition of a Proclaimers song. This wouldn't have been a problem normally, but it felt like the same song had been on repeat for the last two days while we'd wound our way up from London, after already hitting a dozen European cities. Hearing the song again caused raucous groans and laughter from our group.

'You know what this reminds me of?' My best friend Heather leaned in. 'It reminds me of that time in primary school where we had to practice those Beatles songs over and over.'

For months, our class of ten-year-olds spent day after day rehearsing the same four songs, all from the *Yellow Submarine* album, the culmination of which was being crammed on a tiny stage in the town hall to sing for the masses – mostly other schools and mums, but it was our five minutes of fame. One misplaced step saw Heather, the periscope of the submarine, fall off the edge of the stage.

I smiled at the memory. 'I was a bright pink octopus.'

A crackly loudspeaker and the shuffle of feet announced the beginning of the procession and, just like the song, we were on our way. My breath formed small cloudy bursts in front of me and, not for the first time this trip, I was thankful that I'd packed another layer of clothing. Even though we'd been in Europe almost three weeks already, the cold took some getting used to, especially as we were more acclimatised to roasting under the Australian sun at this time of year.

'Josh was seaweed,' I said, the memories of our gone too soon childhood flashing before my eyes. A small child bounced off my leg and collapsed onto the muddy ground, before getting up and running off again. Her exasperated mother was hot on her heels, a puff of fringe and muttered words under her breath.

'Actually...' Heather looked around. 'Where is he?'

Along with half of our tour group, Josh had dispersed as soon as the procession began, blending in with the hundreds of other people joining us for the traditional Scottish event. He was weaving in and out, looking for new, unsuspecting girls to charm with stories of Australian urban legends. Lanky and a little bit standout-ish, I managed to identify him by his *Where's Wally* beanie over by a group of girls. One on each arm, he looked more than happy with how his night was progressing. He turned the corner with the crowd and disappeared towards Princes Street.

Wet roads glistened under street lights, and grass glowed an iridescent shade of green. Everything here just seemed so ... vibrant. From the architecture, to the history, the people, and the fiery shade of red hair over by a first aid station. I couldn't help the small smile that spread across my face as I realised that I was *finally* here.

For almost eighteen months, Edinburgh had been circled on our calendars as the pinnacle of our trip. Heather, Josh and I – friends for most of our remembered lives – had decided we would embark on a European bus tour at the end of our gap year. When one year became two, it only afforded us more time to save, adding more destinations to our trip.

We worked jobs we hated, took late-night shifts, skipped parties, felt soggy food floating in filthy dishwater, and I'd forgone volunteer shifts at our local hospital (the plan was medicine, if they ever let me into university) in favour of forcing smiles at retail customers in the Christmas rush. It was all in the pursuit of adventure. It had paid off.

So far, our trip had been a whirlwind experience in the best of ways. In just ten short days, we'd had a Christmas feast of buttery pastries underneath the Eiffel Tower and battled cheesy woodfired pizza after tossing coins in the Trevi Fountain. Salzburg revived our senses with sweet cinnamon-y apple strudel after shopping the *Getreidegasse*, and hoppy beer in Berlin kept us warm against biting temperatures. I ran my fingers along all the old stone buildings and dunked my toes in all the freezing waters. I wanted to feel it all. The moment we arrived back in London, we boarded another bus for Edinburgh, ready for the biggest street party and New Year's celebration this side of the Atlantic.

The procession came to a quick stop along Princes Street, a neat mixture of Georgian and Renaissance architecture. I wouldn't have known that fact if I hadn't spent three hours battling drizzling rain in a thin plastic poncho on a walking tour this morning. Ornate windows from tall buildings looked down on the street and, while I was busy marvelling at that, a scuffle broke my train of thought and drew my attention back to the here and now.

Josh jogged towards us, nattering nervously about something

happening further up the road. Despite the cold, a bead of sweat rolled down his temple. His brown eyes were wide with … was that fear?

'This dude thinks I grabbed his girlfriend. He's looking for me.' A jittery hand rested over his mouth as he surveyed the scene before us. Heads turned towards him. Everyone could see what was coming before he could.

'What?' Now my eyes widened. 'What have you done?'

Heather did what she does best and gave him a shove. 'You idiot.'

'No, no, it's not like that. I thought she was single.'

He *always* thought they were single.

A scowling boyfriend emerged from the crowd, his own Moses parting the sea moment, complete with hot-pink beanie and clenched fists. He glared at me only briefly, long enough to acknowledge that I was there, before reaching around me for Josh, who was swearing like a stand-up comedian combating a heckler. My pulse began racing.

Heather pulled me out of the way but, I wasn't prepared to spend the night tending to Josh's wounds. I was on holiday, not working, and I wasn't about to let him ruin all our fun. I handed her my torch and made a beeline for the scrum. Both he and Burly Man were very shouty, shoving each other in the tiny boxing ring that had formed around them.

'Josh!' I shouted.

He held a palm out to stop. 'It's alright, Em, just don't worry about it, okay?'

'That's your girlfriend is it?' Burly Man tipped an oversized chin in my direction. 'Some boyfriend you are.'

Grabbing Josh, I muttered something about men and women still being able to be friends in this day and age without having to get naked with each other. I think I might have been louder than expected because, before I could so much as clutch at Josh's jacket, they were jostling again. A rustle of fabric, a flash of dancing footsteps, and I felt a blunt sting across my face. All at once, everything was dark and far too bright, like a child was flickering a light switch. My sinuses were connected to a trip switch in my heart, and each beat offered a sulphuric burn. I was disoriented and, as my eyes watered, I took a wobbly seat on the ground. It may have been cold and wet, but it was better than swaying about.

I knew how these moments played out, I'd seen it a million times before when volunteering with the ambulance. Music concerts were especially healthy for face to fist experiences. Heather was screaming at someone, probably Josh, who was apologising profusely. Her voice was soon joined by the polyester swish of a hi-vis bomber jacket. I blinked away tears, hoping to get a proper look at the face that swam in my vision.

Touching my nose only made my face burn and eyes water all over again. Through damp eyes, he looked like a watercolour painting. Street lights shimmered in one corner, and his hair a wispy flame-red cloud with sideburns that reached down and hugged his face. His blurred lopsided smile was the most beautiful thing I'd seen all night. As he came into focus, so did Josh over his shoulder.

'Oh, Em, I am … fuck … so sorry. Are you okay?'

Heather slapped at him again. 'What do you think, idiot?'

She barely touched five-feet-tall in a line-up. Despite that, she was full of energy and, right now, looked like a mother about to grab at naughty earlobes. Josh inched away from her and, in all this, it occurred to me just how many people were happy to watch what was happening, to whisper among themselves instead of help. I lolled about, steadying myself with a palm on the cold wet asphalt. Dropping on his haunches, the first-aider snapped his fingers in front of me.

'You okay?' he asked. 'Is there any blood?'

I frowned, confused. 'Huh?'

'Are you bleeding?' He flashed a torchlight across my eyes and offered a fistful of tissues.

Squinting away from the brightness, I dabbed at my eyes. Anything near my nose made me want to vomit, but there was a small trickle of blood. 'Thank you.'

'At least it's not broken,' we said in unison.

His mouth twitched, a smile that threatened to widen as he offered me a cold pack. Under the light, his eyes were, in one moment, bottle-green. The next, they were ocean blue. 'What makes you say that?'

'It's not all bent up and I can still breathe.' Through squinting eyes, I waggled a finger at his jacket, complete with reflective patches and a blank space for a name badge. 'It looks just as good on you as it does on me.'

'Is that so?'

My nose burned, and I rolled forward, tissue to my nose. 'At least it's warm, right?'

'You do a bit of first aid, too?'

I nodded, looking about for my friends. Burly Man had disappeared, and Josh was still being reprimanded by Heather. He looked like a small child, hands up around his chest as if he'd physically shrunk against her anger, which was par for their friendship.

Heather and I met in Grade Two, when my family moved to the area. On the first day of school, while I stood the back of the crowd waiting for something to happen, she strode across the quadrangle, shook my hand, and introduced herself as my new best friend. Who could possibly argue with that?

We met Josh a few months later when he started at the school. He came prepacked with a face full of freckles, crooked teeth, and milk bottle glasses. When the other boys picked on him, Heather went into battle for him, and he's never forgotten it. Since then, it had been the three of us. Josh slotted into our lives as if he'd always been there and, when I got my first period in the middle of gym class, he whipped out a small make-up bag from his backpack. Inside: pads, tampons, and Panadol. His mum had given it to him, so he could, 'be a good friend'.

He still carried that make-up bag but, now, it also contained condoms, Berocca, and anything else needed for a quick hangover fix. That was essentially our friendship.

I dabbed at my nose again, resisting the urge to vomit. 'A little. Mostly concerts.'

'Why don't you come across to the first aid station and tell me more about that.' He held out a hand and pulled me to my feet. Did I mention he had wonderfully strong hands? 'My name is William.'

I brushed myself down – anything to avoid touching my face. 'Emmy.'

I followed his jacket through the crowd, the state of my face more of a bemusement and free sideshow attraction to anyone who walked past.

'So, first aid?' he asked.

'Oh, I did get a call up for the tennis in Melbourne last year.' I followed along with pointed finger and stories at the ready. As often as I could explain the goings on to friends, they didn't quite get it. This guy? He spoke my language.

'I am so jealous of you right now.' William ushered me into the first aid station. 'I've often thought of packing up for a summer and heading down for the tennis.'

The first aid station, which probably doubled as a marquee at family barbecues and sports club days, wasn't much warmer than the street, but an industrial heater in the corner at least took the chill off the air. That's more than I could say for the wet patch on my backside. My friends lingered outside, like students waiting outside a principal's office. Our torches had been handed off to others in the heat of the moment. Occasionally, Heather peered inside, her face wrought with concern.

'Jealous of me?' I said with a disbelieving laugh. 'Please, I've just taken a fist to the face.'

'Well—' he shrugged '—besides that.'

'How about you?' I asked, sitting on a chair by the entrance.

He took the seat next to me, bringing water bottles and paracetamol. 'I did Wimbledon last year. Roland Garros the year before.'

'You did not.' Speaking of jealousy.

'Okay, so, Roland Garros was as a spectator but, you know, always on duty.' He swung about in his seat and looked at me. 'Any drugs tonight, Emmy?'

A bright light flashed into my eyes again. God, he was checking my pupils. 'What? No.'

'Alcohol?'

'Too broke for that,' I said.

William gave me a hard stare, eyebrows reaching for the sky. He was having none of my shit tonight.

'Alright, maybe a swig of vodka and a schooner from the cheap bar at the hostel, but nothing to get drunk on.'

He scoffed. 'You and me both. Tonight has been a bottle of raspberry cordial and far too much water.'

'Doesn't pay well, does it?'

'Can't say it does, but I do love it.' For a second, it looked like he'd folded in on himself. He popped a blister pack of painkillers. 'No allergies?'

I shook my head. His fingers grazed my palm as he dropped the tablets in my hand. My toes curled, and breath hitched. 'No, and thank you.'

'You want to hang about for a while, so I can keep an eye on you?'

Heather's eyebrows disappeared up into her hairline and her mouth rounded into a scandalised 'O'. When Josh suggested they leave me, I didn't try and stop them; I was happy where I was. There was a quick agreement that it would be easier if I just met them back at the hostel instead of arranging a meeting point. Before leaving, Heather snapped off a quick Polaroid.

I scowled at her. 'What do you want to do that for?'

'For posterity's sake. Maybe prove to people you got into a scrap.' She grinned, disappearing into the throng of people.

Josh held a steadying hand on her shoulder. I looked back at William, chin buried in the neck of his jacket and wild hair everywhere. I pulled my beanie off, forcing it into an already bulging pocket.

'I sure you'll be fine, but just be mindful of it, will you?' he said, eyes glued to the crowd wandering past. 'If you have a lot of swelling—'

'Or trouble breathing, go to the A&E?' I flashed a stubborn smile. 'I will.'

'You know, it's you who's supposed to be listening to *me*,' he teased. 'And it's definitely not broken if you're laughing at me.'

'Yeah, well. Call me a bitter med school reject.' My nose had settled into a dull throb, the kind I knew would still be around in the morning. But at least the bleeding had stopped.

'Reject? No. They let me in, they should have definitely let you in.'

'You're a doctor?'

'Yup, a junior doctor,' he said. 'And in a couple of years, I'll be a GP.'

'What an effort.' I sighed. 'You love it?'

'Adore it. It's the best job.' He smiled. 'I mean, it's got its moments but …'

I grinned. My nose ached. 'Yeah, I get it.'

My plan, thwarted as it might have been, was to train as a doctor, because how good is it to do things that feel good for other people? Even volunteering, seeing people off into an ambulance, at least I'd been able to help, or make them more comfortable for a few moments in time. Recently, I'd had a call up from the local hospital, allowing me to volunteer in the maternity ward. There was nothing better than my few hours a week spent in there. But I didn't need to explain this to William, he understood.

Instead, we sat quietly beside each other and watched the crowd shift and change. They moved up and back along the street, A bright orange light filtered down the street, highlighting the faces of young and old alike.

Whether we'd been joined by anyone else in the first aid station was beyond my comprehension. There'd been no call to attention, and no one had approached for anything more than paracetamol and water. We huddled in our jackets, watching, waiting.

Fireworks exploded above our heads with a loud crack, ripping through the night sky, and sending rainbow-coloured sparks back down to earth. Conversations stopped mid-sentence as crowds gasped as marvelled. It didn't matter how old you were, fireworks were still a thing of wonder. I looked up in time for another *thunk, whistle, crack, sparkle, fizzle.*

When the last one sizzled into memory, I stood and brushed myself off again. William looked up at me, his face expressionless.

'William.' I held my hand out to him. 'Thank you for your help tonight.'

'Pleasure's all mine.'

For a moment, I wasn't sure what I was supposed to do, even though I'd been in this same situation myself time and time again. So, I went with what was … normal and totally not creepy.

'Well, goodnight.'

His smile reached his piercing blue eyes. 'Goodnight, Emmy.'

With that, I walked away. People were moving back down the hill towards the station, the crowd noticeably thinner and torches snuffed one by one. A haze of grey smoke had settled above the street. I chanced a glimpse back at the first aid station, not knowing what to expect. There he was, hair aflame and smile wide, chatting excitedly and handing out bottles of water.

Smiling to myself despite the throbbing pain in my nose, I turned and walked away.

Dear Reader,

Thank you so much for taking the time to read this book – we hope you enjoyed it! If you did, we'd be so appreciative if you left a review.

Here at HQ Digital we are dedicated to publishing fiction that will keep you turning the pages into the early hours. We publish a variety of genres, from heartwarming romance, to thrilling crime and sweeping historical fiction.

To find out more about our books, enter competitions and discover exclusive content, please join our community of readers by following us at:

@HQDigitalUK

facebook.com/HQDigitalUK

Are you a budding writer? We're also looking for authors to join the HQ Digital family! Please submit your manuscript to:

HQDigital@harpercollins.co.uk.

Hope to hear from you soon!

If you enjoyed *Lessons in Love* then why not try another delightfully uplifting romance from HQ Digital?

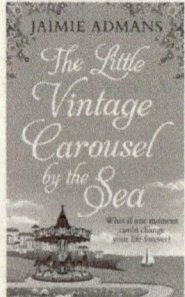